THE VOYAGE

THE VOYAGE

BY

Charles Morgan

It is not wisdom to be only wise,
And on the inward vision close the eyes,
But it is wisdom to believe the heart.

GEORGE SANTAYANA

1 9 4 0

The Macmillan Company » New York

Copyright, 1940, by
CHARLES MORGAN

SET UP BY BROWN BROTHERS LINOTYPERS
PRINTED IN THE UNITED STATES OF AMERICA
AMERICAN BOOK–STRATFORD PRESS, INC., NEW YORK

DEDICATION

*On the 1st of June, 1940, when I finished this book, know-
ing that I might not, without presumptuousness, offer my
work to France in gratitude for the honour she has done me
and the happiness she has given, I dedicated it to a French
man and woman who have deepened my love for their country and given me an insight into human goodness that springs
in them from singleness of heart. If I had been able to write
as they have lived, this tale of Barbet would have been better
worth their acceptance, but I offered it to them as it was,
with all its faults, for the pleasure it gave me to remember
that they were my friends. Their country was overrun
before my letter could be answered.*

*Now, with deepened affection and with compassionate hon-
our, I re-dedicate it to them; but because, if they live, they
are within the power of the enemy, I have for their sakes
taken their names from my page. To-night, the eve of Midsummer, there will be no bonfires on the hills of the Charente,
but, though dark ages intervene, they will be re-lighted, for
France is an idea necessary to civilization and will live again
when tyranny is spent.*

C. M.

July 23, 1940.

CONTENTS

BOOK ONE

The Country River

As in water face answereth to face, so the heart of man to man.—Proverbs xxvii, 19.

Chapter 1

STANDING ON A LADDER PROPPED AGAINST THE white walls of the house, Barbet was re-painting the shutters of the Maison Hazard. His mother had wanted the colour to be grey, and had complained that the work should in any case have been done by one of the day-labourers and not by their master; but Barbet had no sense of his own importance, he enjoyed the task and liked the green he had chosen. He had, therefore, chaffed her for her conservatism and steadily continued, singing small songs on his ladder to keep time with the sweep and patter of his brush.

The house, an old one, had been given by its extensions the shape of an L which included, within its arms, a courtyard facing south and east over the valley of the Charente. Formerly this courtyard had been shut in by the high walls usual in that secretive country-side, but when Julien Hazard died in 1876, his son Théophile, who was called Barbet because Théophile was too grand a name for him, had pulled down the walls to what he called "sitting-level" and for the last seven years had enjoyed an outlook denied to his childhood. The great stone gateway at the south-east corner remained; for a stone gateway, with rounded arch, perhaps suggested long ago by the Romanesque façades of the local churches, was the pride of a Charentais home. Barbet's mother had fought for the walls too, but not with the same desperation as for her gateway, and, when the walls were down, she had been pleased, as Barbet had known she would be, and had clapped her hands at the view. "There," she had exclaimed, "it's like coming out of a box!"

At the back of the L were two walled courtyards. The larger, to the west, had at its farther end, facing the house, the customary

3

gateway, and, on either side, the farm buildings, the stables, the store-houses and the distillery in which the business of wine-grower and farmer were carried on. The smaller, to the north, had once served the same purposes, but in 1826 Barbet's grandfather, Guillaume, a shipper of Roussignac as well as a producer of wine, wishing to acquire the site of the town's old prison-house, which adjoined his own premises there, had suggested—since even criminals must have a roof—that the prisoners should be confined temporarily in cells, which he would provide and secure, in the northern courtyard of the Maison Hazard. He was to be responsible for them and receive an allowance for their upkeep—an arrangement so convenient to a man whose buildings were too large for him that he had taken care that it should endure. It had endured so well that the collapse of the monarchy, the rise and fall of the Second Empire and the reorganizations of the Third Republic had left it undisturbed. No one was interested to disturb it. Julien had succeeded Guillaume, and when, at Julien's death, his property was divided by his two sons, Anton, the elder and richer, had taken control of the shipping business of Hazard and Vincent and the other family interests in Roussignac while the Maison Hazard, its vines, its farm and its prison, had fallen to Barbet, the younger. Meanwhile the central government—all the central governments—being blessedly French, had been content as long as the system worked, and, as for the municipality of Roussignac, for three generations there had been scarcely a man of consequence in the place who was not by birth, by marriage or by dependence an Hazard. When responsibility for the little prison came to Barbet, he disliked it, for he did not see himself as a warder of men, but he discharged it as well as he could and, since he might not release his prisoners, made friends with them.

While Barbet was painting, Lancret, the curé of Roussignac, came in through Madame Hazard's gateway. He might have come by another way but this was the polite method of approach, and, as the Hazards were a Protestant family, though Madame Hazard had been bred a Catholic, he was carefully formal in his friendship with them.

When Barbet heard a footstep in the courtyard and turned, paint-brush in hand, to find the priest's drawn face and quenched eyes looking up at him, it was of the prisoners he thought first—whether he had forgotten them.

"What is the time?" he said, clambering down the ladder.

Lancret smiled at this abrupt greeting and held out his watch.

Barbet took it into his hand. "Good. Plenty of time. I get interested in things, you know, and when something happens to recall me I find I have forgotten the prisoners. But there's more than an hour to their supper. . . . I'm sorry. How are you?" He returned the watch and held out his hand. "My mother and Renée are indoors somewhere. Come in and rest."

"In fact, it was you I wanted to see."

"Good."

"But I am interrupting your work?"

"No," said Barbet, rubbing the muscles of his arm. "I've done enough for a beginner. Besides, if there's a chance, I generally sit down for a little while before supper. On that wall in the sun. It's a good place, looking on to the river. The irises are beginning at last—you can see patches of yellow. Shall we sit there? I'll bring the paint-pot down first or I may forget it."

"Willingly," said Lancret. "You had better put on your jacket, hadn't you? This is April, the warmth soon goes out of the day."

"Thank you," said Barbet, "but I like to have my arms free. I like to feel the air."

The priest climbed over the wall and sat down upon it to wait while Barbet put away his ladder, his paint-pot and his brush. If I can say to him quite simply what I have come to say, Lancret thought, all will be well, and it ought to be easy enough, for Barbet takes everything simply; he is never shocked or supposes you to mean what you haven't said; you can say anything on earth to him as long as you say it straightforwardly; there ought to be no difficulty. But Lancret knew himself and knew that, though the request he had to make was both harmless and simple, he would have difficulty in making it. It touched a subject that his mind hungrily sought after and intuitively shunned. When Barbet was beside him, he began to speak of other things.

"Well," he began in the uneasily jocular tone of a grave man embarrassed, "at any rate you can now sleep quietly at nights."

Barbet, not understanding, raised his eyebrows.

"I mean," Lancret added, "that the distillation is over. You don't have to attend the stills. You must be glad."

"Yes. I'm even more glad I had something to distil. Those poor devils over there"—and he pointed across the Charente to the ridge behind which lay the chalky country of the Grande Champagne—"they are in a bad way. Their vineyards are eaten up."

Lancret's hands tightened on his knees. "Your own are still untouched?"

"Not a speck. This morning I was out hoeing. I like using the bigot and digging out the clumps until there's a pile of earth over my feet. It smells good. As I dug I watched pretty closely. I've not seen healthier vines. Not a speck or a sign."

"It's like a plague," the priest answered. His eyes took rebellious fire against this vine disease, the accursed green fly, the phylloxera, which had brought his peasants to ruin and despair. It was not easy to answer them when they asked: where was the justice of God? To this, as to all else, there was an answer that he, as priest, could give, but, as man, he too rebelled against the misery of a quiet and honest people. His mouth twisted. "It's like the plague," he said again. "It's like looking into your friends' faces for signs of leprosy. Even our people this side of the river are hit badly enough. However, God's will be done."

"There's more hope for us," Barbet answered, "than there is for Segonzac and Cognac. Our people might turn their land to general farming—"

"Except that they are vine-growers, not farmers. It's not a job to learn in a day."

"No. But these new American roots—there's a good chance they may be exempt."

"They die," said the priest impatiently.

"In chalk they do. But not in clay and lime—or so they say in Cognac. That might save our lowlands. And I don't despair even of the Grande Champagne," Barbet said. "Planchet didn't altogether ring it off; that's true. But suppose another mission went to America and found chalky soil the same as ours and studied the native vines that grow in it? What then? Isn't there a chance? Experiment and patience," said Barbet. "It will come if we work for it."

Lancret beat his hand on the wall. "Experiments!" he exclaimed. "Theories and experiments! What do these professors expect? It's all very well for them with their laboratories and their nurseries and their grafting. Meanwhile all the vineyards of France are being eaten up by the phylloxera. The people are desperate—the small men most of all, the ones without reserves from the past. I go from house to house. You don't know."

"I do know. But to re-plant is the only hope."

"And even if the new grafted vines stood against the disease," the priest demanded, "what then? Would they produce a French grape? What should we get—some rank eau-de-vie? And how long would it take? When would there be a vintage again? The peasants would starve meanwhile. Take my word for it: short of a miracle, the whole countryside will be a desert."

"It's odd," Barbet answered, "but I am sure that will not happen. We shall come through this. In time, there will be vintages again as good as before."

Lancret opened his mouth to remonstrate angrily, but looked first at his companion. His anger was checked by something unaggressive and steadfast in this shaggy man who had earned his nickname long ago by his resemblance to a water-spaniel.

"You may be a heretic," Lancret said with a dry smile, "you talk about brains and patience but you evidently believe in miracles."

"I?" Barbet answered, looking up in surprise from the pebbles he had been dropping from palm to palm. "I wasn't prophesying, you know. But I believe in things happening naturally. I can't think that in the end nature deserts you unless you desert her.

Quessot—he taught me the cooper's job and I still work with him on the barrels—he says the phylloxera is a curse of God laid on France because she turned out the Emperor. If Napoleon came back, the vineyards would flourish again. My mother agrees with him; she's a fierce Bonapartist; she says our own vineyards have been spared because she lives among them, but I—"

"Your brother Anton says it's a miracle."

"Does he indeed? I didn't know he believed in them."

"Well, he puts it in his own way. He says you have the devil's luck."

Barbet began to laugh. "He and Mother and old Quessot! I tell them that the phylloxera has hit the Charente because the vines have been starved. People gave manure to the crops in between, but the poor unhappy vines have always had to be content with none at all or a chance sprinkling on the side. Even nature gets tired, you know. I've always given ours something since my father died. Not much. I can't afford to buy more than a little. But something from our own farm and the leavings of the wine-press; it may have helped. And someone had the idea in the 'sixties that if the lowlands were drained they might produce a cognac equal to the Grande Champagne. Father tried it. He cut ditches round our vineyards and drained into the Soloire. I stopped them up. Our roots are under water all the winter and well into March. That may check the phylloxera. The little beast can get to the roots through the friable earth of the Champagnes but mud and water may not suit him."

On this the priest made no comment.

"But it wasn't to talk of the phylloxera that you walked out from Roussignac?"

Still Lancret was silent, remembering Barbet's childhood when he and his brother Anton, now mayor of Roussignac, had been sent to him for lessons. Odd that he, a Catholic priest, should walk for half an hour at the end of a long day to seek that boy's help and should now be sitting on a wall with him, hesitating to ask it. There were many who considered Barbet as almost a simpleton; and perhaps he is, Lancret thought, and a heretic into the bargain, but no one freezes against him, no one is afraid, and he alone can do what I want.

"How old are you, Barbet?"

"Thirty-two."

"It must be nearly twenty-five years ago. How much do you remember of those days—the lessons, I mean?"

"Precious little of the lessons," Barbet answered, pushing his fingers up through his hair as he had when he was floored by the conjugation of a verb, "but I remember Madame Despreux's pastry. I'm glad my father wasn't squeamish about his two brats taking lessons from a priest. The pastor of those days wouldn't have given us sweets. Madame Despreux always gave me a twist of raw pastry with sugar piled on it, and for Anton there were lumps of sugar soaked in coffee from her cup."

It was Madame Despreux who had come in daily to cook for the priest and clean his house. Years had passed since anyone but Barbet had spoken of her to him. That Barbet sometimes did so was a link between them, for a man who must not speak of a beloved woman, who must always divide his words from his heart, is grateful when another speaks of her with natural kindness; and Lancret, when the name of Despreux was spoken, perceived again, amid the winter of his self-discipline, the remote spring of his life. Lest by so much indulgence he should, across the years, again partake of the sin repented and absolved, he would seldom allow Barbet to speak long of Madame Despreux, but now it was necessary, and he said:

"You remember her appearance?"

Barbet shook his head slowly. "I was a boy, you know. It's only an impression I have—great eyes and dark hair—very dark. I used to think of her as a night-creature or a creature of the woods. No, she wasn't beautiful, was she? She was—"

"Ténébreuse?" said Lancret with a smile.

"And one thing I do remember," Barbet exclaimed. "Her ears—small and pearly, like shells; only their tips were pink. Sometimes she let me pull them for a treat, and she'd laugh with a row of tiny teeth. She was proud of her ears; she said they were her pedigree: 'Only my hands are coarse.' "

Lancret shifted his grip to the wall and fastened on its edge. " 'Only my hands are coarse,' " he repeated.

"Sorry," said Barbet. "It's not usually my failing to talk too much."

But nothing could destroy the intimacy or cause embarrassment between them, for each, in his own manner, was a realist; even their silences had the ease of a mutual respect, and Barbet wished only that, for Lancret's sake, he had not spoken of Madame Despreux's ears, which the priest also had touched when they were warm and alive. In May '61, Despreux had died. Barbet remembered the funeral; it had been his first and he ten years old. On Christmas day, the widow had borne a daughter, Thérèse, and had continued to work for the priest, taking the child with her. Often, during the following years, as a boy, and in the intervals of his military service, Barbet had noticed Thérèse at the cottage, at first in a basket on the horsehair sofa, then as a child receiving lessons from the priest as he himself had done. When, a young man, he returned from the awkward business of establishing Thiers in power, he had not at first recognized her, for she had ceased to be a child. "But you haven't forgotten Thérèse?" the priest had said with the care of a father for his daughter, and Barbet, not to hurt man or girl by his forgetfulness, had pulled himself together and said: "You have your mother's ears, Thérèse. They are your pedigree." At the age of ten, she hadn't been much interested in her ears. "Are they? Pedigree? What's that?" But she had demanded in a flash: "Did they sing your songs going into battle?" He had asked who told her that he made up songs and she had nodded impatiently at the priest. "Oh, I don't know. He did, I think, or Mother. Did they sing them, going up to battle?" "Some they did," he had acknowledged, and she had burst out: "Aren't you proud? I should be, if they were *my* songs!"

It had been in '76 that Madame Despreux died. Barbet, by then his father's assistant at the prison and in the vineyards, had gone to her funeral as he had to her husband's. He remembered it because it had been in the year of his own father's death, and for another reason. Exhausted by watching and by grief, Lancret had spoken neither to God nor to the people, but to the earth itself. Opposite Barbet at the grave, had been Thérèse, a girl not yet fifteen years old, long, pale and dark, and Barbet had contrasted her with his own cousin, Renée, who, orphaned a month earlier, had come to live at the Maison Hazard. Renée, though almost of an age with Thérèse, was still a child, a plump thing, like a rosy apple, dressed in black. Thérèse had already entered into her maturity; she was taut and pliant, a birch tree, a knife in the air. When he raised his eyes from the coffin, he had seen her only, and afterwards, at home, Anton and Anton's wife, Bette, and Madame Vincent, Bette's mother, had spoken of the girl with the venom that is always spat by the jealous against supreme vitality. They had been glad that Thérèse, having no father who might acknowledge her, must go as a slave to her aunt Sernet at the Cheval Pie. "She's lucky to find a home anywhere," Madame Vincent had said. "She couldn't keep her eyes still—not over the open grave." "She was lost," Barbet had answered, and he recalled still his surprise at the sound of his own voice. "But not frightened," he had persisted, and his brother, unaccountably angry, had cried out: "If her aunt Sernet doesn't frighten her, no one will. The Cheval Pie won't be a bed of roses. They are as poor as rats. Sernet drinks his own profits and the woman's a tartar. They'll take the whip to her or I'm mistaken." Whereupon, Bette had chimed in. Her voice came to Barbet out of the past with a vindictiveness fiercer than her husband's. "Even when the coffin was squeaking down on the ropes," Bette had said, "she kept turning back her hair with her fingers so that we might all admire her pretty ears."

At this point in his recollection, Barbet turned to Lancret, who at once, with the extraordinary effect of one that had overheard, said quietly:

"Thérèse Despreux has her mother's ears."

"What made you say that?"

"Hadn't you been talking of ears?"

"So I had," said Barbet. "So I had. What has become of Thérèse? Still at Angoulême?"

"You haven't heard from her?"

"I? Not for a long time. Why should I?"

"Before she ran away from the Cheval Pie, it was to you she came for advice—not to anyone else, not to me."

"Oh, you'll forgive me," Barbet exclaimed, "but that's nonsense. She didn't go to anyone for advice. Thérèse wouldn't. It was her secret that night; she was bursting with it; she had to tell someone; I happened to be nearest, so she told me. You forget, she was nearly eighteen."

"So young?"

"I didn't mean 'so young.' I meant: old enough to make up her own mind. . . . No," said Barbet, aware that it was an old wound in Lancret that Thérèse had come to him neither as priest nor as man. "No, you must understand this, my dear abbé. Thérèse doesn't spurn or neglect you. She's of a kind that can't be helped much by anyone's advice. Certainly she didn't ask mine. I had recently been in Paris, visiting the merchants at Bercy; it was four years ago this spring. I remember because there had been the great vintage of '78, the last great vintage, and distillation wasn't done. One evening I had been in Roussignac. I don't like the Lion Rouge, never did; it was too pompous for me; so I went to the Cheval Pie for a moment before starting to walk home. Frédéric served me; I didn't see Thérèse but she must have seen me. I came back by the path through the Long Wood. I heard footsteps behind me. It was dark, so I turned round. 'Monsieur Barbet! Monsieur Barbet!' There she was, breathless. 'Have you been to Paris?' she said. 'Have you?' When I answered yes, she said: 'How could I get to Paris?'"

The priest threw an envious glance at Barbet. "What did you say to that? I shouldn't have known what it would be best to say. She would have thought I was preaching at her. It would have done no good."

"Well," Barbet replied, "what I said was: 'Just go, Thérèse, if you can pay your fare.' Then she came close to me. 'Tell me about it,' she said."

"You are a very fortunate man," Lancret remarked with a sigh.

"Am I? Why?"

" 'Then she came close to me.' And ' "Tell me about it," she said!' A priest who could do that—but never mind. Go on with your story."

"I told her what came into my head—just what I'd discovered myself—the smell of the place, bits of detail all higgledy-piggledy: brass rims on café tables, the street of books at the back of the Rue Bonaparte, the Quais, the Île St. Louis growing out of the Seine, the boats, the noise, the glistening spokes of carriage-wheels, the huge hats, the cut of the beards—and I told her about the woman I saw in the Abattoirs with eight small pigs running ahead on a string like ponies in a circus. . . . And when I'd finished, she was silent a bit. Then she said: 'Does it shine?' "

" 'Shine'?"

"That's what she said. 'I shall go there. I will! I will!' Then she told me she would be eighteen at Christmas. Didn't I think she could earn her living in Paris?"

"I hope you said—"

"It's no good lying to people, particularly when they know the answer. She could earn her living anywhere. I said so. That surprised her. I asked her: 'Did you expect me to try to stop you, Thérèse?' She shook her head. 'Did you want me to?' At that she laughed out loud. 'No. No. I didn't want anything—not you, not anything except—' "

"What did she want?" said Lancret. "If her mind was made up, why should she come to you?"

"She wasn't asking me. She was telling me," Barbet replied, delighted by the recollection. "What she wanted was to say the word 'Paris.' And two days later off she went."

"Only to Angoulême."

"Does that make any odds? I think she's one of those who go on voyages, you know."

"Voyages?" said the priest.

Barbet shrugged his shoulders. "We all do. At last, one day, it becomes necessary, it becomes natural. Then difficulties vanish. You just walk out."

"From what? To what?"

After a moment's hesitation, caused by his surprise that the question should have been asked, Barbet replied: "From one way of living to another."

"The road to Damascus, I suppose?" Lancret said with irony.

"Or to Angoulême," Barbet answered, smiling at the priest's solemnity in a way by which Lancret himself was disarmed. "Or if you're a bird you migrate. I suppose for a long time it seems natural to a swallow to stay where he is and be what he is. Then it becomes unnatural and he goes on a voyage."

"But young women are not swallows."

"No."

"They have responsibilities, they have ties, homes."

"But so have swallows. . . . Oh, I know there are always reasons for *not* making a voyage," Barbet continued. "Good reasons. Unselfish reasons—that's why they are so strong. We invent and imagine them—that, too, is why they are strong. But in the end, you know, we just walk out."

"Dying?"

"Ah well," said Barbet, "that's a voyage too. But there's no need to wait as long as that. Thérèse—"

"What I came to tell you was that she had come back," Lancret exclaimed, taking the plunge before which he had so long hesitated. "Did you know that?"

"To the Cheval Pie? When?"

"Last night."

"Why has she come?"

"Since Sernet died, there's been no one but the boy, Frédéric, and Madame Sernet herself—and she's bedridden. Custom has almost ceased. They are near to starving. I should have thought Thérèse might have served them better by continuing to send them part of her earnings in Angoulême. But no: she had her own ideas. She says she has a scheme. She won't tell me what."

"I see," said Barbet. "But why should you suppose that I of all men can be of any use to her?"

Lancret stood up from the wall and walked a few paces away; then swung round. "She's like a tigress. She thinks the world is going to attack her. She knows that I disapprove—that I am bound to disapprove—the life she had been leading in Angoulême. She's shut against me." After a long silence, he added: "That is my punishment."

"What do you suggest? Am I to tame her?"

"Go to her and see her, Barbet. Try to persuade her to do nothing violent, nothing rash, nothing wicked. Perhaps she will listen to you. Perhaps if you were to say——"

"It is true," Barbet interrupted, "that people are always ready to attack her. Perhaps they are frightened themselves."

"It's her own fault. I! I! I!—she is an insane egoist. And it isn't that she's a fool," the priest continued. "She can talk of general subjects with remarkable intelligence. But in life she's like a bad actress on the stage—she can't listen; with her ears, yes, but not with her mind. When she was a child, if you talked to her of the Crucifixion, she was only waiting to tell you what *she* would have done if she had been Mary Magdalene."

"But I should like to know what she would have done if she had been Mary Magdalene," Barbet said, meditatively stroking the end of his nose, but the priest was too excited to regard him.

"I! I! I!" he exclaimed again. "It's a kind of madness. It's a blind insensitiveness to the effect she is producing on other people. In the days when she confessed to me——" He put his hand to his throat. "But she is sensitive enough to know that she multiplies enemies. She doesn't know why. She thinks it unjust. And so she challenges, she defies; she defies because she is afraid; she does dreadful things and says dreadful things of herself. I have heard her say that she has a devil in her."

"But you love her?" Barbet asked suddenly.

Lancret swerved from the question. "I am responsible. From the beginning of her life I have been responsible as her priest and as——"

"No," Barbet said. "She is responsible. That is the virtue and the strength of her. She takes responsibility for her own life. She goes on her voyages. You must give her credit for that."

"Or is she irreclaimable?" Lancret replied. "Incapable of repentance? Rotten at heart?"

"If you believe that——"

"I have no right to believe it of any human soul. My sin is greater than hers," Lancret cried, moving up and down with short steps, unable to control his voice.

"If you believe that, why did you come to me?" Barbet persisted. "Certainly, it has never worried me that she talks about herself. Too much, I grant you. But after all it is an interesting subject."

At that the priest was able to smile again, and, when he said that he must return to Roussignac, they walked together to the edge of the wood.

"You are more patient than the rest of us," he said. "Do you remember the story of Flornoy's father? He was in India—or was it Burma? One day, he met a tigress. Instead of trying to fight or run, he went on quietly. The tigress turned and accompanied him. He and she went for a walk together."

"Bless my soul," said Barbet. "Isn't it natural? What else could the chap do?"

He walked slowly back to the house when the priest's tall figure had vanished among the oak-trees, and seated himself on a wooden bench at the edge of a grassy clearing outside the walls. At this point the ground fell away steeply, allowing him to see the river over the heads of the pine-trees which grew exceptionally in the neighborhood of the Maison Hazard as they do in the region of Garde Epée. He lifted his hands to his face and, finding that they were not rid of the smell of paint, began to wave them in the air. This producing no effect, he fetched two handfuls of pine-needles, returned to his bench and rubbed them slowly between his palms until all were fallen. After that, he drew his feet up under him, and, having smelt his hands again, wrinkled his nose and gave up his attempt.

His brown hair threw out, here and there, upward twirls of no great dignity, and his face—a blunt-angled face that retained the chunkiness of a boy's—was almost as brown as the hair. The warmth of its colour gave a special emphasis to eyes not brown but blue and far-looking, with a steady liveliness of their own—the eyes of a northern seaman who surprisingly inhabited the body of a brown bear.

After a little while, he pulled his shirt away from his ribs and wriggled himself that the air might move across his flesh; he revolved his arms slowly with the same purpose; he sniffed the pine-trees. There couldn't be a better evening, he said to himself, and was grateful, and still.

Far below, the reedy waters of the Charente were sunlit on their farther bank. A meadow extended there, with a great double procession of Lombardy poplars running beside it up the southern hill, and beyond the meadow to the west were squares and triangles and long slices of cultivated land divided from one another by hedges blurred in the whiteness of hawthorn. Crowning the landscape was the wooded ridge which marked the main road from Cognac to Angoulême, now puffy with new foliage and the late gold of the sun. A barge was being towed down-river, dragging behind her a double wake that shone like the track of a small snail. While Barbet watched her, she nosed alongside, and tied up for the night. The ripples vanished, the water settled to the gleam of rubbed silver, the willows on the bank reappeared in it, standing on their mirrored heads. The tiny figures of the bargees could be seen making fast and, presently, moving away with their two horses towards the opposite village of Bellis. Perhaps they lived there and this was a fortunate stopping-place. Barbet watched the pencilling of their shadows before them and the slow flicker of light between their legs as they walked.

From behind him, the smell of cooking came out from the Maison Hazard, for the prisoners' supper was being prepared. Fontan, in the first cell, would be impatient for it, not because he was hungry but because he was still new enough to count the hours

There's not much you can give him to do, Barbet thought. He won't read—or can't. For him there are women in every book; his Eugénie is in every book, even in the Gospels. Anyhow, he's no good with his hands except at music, and what instrument can he have that won't infuriate the others? Even the mandolin, he'll play for hours on end if he's given the chance—the same passages over and over again. Marcotte, Heim, Balze, even Autun at last, begin to shout him down, and at the first twang of the strings Blachère hammers at his door and howls like a wolf.

There was a sudden arrest of Barbet's mind at the thought of Blachère. At first encounter, he had recognized the others; their reputed evils, their angers, follies, freaks, were the disguise that a man put on or that circumstance puts on him, but their own realities, they themselves, were plain through their disguises. Fontan was a small boy, frightened and defiant, looking for shelter. Marcotte, a peasant strained to cities, had the earth in him—spring and warmth, a fecund darkness, under the cruelty of paving-stones, and, in seeing Marcotte, it was not only the disguise of the cruel mouth and slit eyes that Barbet saw, but this earthy figure, this innocence overlaid. Balze, Heim, even the sleepy Autun—each looked out through his disguise into Barbet's face. Only their disguises might be condemned or forgiven; their essences, like birds and trees and night and morning, were not to be judged but perceived. To think of his prisoners was, for Barbet, to look through open windows into rooms of his own house. To this, Blachère was an exception. To think of him was to strike a wall in darkness.

His thought retreated from Blachère. He remembered a conversation with Fontan:

"But you didn't kill her . . ."

"No. She's alive still," Fontan had replied, as though the knowledge tormented him.

"Why don't you make a voyage with her?" Barbet had asked.

"Make a voyage?" cried Fontan, and Barbet had said that his own voyages might begin anywhere—at a side road, for example. You said to yourself: if I went up that road and straight on, soon there'd be no time or distance. "But I never see a side road," Fontan had answered. "I'm shut up in this place," and Barbet, finding that he could not explain his idea to Fontan, had said only: "I make up journeys. I did when I was a boy. I do still."

"What's the point? Where to?"

It had been the priest's question—"From what? to what?" he had asked, and to him Barbet had been able to reply: "From one way of living to another." He had found that he was prevented from giving the same answer to Fontan, and now, remembering this failure, he understood the reason of it: in his relationship to Lancret, he was free, but, in his relationship to Fontan, bound, for how can a gaoler who does not cease to be a gaoler speak to his prisoner of moving from one way of living to another? The truth dries on his tongue because he himself does not live it. And yet, Barbet said to himself, though I should cease to keep the gaol, Fontan would remain a prisoner. The problem troubled him, not because he believed it to be insoluble, but because he knew that he was taking too complex a view of it and had not yet enough simplicity to solve it.

By the time he had ceased to think of Fontan, the barge was like a black twig among the reeds, the men and the horses had disappeared. The village itself was passing into shadow as his mind gradually emptied itself of all these things.

Chapter 2

"THEIR SUPPER WILL BE READY IN TEN MINUTES, Barbet," Madame Hazard called from the kitchen door. "It's time you went round the walls." Her son did not move. His legs were still drawn up under him on his wooden bench; his body was straight, his head erect, his hands now were grasping his feet. "Ten minutes, Barbet," she repeated. "Renée will take the stew off then."

What she saw of him was his back, his faded shirt of blue linen tautened by the forward drag of the arms, and his head, broadening above the ears, tufted at the crown. She knew that he was within earshot, and was on the point of shrilling her voice to break his concentration, when the crest of hair, a loose plume raised up into the evening light, saved him, as it had often, and against all reason, saved him from her anger when he was a boy.

"Shout at him, Aunt!" cried Renée. "He can hear all right if he wants to."

"Oh, yes, he *can* hear," answered Madame Hazard, "but he doesn't, you know."

"Well, make him!" exclaimed Renée, who, though younger by ten years, felt for Barbet the affectionate intolerance of an elder sister. "When we are ready to serve, he won't be. With Madame Vincent coming to supper, I want time to sit down and cool off a bit."

She left the stove and went to the window, intending to give her cousin the edge of her tongue. Her heels beat out her irritation on the stone flags; the great spoon in her hand lashed at an assembly of flies on the drying-board. "I'll stir him," she muttered, thrusting out her head, but when she saw him, perched there on the bench, she was at first silent, as her aunt had been, then laughed and shrugged.

"Bon," she said, swinging back to her task, "let him alone, if he must be such a fool," but there was no venom in the word "fool," and, when she clattered a saucepan to show how angry she was, she found that she was not angry at all.

"Did you see," said her aunt, "he has that paint on the seat of his breeches?"

Renée nodded. "You may be sure. He never gives a thought to the seat of his breeches. . . . What does he do with the paint, anyway—sit in it?"

"God knows," said Madame Hazard. "He is very foolish. And yet he does his work well—and more than his share of it."

She had done her part of the cooking and stood now in silence at the doorway, feeling the jets of cooler air flow in through the gaps of her teeth, looking sometimes at her son, sometimes at her niece, but only at their appearances. She did not look into or deeply compare them, being interested only in the plain facts that the girl, with her bare arms and long, striding legs and little beads of sweat in the groove of her lip, was never still, while the man was more still than a rock. His stillness had life in it; he was as still as a bird in the instant before flight.

Madame Hazard was extremely small, but with the smallness of a miniature, not of a dwarf, the proportion of her youth surviving even in the shrivel of her age—a pretty girl who had grown old but felt still the pretty girl within her and looked out of the shell with that girl's eyes, and pouted with her lips, and cackled with her laughter. Her arms, clasped at the elbows, now rested comfortably on the ledge of her apron; below them, her black dress fell in deep, shiny folds; and, above her waist, the diminutive body was still graceful and with a kind of frozen pliancy.

The years had done little to change the expression of her eyes, which retained all the petulance of her girlhood. At sixty-two, she could still use ill-temper as a privilege, her lips sullen with the arrogance which, when the lips themselves had been full and red and smooth, had turned the head of Barbet's father thirty-six years ago;

and, though she had learned that to scream at her son was a waste of breath, she did not know why. His immunity baffled and irritated her. What was she in the world for, if not to set men by the ears?

"After all," she said at last, "he's old enough to know better."

Renée replied that, for herself, she wouldn't have cared, if Pierre Vincent's mother hadn't been coming. If Barbet was late taking supper round the cells, everything would be put back. Blachère would start kicking his door and shouting. "You know how it is—once he starts that game, he keeps it up, and it makes no odds how we have supper—with the courtyard windows closed and the shutters across—still she'll hear him. She always pretends to be startled. Down go her knife and fork, and she cocks her head like a terrier." Madame Hazard began to chuckle at the familiar scene, for Madame Vincent, with her long nose and freckles, was, to her, ridiculous, in common with all ill-favoured women. "Can't you hear her?" Renée continued, encouraged to mimicry by her aunt's applause. " 'What can that noise be?' she'll say—as if she didn't know we kept a prison! Then everyone will be quiet. Blachère's voice will come through—the filthy words—right in her ear."

"Serve her right!" said Madame Hazard.

" 'Serve her right!'—I dare say! But it's not you wants to marry Pierre," Renée retorted. "Every time she has her ears scalded by Blachère, she holds out again, and there's another five hundred on the dot. . . . I'm twenty-two, and with Pierre living in the house—"

"La, la, la! You're too hot—that's why she holds out. Blow cold a bit, girl. Then she'll come to."

Renée sighed over such patient strategy, impossible in her. "All the same," she said in the tone of a little girl wishing that her family drove out in a glass coach, "I do wish we didn't keep a prison."

"Nonsense!" cried Madame Hazard, who enjoyed the prison when it infuriated Madame Vincent. "Don't you believe it. Prison or no prison—it's all the same to her. If we kept a cathedral, she'd find something to complain of in that. She's not good enough for us and she knows it; that's why she's a duchess with one nostril and a republican with the other—and both with her nose in the air! Her father was a shoemaker at Angoulême; mine was a sergeant at Quatre Bras. And if it comes to prisons—isn't Pierre her own son, and isn't he warder here and overseer and handyman all rolled into one, and isn't it my son who's his master? Barbet's too soft. I'd soon let your Pierre know his place—"

"It's not *his* fault!"

"Well, his mother, then. Can't a place be found for him in the office at Roussignac? With his brother Anton's partner and his sister Anton's wife, you'd have thought a desk could have been found for Pierre."

"He doesn't want a desk. He likes work on a farm."

"Nonsense, child. He must take good money where he can get it, particularly if he wants to marry you. . . . Anyhow, why does his mother let him take our wages if she's so ashamed of prisons?" The little woman shook with anger, tramping with her feet and rolling her body from side to side. "Pah-pah-pah!" she exclaimed—a noise like the struggle of water in the neck of a full carafe. "If she had had a daughter to marry, she'd have haggled with Bonaparte himself because he was a Corsican. She is that kind of woman."

"And who would want to marry Bonaparte?" asked Renée slyly.

"And why not? Why not, pray?"

"He had such a belly on him," said Renée.

"Belly!" Madame Hazard exclaimed, drawing up all the inches of her Bonapartism. "Not at Lodi! Not at Marengo!"

"It must be time," said Barbet, appearing at his mother's side. "They have their bowls, haven't they, Renée? If you'll give me the tureen, I'll take it round. Is it a good stew?"

He drew a bunch of keys from within his shirt and allowed it to dangle before him on its cord. Both hands were free for the tureen and he held them out.

"How you can go about with those digging into you all day, I don't know. All night too," Renée added. "No wonder you're a bachelor."

She took the keys and allowed them to fall with a clink against the buckle of his belt. "What is it? Are you so afraid to let them out of your sight?"

He smiled at her. "You give me the stew, or Blachère will be kicking the place down. You won't like that with your mother-in-law coming to supper."

"My mother-in-law!" She gave him the stew. "She's not that yet, and won't be if you can't keep your circus in order. Go on with you, and don't forget you have the round of the walls to do before Madame Vincent comes."

Carrying the tureen before him, he walked to the farthest of the kitchen's three doors. It stood open upon a covered way which Julien Hazard, wanting direct communication from kitchen to prison so that supplies might not be carried through intervening rooms, had clamped on to the west front. It was, in effect, an external passage which led round the angle of the house, to the prison courtyard at the back of the north wing.

"And don't you forget," Madame Hazard called after him, "that this is not one of the evenings on which you invite the circus to have its supper in the open. If you do, Blachère will come up to our windows and shout."

"It's hot in those cells," said Barbet. "If I let them out into the courtyard for their supper, they'd be quiet. I'd tell them Madame Vincent was coming. They are reasonable men."

"Really, Barbet," his mother intervened, "if they were cattle, you'd say they were reasonable cattle."

Interested at once, Barbet put down the tureen. He wished to point out that everything depended on whether you felt that you were separate from the cattle or of the same nature with them. He began to remind his mother of the story of Flornoy and the tiger, but Madame Hazard knew to what such argument led.

"In any case," she said, "cattle or no cattle, reason or no reason, you promised Renée not to let them out this evening. It's her evening. Pierre has taken the gig over to fetch his mother now. You gave your word, Barbet."

"I know," he said, remembering. "Well?"

He picked up the tureen.

"But will you keep your word?"

"Entendu, p'tite mère."

When, after leaving the kitchen, Barbet reached the end of the covered way, he turned into a vaulted stone passage which penetrated the structure of the building itself and, being stopped by a thick, bolted door, was lit only from its outer end. In a niche beside the door was a box containing the pistol he should have put into his hip-pocket before going to the prisoners; another, for Pierre Vincent, lay beside it. His father had always gone armed into the prison courtyard, and, if one was to be a gaoler, one might as well be a competent gaoler, but on this occasion, as on many others, he left the pistol in its box, for he had no sense of risk to remind him of it and had enough to do with the tureen.

When he had passed through one door, another confronted him, for Julien Hazard had built a second barrier into this passage, that one might always be shut before the other was opened. A grille in the second door commanded the quadrangle. Barbet looked through it, not, as he had been taught, because the prisoners might have broken loose, but because it pleased him to watch, through this wooden frame, the birds in the courtyard or on the roof. They seemed to prefer the eastern roof, above the occupied cells, where they could not be observed by the prisoners. This puzzled him, for he believed that birds were little conscious of the human eye. Considering this problem, he entered the courtyard itself, set down the tureen again, and locked the door behind him.

In his grandfather's, and at the beginning of his father's time, the place had been crowded; now it contained only six prisoners. At its northern end were a disused lodge and an entrance gate, now permanently shut; to the south, beside the area of stone-paving on which Barbet stood, was the back of the Hazards' living quarters, its lower row of windows protected by bars and interior shutters and its original door bricked in. On either side, the farm buildings and store-houses of the old courtyard had been converted to the uses of a prison, and above them were false walls, built sixty years ago when a prisoner had escaped by scaling the roof. To this precaution another had been added. Wherever a man might dare to climb, inward-sloping prongs had been embedded in the stone. The coping of the false walls and the edge of the roof bristled with them, giving, to one who stood within, a sense of being enclosed by a square of rusty bayonets. These spikes were of value to Barbet as apparatus for his study of birds. Reconciliation and exile, happiness and mourning, war and peace—every kind of domestic or foreign crisis might express itself in the choice of a prong. Some he had made convenient for the gregarious by small wooden platforms attached to them; a few were equipped for the solitary by having had circular barriers, like the hand-guard of a sword, slid over them to such a distance as allowed one bird, and one only, to perch on the secluded tip; from half a dozen were hung split coconuts, tin baths and other conveniences that served also as swings. Barbet was at once aware of it if a thrush changed his club.

On his way to the cells, he crossed the grassy central space, a small, rectangular meadow, shaded by cherry and apple and by an enormous ilex, so old that the courtyard must have been built round it. This evening the birds sat up aloft in rows to stare at him. Two came nearer, but, finding that there was nothing to please them in the tureen and that heat rose through the ladle-slit, they flickered about his shoulders and away. Even the tit in her bath did not pause for him, and he was glad. Birds were not pets, like Renée's dog; if they became dependent on him, they would by that dependence separate him from themselves. To tame them, to compel them to his plane, would have been shameful; and if, in winter, he gave them food, he gave it with what secrecy he could, dissociating himself from it, never pausing as their host, or persuading them to himself. He loved them for what, in themselves, they were, not for what he might lure them into becoming, and so glad was he now of their independence—an assurance of liberty in himself and of his unity with them—that a tune sprang up in his head. It became a song; words flowed into it which were, in his mind, a rejoicing that men and birds in their differences mark the span of nature's including hand. By the time he had reached Fontan's cell, he was

singing as happily and with as little consciousness of an audience as
he did when going about the country alone.

"That's new!" Fontan exclaimed with the querulous intonation
of one who had been unjustly kept out of a secret. "The tune, I
mean—I haven't heard it before."

"Nor have I," said Barbet. "Look, here's your stew. I mustn't
keep the others waiting now. There's the cheese and fruit to get
and I haven't long to-night. Madame Vincent is expected."

"Madame Vincent is expected!" Fontan echoed with bitter
scorn, as though Madame Vincent, of whom he knew little but the
name, were his enemy.

Everyone has his misfortune, his special kink, and it was Fontan's
to believe that men were in conspiracy against him: not that Fate
had overpowered him—a belief that gives a man, after all, a repose,
a certain final dignity of the vanquished—but that everyone's hand
was against his class, against him personally, that laws were designed
to cheat him of his rights and squander his powers. He had the
gnawing grievance of those who, hating privilege, desire nothing so
much. Barbet knew that he was harmless. A man who believed
that the world existed to ensnare him was afraid of life itself and
dared not act. "Il n'est pas dangereux, ce pauvre Fontan."

But Fontan did his utmost to appear menacing. He leaned
against the table of his cell, clutching its edge with fingers like sticks
of ivory. His head was thrust forward; the evening light glistened
on two bony protuberances of his forehead. Suddenly he shot out,
from under black, meeting eyebrows, the absurd, ferocious glance
of a violinist who, unsure of himself, tucks his fiddle under his chin.

"Hum it again. You'll forget the tune. Go on—then I'll have it."

Barbet knew that what Fontan wanted was the mandolin. He
would pick out the tune on it, then forget this tune and play others
from the past—tunes recalled from the time when he was a teacher
of music and Eugénie his pupil—until he was lost in a frenzy of remembrances, and bliss and misery were confused in his brain. Well,
he can have it for a little while, Barbet decided, and fetched it from
a spare cell.

He hummed the tune again. "But it ought to have little trills, high up, always going on behind it," he said, becoming eager himself. "And others behind that, higher and higher until you can't hear them at all—a lark so high you can't hear him. I can't hum that."

"I could play it if I had a fiddle."

"No one could play it," said Barbet, "except—"

"Mozart!" cried Fontan.

As if the other had not spoken, Barbet smiled, not at all in self-pity, but with the special radiance of those who feel but do not envy genius. "There," he added, "there's the mandolin."

On Fontan's chair, he sat down to listen. It surprised him to hear his tune under Fontan's hand. A moment ago it had come to him out of the air. What he had sung had been a stumbling shorthand for what he had heard, and now Fontan was transcribing the shorthand as if it were all. But how clever he is! Barbet thought, who could play only the gavotte that had been drilled into him in his boyhood and a few melodies, laboriously picked out, that he had heard in the café concerts of Angoulême. That *is* the tune, he repeated to persuade himself, lest he should do injustice to Fontan's talent. He sang the words in proof that he was grateful for the player's skill and kindness, and the tureen would have been forgotten if a mutter of protest from the neighbouring cells and a howl of rage from Blachère's had not silenced the mandolin.

Barbet then made haste from cell to cell, carefully locking the doors again, when he had ladled out the stew. They were in the right; it was their supper-time; he was sorry. Marcotte, a grizzled labourer, put his finger in the stew: "Still hot," he said. Autun, who had been an official of the post-office in Roussignac and was imprisoned for having stolen the cash, pulled one of the long grimaces that had been accounted to him for humour in his days of prosperity, and said nothing. Balze and Heim, leader and led, clerks to the same notary, who had planted the scrip of the Union Générale throughout the neighbourhood before the crash in '82 and had mixed with it a forged scrip of their own, said much, for it was their profession. Supper was late; the cells were too hot to breathe in.

"Aren't we to have the courtyard to-night?" said Balze as he heard Marcotte's door being locked.

"And why not?" said Heim.

"Why not?" said Barbet. "There couldn't be a lovelier evening," and not until he had let them all out of their cells did he remember his promise to Renée. It was Blachère who reminded him.

"And what will Madame Vincent say?"

It was said in that tone of false good-humour, intended to flatter the many at the expense of one, which is the mark of a bully among boys and men, and was accompanied by a facetious tilting of the head on a short, rolled neck—a head which, now that it was partly bald, was seen to have a cushioned fatness and whiteness and looseness, so that it was like a wrinkled ball of lard on which bristles were growing. Blachère had been a professional strong-man, a travelling showman, and, he said, in his time a bear-tamer, but this Barbet wondered at—how could a man have tamed bears without learning to despise himself, and Blachère bragged of his bears. He wore a black moustache, now streaked with white, twirled high about waxen and pitted nostrils; his mouth, separated from his moustache by a rim of lip, was full and purple, like a sliced steak; and about his eyes, small and close-set, were long black lashes, which to other eyes might have given an expression of tenderness but to his were a dressing of the grotesque. Being muscle-bound, he held himself stiffly, and had, in general, the appearance of a depraved doll.

"What will Madame Vincent say?" he repeated.

"She's of no consequence," replied Barbet at once. "You can have your supper in the yard if you'll be quiet."

What had made him say this, he could not afterwards have told. If he had ordered them back into their cells, they would have obeyed —even Blachère, who had expected it. Barbet did not even reflect that his yielding might be interpreted as submission to Blachère. He had none of the self-consciousness of power, and found it so necessary to laugh at himself that he had not the least fear of being laughed at. In spite of his promise to Renée, it was in the open that he had imagined the prisoners having their supper.

When he returned to the kitchen again for cheese and fruit, he drew Renée aside.

"I have let them out."

"But your promise?"

"I have broken it."

"But why—why?"

"It happened so."

She looked at him. "You are mad!"

"No," he said, "but Madame Vincent's not important—even to you."

"How can you say that?" she exclaimed. "If there's a rumpus to-night—"

"Will Pierre love you any the less?"

"No."

"Or you him?"

"No, but a promise—"

"Yes, Renée, but now it's broken, you don't care. You're not angry. You are only telling yourself you ought to be."

She stared and choked and laughed aloud. "Oh, but it's true, you're mad, Barbet!"

He took the cheese from her. "Bless you, Renée. You're good about my promise. You don't make scenes."

"What's the good—if you're mad?" After a silence, she said: "That man frightens me, Barbet."

"Which man?"

"Blachère. Not the others, but he does. Some day he'll kill you."

"No."

"He'll try."

"Why should he?"

"Because you're alive and he's dead."

"Good God, Renée, what made you say that?"

She shrugged her shoulders. "Is it true?"

He did not answer but returned to the courtyard. The prisoners were gathered at a table under the ilex; they had carried the tureen with them. With Heim and Balze applauding him, Blachère was plying Fontan with tales of women. Autun sat a little apart, a grimace fixed about his mouth. Old Marcotte had his head down to his bowl, supping from a greedy spoon, but his eyebrows were up, his gaze tied to the speaker. Fontan's eyes were shut, his face twitched, and he forgot to eat until Barbet reminded him.

Chapter 3

IT WAS NOT TRUE THAT MADAME VINCENT'S father had been a shoemaker in Angoulême; he had been a worker in leather, a maker of harness, and, for the love as well as the profit of it, a binder of books. Reading the books he bound, he had dinned it into his daughter that she should do likewise.

When she married Vincent in '46, she brought with her seven thousand francs and a memory at once prodigious and useless. She remembered scraps from everything she had read but was without care for meaning or context. Poor Vincent had been overwhelmed by her quotations, not because they were apt, but because they had, on the contrary, no relevance to the subject discussed and produced upon his mind the cumulative effect of a spell. "Why do you say that, Emilie?" he would ask at first, lifting his head from the pillow. "Because it is true, Vincent!"—and the alexandrines would roll again like thunder around the canopy of the bed. "But it has nothing to do with us," he would protest. "I've had a long day. I want to sleep. I can't make out why you say it *now*." "Because," she replied, "it rings in my head."

After a little while, he set himself with desperation to beget children, and his nights were subsequently quiet; but though, as he told himself, he thus employed the only means by which a woman's silence may be assured, he had little profit of his exercise; for afterwards he himself began to lie awake, troubled by social conscience and wishing that he had been better educated. The years passed; Victor and Bette and Pierre were born; the flood of quotation continued and no remedy appeared. At last he fell sick and was near to death. One night, stirring in the small hours and seeing Emilie awake beside him, he asked what time it was. She looked at the watch and said it was one o'clock; then, in a voice of doom, continued:

"Mademoiselle d'Esgrignon, prions Dieu que cette heure ne soit plus fatale à notre maison. Mon oncle, Monseigneur l'archevêque, a été massacré à cette heure, à sette heure mourut aussi mon père. . . ."

Vincent had protested feebly that none of her uncles had been an archbishop; then, perceiving through the mists of consciousness that once again he had missed his cue, he had hid his face in his pillow and died, feeling that this was the least so ignorant a man could do.

A man may die of worse diseases than a surfeit of Balzac, but Madame Vincent did not fail to mourn her husband, for she was not a woman to neglect an opportunity, and no subject has a richer literature than bereavement. When at last it was exhausted, she turned to marriage, wishing to dispose of each of her children in turn. Bette fell in with her plans, but Victor, the eldest, had no taste for women, and Pierre would have none but Renée. Madame Vincent had no objection to Renée, or, as Madame Hazard was aware, to the prison, but she had found a profitable bed for her daughter with Anton Hazard and was certain that, in the matter of dowry, Barbet could be squeezed on Renée's behalf. This was clearly though silently understood between her and Madame Hazard; there was a bargain to be struck and they would take their time about it. Meanwhile nothing was too hard for them to say of each other, but they were very good friends. They had much in common: avarice with good-humour, scepticism with ignorance, bawdiness with refinement. Madame Hazard felt superior because she had been pretty; Madame Vincent because she could quote; they were thus bound together by that strongest of ties, a contempt for the rest of the world. Whenever anything was mentioned, except property, that men have lived or died for, they celebrated their scepticism with a wink.

"The curé," said Madame Vincent after supper, with just such a wink as this and a drumming of her finger-nail on the edge of her coffee-cup, "will have to mind his Ps and Qs. He thought he was rid of her, I'll be bound."

"Of her?" said Renée.

"Now, Miss Innocent, don't you pretend!"

Madame Hazard pursed her lips. "I don't suppose Renée knows anything of it—unless Pierre told her."

"And I suppose Barbet doesn't either?"

"I'm sorry," said Barbet. "What were you talking of?"

"Thérèse Despreux. She's back at the Cheval Pie. Home for the pickings. It didn't take her long. She was back before Sernet was cold."

"There's not much pickings," said Barbet. "There's nothing left. Madame Sernet's useless. The Cheval Pie is on the rocks. Whatever sent Thérèse back, it was what she can bring, not what she'll find."

"Pah, pah, pah!" his mother exclaimed. "She's no good that girl—never was."

"But the curé?" Renée demanded. "What's it to do with him?"

Madame Vincent laid a finger beside her nose. "Perhaps Barbet will tell you."

"She means," Barbet said, "that many people think Thérèse Despreux is the curé's daughter. You wouldn't remember, Renée. You're no older than she. How old were you when you came to live with us?"

She counted seven years backwards on her fingers. "Fifteen."

"There, you see. The scandal was stale by then, and Thérèse—"

"But I was here when her mother died," said Renée. "I was fifteen and Thérèse only a few months younger. I remember the widow Despreux's funeral and thinking how much dumpier I was than Thérèse. It's almost the first thing I do remember in this place. O but she was espiègle! Always so full of games and sayings, she could drive us mad! Black hair in a mop and green eyes. And thin —like a boy. At the funeral, she stood with her feet together and her hands clasped—and glinted! And sometimes she twisted her hair back to show her ears. The more piously she behaved, the more certain you felt that for two pins she'd throw a cart-wheel."

Pierre heaved himself out of a long silence. "That's about what

she has been doing by all accounts, since she went off to the milliner's
at Angoulême—throwing cart-wheels. It's not four years ago and
she's come back looking like—" He gave a long whistle. "Espiègle!"
he said.

His mother repeated the word. It found response in her memory.
She rumbled like a musical box whose works have been stimulated
by the insertion of a coin.

> " 'Cœur d'ange et de lion, libre oiseau de passage,
>   Espiègle enfant ce soir, sainte artiste demain.' "

It was said as though it were an imprecation, and, accustomed
though they all were to Madame Vincent's outbursts of irrelevance,
it took them a little time to understand that only one word, espiègle,
had for her a present meaning; the rest were the cotton-wool in
which she happened to have found her peach.

"I disagree," said Madame Hazard.

"And what do you disagree with?" Madame Vincent demanded.
"One can't disagree with Musset. One can't disagree with poetry.
One can dislike it; one can be ignorant of it; one can be a plain fool
about it; but one cannot disagree with it. There is nothing to disagree with."

"I disagree," said Madame Hazard. "Angel and lion, indeed!
Libre oiseau de passage! A girl who works for four years in a milliner's and then comes home to rub her knuckles off swilling glasses at
the Cheval Pie! Angels and lions—what have they to do with her?
Tell me that."

"Nothing," said Madame Vincent.

"And if you ask me," cried Madame Hazard, "the girl's none the
worse for that."

Madame Vincent's freckled nostrils curled in derisive triumph.
"A moment ago," she exclaimed, pouncing on her opponent, "there
was nothing bad enough you could say of the girl. 'She's no good
that girl, never was'—your own words. Can you deny it?"

"I disagree," said Madame Hazard; then resumed the attack.
"And don't you dare to quote me! The poets if you must, but me—
to my own face! It is too much!" Her old cheeks were a fierce pink,

her eyes flashed, her hands, in an ecstasy of wrath, were pawing the stuff of her company gown. This was an evening to remember—as rich and reasonless a quarrel as ever they'd had. What was it about? . . . That Thérèse Despreux. . . . And how had Thérèse come into it? . . . Angels and lions? Her anger ebbing, she began to feel old, tired, confused; then, suddenly, she jerked up her head, stiffened, gazed, and threw in the Old Guard. "In any case, she has a pretty nose, and if she's good she's good in spite of it, and that, Emilie Vincent, is more than all of us can say. To resist temptation is one thing and no doubt God rewards it, for men don't. But never to cause temptation is another, and, if there's a prize in heaven for that, the angels keep it to themselves. . . . And you," she cried, rounding on Pierre, " 'cart-wheels' you said, 'throwing cart-wheels in Angoulême'—what d'you mean by that? Pleased enough you'd be, with your sheep's eyes, if any girl worth her keep would 'throw a cart-wheel' for you. What are you—a cardinal?"

"Well," said Pierre with a conciliatory grin, "it was pretty hot, I gather."

"Hot!" said Madame Hazard. "Isn't she twenty-two and a priest's daughter? What do you expect—a nun or a cuttle-fish? Look at your own Renée! Is that cart-wheels? Look at her cheeks!"

And, indeed, they were pink.

"There," the old lady exclaimed, "upon my soul, I'm warm myself." She hauled up a fan that was hanging on a cord from her waist and began to cool her cheeks. The fan had a pleasing scent which reminded her of parties in her youth. She smiled, put her head on one side, and forgave her guest. Madame Vincent, in her turn, scowled and forgave her hostess. "I think," said Madame Hazard, "that Madame Vincent would join me in a game, if you'd be kind enough to bring the cards, Renée. And, perhaps, dear Emilie, a little glass of something de derrière les fagots?"

Chapter 4

WHEN THE LADIES WERE SETTLED TO THEIR game, and Pierre, with Renée, had escaped into the pine-wood, Barbet sat for a little while on a straight chair against the wall, watching cards slide in the lamp-light.

"Ne vaut pas," said his mother.

Madame Vincent continued to announce her hand.

"Egal," said his mother, and Madame Vincent, baffled, tapped her cards with her finger-nail and began to talk.

"I want to have a little conversation with you, Chouquette, before the evening is out," she said with an eye on Barbet.

"About what?" asked Madame Hazard.

"An old subject, my dear. My son asked me to speak of it."

"Which son? Victor or Pierre? If Pierre, it's Renée's dowry. If Victor, it's this idea that Barbet should sell the house to Anton. I know, I know, I know."

"Well," said Madame Vincent, "with the phylloxera threatening, the price—"

"Pah! The phylloxera won't touch the Maison Hazard as long as I live in it. Besides, the price has risen."

"Now listen, Chouquette. Be reasonable."

"I won't listen. I won't be reasonable," Madame Hazard exclaimed. "We are playing piquet. Look at your cards, Emilie."

Madame Vincent surrendered. Silence fell. Piquet was Barbet's own game, and he could have watched it peacefully for an hour. But he had not yet made his round of the walls, and, drawing his eyes away from the glitter of the cards, he stood up and shook himself and went out to the small courtyard in which Lancret had found him. The cooler air carried in it the night-scent of pine-trees. Muffled laughter, instantly suppressed, came to him from the increasing darkness. Pierre and Renée were not far away. And will he remember, when they come in again, to brush the pine-needles from her shoulders? said Barbet to himself.

In this courtyard were three trees—a vine over the door, a fig against the north wall, and a pomegranate. At the foot of the vine Barbet found a stable-lamp in its accustomed place. He lighted it and, as he walked, turned over peacefully in his mind the work he had done earlier that day with old Quessot in the coopers' shed. As a boy he had been, first an admirer, then an apprentice, of Quessot, and now, except at the time of the vintage, few days passed in which they did not work together. Barbet was proud of his skill in this ancient craft which no machinery could replace; in the uses of the "bear" and the "dove," in binding the chestnut hoops with the bark of osier, he was the old man's equal, and, when the fire was blazing inside the unfinished barrel and the hoops were being driven on, he could bend his back more easily and was quicker with the mallet; but, as long as I live, Barbet thought, or as long as he lives, when it comes to paring the staves, Quessot will be my master with the chipaxe. Still, thank Heaven, I can hold my own with most people even at that job, he added, and if ever I were to sell the place to Anton as he wishes or if the phylloxera eats up my vines, there are few districts of France where a cooper can't earn his living with his hands.

This conclusion was enough to banish care. He and his lamp swung through the gateway without a trouble in the world. Soon he came to the cell windows in the eastern wall, which it was his duty to examine. As he approached them, he turned his head suddenly, but none had called him. Only an inhabited silence flowed up from the wood, and he did his task. By the time he had made sure that the bars had not been tampered with, a moon was up, but he kept his lamp burning and began to walk home, looking now and then across his shoulder into the wood.

There was nothing in the air he breathed, or in his shadow on the prison wall. or in the smell of earth, nothing in the warmth of the lamp on his knuckles, to distinguish this night from others of spring; but he heard his own voice say aloud: "I shall remember to-night." As he said this, Lancret, who had been absent from his mind, so powerfully returned to it, that he raised his eyes sharply as though his name had been called from under the blossom of the cherry-tree.

But that is absurd, he couldn't be walking here in the dark, Barbet reflected. Lancret, certainly, was at home, a book before him on the white oilcloth of his table, one hand propping his head, the other stiffly raised to guard his eyes against the candle-glare. The uplifted hand came down to the corner of a page, the head for a moment was tilted as though to the sound of a footfall; but there was no footfall, the page was turned, and the reader with a sigh continued his reading. Barbet was halted; he had seemed to be a spectator at Lancret's uncurtained window; and, submitting himself to so clear a summons, he turned in the direction of Roussignac.

In the Long Wood he had need of his lamp. The path was ribbed by moon, thinly and at long intervals. A clinging bramble checked him. While he freed himself of it, he saw, in a ray of his lamp, an exposed root with two steep angles like the letter W, the same coiling root which had lain between him and Thérèse Despreux while she asked of Paris on the eve of her flight to Angoulême four years ago. He had long forgotten but now slowly recognized it, and, his thought being directed to Thérèse, he knew that it was for her footfall that the priest, her father, listened while he read, while he prayed, even while he slept, always in vain for she would not come to him, always in confusion of spirit for, though she came, still she would carry his sin within her. Her life itself was his remorse, yet she was the emblem of what earthly happiness he had known, his vindication as a man. Poor Lancret's heart cried out to her as a body in a dark place cries out for the sun, but each impulse of affection, each secret pride in his daughter, appeared to him as renewal of the sin in which she had been begotten and a denial of his repentance.

When Barbet had passed through the Long Wood, he came at once to the outskirts of Roussignac and blew out his lamp. A few minutes in the deserted road brought him to the church which stood in a small square and was protected from wheeled traffic by a surrounding pavement, raised a step above street level, and by a ring of plane-trees. The church itself was octagonal and from each of its sides a semicircular apse swelled out under a steep roof. This roof was supported, where it overhung the walls, by corbels variously carved with angels and men and animals, a delight of Barbet's childhood and a delight the greater because it had not been thought wise that a Protestant boy should stand gaping at a Catholic church. He paused now, outside the west entrance, to discover, on the first corbel to the left, a squirrel to whom the ancient sculptor had given a straight face, like a horse's. Shadow was on the face, but the great bushy tail was in full moonlight, and Barbet remembered that he had always intended to ask the priest if there was a legend about the squirrel. I'll ask him to-night! He rounded the church and entered Lancret's small garden. There was light in the uncurtained window. He rapped on the pane. Lancret turned and gazed. He pressed his hands flat to his cheeks, thrusting his lips forward, and rocked his head to and fro as though awaking from a dream. Then, possessing himself, he rose, disappeared for a moment from Barbet's sight, came to the door and opened it. His height filled the door.

"Come in, my son."

He was spare and wiry of body; his eyes were sunk, his neck was so thin that the skin of it had fallen loose, and when he smiled his eyelids did not lift.

"How can I help you?"

"It's not about myself," said Barbet.

They had edged their way through the passage, each bidding the other to go before him, and were in the priest's room under a small portrait of Leo XIII and a larger one of Pius IX which still held the place of honour that it had occupied in Barbet's childhood. Lancret closed the door and, without a word, seated himself in a high-backed wooden chair. There he began to smooth his knees outwards with the palms of his hands, and at last raised his eyes to his visitor. "Well?" he said.

"I was going the round of my prison walls," Barbet explained. "It came into my head that we hadn't finished our talk of Thérèse Despreux."

One of Lancret's hands went up from knee to throat, eagerness came into the eyes, the lips parted. How much he wishes to speak of her! Barbet thought. He is like a man secretly in love; nothing interests him except the subject he must not speak of; speak her name, and his agony shines through all his concealments. He may banish her from his lips but not starvation from his eyes.

But the priest was old in self-discipline. Age, like a curtain, was lowered over the face again, and he said: "Perhaps not," admitting nothing, denying nothing; and he continued: "What do you wish to add? You tell me she is a young woman who takes responsibility for her own life. Certainly, she hasn't come to me. As for you— you were no particular friend of hers before she went. Why did she tell you she was going?"

"You asked me that question this afternoon. I think I answered it."

"Perhaps I didn't understand the answer."

"Well," said Barbet, puzzled by the coldness of the priest's demeanour, "she had to tell someone."

Lancret pursed his lips.

"Oh, yes," Barbet continued with a smile. "When you're that age, there are secrets too exciting to keep. Someone had to be told that she had decided to capture Paris."

"But why you?" Lancret persisted. "That seems odd to me."

"Not in the least," said Barbet. "When I was a boy, I used to tell my secrets to the dog."

Lancret grinned at that. "But you were wrong to let her go," he began after a silence. "She was too young. She has ruined herself." His face was working and his voice rose, for he could not endure his remorse unless he dramatized it.

"She's still the same human being," said Barbet. "At any rate, she may be."

"No woman can be the same who—"

"She is, if she sees herself so. At least, that's how I read the gospels."

Lancret's eyebrows went up. "That truth is in the imagination, not in the deed? All these are words that need to be defined, my son, if we are not to deceive ourselves and think we are wiser than the Church."

Barbet acquiesced silently. He had respect and love for the priest and no pride in dispute with him or with any man. He watched him rise from his chair and nervously divide and re-divide the pages of the book he had been reading. Suddenly the eyes came up.

"Her mother used to sit on that couch where you are sitting."

Barbet nodded, but did not reply.

The priest closed the book with a thud. "Why was the girl brought into the world?" he said. "Every sin she has committed has its root in that. If she were to come to me for absolution, I—"

"Don't speak," Barbet interrupted at once, seeing that his friend was beside himself. "You will hurt yourself by speaking. If she came for absolution, she would not come to you personally, but to the priest of God."

At this Lancret recovered himself. "That is true," he said. "You have a quiet mind. May God keep you in it." Then, roused again, he burst out: "She boasts of her vileness. Not one man but many. You are too young!" he cried. "How are you to know that there are some whose shame itself is a drug? They revile themselves as others praise themselves. It isn't their lust they can't abandon; it's the terror and excitement and perverted vanity of their shame! There's a devil in them that nothing can cast out."

"Come and see," Barbet answered.

The priest returned to his chair and sat in it trembling and exhausted. Barbet knelt before him, took the slippers from his feet and began to fasten on him the shoes he wore out of doors.

"You don't understand what she has done!" Lancret cried with the petulance of a mind deeply confused.

"Is she proud or cruel or mean or cowardly?" Barbet asked. "You have often said that they are the sins of the spirit."

The priest seized him by the shoulders and repeated: "You don't understand what she has done! Are you a simpleton? What she has *done!*" he cried as though her sins of the flesh were visible before him, and he repeated again and again: "What she has done! What she has done!"

Barbet had fastened the shoes.

"Now we can go out," he said in a matter-of-fact way, and, without change of tone: "Certainly, we don't yet know what she is."

The priest stared at him. "What do you propose to do?"

"Go and see," Barbet answered.

They walked through Roussignac together. Their way led them through the market-square, where Anton Hazard's inn, the Lion Rouge, looked out, with the frowning solemnity of grey stone, on a statue of Guillaume, his grandfather. It was the centre of life in Roussignac; here carts and gigs drew up on market day; here small producers brought their samples of new brandy to Anton himself and his fellow merchants; and here, as in the Chalet at Cognac, distillers on the lookout for wine to distil sat to make their bargains. This evening, because it was warm, the tables on the pavement were full. To avoid notice, Barbet and the priest walked on the other side of the square and turned abruptly down a cobbled slope that led out of it. They came, at the bottom of this slope, into a much humbler square, called the Place du Cygne. Little more than a large courtyard and irregularly enclosed on three sides by ramshackle houses, it lay open on its farther side to the river. The last building on the left was the Cheval Pie. Its low, tiled roof, its squat, oblong face, and the round window under its central gable lent it the appearance of a high-shouldered dwarf with a single eye. Above its door was a narrow balcony of green slats pierced into a lacy fragility; the shutters were of the same design; the eaves were fringed with scalloped boards, and the whole place gave an impression of being dirtily befrilled. In front of it a space studded with plane-trees and rusty tables was enclosed by a trellised fence, and behind it, where the Place du Cygne was merged in the grassy approach to the river's bank, was a little wood cut by two tiny rivulets which enclosed an island. The plane-trees, the convenient wood, the rustic bridges and no doubt the frogs and the nightingales had, amid the glories of the Second Empire, won for the Cheval Pie a cheerful riverside reputation now departed. There was not a customer to be seen.

"I can't come to a table with you," said Lancret. "There's a bench over there on the grass. Sometimes I talk to people there; no one will be surprised; we shall see all that passes."

The door of the Cheval Pie stood partly open and a gleam shone from it on to the nearer plane-trees. Two figures came out—a young man's and a girl's. As they went from empty table to empty table, there was a clinking sound, as though they were setting down drinks before imaginary guests, and Lancret said: "What are they putting on the tables?"

"Saucers," Barbet replied. On each table not blackened by the moon-shadow a white rim appeared.

The figures went indoors and came again. The girl's voice could be heard urging Frédéric to make haste; it was uplifted, as though she were in the excitement of a party. "You'll see! It will be brilliant when it's done—like a place in a city. It will be sparkling and everyone will say—" By this time they were indoors. There was long darkness and silence. At last they came out, struggling under a burden so heavy that it dragged them down and toppled and would have fallen but for the wall of the house.

"Where is it to be?"

"There!" said Thèrése instantly. "You see—the hoop of the tables."

In the place she had chosen, where the earth was hard and smooth, the piano was set down. She straightened behind it; her face had in it the fierce tension of one pursued—a defiance, an assurance, a glee. She laughed, and ran into the house. Frédéric, limp and pale, his hair forward across his brow, stood and shook and followed. They came out with candles, an armful, she with a lighted taper. In each saucer a candle was fixed in its grease and extinguished; the piano was decked with them. Then to some of the wicks she put flame, her lips parted, a deep smile upon them, as though her whole being were pledged in this adventure, and when it was done she stood back, throwing out her arms so that the taper dripped from her hand, and cried: "Walk up! Walk up! The show is open. Thèrése and Frédéric! Thèrése Despreux—mesdames, messieurs, the first of a thousand nights. . . . *Now*, Frédéric, play!"

"There's no one to play to," said Frédéric.

"There never is until one plays. . . . There's an audience at the Lion Rouge. Play to that!" She threw her arms about him, kissed him, and sprang back. "There's an audience in Paris. Play to that, Frédéric! If I sing, they will come."

She pulled on her aunt Sernet's red mittens, made her hair grotesque and thrust white flowers in it, stripped off her bodice and stood, bare-armed, in a chemise and skirt. "Now, Frédéric!"

He played, at first timidly, then louder. She sang: "*'Last night I met a sergeant . . .'*"—the whole song, fourteen verses.

"God protect her," said Lancret, "it needs courage to sing to no one. If there were no congregation, should I preach?"

"She has a way with her," said Barbet. "We are seeing something to-night."

"But it's done," the priest murmured. "The song's over. No one is here."

"Bis! Bis!" cried Thérèse, and sang again: "*'Last night I met a sergeant . . .'*"

"Look," said Barbet.

On the cobbled slope which led down from the large square to the small, a group was assembling, between the walls of the houses. They came forward in pairs and in threes, crossed the square and stood like oxen at the palings of the Cheval Pie.

"Someone is needed to walk in, to order drink, to be the first," said Barbet. "You will not come?"

"No," said Lancret, as if he were going to the stake. "I cannot. But I will watch from here."

"Light all the candles!" Thérèse commanded. "They are coming. Light all the candles, Frédéric. . . . No. Stay where you are. Play the piano. Play like hell." She ran from her place, thrust the taper into Barbet's hand. "Light the candles," she said, and ran back and began singing.

The audience came, like moths. In each break of the entertainment, Thérèse and Frédéric brought them drink. Before half an hour had passed, the priest rose and went off across the square. Barbet stayed to the end. The songs she sang, all of them stale from the music-halls, were but part of her entertainment; she danced as well, body and head thrown back, her legs prancing like a wild pony's, and because her skirt impeded her she threw it off and danced in a swirl of white frills that sent a growl through her audience like the swish of a gravel beach.

"And who paid for them, I ask you?"

The dance over, she went from table to table, talking to everyone, pretending to drink with them all.

"And who *paid* for them, I ask you?"

"Ah, Mademoiselle Thérèse, he was a lucky man!"

"Who?"

"He who gave——"

Another youth chimed in. "And he who took away."

She was asked if she had no new songs, and hesitated, suddenly put out, like a child scolded for its lessons and stung by injustice; then, woman again, she replied: no, but soon she would have. She was asked who had taught her to sing and, being tired, flashed back. Soon her good humour was recovered, but too late. The men at her table laughed; one of them rose and gave an imitation of her; and when she commanded herself to say: "Good night, messieurs. Good night. You will come to-morrow?" there was almost a snarl in the reply: "I'll look in for the new song you promised us." But there were others that praised her; for them she sang again; when they were gone and only Barbet remained at his table, she said to Frédéric:

"Was it all right? Was it? Oh, Frédéric, say it was, even if——"

"There's someone still there," said Frédéric.

She came over. "It is Monsieur Barbet!" She snatched her skirt and wrapped it about her.

"So you have come back from Paris, Thérèse."

"Paris? . . . Angoulême."

"They are the same. But you said Paris to me. Have you forgotten?"

"Well," she said, "I wasn't yet eighteen. I had big ideas."

"Do you make voyages still?"

Her great eyes widened; then, with swift recall, she narrowed them and her mouth became hard. "Make no mistake about me. I've come down to earth." She began to move from table to table, puffing out the candles. "That was to bring them in; can't afford candles every night; look how they gutter—and you'd have said there wasn't a breath! But there is one thing you can do for me," she said, returning. "Lend me a mandolin. That would give the grumblers a change."

"Yes," said Barbet. "There are two at home. Frédéric can come in the morning."

"I don't want two in the morning. I want one to-night."

"But it's too late." He started up, watch in hand. "Look how late it is! And I haven't shut my prisoners up."

"I want it to-night!" she exclaimed. "Why not? Frédéric and I will walk out with you and fetch it. Yes, Frédéric! It is I who should be yawning!"

"But Thérèse—" Barbet began.

"Oh," she cried, "you men are all the same. To-morrow, to-morrow, to-morrow! Your promises—nothing comes of them."

"Then come with me now and fetch the mandolin."

She went into the house, re-dressed herself, and came out a new woman.

"This will be fun," she said. "It's lovely to begin something fresh just when it's time to go to bed."

As they went through the wood, Frédéric carrying the lamp before them, she stopped and leaned against a tree.

"I could sleep standing."

But no sooner had Barbet moved towards her than she sprang to life again. "No, no, leave me alone. I can do it myself. I always have."

"Do what yourself?"

"Walk. . . . Everything!" Then, from behind him, quietly: "Barbet, how much further is it?"

Because she lagged behind but was now come so far that she would not return, he loitered to give her time, collecting glow-worms in a card-board box that he produced from his pocket. While he stooped, she waited, puzzled, and asked:

"What do you want them for?"

"My mother likes them in the small courtyard. She says there aren't as many as in my father's time."

"Do people always laugh at you?"

"Often," said Barbet.

"And you don't mind? The people I know would think you mad."

"The grand people in Angoulême?"

"Well, they're not so grand. But they don't pick glow-worms. Look!" she exclaimed, "there's one! Where's your absurd box?"

He held it out. "Thank you, Thérèse. Would they think you mad for helping me?"

She did not answer, for at that moment both were still, there was no rustle of the undergrowth, even Frédéric was motionless ahead of them, his lamp at his knee, and a low ululation came from beyond the wood.

"Listen!"

"It's the prisoners," said Barbet.

"Rioting?"

"That's a big word," but he slipped the box into the pocket of his jacket, overtook Frédéric and, seizing the lamp, went on at mended pace.

Madame Hazard's parlour was lighted but empty. She, Madame Vincent and Renée were in the kitchen. At sight of Barbet, his mother trotted towards him, her lips wet with indignation, her little hands beating the air.

"You see," she cried, "what comes of it? 'They'll be quiet,' you said, 'they are reasonable men,' you said. And now for nearly two hours— Where have you been, Barbet? How *could* you? Where have you been?"

"Here is Thérèse Despreux, mother. And young Frédéric. They have come to borrow a mandolin—"

Madame Hazard stamped her feet. "Mandolin! This is no

time for mandolins! Inside there is the Commune! For two mortal hours they have been shouting at our windows, beating at the doors, raging and tearing—" Excitement choked her. She had no anger left. "Listen," she said, whimpering with fear.

Madame Vincent, who had seemed calm because she did not stir from her chair, said without turning her head and in a blurred voice not her own: "They must be taught. They must be taught. Their blood or ours!" Her bulk underwent a series of slight but regular convulsions, like the contractions of a great jelly-fish, and each convulsion squeezed from her the same breathy phrase. "Their blood," she said, "their blood." Her fingers contracted and loosened on the chair-arms, like the paws of a cat; beads of froth were pushed forward by the champing of her lips; and Barbet understood that she and his mother and Renée were in the tide of fear.

"Pierre! Pierre! Pierre!" cried Renée.

"Where is he?"

Renée stretched out an arm at the two older women. "They made him! They goaded him!" she exclaimed. "He's going in now."

"Where?"

"To the prisoners."

"But he will have his pistol," Madame Vincent cried. "That will teach them. Their blood or ours. Their blood."

Barbet looked from one face to another. Even Frédéric had taken the infection of terror; his shoulders were pinched forward; he was plucking the skin on his finger-joints. At his side Thérèse was standing. Her expression was not of fear but of profound interest, as though she were discovering something that at once awed and amused and delighted her. Barbet observed with surprise that her attention was fixed upon his own face.

"They'll kill him," Renée cried. "They'll knock the pistol out of his hand."

"Nonsense," said Barbet, "it's not a question of pistols."

He went at once into the covered way. When he came to the first of the two doors, he saw Pierre stooped beside the lock, fumbling in the upward glint of a lantern that threw the greater part of its light about his feet. He was trying to fit the key left-handed, for in his right was a pistol. "Wait, Pierre!" Barbet said, but Pierre was beyond hearing him. The voices of the prisoners, though nearer, were less distinct than they had been in the house; their noise, muffled by two intervening doors, was the animal noise of a pack, now almost silent, now falling to a deep, angry pulse or rising to a howl; and from time to time Pierre shouted back the threats of panic, screaming to the unseen men, who could hear no word of his, that he was armed, was armed, was armed; the first who touched him should die!

Barbet took his wrist and opened the fingers that were grasping the pistol. Pierre sagged against the wall, panting, incoherent. His tumbling words had no meaning but that, thank God, there were now two of them—two pistols—two men—two pistols—a massacre!

"You have lost your head," said Barbet. "Go back to the house."

Pierre would not go; if necessary, he said, flourishing his arms, he was willing to die, but he would not go. A desperate, theatrical valour had sprung up from his fear. Nothing would persuade him, he cried, to allow his master to go in alone, and Barbet, smiling at the word master, never before heard on Pierre's lips, said to quiet him that he had no intention of going in at all; it was unnecessary; the prisoners could not escape; they might be left to howl until they were tired; in the morning or sooner help would come from Roussignac.

Pierre gazed at him with the sick relief of a man who wakes to find that all his terror has been a dream. "Not go in. Not go in," he repeated with a mounting, bewildered joy. A look of cunning came into his face. "Yes, we will leave them to shout. That is clever. We will leave them to kick and swear. In the morning, they'll have their lesson."

"Go back to the house, then."

"But you?"

"I shall follow."

Believing or not, Pierre obeyed. At the turn of the passage, he hesitated and looked back; then went on, leaving Barbet alone.

After a little while, Barbet was surprised to hear his voice say: "That's extremely odd. I have been lying to myself." As he was not conscious of having argued with himself at all, this was an embarrassing remark for Barbet to make to Barbet, and it took him a little time to perceive that when, to be rid of Pierre, he had said that it was unnecessary to enter the courtyard, he had not said this only to be rid of Pierre but because the idea of calling in others to arrest and punish his prisoners had presented itself to him as a comfortable and reasonable way out of his difficulty.

After all, why not? He and Pierre might easily patrol the outer walls and have the prisoners observed from the windows overlooking the courtyard. Time would pass, reinforcements come, and responsibility be lifted from him. That's the sensible thing to do, Barbet thought—not to go blundering in on them single-handed while they are in this mood; and the part of him that wished to do, as a gaoler, what his father would have done, that modesty in him which respected the common sense of others and was inclined to regard as spectacular his own original impulses, was tempted; but he could not escape the remembrance that, when he was in his mother's kitchen amid the panic of women, he had suddenly, without astonishment, seen himself entering the courtyard alone and had perceived beyond argument that this was necessary and right. What he should do after going in, he had not known or asked.

But at this moment, while he stood in the narrow, vaulted passage, grasping the pistol he had taken from Pierre, nothing seemed natural or simple. He was without direction, like a ship in irons. He looked at the pistol and jogged it in his hand: this at any rate had nothing to do with him.

If he went back, he would not use it; if he went on, still he would not use it; it had no part in his idea of himself, and he put it away.

He opened the first door and, having passed through with his lantern, locked it again. As he faced the second door, his eye fell on the sliding cover to the grille through which, in the past, he had been accustomed, before visiting the cells, to watch the birds in the courtyard. His hand went up to open the grille; through it he might reason with his prisoners; but to argue with them through a slit in a door would be useless, and he dropped his hand. He put the key in the lock, turned, withdrew, and hid it on a protruding brick above the lintel; but this marked no decision in him; the bolts were still shot and he knew it.

At the grating of the key, the prisoners abruptly became silent. Believing him to be armed, they would spring upon him as he entered. He began to reason with himself; the pulse of imagination weakened within him; the confidence of his spirit ebbed, for what he had known in his heart was turned to ridicule by his mind. All that evening, from the moment in which he had begun to make his way towards the priest's house, it had been as if everything he did were part of a designed pattern of which the unity and value were not in doubt. Now this certainty appeared as arrogance in him—as ridiculous as the notion that had come to him one afternoon of his boyhood to walk on the water of the Charente. He had stepped out of his boat, and, after a moment in which the water seemed to carry him, had thought: How stupid! and laughed at himself, and sunk, spluttering. He would have been drowned if he had not been able to swim—and, once in the courtyard, no swimming would save him. I can do no good, he thought; it will be better for them not to be given a chance to attack me; to go in is false heroism, a futile rashness; it can do no good, it is against reason, the act of a fool.

And now I'm lying again, he said to himself in cheerful patience, for it had been clear to him once that only by confronting his prisoners could he heal their rage or be atoned with them. If he used force against them or allowed others to use it, certainly he took arms against mankind and against himself. Whether force was of itself evil in men that had no other instrument, he did not now ask; but he knew that in himself it wouldn't work; it was a corruption of his imaginative life, which offered another way to him. And yet, it isn't reasonable to go in unarmed, he repeated. It isn't reasonable to go in at all. What good can it do? What possible good to them or me?

The simplest acts of the imagination always appear to be useless until they are completed and fulfilled, and Barbet hesitated.

Now, if I could stop arguing with myself, I should know, he said; if I could stop being clever, I should have a chance to be wise; and he put consequence from him and made himself still. Because nothing had followed upon the grating of the key in the lock, the prisoners set up their howling again, and Barbet heard it; but now it had little effect upon him either of intimidation or of challenge, and, at last, none. He was reckless of it; he ceased to care what his father, or any reasonable man, might have thought of him; he ceased to fear and, even, to pity the men kicking at the door, feeling of them that they were submitted to the same power and the same mercy that encompassed him; and he saw that what would happen after he had entered the courtyard was not to be asked. Really, he thought, if a fledgling always asked: what will happen afterwards, no sparrow would ever throw itself upon the air. Nothing is simpler than to draw those bolts, and he drew them and went in.

The prisoners, seeing him, held back. The courtyard surprised and dazzled him by its moonlit brightness; the men's heads were like steel casques with a rind of light at their edges, and above them, at an upper window of the dwelling-house, a girl's face, arms and shoulders had the watchful composure of stone. Behind the men arose a white and seemingly gelatinous shape with Blachère's mouth in it, which opened; at the sound of his voice the group twitched, swayed and lurched forward clumsily, but could not advance, for their eyes were upon Barbet's, they were frightened by what seemed to them an unnatural acquiescence in him, they stood rooted by the shock of his disregard, and, when they perceived that he was looking at an object behind them, they followed his gaze to the window, but could see only a woman leaning on the sill. So they turned back, and Blachère, who alone had not been diverted to the window, cried out to them again: on, on, the door was open! but he would not go first, or move except to drive them forward, believing that Barbet was armed.

They obeyed him, blindly, heads down, crouching forward under Barbet's eyes, plunging as though they had been dragging at a rope that was suddenly released. They did not lay hands on him or look at him, but came forward, compelled and reasonless, a wedge of shoulders, a scuffle of boots. Borne away by their thrust, he was carried against the wall flanking the door, where, twisted round, his cheek flat against the stones, he was for a moment held up from the paving and rolled in their advance until, their pressure released, he fell, and was in a heap with Fontan and old Marcotte. Autun, Balze and Heim, believing that they were free, hurled themselves through the open door. The second was closed. They screamed their disappointment, pounded with their fists.

"He has the key!" Balze cried. "Make him give it up!"

The three of them came tumbling back into the courtyard again, and flung themselves on Barbet to have the key from him. His cheek and mouth were bleeding but he did not know it; he knew only, as their impact struck him down from the upright position into which he had struggled, that, against reason, all was well. He made no resistance, had no plan; as their weight and darkness fell upon him, he yielded to it; it would be lifted, the wrath and confusion would end, there would be peace suddenly, like the drop of a gale.

Blachère was setting them on like dogs to their quarry. Dragging at Barbet's pockets they would have torn his clothes from him, but he was thinking that to-morrow he would go out in his boat and cross over to Bellis and stand in a place he knew of to watch the migrants arrive. It was a pocket in a tall hedge which concealed him completely unless he mounted on a stone and stretched upward, and so necessary was it for him to stand up to see the imagined birds that he stretched upward now, and passed through the groping hands and was above the men; they fell away from him.

"Stand back!" Then, in a new panic—"On to him! On to him!" Blachère cried. "Look, he's armed!" Springing aside, he flattened himself against the wall, his hands spread out, his head lolling, for Barbet was fumbling in his pocket and now said: "Be careful. You will hurt them."

"Close with him!" Blachère shouted, and Autun dragged wildly at Barbet's head, Heim and Balze pinioned his wrists.

"It is in his pocket," Blachère said. "Take it. The filthy hypocrite! The unarmed, the peaceful gaoler! The innocent swine! You said he was never armed. His hand was to his pocket. Take it, Fontan. . . . I will take it myself."

In Barbet's pocket he found only a box, and would have thrown it down or in some way concealed it, but the others cried "Show it," and he held it out on the great palm of his hand. "Open it," they said. "What's inside?"

"Nothing, nothing," but they would have him take off the lid and in the leafy dark of the box there were glow-worms shining.

Heim and Balze released the wrists they held. Autun stood back, opened his mouth and shook.

"The pistol! The pistol!" cried Fontan in delighted mockery. "There is your pistol, Blachère! Stand away! Stand away! The glow-worms will bite you." Old Marcotte began to cackle. Suddenly the whole group quaked. Blachère, enraged, threw down the box. The glow-worms were scattered. Barbet fell on his knees and began to gather them in. When the men had done laughing, they went down beside him on the stones.

"Look," he said, "not one of them is hurt."

Then he sat back on his haunches, like a boy playing marbles, and looked from face to face without surprise.

"No one is hurt," he said. "Look, if they are put down on the cracks between the stones they will run races."

Because the day was over and his imagining worked out, a tune came into his head. As the glow-worms moved on his fingers, he began to sing it under his breath. Fontan listened and sang with him.

"Who is that at the window?" Balze asked.

"At the window?" said Barbet. "Oh, that is Thérèse Despreux. One evening she will come into the courtyard and sing and dance for you."

He sat back on his haunches again and stared across the grass at the ilex. He talked to the men of Thérèse, as though she were among them. They did not know when she left the window, and listened as though he were telling a story.

Not long afterwards, Marcotte said: "It will be morning soon."

A pale sky was above the roof of the cells, a rosy edge to the stone; a cock that had been crowing in the night, crowed again. Barbet knew that he was tired and, wondering that he had found tongue to speak so easily to the men, he took up the glow-worms and let them go in a green place near an apple-tree in the courtyard. The prisoners went to their beds. When Barbet had taken water to them and spoken to Blachère, who gave no answer though the white of eye proved him to be waking still, he returned to the kitchen. Only Pierre awaited him.

"Did Thérèse have the mandolin?"

Pierre growled and stared; he would have spoken then what was in his mind; but Barbet, not receiving his anger, passed by him, and went to his own room. The window was a sheet of morning; a breeze from the river touched his forehead and his upper eye as he stretched himself on his side; the field-crickets and the tree-frogs made themselves heard for a moment before he slept; the spring night was full of vibrations.

Chapter 5

IN THE MORNING, HE FOUND HIS MOTHER ALONE AT
the kitchen table. She was sucking a crust dipped in coffee and
milk. When he kissed her, she put up her forehead, blinked her moist
eyes and was silent. This was not unusual; she did not mix her pleasures, and seldom chattered when there was food about. Not dreaming that a storm was about to break upon him and with no thought
but of the day's work that lay ahead, Barbet took his coffee and sat
down.

"This is money-day," he said, meaning that before nightfall, perhaps during the forenoon, he must go to the Lion Rouge and receive
from Anton, in his capacity of mayor, the money due for the
prisoners' upkeep. If his mother had any commissions for him in
Roussignac, she would speak now. She looked at him but said
nothing.

Renée presently came in from the stables, her hair about her
forehead. She thrust back her hair, returned Barbet's good morning
with a word half uttered, took her seat and gazed; then turned her
eyes upon her cup and looked out no more. When Pierre returned
from his visit to the cells, Renée handed him the glass of white wine,
the tuc-ver, that he expected, and Barbet asked, as he did each
morning, if all was well. Pierre halted; his eyes, under their blond
lashes, became wider and whiter in a reddening face; he had the
appearance of a young bull being suffocated until at last he was able
to say: "How can it be? Well! I like that! You ask me if all is well!"
and the flood of his anger was released, like water from a jolting tap,
in ponderous spurts of exclamation from which it appeared that he
had been cheated, fooled, humiliated, and that last night Renée had
called him a coward.

"No, no!" Renée exclaimed. "I never said that, and if I did it was without thinking." To prove her loyalty to Pierre she joined in the attack on Barbet who sat astonished, his spoon in the air.

His mother said nothing. Looking from one speaker to the other, she clucked her tongue in a way that proved she would say much when her coffee released her. It was the name of Madame Vincent that brought her into action.

"To go in to them unarmed—not meaning to fight—well," Renée exclaimed, "that was a milk-sop thing to do. No true French-man would do it, Madame Vincent said. She was furious—wasn't she, Pierre? You heard what she said."

"And I heard it too," Madame Hazard replied, bobbing in her wooden chair as though she were on springs. "Every word of it! She was afraid for her skin. 'They will get out!' she said. 'You mark my words,' she said, 'they'll be in this room and tear our clothes off our backs!'"

"You were just as frightened yourself, Aunt!" Renée retorted. " 'He will be killed! He will be torn to pieces!'—and you ran up and down the floor like a hen in a barn."

While the voices of the women were raised in high dispute, Pierre plodded on with his grievance, which was that, by quelling a riot without his help, Barbet had made him a laughing-stock. But this was not Renée's complaint, though she had, indeed, said hard words to Pierre when he had returned alone to the house. What angered her was that Barbet had been up to his tricks again. Why couldn't he behave like other people? Why couldn't he do what was expected of him? Why must he always make the neighbours talk? It did a girl no good to be the cousin of a freak!

"But, Renée, what have I done wrong?"

"It's not that you have done anything wrong. It's the way you did it. Everyone will know that there was a riot in the prison last night. Thérèse will have a story to tell! And when it goes round that you didn't stand up to them—"

"They went quiet to bed," Barbet observed.

"That makes it worse!" said Renée.

"Ah!" Pierre cried with as much irony as his blurred voice would permit, "that was a miracle! God, no doubt, was on Barbet's side! He is always on the side of fools! Next time the Prussians come, Barbet will show them his glow-worms and back they'll go across the Rhine without a bayonet to stick them."

Never had Pierre spoken so many words consecutively. Embarrasssed by his own eloquence, as a child may be by a fit of temper, he sat drumming on the table and kicking his chair-legs with his heels. Barbet made no answer; the women were astonished into silence; and Pierre began to repeat himself. "Ah, yes, that was a miracle! That was a miracle no doubt! My mother will be proud to know you have a saint in the family."

Whether or not it was this reference to Madame Vincent that inflamed Madame Hazard, certainly by Pierre's word she was changed. Her little body became still and stiff; her eyes blinked rapidly, then opened and blinked no more; by the pressure of her hands on the table she partly hoisted herself from her chair, and remained suspended, neither sitting nor standing, like a little, bristling dog, half-raised on its fore-paws at sight of a ghost.

"Who knows?" she said in the voice ordinarily used by her only when speaking of Napoleon the First or of her father, who died at Quatre Bras. "Who knows, Pierre? It may be that you have spoken the truth."

To what truth she referred, Pierre could not guess. No one at that moment was further than he from looking for a halo on Barbet's head. Indeed, in Madame Hazard herself, after her first moment of pride, scepticism almost reasserted itself. She crumpled a little; the tension of her body was relaxed; when she looked at her son, the worker of miracles, she saw that the cockade of hair to which she was accustomed sprouted as foolishly as ever from the crown of his head. Saint or not, he was uncommonly like Barbet; but, before she sat down, regardless of the Protestantism assumed for her husband's sake, she crossed herself to be on the safe side.

It was a gesture she might have conveniently forgotten, if a visit from Madame Vincent had not driven her to justify it. After breakfast, Barbet, having renewed an earlier acquaintance with a redstart who was singing monotonously on the roof, set out for Roussignac, and Pierre, with Renée at his heels, for the vineyard, to work the heavy clots of earth caused by the unshoeing of the vines. Madame Vincent, driving up in a red-wheeled tilbury, with her elder son, Victor, at her side, came upon Pierre and beckoned him away from his labourers. "What now?" she said, for she was puzzled and, in spite of herself, a little impressed by what she had seen through the barred window and the curtain-chinks of the parlour. If there had not been early work to do in her own home, she would have waited last night for Barbet's return from the courtyard; she had left in a torment of curiosity. "What happened after I had gone?" she demanded.

"How should I know?" Pierre grumbled. "It was I drove you home. When I came back, the prisoners were in their cells. That's all I know. And now the old girl says it was a miracle."

Renée's quicker tongue told the story, to which Madame Vincent gave an attention graver than they had expected of her.

"So!" she said, when the tale was done. "And what does Barbet say? Does he believe it?" Then, rousing herself, she threw off superstition: "Or is it only that fool mother of his?"

"Well," Pierre admitted, "he has said nothing about it. He just gave her a second cup of coffee and went off to Roussignac."

"Then how does he account for what happened?"

"He doesn't."

"That is ridiculous. He must be made to account for it. Isn't that so, Victor? You are a man of the world."

"Yes, mamma, certainly, but all the same—"

"What?"

"I am not sure in what way it concerns us."

"That Pierre should marry into a blasphemous family and the whole country laugh at him! Doesn't that concern us?"

"Oh, certainly it does. But I am not yet sure what use to make of it."

Victor considered this problem carefully, stroking flies off the pony's flank with the lash of his whip. He was smaller and narrower than Pierre, very dark, with a sharp nose, bright brown eyes, and an air of being town-bred and dapper. If chance had not made him Anton's partner, he might have been a banker or a sceptical priest. His special gift was to treat his mother with an extreme formal deference, which led her to believe that she ruled him as she ruled Pierre and Bette, while going his own pernickety way in spite of her.

"You see, mamma," he said with that flicker of his brown eyes which served him for a smile, "we must learn of the philosophers," and he waited the effect of his remark with the curious interest of a doctor who has administered an emetic.

For a moment Madame Vincent was at a loss. "Learn of the philosophers!" she repeated. Then, almost with passion her memory gave up its dead. " 'Learn of the philosophers,' said the Count de Gabalis, 'always to look for natural causes in all extraordinary happenings: and when there is none, fall back on God.' "

"Precisely, mamma," said Victor. "If Barbet did not perform a miracle, nothing unusual has happened; if he did, what blasphemy do you complain of?"

"Enough! Enough!" Madame Vincent exclaimed, seizing the reins from him. "I never heard such nonsense. Is this France? Is it the nineteenth century? A miracle, indeed!"

"Still, it would be annoying, mamma, to be among those who failed to recognize a miracle before their eyes. There have been so many in history. They are always the fools of the legend."

Madame Vincent knew he was laughing at her, but with which side of his mouth, how could she tell?—for he was a trimmer, and could not himself have told. There was nothing to be done with Victor except shout him down.

"There is no such thing as a miracle," she said, "and if there were, it's nothing to boast about in one's own home. Have you ever heard of a saint who didn't get his family into trouble?" and, as a mark of her disapproval, she left Victor outside while she called upon Madame Hazard. He strolled back to the vineyard, and infuriated Pierre by paying elaborate compliments to Renée, though he had no interest in her or in any woman.

The two mothers meanwhile seated themselves face to face at the parlour table. An épergne, empty of flowers, intervened. It stood on a mat of crocheted silk. Madame Vincent twisted the tassels.

"And now, my dear Chouquette, what is this I hear? You have changed your tune since last night."

Madame Hazard was aware of this and deeply embarrassed by it, for consistency was to her a supreme virtue. "What I have said I have said," was among her favourite expressions, and there was now no denying that, last night, she had called Barbet a rascal, and, in the morning, a—but had she used the word "saint"? Certainly not. What the others might have understood was their concern; what she herself might, in a rash moment, have felt was her own; if she had not spoken the word "saint," she might still wriggle.

"Listen," Madame Vincent continued, "listen, Chouquette, and tell me what it is you say now. Did your Barbet put the prisoners to bed by force?"

"No."

"Did he command them?"

"No."

"Did he call upon Pierre for assistance?"

"Dieu Jésus—non! That he did not!"

"Then," said Madame Vincent, looking around the cherubs of the épergne with the triumph of an advocate who has cornered his witness, "does it not follow that he put them to bed with the help of God?"

But Madame Hazard smiled as she did when her opponent played a wrong card at piquet.

"Is there anything, dear Emilie, that we do without his help?"

"That," cried Madame Vincent, springing to battle, "is cant and hypocrisy. You know perfectly well that there is a difference between the things one can reasonably expect of God and the things one can't."

"Oh dear, oh dear," Madame Hazard exclaimed, suddenly cackling with merriment.

> " 'If the cherries in your hat
> Jump about like that'

we shall have no need, my friend, to put flowers into the bowl of
the épergne."

She closed her eyes, put her hands on her hips and began to shake
with the laughter of the frivolous minx who inhabited her.

"And this is the moment you choose to quote a patter of the music-
halls!" she heard Madame Vincent cry in indignation. "A lewd
patter, too, if you went further with it—as well you know! I can
see nothing to laugh at!"

"No, Emilie, you seldom can. That is one of the things one can't
reasonably expect of God."

"You, a relapsed Catholic," Madame Vincent retorted, "—I am
astonished that you believe in saints."

This was too much. Tears started to Madame Hazard's eyes.
Being of that frail nature which enchants men by its variable ease
but being also a woman who hoped intuitively that in a predomi-
nantly masculine heaven a place would somehow be found for her,
she always paid for her moments of irresponsibility with moments
of panic. In her girlhood, she would go in icy dread from her naugh-
tiness to the priest, only to look out from under a repentant bonnet
on her way home and run hot-foot from the priest to her naughti-
ness; and though she could not help mocking her stern neighbour
now and then, she had a feeling of almost superstitious reverence
for Madame Vincent, because, poor thing, she was, and had always
been, so ugly; because, whenever you giggled, she looked at you
over her great nose like a large and reproachful mare. It brought
Madame Hazard to her senses to discover, when she opened her eyes,
that the épergne, her bulwark, had been removed to the end of the
table and that she was looking straight into the long brown face. It
was like waking in a meadow to find oneself being snuffed by a cart-
horse.

"Forgive me," she said, hoping the face would relax, and wishing,
in another corner of her mind, that she was young enough to jump
up and dance round the table, "forgive me, Emilie. Let us talk of
this as friends."

The face did not relax.

"Very well," said Madame Vincent, and, having made sure, with a modest glance, that there were no men in the room, she sat back from the table and crossed her legs.

And now, because she had been frightened, because she was hard-pressed, above all because she had made a fool of herself, Madame Hazard knew what she must do. If she gave signs of retreat, Emilie would pursue and trample her. At all costs she must attack.

"Listen," she began demurely, pulling the crocheted mat towards her and smoothing it with her little hands, "I will confess to you that I am troubled in my own mind. I am not as learned as you are." She looked through her eyelashes to mark the effect of this and, judging it to be satisfactory, continued: "I have not the advantage of your reading. Sometimes, as you have told me, I flutter like a moth. It would help me, my dear, if you would answer a few questions."

"Certainly I will answer," said Madame Vincent.

"Then, first, I will ask you this: Did Barbet put the prisoners to bed by force?"

"No."

"Did he command them?"

Madame Vincent moved suspiciously, hearing her own questions return to her, but she answered firmly: "No, Chouquette."

"Did he call upon Pierre for assistance?"

"No, but—"

"And the prisoners were fierce?"

"Indeed."

"Rebellious? Defiant? Murderous?"

"Indeed! Indeed!"

"Then can you suggest, Emilie, any natural reason for their sitting on the ground to study glow-worms? Can you tell me, in a few clear words, in what way this story differs from that of Daniel in the lions' den?" And suddenly, while asking this question of Madame Vincent, Madame Hazard asked it of herself and could find no answer. Her heart beat faster; a thrill of wonder ran up her spine to the roots of her hair; she saw before her, in imagination, the tranquillity of those men who had fallen upon their knees with her son in the moonlit courtyard. It was glow-worms, not prayer, that had brought them down—still, upon their knees they had fallen, and she saw again that crouching group and remembered the long silence that had followed and, when she had thrown up the window, the distinct murmur of Barbet's voice. Now she was passed beyond the persuasion of Madame Vincent and all fear of her. She was possessed by the assurance of wonder, as she had been when she had emptied her first cup of coffee, and the assurance transformed her.

"Can it be," cried Madame Vincent, "that you believe this thing?"

"Can you," Madame Hazard demanded, "look me in the face and doubt it?"

"In five minutes," said Madame Vincent, with more gentleness than was usual in her, "you won't believe it yourself, my poor Chouquette."

"But you will—*you* will—though you are too stiff-necked to admit it."

Madame Vincent did not deny this, but shrugged her shoulders. The mother of Barbet gazed at her.

"What is belief?" she asked. "What is belief?" Her old face blushed and crumpled, as though she were a girl scolded for her love and faith. With a little cry of joy, she burst into tears and trotted out of the room.

Madame Vincent arranged the crocheted mat in the centre of the table and returned the épergne to its place. She would have liked to have done more for Chouquette, but did not know how; so she went into the vineyard and bullied Pierre because she loved him and because he could not perform miracles.

Chapter 6

IN MADAME HAZARD'S FANTASTIC BELIEF THAT HER
son had worked a miracle and in the incident from which that
belief had sprung, Victor saw the opportunity he had long been seeking to drive Barbet from his home.

In 1876, when Julien Hazard died, though the phylloxera was
known, it was not a present menace to the district of Cognac. The
Maison Hazard, its farm, its vineyards and its reserves of brandy,
were believed to be worth two hundred thousand francs, though
their admitted value was less. Barbet had accepted them as his share
of the inheritance, and at his father's wish, so that the family property should not be divided, had joined Anton in an agreement, an-
nually renewable, by which Barbet, if at any time in the following
year he decided to sell, would give Anton a first option to buy at a
price stated in the agreement. Since then, because wine for distillation and cognac for blending had been made rare by the disease of
the vines, Barbet's property, seemingly exempt from the phylloxera,
had increased in value. Each year he renewed the agreement without raising the figure above the hundred and sixty thousand francs
suggested by their father as a fair price between brother and brother,
but nothing would persuade him to sell. To compel him to do so, to
win profit for Anton and commission for himself, was Victor's
purpose.

He had a genius for suspicion, an invincible assurance of human
baseness. Making it his art to know what each man and woman
lusted after or feared, he was a collector and connoisseur of secrets,
the more successful because he was an honest blackmailer who never
blabbed without reason and did indeed give silence in return for his
price. These qualities had enabled him to establish, in Roussignac

66

and the district surrounding it, a network of petty powers; he knew the infidelities of wives, the dishonesties of clerks, even the agonized shames of children, and traded in them as only a man can in whom avarice is the least of his vices. He valued money, not as a miser does or for what it could buy, but as evidence of his triumph and of others' submission to him. To extract payment from a frightened woman gave him the pleasure that a snob might have in a new decoration or a pedant in a new degree; it was useless, but a feather in his cap, a title to self-esteem, and self-esteem was necessary to him as a narcotic to his self-hatred.

To this entanglement of obscure pressures and secret commissions he gave a name. He called the thing his system—"le système Vincent"—and ruled his secret empire with the pride of a Talleyrand, keeping a journal which, when posterity discovered it, should earn for him the immortality of a Fouché. But he had not Fouché's restraint. The greatest intriguers are they who remain unknown. The rest grow weary of the very secrecy on which their intrigue depends; they crave for that recognition which is, in its nature, fatal to them; and Victor hated Barbet because he was unresponsive to his malice, deaf to his schemes, behaving in all things as if le système Vincent did not exist.

Victor had material reasons also for wishing to force Barbet to sell the Maison Hazard. Anton desired it to appease his hunger for property; his wife, Bette, to crown her prestige as queen of Roussignac. From so large a transaction there would be rich pickings for its negotiator, and Victor laid his plans carefully. For more than a fortnight he exploited his system in a series of visits, of casual meetings at street-corners, of little threats, flatteries, bribes and rumours. To one he held up Madame Hazard's belief as blasphemy, to another as madness, to envious women as intolerable arrogance. To some he represented it as Barbet's own claim, adding that the little man had become impious and intolerable, that he "heard voices" and "had chats with angels," that he combined fantastic assertions of holiness with secret debaucheries at the Cheval Pie. It was not easy to stir up opinion against Barbet personally; he was loved, and even those who considered him extremely odd were more inclined to smile at than to condemn him; but when Victor hit upon the device of linking the names of Barbet and Thérèse, he found that his course was clear. The sour, the disappointed and the repressed among the women of Roussignac loathed "the tart from Angoulême"; the good wives distrusted her. Victor told how she had followed Barbet into the woods by night, how she had borrowed and was even now using his mandolin, and how Frédéric had said— The gossips of Roussignac lent ear, and the way was prepared for Victor to call upon his sister one morning in her grand house with gargoyles behind the Lion Rouge.

Bette, a woman with high, ruddy cheeks and yellow hair which grew so far back on her forehead that she seemed to be wearing a slipped wig, received her brother as a monarch might receive the head of her secret police—that is, with patronage and fear, an elaborate mingling of affability with dislike; at which he smiled thinly, seated in a gilded chair, inhaling the smells of camphor, beeswax and lace curtains that were her drawing-room.

She began at once to chatter, eager to know but afraid to hear why Victor had come. Two years ago, she had gone for a walk in the woods with Henri Flornoy, the doctor—he whose father had gone for a walk with a tiger. They had rested in a deserted hut, and Henri had begun to tell her what happiness it was for him to find, in so dull a place as Roussignac, a woman of high intelligence and sympathy, in whose company he felt himself to be always at ease. "Then shall we sit down?" she had said, for Henri was sentimental and might have talked standing for an hour. They were seated on the ground together, he admiring the peculiar expressiveness of her hands, when Victor walked in. Afterwards, she had explained everything to Victor. Whether he believed her or not, she did not know. Certainly he had said nothing to Anton, which, at the time, had surprised her; but he had not ceased, whenever they met, to remind her of his knowledge. He did not threaten; he made no direct statement of any kind; but sometimes he would speak of woodland walks, sometimes of the danger of women falling in love with men younger than themselves, and sometimes, in the company of others, just when she was a little boastful, a little gay, perhaps a little neglectful of him, he would take her hands and bow over them and declare that in all his life he had not seen hands as expressive as hers. Flornoy's name was not mentioned. Victor would speak mysteriously of the Count Fersen, and Bette had had to go to her books before she discovered that Fersen had been doubtfully spoken of as the lover of Marie Antoinette. Now the reference was clearly understood between them. Bette did her utmost to pretend that it was a good-humoured joke.

"And how, dear sister, is the Count Fersen?"

"Victor, how foolish you are! There was never anything in that."

"That is why I speak of the Count Ferson. No one but Marie Antoinette herself will ever be sure."

It was said with a dip of his empty glass that was almost an obeisance. Bette's nostrils flickered. A likening of herself to that unfortunate queen pleased her in spite of the context, and she begged him to take another drop from the decanter beside his chair. First he filled her glass, then his own.

"I have a suggestion to make to you," he said, but it was long before he made it. Once her curiosity was roused and her fear awakened, she became voluble, and Victor had only to be patient; her knowledge would be poured out; relevant or seemingly irrelevant, it was all grist to his mill; he stored it in his orderly memory until its use should appear. Though she was a fool when he played her, and had the weakness of supposing herself to be astute, she was by no means valueless to him, for she knew how to play others— young Flornoy for example—and had a judgment not sapped by pity. She might or might not have employed the man for her pleasure; Victor did not care so long as she was able and willing to use him for their common advantage. Though carnal desire had no meaning for him personally, he accepted it in others as a fact; it was no bar to his alliance as long as it was uncorrupted by romance. Being himself unfruitful not by physical defect but by that avarice of spirit which turns lust inward upon itself, he was disgusted by all things generous and naturally productive.

Even Bette he had avoided when she was pregnant and nursing. He could not endure the sweet, mealy smell of babies or the sound of their gums at the breast. To account for this in himself he had woven a philosophy of frustration into the pattern of his life. All faith was hypocrisy, all achievement contemptible. Any man who succeeded and any woman who loved became a target for his enmity. He loathed the prolific. When his mother spoke of Hugo or Balzac, he said they "spawned." He was afraid of the sea, even of the lake—they were too large, but he kept goldfish in a bowl and tickled them with the back of his finger-nail. His political opinions were governed by dislike of those in whom he perceived the lie of idealism, and nothing gave him more pleasure than to sterilize aspiration by ridicule. Even his feet were consistent with his theory; there was no spring in them; they did not stride, but picked their way, each step an avoidance; and whichever of them was in air when he crossed his legs drooped like the tail of a limp cod overhanging a fishmonger's slab. While his sister talked, he stroked the dusty upper of his boot, designing a little pattern upon it.

She knew what he was waiting for and allowed him to wait, telling him of all the other inhabitants of Roussignac but saying no word of Barbet or Thérèse. At last she said that on Friday, while she was checking the cash-book, Thérèse had come into the store.

"For what?"

"Underclothes."

Victor asked for details—their price, shape, colour. With frills or without? Bette answered him unsmiling, as though she were stock-taking. She understood perfectly that, if one intended to have power over a woman, all information concerning her was of value.

"I think," said Victor after an impressive pause, "I see at last a way to your becoming mistress of the Maison Hazard."

She sighed. "Barbet will never sell."

"I think in the end he will," said Victor and he explained to her again, with new and persuasive detail, how he had worked upon opinion in Roussignac. It was beginning to be said that Madame Hazard was mad; soon Barbet himself would be included in the charge; already there were boys who cried out "Saint! Saint!" as he passed, and laughed at him.

"Victor," said Bette, "if you think you are going to drive out Barbet by ridicule, you have mistaken your man."

Her brother was for a moment taken aback. "You think so? Perhaps you are right. But if his mother is ridiculed? If Thérèse Despreux is persecuted because of him? If the story of that prison revolt grows and grows until he himself begins to wonder whether he is not unfitted to look after prisoners? Listen, Bette," he continued, leaning forward and touching her knee, "you must give me credit for not being a fool."

If she had dared, Bette would have shrugged her shoulders. Instead she leaned back on the sofa, allowing her chin to sink until she could feel under it the beads she was wearing.

"You know," she said, "Anton doesn't despise Barbet."

"What do you mean?"

"Anton dislikes him. Anton can't make head or tail of him any more than we can. They're as far apart as it's possible for two men to be—but Anton doesn't despise him."

Victor curbed his impatience. "Still I don't understand what you mean."

"Only that I think we should be wrong to under-estimate him. I don't believe he can be threatened or bribed."

"Who has spoken of threats or bribes? But we can induce him."

Bette lifted her head. "Can we? How?"

"By combining the two purposes—the Cheval Pie and the Maison Hazard. Have you spoken to Anton again about his buying the Cheval Pie?"

"I have. He grinned."

"Well?"

"Oh, I don't say he's against it. He's always willing to buy local property at a price."

"But does he not see that the Cheval Pie will become a dangerous rival to the Lion Rouge—more and more dangerous as long as the girl is there?"

"The girl," Bette repeated. "So we come back to her."

Victor had other motives than his desire to turn out Thérèse, but he was willing that, for the time being, his sister should concentrate upon it. He had already interested his friend Georges Hurtaux of Angoulême in the widow Sernet's property; he would bid up Hurtaux against Anton while appearing to act as buying agent for each; he would take commission from whichever would pay the more and, as selling agent, commission from the widow Sernet as well. As for the Maison Hazard, the difficulties were greater but not insuperable. The price was fixed; the conditions were agreed in detail; nothing was needed but Barbet's consent to sell; and Victor had decided that this consent could be obtained from Barbet, if not by threat or appeal to avarice, then by working on his conscience.

"I think," Victor said, "you understand me very little, Bette. It is true, I wish to be rid of the girl, but there is a connexion between the two projects."

"Between the Cheval Pie and the Maison Hazard?"

"Certainly: drive out the girl, the man will follow."

She was incredulous. "Barbet? Thérèse Despreux? You believe that?"

"Who knows? Men of his sort are often trapped by extremely animal women."

"But she—why should she look at him?"

"Because, my dear Bette, he would be a new experience for her. Gluttons like a new dish. That in the first place, and afterwards—well, she would discover that he was kind to her." The tension of an extraordinary malice drew his eyelids together and he said: "The great whores have always lighted candles to the saints not for the forgiveness but for the understanding of sin."

Bette regarded her brother with bewilderment. His meanness she knew; his cleverness she knew; his limitations as an intriguer she vaguely apprehended. She feared, admired and despised him— admired his persistence, his memory, his unswerving materialism, while despising the pettiness of the man and the absurd pretensions of his system. It had amused her a little, though she wanted the Maison Hazard if she could get it, to think that, in attacking Barbet, her brother would find himself out of his depth. She disliked Barbet because so evidently his life rested upon values that she did not understand; but she respected him, as Anton did, because there was something formidable and, above all, unaccountable in his "fanaticism."

Now she perceived for the first time in her life that Victor also was fanatical—something much more than a village blackmailer who gave himself the airs of a Fouché—and she was afraid with a new fear. Hearing what he said of Thérèse Despreux and watching his face as he spoke of the great whores that lighted their candles to the saints, she understood that power not his own, not the product of his scheming or of his conscious mind, was awake in Victor. She looked at him cautiously. His eyes were open again; with the little finger of his left hand, he was picking his ear; nothing in him appeared to be abnormal and she drew breath in a long sigh. Then she asked him, as casually as possible, why he disliked Thérèse so much. To her surprise, the question seemed not to exasperate him. He replied in an even voice, as though he were discussing the anatomy of an animal, that the girl differed from other sensual women in this—that while they were possessive, she gave out. As he said this, his hands made an outward, flowing gesture from his body, and he asked:

"Have you ever seen blood pumped from an artery?"

Bette answered "No," but he did not hear her.

"It is like that," he continued. "To be near her is like being spurted with blood."

Still outwardly calm, he passed his hands over his face, wiping it, and allowed them to rest upon the arms of his chair.

"That, you see, is what they have in common."

"Who?"

"Barbet. Thérèse. It gushes from them."

"What gushes from them?"

He wished to be silent, not to confess himself even to his sister. She watched his lips parting and closing, and his tongue come out to wet them.

"Life," he said at last, and no sooner had he said it than he began to stretch himself and smirk and jig in his chair, for fear that she might understand him too well.

That morning Barbet had walked to the Lion Rouge to collect the money due to him for the upkeep of his prisoners. He should have come three days earlier and his brother shouted at him: "How do you expect me to keep my accounts in order if you let things run on in this way?"

Barbet said he was sorry to have been unpunctual, took the money and signed a receipt for it.

"Sit down," said Anton. "I have a few words to say to you. Is the door firmly shut?"

Having tried the door, Barbet seated himself opposite his brother at the varnished table. Only the upper wings of the shutters had been thrown back; the floor, the table, the empty stove and a pair of riding boots drooping against the farther wall were in a half-darkness pierced by slender beams that fell through shaped apertures in the lower shutters; the body of light from the square struck across the room horizontally, and when Anton stood up, as he always did when he was about to orate, his face and shoulders were unexpectedly plunged into it; it slapped him in the eyes and he sat down again, blinking, as if he had hit his head against the ceiling.

He had the gift, necessary to ambitious men if they are to pillage the world with a good conscience, of believing that he was a benefactor of the human race, particularly of the section of it that lived in Roussignac. Being its benefactor, he had a right to lecture it and to expect it to respond gratefully to his enthusiasm. If attendance at the Lion Rouge or purchases at the Magasin du Lion fell off, he was distressed by the ingratitude of his fellow citizens, for was not his inn "the centre of their civic life" and his store "organized to serve them"? In private business he was brief, shrewd and not dishonest; in private life, close but not unkind; it was only in his capacity of mayor or as head of his family that he became fuddled by a sense of righteousness. "There are times," his mother had said to him when he had pointed out to her that it was her duty to persuade Barbet to sell the Maison Hazard, "there are times, dear Anton, when you behave as if God and not Victor Vincent were your go-between. I will not have you talking to me as if you were a statue in the market-place. The old man on that pedestal was my father-in-law. Sit down, for heaven's sake! Don't hold up your left hand like a marble orator as if you expected the pigeons to anoint you."

"I am sure," Anton had replied, "that every word was spoken for your good."

"Justement," said Madame Hazard. "That is what I complain of. . . . And there are too many words."

There were always too many words when Anton spoke for the good of others.

"I am being reluctantly compelled to believe," he said now to Barbet, rising again from his chair and cautiously arranging himself so that the sun warmed the back of his head and threw forward deep shadows from the flesh of his jowl, "that the conduct of affairs at home is falling into a condition of—I will not say confusion but certainly of irregularity. I will not conceal from you that since our last discussion of that unhappy incident . . ."

"What unhappy incident?"

"The outbreak."

"You can call it what you like, Anton, but it wasn't unhappy."

The mayor smiled as men do when patting a dog they distrust. "I am not an intolerant man, Barbet," he continued. "I hope I shall never be accused of being a worldly one, and it is my duty, as head of our family and indeed—if I may say so—as father of Roussignac, to recognize the validity of many points of view not my own. I am fully aware of what you feel about the revolt, but you must allow me to insist that, from the standpoint of discipline and good government, its outcome was extremely unhappy."

"The prisoners are still there and in good order."

"So it may seem to you, but to Pierre Vincent . . ."

"Ah," said Barbet, "but that is because he has become afraid of them—and afraid of me. You see, he has become very confused. The curé says he is like the modern world: he is both superstitious and sceptical. Poor Pierre! He half believes I performed a miracle and, because he will call it a miracle, he is quite sure it wouldn't work again."

"Well, would it?" said Anton in spite of himself, his human

curiosity overcoming his knowledge that the only way to preserve official dignity in Barbet's presence was not give a chance to his unexpectedness.

"I thought *you* were lecturing *me*?" Barbet replied.

Anton drew himself up. "You mistake me. I may be mayor of this place—and a heavy task it is—but I am still your brother. It is my duty to understand you. Tell me what you believe." It was an order.

"I will tell you. Plainly this. If I had anything I valued that Blachère could take away from me, then I might have to use pistols to protect it. There's no need to use force if I haven't.""

"But you have."

"What?"

"Your life. Don't tell me you don't enjoy living. I've never known anyone who seemed to enjoy it more—though what you get out of it puzzles me. Your life was in danger."

"But then you see," said Barbet, "I don't count that as a personal possession."

The large head twisted in the sunlight. After staring for a moment at his brother, Anton decided not to reply. He came out from behind his table, walked with determination across the room, halted in front of a wall map of the district and said abruptly over his shoulder:

"In any case, my poor Barbet, we have practical things to consider. I had been about to warn you that, though you seem not to care or not to have noticed it, this unhappy incident—this incident is being very much talked about."

"Victor sees to that."

"Ah!"

"Oh, I'm not asleep, Anton. I have eyes and ears. As I came here, two boys shouted after me: 'Show us a miracle! Show us a miracle, Monsieur Hazard.'"

"There, you see? You see how the family name is dragged in? And what did you say? Took no notice, I hope. That is the only dignified way."

"I took notice all right," Barbet answered with a grin, hitching his heels on to the bar of his chair and hugging his knees with clasped hands. "I took them back into the woods and told them all they wanted to know about birds, and a bit more. We parted friends."

This was another diversion. One found, with Barbet, that one was continually led into talking about what interested him. I will say what I want to say, Anton thought. Twice I've tried. Now I'll make him listen.

"Listen to me," he said, the wall map deserted. "Very strong representations have been made to me as mayor of this town that you are not a fit and proper person to be in charge of prisoners. In fact, I have been asked to recommend the authorities to make a change. I refused, of course."

"Thank you. . . . Why did you refuse?"

"Because you are a member of the family. Whatever personal differences—"

"Only for that reason?"

"Isn't it enough? Mother is positively hostile to me, but she is my mother, I refuse to quarrel with her. I am, after all, a Frenchman. What would be thought of me if I ceased to visit her on the appropriate occasions or deprived my own brother of a source of income? Though I take this opportunity of saying that neither you nor she makes much response. I am told that you go to the Cheval Pie."

"My good Anton, I don't spend five francs a week on drink. I'll willingly give you as much."

"It's not a question of five francs or five hundred francs. It's the impression it creates—my own brother in the enemy's camp."

"I like the music and the open air. The Lion Rouge is too important for me, too much like the Senate—or the Bourse."

"And you like the dancing?"

"I do indeed."

"And the girl? I hear you have lent her a mandolin."

"Is that a sin?"

"It is indiscreet. You have been seen in the woods with her. That night she was at the Maison Hazard."

"That's all one with the mandolin. She and Frédéric came that evening to borrow it."

"She is a corrupt woman."

"No," said Barbet.

"She is a harlot."

"No," said Barbet.

"You will be telling me next she is a virgin."

"Ah, no," said Barbet with a smile, "that would be expecting too much of mankind."

At this point, Victor's head appeared round the door.

"I beg your pardon. I see you are engaged. I looked in with a message from Bette."

Barbet rose at once, glad of the interruption, and went out. As soon as he was gone, Victor began :

"That girl Thérèse—"

"You have been listening," said Anton.

"Listening? Bette and I have been discussing her. She is a great danger, Anton. She has ability that girl. Leave her there and she will work up the Cheval Pie until . . ."

"Nonsense. Her songs are stale. People will soon tire of her. Besides, the Cheval Pie is falling to pieces. All very well in spring and summer but in winter they'll feel the pinch. There are holes in the floor you could fall through and the roof leaks. She can't work up the Cheval Pie without half rebuilding it—and where's the capital coming from?"

"From you, Anton, if you're wise."

"I'm wiser than that. Let the thing die, I say."

"But if someone else—"

"Who?"

"Anyone with a little money, a little enterprise and an eye for that girl. Anyone from Angoulême or Limoges—perhaps even from Bordeaux."

Anton ceased instantly to be the benevolent mayor of Roussignac.

"Now," he said, "come to the point. Sit down." He had remembered suddenly having been told that Hurtaux, of Angoulême, had visited the Cheval Pie. Hurtaux had enterprise, was a speculator in

all trades; he had money—or he knew where to raise it; certainly
he had an eye for a girl. They talked for half an hour and more,
each determined not to mention the name of Hurtaux. At the end
of the conversation, Victor went off to visit the widow Sernet, so
satisfied by his morning that he threw up his head as he entered the
square. Above the roofs was a cloudless sky of May with the depth
of a receding paleness and an absolute calm. Remembering what
Hurtaux had said of Thérèse, he thought that he would have a few
words with her before visiting Madame Sernet. She was a greedy
animal and would eat out of any dish.

Chapter 7

AFTER LEAVING HIS BROTHER, BARBET HAD GONE
to the Cheval Pie. At this hour of the morning the tables were
empty. Frédéric, in shirt-sleeves and apron, was washing them and
the zinc chairs; he had tipped them over that they might dry more
easily, but he found a place where Monsieur Barbet might sit with
his head in the shade of a plane-tree but his knees and hands in
the sun.

"How is business, Frédéric?"

The youth smiled at him, showing his teeth like a young white rat
prematurely aged, and said that sometimes it was extremely tiring;
then, as though he feared that this might be taken as admission of
defeat and so as an act of disloyalty to Thérèse, he added, echoing
her optimism: "But new people come. They seem to be interested.
A very rich stranger has been here twice. Thérèse heard of him when
she lived in Angoulême. Hurtaux, he's called. But I don't know
what will come of it all."

"Of what?"

"Well, you see, it leads to nothing, does it? And Thérèse is
always thinking that it will. She works and works. She's strong.
And she has what she calls 'her star.' But I haven't. . . . Do you see
what she has done about the piano? No, it's indoors now. But you
see that wooden slope, down from the doorstep? She made it, and
put the piano on wheels. We don't have to lift it now. And she says
she's going to make a platform so that when she dances everyone
can see her feet."

Frédéric's eyes were wide in admiration of her energy, but his
body drooped at the thought of it. He brought out a pink sirup on a

saucer. "Your grenadine," he said, and, having set it down, continued as though he had not been interrupted:

"She's mad, I think. Do you know—while I am going round the tables each evening to see that everyone has his drink before the first song begins, she sits in that little room on the right of the door with her face between her hands and her cheeks pressed up by her fingers. I don't know what she thinks about or how she does it, but when I go in to say everything's ready and she stands up, she's two inches taller and her eyes flash and sometimes she says it's the Bois and sometimes it's a place she's heard of in Montmartre, and she knows who's there and what they're wearing, and they are all waiting for *her*. She says most of them are half dead; she says their blood doesn't flow; she has to make it. Then she says that's why they hate her and always will. Do you know, Monsieur Barbet, once she said to me—to *me*: 'That's why *you* hate me, but you don't know it. You do whatever I tell you and so will they, but what they *love* is someone who is so nearly themselves that they don't feel the drag. People want you to tuck them up and let them sleep,' she said. 'They hate you inside themselves if you raise them from the dead.' "

"You remember it all," said Barbet, "word for word."

"Oh, yes," Frédéric answered. "You see, I'm consumptive. I shan't live long." He wandered off and began to set the tables upright again in readiness for the customers who might come in a little before noon.

Above the houses opposite the Cheval Pie the sky was emptied of the blue that had made it opaque an hour earlier. Its transparency drew on the eye; there was no longer a roof above the earth but space itself; and Barbet did not hear Thérèse approach him.

"Good morning, Monsieur Barbet," she said. "Now it is you who are going on a voyage—and further than Paris!"

He had supposed her chair to be empty, but she was seated opposite him and he looked at her without surprise.

"It wasn't much of a voyage," he said. "I was thinking about the vineyard as far as I remember."

Wishing professionally to entertain her customer, she began by asking him about the vines. He said that, if there was no setback, the season would be early this year; already the vines were in leaf, and that morning his mother had heard the ortolan. "At least, I suppose she did. Often she's deaf, or seems to be, but she's always the first to hear the binetu." Thérèse listened, at first with politeness only; she was worried about her dancing shoes, a heel had loosened, she had secured it, now it was loose again; she must have new shoes. The thought of what they would cost tugged at her mind; she defied it, as she did all her present troubles, by saying to herself—it's quite sensible, it's not extravagant really, it's a professional expense, and she drew courage from her future, from Paris, from the fame and glitter that would enable her to look back on the Cheval Pie as—I wonder, she thought, whether I shall remember this particular morning, sitting here, the iron leg of the chair against my ankle, and worrying about the heel of my dancing shoe. "Oh, yes," she said, "the binetu."

Barbet smiled at her polite failure to be interested in the bird.

"Can you imitate him?"

Her face became animated at once. She forgot her shoes.

"Of course I can!" she exclaimed. "Been-been-been-towoo-woo! Been-been-been-towoo-woo! Is that right? Have you ever thought how funny it must be to make that sound from inside yourself? I mean— No, I suppose it isn't funny really, not if you are a binetu, but—" She broke off, shaking her head. "That's what's wrong with me. I haven't any imagination—except my own kind."

"What is your own kind?"

"Oh, Paris. On and on—always the same—me, me, me. If you go on imagining the same thing always, it's like being shouted at, it's like hammers inside your head. What was Frédéric talking to you about?"

"He's tired," said Barbet.

She was pitiless. "Tired. So he ought to be. I have to drive him if we are going to run this place between us and look after that old thing upstairs. Then he says: 'Suppose you do succeed. Suppose you do get to Paris. What will happen then?'"

"What will happen?" Barbet asked.

"Someone will buy the Cheval Pie. Your brother probably."

"But Frédéric?"

"Oh," she cried impatiently. "I can't look so far ahead. He's dying anyway. So is the old woman. Let's hope they both go out together. That's cruel and heartless, isn't it? Well, now you now— I am like that."

"No," said Barbet, "you are not. If you were, you wouldn't boast about it."

"You see," she said, taking no notice of this, "I'm not really a coward, but I get panics. You have money and a settled position and a job that goes on day after day, week after week; it's easy for you not to be frightened. . . . No it's not. It's just as hard for you as it is for me. I suppose, if I was really any good, I should *know* that Paris was coming, just as you knew, when you walked into the courtyard of the prison, that Blachère and the rest would eat out of your hand. . . . Sometimes I do know; then I'm happy, and I'm kind even to Frédéric; but sometimes it seems hopeless. How do I ever begin? How do I get out of this place?"

"By being yourself," said Barbet.

"That's not how it's usually done. It's done by being what audiences expect you to be."

To his own astonishment, Barbet slapped the table with his hand. "Why do you lie?" he said. "You're not cruel. You're not heartless. You don't know as much as a tenth-rate girl in a chorus about how to flatter an audience. If you did, you'd sing your songs better."

She opened her eyes and smiled broadly. "They are not my songs. They are someone else's songs. They're stale songs. That's why. If they were mine—"

"That's what I was saying," Barbet interrupted. "Now you have said it yourself. And I want another grenadine."

"You shall have it on the house," said Thérèse.

When she was gone, he thought: it wasn't really a good imitation of the binetu she gave; it should be a single, not a double note at the end of the call—not "towoo-woo"; but the sound she made was more than an imitation; it had herself in it, her own sadness and gaiety. At first, people would say: That's wrong, that isn't the bird-call; but soon it would give them more of the binetu than their own memory of him, and, when they heard him again in the vines, they would miss the double note and say: That's odd, the binetu is different this year.

He would tell Fontan of Thérèse's version of the binetu and Fontan would pick it out on the spare mandolin or on a fiddle. Barbet began to hum a song—a rambling, improvised narrative of the vineyard, with a soft lilt as its undercurrent and now and then a bird-call to break the lilt and point it. The bird-calls existed chiefly in his mind; he had little voice to reproduce them, so he drummed them on the table with his fingers and breathed them almost soundlessly with his lips, cocking his head and hearing them with the ears of his imagination. His songs were of two kinds, Fontan said—the tinklers and the throbbers. This, being a narrative, was grave and throbbing, though not, for Barbet, less happy than those he sang to livelier tunes. It might have continued for a long time, verse after verse strung together on haphazard rhymes, like the voyaging tales he had chanted to himself when he was a boy, lying in his bed, awake by daylight; but Thérèse returned with his sirup and, after a couple of verses in her presence, he came out of the vineyard and stopped.

"Sing another," she said.

"There isn't any more. I make it up as I go along."

"I didn't say 'more,' I said 'another.' "

"Oh, well," said Barbet, "most of them go as fast as they come. Fontan has written some down.

> " *'There was a lady sat in the shade*
> *With her feet in a patch of the sun. . . .'* "

He wondered if she was still interested.

"Go on," she said. "What is that one about? What happened to the lady?"

"That depends," Barbet replied. "It depends on who she is. As far as I remember, the first time I hit on that one was on a winter's afternoon, walking back from Roussignac in the snow. I had been in the church to find the curé, but he wasn't there, and I had stood staring at the picture of the Annunciation. . . ."

"I like that picture too."

He nodded. "The song was about that. But it's been about other things since. There are dozens of versions, I'm afraid. When you come to think of it, there's scarcely any story that might not begin:

> *" 'There was a lady sat in the shade*
> *With her feet in a patch of the sun.'*

Or there's the Reed Song; Fontan likes that; it's about starlings, but it's about battles as well. Or there's a crowd of little songs about swimming—there's one about the water that was lying still, suddenly I jumped in and began to swim, and the song isn't about me but about the water. Then there are dozens of songs of not more than four or eight lines each, and some of them don't even rhyme; some aren't verses at all and don't pretend to be. Things that came into my head with a tune attached.

> *" 'I have two oars in my hands. Why do I feel that I must be fair to them, as if they were alive?'*
>
> *" 'I said a stupid thing. I wish I could unsay it. But you alone can unsay it by not remembering my foolishness when you remember me.'*
>
> *" 'Now I shall lie down but I shan't fall asleep haphazard. I shall watch myself falling asleep; then I shall sleep well. I shall watch myself falling asleep, like a bright coin twisting through clear water until it is a gleam and disappears.' "*

"That would be a song to end a programme!" Thérèse exclaimed. "Sing it now, sing it to your tune. Then I will *make* it." She sprang up. "Come to the piano. Try it. Let me try it. . . . Frédé! Frédé!"

In the little parlour at the entrance of the inn, Frédéric was set down on a creaking piano-stool. He stumbled laboriously into Barbet's tunes. Thérèse swept him aside as soon as she had in her head enough words of each song to enable her to experiment with it. Nothing came from her as Barbet had expected it to come. The grave lilts she quickened; the simple, meditative words she delivered with a violent accent of mockery; the cheerful ditties she sang with the solemn intensity of an awe-struck choir-boy—changing everything, exaggerating everything.

"I know! I know!" she cried. "I know I am overdoing all of it. I want it loose! Then I can shake it into my own pattern."

After a little while, letting her hands fall from the keys, she gazed at Barbet.

"You are patient. You don't seem to mind."

"Why should I?"

"These are your songs! I'm not singing them the way you wanted them."

"Not yet. But you will."

She shook her head violently, determined not to deceive this considerate author.

"Oh no I shan't. Never. I shan't sing them like *this*. This is all ragged and extravagant. But I shall still make the solemn ones gay and gay ones solemn. That's *me!* That's my invention about your songs. That's how to treat them." She awaited challenge.

"Of course it is, Thérèse," Barbet said. "Gay and grave—of course, in my songs, they're interchangeable. Thank you for telling me."

She asked seriously if she might use his songs. Might she have the music Fontan had written down? Yes, Barbet said, but would she, in return, sing and dance one evening in the courtyard of the prison? She clasped her hands in her lap and moved her head slowly in refusal. Barbet observed her with astonishment.

"No?" he said. "I don't understand. Why not? Why won't you give a performance in the prison? Not now. In June perhaps. Or in the hot weather—in July. You are not frightened? Good heavens, they won't hurt you!"

"I know that." She made no further reply, but twisted round on the music-stool and jerked her head up and away from him so that the muscle of her neck was as taut as her straightened arms.

"Why?" he asked.

"Because—why do you want that?"

"So that Fontan can hear. It's partly his music."

"Is that all you can think of?"

"What else is there?"

She closed her lips. Then suddenly she exclaimed, struggling with herself: "It's the devil in me makes me want to say 'yes.'"

"Oh," said Barbet, "we all flatter ourselves about our devils," at which she turned on him a face transformed, lit with a terrible animation, a lamp flashed violently in his eyes.

"They are shut up, your prisoners. They are men. Are you blind?"

"No," he said. "I'm not blind. And I'm not afraid. All men are prisoners. That's no reason to use one's prison as a hiding place."

"On your head be it, then."

He laughed at her. "How you dramatize yourself—your devil and your prisoners! On my head be it, certainly. Besides, it was all a lie—you wanted to come, you—"

"I said so."

"You meant to come?"

"I suppose so. I—"

"Then why lie about yourself? Why pretend to be afraid of your own power? You're not, you know."

"Oh," she cried, "very well. You know too much for a man. I'll come. If I'm a genius, I'm a genius; and if I'm a bitch, I'm a bitch. Tant pis! But it won't be a performance for monks and little girls."

Turning to the piano, she laid her hands on the keys, then swerved to him.

"Other people are afraid of me," she said. "Why aren't you?"

"You try that song," he answered. "It's only the sham people who talk about their own devils. You'll drive them in harness—or drink yourself to death."

She leapt to her feet and seized his shoulders.

"My God! What are you—mad?"

"No. Sane. So are you. Now, sit down and sing."

She obeyed but mocked him. "Would you like to hear it as if an angel were singing it—a sane angel, not given to drink?"

"Yes," he said, "I should, if angels are in your mind. Not otherwise."

While she was singing this song, Victor came to the Cheval Pie. Other customers were before him; they and he were served by Frédéric; and Victor, as soon as he had sipped from his glass, went in the direction of the music. Standing a little aside from the window, he looked in attentively. Barbet was leaning against the wall beside the piano, his face lighted, his eyes upon Thérèse, making no attempt to conceal his eagerness for her song—or was it for the girl herself? Sometimes he intervened with that swift assurance, that absence of self-distrust, which seemed to Victor inexplicable in a man so unassertive; and Thérèse listened, almost in submission, while he sang his version of the song, before throwing up a defiant head to sing her own which, though all her own, was yet an interpretation of his. They clashed, disputed, interrupted each other, but from their clashes agreement sprang as though there were in each song a hidden perfection that yielded itself to neither singly but was recognized by both in the instant of its emergence. Victor had the impression that he was watching something altogether new in his experience of human nature, as though the two figures, whom the window framed, were not the Barbet and Thérèse whom he knew separately—the wiry little man whose independence was like a flame, the lustful, fierce girl with the guile of a gipsy and the dark wariness of an animal at bay—but two beings appeased in each other's company, not held in the tension of their differences, but at ease with the profound ease of two friends met after long division or of two poplars swaying in the same wind. To Victor the sight was intolerable. He went in, and no sooner had he slid open the parlour door than the music ceased abruptly; he saw what a fool he had been, for Barbet was precisely what he had supposed Barbet to be and Thérèse was the girl he knew—with a flashing, wanton pride as her advertisement and her defence. Victor decided that she was trying to seduce Barbet because he had money and was easy prey. He hoped she would succeed, for Barbet was of the kind she might destroy.

"Don't let me interrupt you," he said. "My dear Barbet, I beg you not to go on my account."

"It's not on your account," Barbet answered. "It's time I was on my way home."

Victor plied Thérèse's curiosity. "I wanted you alone. A little matter. I have something to say to you." She came to his table, accepted absinthe, listened with animation. I could have her myself, Victor thought; the idea fascinated and revolted him; he would have liked to humiliate her, to throw her down and leave her, to count coins into an abject hand. "You have such talent. You are wasting yourself in this place."

She smiled, an easy dupe. "My songs or my dances? Do other people say so? What did Monsieur Hurtaux say? Hasn't he a share in a café concert at Bordeaux?"

Victor was not yet willing to advance as far as Monsieur Hurtaux.

"Your songs and your dances—well yes, of course they will come. You are inexperienced as yet. But they will come." He turned his eyes full into hers. "It wasn't of them I was speaking."

"Of what, then?"

"Those eyes tell me you know well enough, my dear."

"Indeed, no."

"I will be explicit then. All the men in Angoulême, in Cognac, in Roussignac itself are not those who come to gape in this garden when you kick your skirts in the air. Even the most beautiful picture must be brought to market. Every business needs management. Now—"

"Are you proposing yourself, monsieur, as a lover or as—"

"An agent," said Victor with a little bow.

"To bring men to *me* !"

"Precisely."

She gave no sign of anger. "To *bring* them," she exclaimed. "Ah, that is a good joke! . . . It is a joke that wouldn't have occurred to you, monsieur, if you knew how men were made. Why do you not propose yourself as agent to the honey? What commission would you charge for the introduction of each bee?"

Victor controlled himself, not because he believed Thérèse to be other than a harlot. She had repulsed him now—that was her little vanity; she would value his services in time. Had not she herself spoken of Hurtaux? No doubt she was casting her line for him— a big fish. A diseased one, too, Victor reflected in satisfaction, a man of unusual tastes, not gentle with his women. Very well, if it was Hurtaux she wanted, Hurtaux she should have. And, in any case, Victor had other business at the Cheval Pie.

"I promised to call upon your aunt," he said, setting down his empty glass.

"Good," said Thérèse, "you know your way."

He entered the inn, climbed a double flight of stairs and knocked.

The widow Sernet was saved from baldness by a wisp of mottled hair down the centre-line of her head. Victor inquired of her health.

"Now," she said, "what offer have you?"

"From Anton Hazard, I regret, as yet, none."

"Then why are you here? It is always the same."

"I spoke to you of Monsieur Georges Hurtaux. He has been here more than once. I think he is interested."

"Interested?" the old woman exclaimed. "In what—the house or the girl? From what I know of Hurtaux—"

Victor with a smile acknowledged her shrewdness. "Primarily," he said, "in the house, I think."

Madame Sernet began to chuckle. "Well, the girl goes with it. That noise in the garden up to all hours! And there's a young man comes creeping back when the rest are gone."

"One?"

"It may not always be the same one. But if they're different, they all make the same noise, coming and going. She makes him take his shoes off—but I hear every whisper, every creak of the stair. I can hear her shoulders drop against the wall when he kisses her."

"Still," Victor suggested consolingly, "it brings in money, I'll be bound?"

"Not a sou."

"She keeps it from you—all of it?"

"She don't take it."

"You believe that?"

"Believe? I know it. She's that kind of a fool."

"Then why—"

"You ask 'why'? Why do men and women do what they do? You can look at Thérèse and still ask why she opens the door at night!"

"A romantic," said Victor, "an animal." He spoke each of these words in a zoological tone, as if he were reading the label on a wild beast's cage. From so foreign a subject he turned to ask politely: "It prevents you from sleeping?"

"Nothing stops me sleeping if I want to sleep. But I'd like to get behind that girl as I did when she was younger. Only the switch would quiet her then. . . . You give her to Hurtaux. I shall enjoy that in my grave. . . . And now," Madame Sernet continued, "how far has it gone? Has he mentioned a price?"

Chapter 8

BARBET'S HOUSEHOLD AND HIS NEIGHBOURS WERE greatly confused by his quieting of the prisoners, for the deepest prejudices were stirred by it. To rationalists it appeared as a cheating of reason; to the conventional as a disgraceful impudence; to sentimentalists as a kind of witchcraft; to the sceptical as a lie. Few perceived that Barbet's method, though it would have been surprising in themselves, was natural and spontaneous in him, and that its effects were neither more nor less miraculous than the growing of a flower from its seed.

Madame Hazard, because a scepticism was overthrown which she had hitherto considered unassailable, rushed to an extreme credulity; in the intervals of her work as housewife, which fortunately did not flag, she would sit with her hands lying palm upwards in her lap, as if she were nursing a baby, and was shocked by the blindness of the pastor and the curé who treated her with none of the reverence due to the mother of a saint. Pierre continued to believe that he had been cheated. What authority he had had over the prisoners seemed to him to have been undermined. Before them he felt a fool and so became one. Even Renée could not reassure him, and he was so evidently unhappy that at last Barbet said: "Renée, if you want to marry him, I will arrange your dowry." There was a cottage among the vineyards in which they might live, and work enough on the land. Pierre need never face the prisoners again. "And he needn't come into the house either!" cried Madame Hazard, who regarded his and Renée's going as a purge of unbelievers. "We know well enough that Barbet can manage the prisoners alone."

Roused by this fling at Pierre, Renée answered with spirit: "And I suppose he will cook their food and do the washing and clean the house?"

"Madame Garbut will come in by the day."

"You have arranged that?"

"Not yet, but she will come."

"She's stone deaf!"

"Barbet," said Madame Hazard with mysterious impressiveness, "will make her hear."

"Heavens above," Renée cried, "he'll have to shout!"

She and Pierre began to prepare for their marriage and departure, giving out that they were glad to dissociate themselves from Barbet's household and had consented to occupy his cottage only in loyalty to the family. Their behaviour was much applauded, for Victor had done his work well, and many who loved Barbet were afraid to say so lest they should be considered enemies of the established order or be laughed at as dupes.

In the prison itself, that evening of rebellion had an enduring and subtle influence. Blachère, his leadership gone, isolated himself from the rest. When they were allowed the freedom of the courtyard, he would often remain, cowed and sullen, at the back of his cell, making no comment, even on his food. The others had expected that Barbet would speak of the incident and punish them for their share in it; if he had done so it would have been a relief to them, for they found that they could not speak of it among themselves. It baffled them and made them shy of speech. What had happened? In what way had they been fooled? They had been shouting in the courtyard—so much they knew clearly. They had believed that they would break free, had been under Blachère's sway—they remembered the sick frenzy of it. Then stillness had come upon them, an end to hammering in the brain; there had been glow-worms at their feet and they had kneeled, like fools, like children; and suddenly they were back in their cells, breathing slow and long, like children cooled after a fever. Now, whenever they began to speak of these events or to blame each other, shyness came into their throats. They were glad to cover over remembrance of this remembered thing.

Though they were not told that Pierre's duties were soon to come to an end, they seemed to be aware of it; for they paid no heed to him, asked him no questions, and treated him as one who had no further share in their lives. Their attention was focussed on Barbet. He told them that before long Thérèse Despreux would sing to them in the courtyard. As the time came near, a piano was brought out and covered by a tarpaulin.

"Can you tune it, Fontan?"

"If you bring me the tuning hammer and wedge."

To her surprise, Thérèse was unable to empty her mind of Barbet, or, when others sneered at or blamed him, to hold her tongue—until, suddenly, she found that she held her tongue always when his name was bandied across the tables of the Cheval Pie, as though what knowledge she had of him were secret.

He brought her his songs, and sheets of music scribbled by Fontan in violet ink. When she tried them in private, they transformed themselves; new speeds, new emphasis, new twists of meaning leapt into her mind. Because she could not write down the changes she made, she played them again and again until they were fixed in her memory, and three times, in the heat of the day, took train for Angoulême to visit Raymond Truc, her former music-master, and returned in time for the evening customers. Seeing her again, Raymond assumed that the idea of his writing music for her was but an excuse for her coming. He dragged curtains over his windows, though they looked to the north, and on a fringed table beside the sofa set down two long red glasses with gilded rims.

"Our special glasses!"

"No one," he said, "has been allowed to drink out of them since you deserted me."

"Am I expected to believe that?"

"How can you not believe it!"

"Easily," she answered, and, rising from the sofa as he approached it, drew back the curtains.

Everything in the room was familiar to her, the mat before the piano rucked by his pushing back the stool as she entered, the best chair in which the governesses sat when he was teaching young girls, the shelf of tattered paper in which his music was stored, the basket in which his dog slept—on all these had rested once an enchantment of squalor, which persisted now, for in her nothing died, no intimacy was utterly lost, all her lives were continuing parts of her life, and this pale young man with heavy eyelids and flushed cheeks, whose tongue was moving over his lips, had pleased her once. Because of her he had come to life and before her eyes was coming to life again.

"Give me your hand."

He stretched it out. She carried it to her cheek, then to her lips, and released it.

"Sans rancune?"

"Ah—mais—"

She took him to the piano and set up the sheaf of music she had brought with her.

"Now, listen," she said. "This is serious. If you can give me this music written down in the way I want it, I—"

The sentence remained so long uncompleted that he prompted her, but her imagination had run out beyond the phrase of swaggering ambition she would have used. In these songs was not Paris only, or her fortune only. In these songs—

"My God!" she exclaimed, "there'll be nothing in them if we don't work! This—it's like a psalm. I want to keep the tune, but break the rhythm. I want the beat of a lame horse at the gallop. . . ."

She played it, sang it, turned to him: "Can you write that?"

"But you are distorting it!"

"He says not."

"Who?"

"Barbet."

Raymond shrugged his shoulders. "They say he's mad."

Thérèse closed her lips. Then she said: "Well, make some notes.

There's Fontan's version." She thrust a pencil between his fingers. He listened and wrote obediently.

"Enough? Can you work on that? Now the next. Listen."

For three hours she drove him. At her second visit, he needed no driving. He was so proud of the result of his labour, so eager for more, that, having kissed her, he made no attempt to draw the curtains or bring out the ruby glasses. At once she asked for them.

"And when, last time, I drew back the curtains, confess—you were a little relieved?"

His grateful vanity accepted half the implication. "But what I said of these glasses was true!" he assured her, and to prove his gallantry he splintered his own against the wall.

At the end of her third visit she had what she needed. As she walked out, with a sheaf of music under her arm, she saw, in the window of the clockmaker's, that she was too early for the train, and loitered to watch the movement of an eighteenth-century clock that he had set out for display. A shoulder touched hers. She looked up into the grey nostrils and black eyebrows of Georges Hurtaux.

Her mind was instantly made up that he should employ her, and she gave him a welcome that bared his teeth.

How much he had admired her performances at the Cheval Pie! Indeed, he assured her, several of his visits to Roussignac had been made for no other reason than to see her. But she distributed her favours so evenly among her customers—the eyebrows curved upward under thick creases—that she had little time for strangers! He was staying near by at the Hôtel de France. Perhaps, if she was not pressed for time—

She was not pressed for time, but had been working indoors all the hot afternoon, and if monsieur thought that a glass of lemon and water under the shade of that awning—

She was thirsty; it was a delight to be waited on; she gulped her drink like a schoolgirl and, when her glass was empty, accepted Hurtaux's suggestion of absinthe. She sipped hers.

"But you are not drinking your absinthe."

"I'm not thirsty any more."

What work had she been doing in Angoulême? Wasn't there work enough at the Cheval Pie?

"But I shall not spend my life at the Cheval Pie."

She knew that she must be very guarded in Hurtaux's presence. She must be professional, not too young or too eager; she must not give herself away; but he said that, when she sang, she had a style of her own which she must cultivate, and he defined her style with such accuracy, such intelligent insight, that she said to herself: Here is a man who knows!—and poured out her plans.

"It is not," he said, "at present everyone's style. That, precisely, is why it might become so. You see, my dear, what people think they want at a café concert is to be horrified or to be amused, but what they really want, if they are made to want it, is all of life in twenty lines, and then again all of life in ten lines, and then again all of life in five—to laugh when they're frightened, to shudder while they laugh. A great diseuse keeps the coin spinning. You can't be sure which way it will come down, and yet, when it's down, you've always won your bet. Now you"—and he laid his hand on her knee—"when you sing, you are very still. You are not pretty. You have a beautiful body when you dance, but when you sing you use it seldom." He slapped her thigh. "Now, tell me, why is that?"

"It's not true!" she cried. "It's not true! I do use my body. It's my hands I don't use—not much. My body and my face are *me!* When their eyes come up from my middle to my face and stay there —that's half the battle. And when I *do* use a gesture it is a cord."

"A cord?"

"To pull them!" She rose beside the table and with fists clenched and arms moving at the level of her breasts dragged in to her the invisible world. From her breasts, her hands slid down until her arms were straight, the palms turned forward. "And then to give them themselves again," she cried, throwing out her hands from the centre of her body. "To give them themselves *new*. That's what I want. I have it in me." She sat down and lifted her glass to her lips. "But I have to *learn* how to give it out."

"It is I," said Hurtaux, "who could give you a chance to learn. And, if I may say so, you please me, mademoiselle."

He explained, in the language of a company promoter advancing a prospectus, that he had inherited his father's business in the manufacture of paper, had expanded it, was rich. He and his brother Henri, a restaurant proprietor in Bordeaux, had determined to extend their activities to the business of entertainment. Already, in Bordeaux, they had established a café concert. Now they were planning another in Angoulême, perhaps a third in Limoges, both feeders to the Boîte d'Argent at Bordeaux. And some day, Lyons and Paris! A network of entertainment throughout France—a web with its centre in Paris. Like the organization of an army, said Hurtaux, the companies moving under orders from place to place, promotion following promotion, every dancing-girl with a chance to become a star.

In spite of her resolve not to appear too young or too eager, her eyes became fixed on his face.

"Could I have a chance in Bordeaux?"

"In Bordeaux! You must be patient, my dear. You must wait until we open a Boîte d'Argent here. Angoulême is where you must begin."

"When?"

"Perhaps in the autumn."

"Perhaps in the autumn!" She shook her head, and pushed towards him the pile of music on their table. "I have my songs now. I am ready for Bordeaux. I will ask Barbet to let you come to the prison when I sing there. You will see that I am ready."

"All things are possible," he said. "Or perhaps could be made possible."

"How?"

"I could write to my brother at Bordeaux."

"You will? You will? Oh—"

He waved his hand as though it were the wand of a magician and set his eyes on her. "It is understood, then?"

"What?"

"It is understood between us?"

There was no mistaking him now. She did not blame him or pretend that she did not understand.

"Why do you want that?"

"Does it surprise you?"

"No." With a sincerity that persuaded him, she added: "But I hadn't expected it. I was thinking only of the work. I wasn't thinking of you at all."

"It will be necessary to think a little of me."

"No," she said.

"Am I repulsive to you?"

She looked at him attentively. "No."

"Or you virgin?"

"No."

"Well? Come—"

"No," she said. "It is impossible."

"And why? What is it you want—a contract? You shall have it." Her eyes met his. "For Bordeaux," he added. "Three months —to sing and dance."

"Not for a contract. Not for money."

So improbable a scruple puzzled him. "For what, then?"

"Not for a contract. Not for money," she said, gathering her music under her arm and forcing herself, in control of stormy disappointment, to repeat aloud an incantation of her mind. "Oh," she said with a smile, "it isn't nobility of soul. I expect it's only superstition."

"Unprofitable, mademoiselle."

"Not in the end."

"The end?"

"You are not a fool, monsieur. In the end, a whore buys contracts for a whore, but an artist sleeps in what bed she pleases."

"Perhaps—in the end," said Hurtaux with good-humour. "But even an artist must begin."

When she left him, she went on to the ramparts and looked over their edge on to the shelving house-roofs and the great plain below. She was tired; there was half an hour to spare, and she sat down on a sun-peeled bench. The heat of the day was past; a cool, peaceful breeze moved on the ramparts, stroking her cheeks and ankles. She closed her eyes, and imagined the gritty courtyard of the Cheval

Pie and the heat of the kitchen while she prepared her aunt's supper.

But afterwards I shall sing and dance!

Even the idea of performance struck no fire in her. Imagination gave no response. By now Hurtaux was in his bedroom at the Hôtel de France. He would find another girl, and she be left for ever in Roussignac. Her feet were sore; her chemise was sticking to her; her finger-nail was caught in a paint-blister on the bench.

It seemed to her that her refusal had been hypocritical, the product of a false and unintelligent pride. "Not for a contract! Not for money!" No virtuous woman would give her any credit for that.

It's time that you, Thérèse Despreux, stopped whimpering. She shook herself defiantly. What did she care for the opinion of virtuous women? They weren't artists; they had no blood in them. . . . And that, she thought, is an ignorant, stupid, extravagant thing to say. I wish I were good. No, I don't. I wish I wanted to be good. No, I don't. "Not for money! Not for a contract!" God, I'm tired.

She looked at her watch, and, raising her eyes from it, saw at a distance Barbet's hatless and shaggy head. She was not in a mood to speak to him; if she was still and lowered her head, he would pass. She tucked her hands under her and watched his approaching shadow. It halted. She felt his weight upon the bench.

"You look very fresh and alive," he said. "Even at the end of June, are you never tired?"

She gazed at him in astonishment.

"You still sit on your hands," he said. "You did that when you were a little girl."

She began to laugh. " 'Fresh—alive—not tired!' "

"Isn't it true?"

"You imagine things."

"But isn't it true?"

"For you it may be."

"Not for you?"

But she would not admit it. "There," she said. "It's time we started for the station if you are coming back by this train. What have you been doing in Angoulême?"

"I have a yearly agreement with Anton about the sale of my place. It has to be renewed. I have been to the lawyer."

"I have been to a music-master," she said. "I wanted a setting for my songs—your songs."

On their way to the station and on the platform she told him as much as she chose to tell of her adventures.

"Thérèse," he said as the train started, "what happens when people come to you with their troubles?"

"The great Hurtaux," she replied with a swift, ironic glance, "was kind enough to say that I had humanity."

"Ah well," said Barbet. "Humanity? That may be. When you suffer, you write the suffering off. You don't hate. Isn't that true?"

"I hate furiously for a bit," she answered. "Then I go on to the next thing."

Barbet considered her with attention: "But you are always acting. You are acting now."

"Is it *wrong* for *me*—to *act?*" Barbet grinned at her emphasis. "Why is it wrong—even if it's true?" she persisted. "Why mustn't I act—in life?"

"Because, if you do, no one but a fool will have the courage to trust you, and you may break your heart before you find one with courage enough."

She was afraid and shook her head and answered: "I shall still have my acting."

"No," he said, "you may ruin that. Acting must always be larger than life, and if your life is itself a part—well, your acting will have to puff itself out like the frog in the fable."

"Then," she asked, "what must I do?"

"Be yourself and give yourself away. . . . There," he added hastily, "I don't know why I should have said that. I have no authority—certainly none to teach you your job. You might as well teach me how to be a cooper."

"Or a gaoler?" said Thérèse.

She had expected him to flinch, but he answered with unperturbed and thoughtful candour: "You think it is wrong?"

"I shouldn't have thought it was your job to keep even animals in cages."

"Well," he said, "the thing isn't as simple as that, just as the question whether a man should refuse to fight in battle isn't as simple as some people imagine. To refuse to kill, to refuse to possess, to refuse to keep a prison: there's an easy vanity in all those negatives that puts me in mind of the scribes and pharisees. Besides, you know, I'm not really an argumentative man. I am not at all clever. I'm not even clever enough to be persuaded by other people's arguments. All the way from here to Roussignac, you could give me reasons against my keeping the prison, and I dare say I should be unable to answer you. But do you think that would make any difference? I should be the same at the end as I was at the beginning. Perhaps that is a weakness. What really persuades me to change something is that suddenly I see it changed in my own mind. It's the same with birds. I know how to find birds in special places, not because I've thought out from experience: such a bird is likely to be in such a place at such a time, but because suddenly one evening a corner of the Long Wood comes into my mind as I'm ladling out the prisoners' supper —the trees, every branch, every leaf, the smell, the sound of it, and there are the birds, and, if I go to find them, there *are* the birds."

"Always?"

"Yes. If the imagination was—ah!" he exclaimed, "but you know the difference between *that* and fancying a thing without truth in it. You see," he added, "that was why I went into the courtyard as I did on the evening you came for the mandolin, and why everything happened as it did. All this fuss people make—my poor mother, too! Was it a miracle? Was it this? Was it that? It was no more a miracle than making a good barrel, or your finding yourself in Paris because you have already seen yourself in Paris."

Nothing gave her more pleasure in his company than that he was one of those human beings who do not always expect to be answered. She said nothing, but wondered whether Barbet would despise her if he had overheard her conversation with Hurtaux, above all if he had known how little discriminating between man and man had been her reason for refusing him. "Not for money, not for a contract."

It wasn't a romantic reason for chastity, but it was her own reason, valid for her.

"How shall you live in Paris when you get there?" he asked, looking up from the roll of music that he had been balancing between his hands.

"Probably with men," she answered, trying to provoke him. "Are you going to tell me that that is wrong—if I keep myself by my job? I wasn't created to be a nun."

"No," said Barbet. "I wasn't thinking about right and wrong. But it seems to me that, for you, it might be more lonely than being alone."

She caught her breath. "That frightens me. . . . You say things sometimes," she continued slowly, "that sound as if I were saying them inside myself—or would some day."

"But it was you who said to me that it was wrong to keep animals shut up in cages."

"Oh," she cried, "we say and say—but nothing means anything until we say it to ourselves. . . . I suppose it's true. I have imagined myself that way—anyhow the flowers and the carriage and the yellow gloves and a bed the size of a room and lace pillows and an enormous tiger on the hearth."

"A tiger?" said Barbet.

She rose and stretched herself. "An enormous tiger. I've imagined it all. . . . When we arrive, are you going to walk up with me to the Cheval Pie? If you do, it will look as if we had been to Angoulême together."

"Instead of which, we have been to Paris," said Barbet. "Are you tired now?"

"Tired? No." She looked at him. "I was."

"Who else was in the train?" Madame Sernet inquired, but, though Thérèse recalled the names of a few fellow passengers, she had nothing to say of them, no gossip, no comment on their appearance, nor would she give a good reason for her having lately visited Angoulême three times. "Surely," said her aunt, "it can't be that Barbet Hazard is your latest victim?"

"Victim? . . . Oh, that! No."

It had not entered her mind. The corners of her mouth drooped in a rueful and secretive smile. How odd! She set herself to imagine Barbet as her lover, for it was part of her bitterness—of her pride, she would have said—that no rule forbade her any experiment, but the ugly, drooping smile vanished, and, as soon as she was gone from her aunt's room into the open, she sat down at a zinc table and stared. She did not think of Barbet, but of herself as she had been before men had known her.

The recollection was not idyllic or sentimental, not even happy, but cool and hard. It was of a girl who, in face of a world that gave her little affection and not enough to eat, had held her own with intuitive self-reliance, as though she were living in an impregnable fortress to which, as long as she held it, God, who knew her state, would bring supplies. The fortress was hers still; it was in fevered proof of ownership that she ran up all her flags of defiance and courage; but she knew that it had been undermined. Each man who had taken her and gone, each from whom she herself had taken—what were they? men—one a better or a worse lover than the last; she bore them no grudge; they had been her pleasure as she had been theirs; she had surrendered *herself* to none—and yet her fortress had been undermined by them; though none had left an individual mark upon her life, and she remembered each less by his character than by his physical attributes, the nature of her security had been affected by the cumulative disturbance of their shifting tenancies. She hated them collectively for this, though towards any one of them she was without resentment, and whenever she accepted a new lover, impelled by a desire for experiment, by heat of blood, by the cry of age at her heels, by delight in the present beauty of her body, a dazzling answer to all criticism of her face, she was thrilled by her helplessness and power, as drug-takers are by theirs. She observed, with painful detachment, whether the man was afraid, shy, brutal; whether he was proud of his hands; whether he emptied his pockets always on to the same shelf; what he did with his shoes—a detachment so precise and so full of wry amusement at the repetitive behaviour of the male animal in his lusts, that to the particular owner of the shoes and braces she yielded herself with a passion which alone could blot out for an hour knowledge that her integrity was being sapped. He was enchanted, supposing that he was specially favoured. He preened himself on his conquest, not observing how, when all was done, she turned her head on the pillow, away from him, away from man, facing herself in her fortress. Though she had imprisoned him, it was she, none the less, who had been invaded. She would turn her naked back upon him and withdraw, not into the vapid regrets of spent desire, but into her own secret, as a captive animal, remembering the jungle, withdraws into the darkest corner of his cage. There was no revulsion from the man. To prove it, she would turn like a panther, gather herself into his flattered arms and swear she loved him. Poor fool, he took her at her outward valuation of herself—no blame on him. What did he know of the fortress? If he had known and stormed it—ah, that would be something! He didn't even suspect its existence, yet he had trodden within it. This was her private hell—that all men, all, all, even when they said and believed that they loved her, were unaware of—what? was it real? was she lying to herself? Doubts came; her being shook; she would begin to cry. Then after a little while: "No! No! I'm sorry. I didn't mean to do that. I was only crying because—" It was a sentence she had never finished.

Now, at her table under the plane-trees, she rubbed the pinkness of her elbows, for the weight of her head had been upon them, and remembered the railway carriage and Barbet's head and the eyes looking out from it. He knows where he treads. He recognizes me. He's not an enemy.

"You fool!" she said aloud. "He's like the rest. He's like the rest. He's like the rest."

She started up from the table and returned to her work, shouting for Frédéric.

Chapter 9

IN THE DAYS THAT FOLLOWED, SHE EXPERIENCED
for the first time in her life an appeasement, as though a wind had
dropped. She sang Barbet's songs at the Cheval Pie. They were
applauded, for her audience knew her; but whoever considered that
he was privileged to give her advice, said in her ear: "That and that
and that were charming, but *this* surely was wrong," praising the
familiar tricks that a hundred competent diseuses could do as well or
better, resisting what was her own. In every song, what stirred hostility was the one quality—a lilt, a poise of body, a flash of mind—
that sprang fresh from inside herself.

"But if I don't do that, it's not *me*!"

"Come, my dear, no audience would accept it. No audience but
this. We swallow the pill for the sake of the jam."

"O God," she exclaimed, "anyone can give you the jam."

At this stage of her experimenting with Barbet's songs, she was
fiercely stubborn. Whether criticism was good or bad she did not
stay to ask, but flouted it violently. Her own ideas were in flux;
criticism confused and arrested her, as comment over a painter's
shoulder, while his struggle has scarcely begun, is, to him, valueless.
Even goodwill so delivered she flung back into the giver's face as
though it were an insult, for she had not that craftiness of concilia-
tion which would have enabled her to say: Thank you. I don't know
yet whether you are right or wrong. Thank you—but I must find
out for myself. She made herself hated by those who failed to understand that this seeming arrogance was but a defensive cry that she
was still in rehearsal.

To Barbet she confessed her rages.

"Oh well," said he, "it's not to be wondered at. I rage myself when someone standing beside my chair tries to play my hand."

"But you are wise," said Thérèse, gazing at him as though he were a surprising creature of a different species. "You don't shout at them. I do! I can't help it. It's physical. Oh, I wish I were *circ*umspect!" She rolled out the long word with elaborate intonation. "I make people *hate* me, because I'm earthy. I'm an animal. I bite. I can't help it. And yet I like almost everyone. I suppose that's a fault, too?"

In spite of her "rages," she was inwardly calm. Nothing was of importance to her but her songs. She forgot Hurtaux, and, when he appeared again at the Cheval Pie, recognized him without a tremor and spoke to him without embarrassment, as though their conversation in Angoulême were of the remote past. Victor's malice left her untouched, and when Anton, in his capacity of mayor, sent for her in his office to reprove her for the breach of a trifling rule, intending to provoke her, she accepted her scolding with a submissiveness that disarmed him. Now, what is happening to me? she asked herself. I have never behaved so well before. I must be dying.

Victor was active meanwhile. He visited Angoulême, intent to discover Barbet's reason for going there, but could find only the reason openly professed—that the time had come to renew the agreement about the Maison Hazard. "It's plain enough. He went to visit the lawyer," said Anton. "It was arranged between us. I had been a week earlier. Good heavens, man, what do you suspect him of—a murder?"

"He came back with Thérèse Despreux," Victor answered.

"Bless you," said Anton, "if you are going to put Barbet to bed with the Despreux, you—and she—are cleverer than I take you for. And if it were true, what then?"

"What then?" Victor exclaimed angrily. "Even Barbet can't ride a dozen horses at once. A keeper of a prison, a lecher and a saint! Prove him hypocrite as well as blasphemer, and that will be the end of him. You are mayor. It would be your duty to act."

"He is of my own family," said Anton.

"It would become your duty," Victor repeated. "After all, you owe your place to public opinion."

"Which you provoke?"

"I have a trifling influence," Victor said in a voice of menacing humility. "The priest has more."

"So you have been to Lancret?"

"Bette has spoken to him."

"And you?"

Victor raised his shoulders. "If it is necessary. . . . You don't understand, Anton. It is to your own interest. You want the Maison Hazard. You want the Cheval Pie. I intend no unpleasantness to Barbet. When he sees that it is advisable, he will go. I wish only to persuade him that it is advisable. As for the girl——"

"As for my brother," Anton interrupted. "I know him and you don't. If you think a hue and cry will drive him out——"

"Stubborn, I admit," Victor conceded.

"No. Not even stubborn. But he won't *hear* your hue and cry. Don't you see that? You're so clever, you don't know your man. Nor your girl." Anton rubbed his hands. "I know women. . . . But go to the priest if it amuses you."

Victor went to the priest and, in his presence, was a changed man —a miserable sinner by eager admission, a determined, wet-lipped penitent, careful to confess always those drier sins by which Lancret personally was least disturbed.

The man in Lancret was uneasily aware of being duped, as school-masters are sometimes aware, without admitting it to their scholastic selves, that they are duped by their favourite pupils; but the priest in him approved Victor's rigid orthodoxy and his refreshing habit of confessing always to something else than lasciviousness. Lancret was extremely tired of lasciviousness in men and women; the story was so old, and the less welcome because it had been his own. It was re-assuring to find in Victor one parishioner whose chastity at any rate might be assumed.

When Victor had received absolution, he walked to the priest's house, and proceeded, as his custom was, to discuss the affairs of the parish, approaching the subject of Barbet not directly—for he knew that the priest had a liking for Barbet—but by way of the approaching marriage between Renée and Pierre, a legitimate topic, for the Vincents were Catholics, the Hazards Protestants; Renée was about to be received into the Catholic Church; and Pierre, though a dolt in Victor's opinion, was after all his brother. The marriage would leave Barbet to look after the prisoners single-handed. In the circumstances, was that wise?

"In what circumstances?" the priest asked.

Victor was silent. When pressed, he said modestly that any opinion of his must be discounted, for he and Barbet were of opposite temperaments and there were, in any case, differences between the families of Hazard and Vincent.

"Which this marriage," said Lancret, "will do nothing to heal?"

"On the contrary," Victor replied.

Renée, he explained, having become a Catholic and not being, in any case, Madame Hazard's daughter, would throw in her lot with her husband, and Pierre, though he had no present alternative to employment by the Hazards, would work in the vineyards and the farm only. "Once they are clear of it, Pierre and Renée will not set foot in that house again except, perhaps, on special occasions. I have told Pierre," Victor continued, "that I think he is going too far."

"A storm in a tea-cup," said Lancret, and added disconcertingly that Barbet seemed not to have behaved badly in the matter. Was it not he who had made the marriage possible? Wasn't Renée's dowry his money? Wasn't it in his cottage they proposed to live? There seemed a certain generosity—

"Perhaps you are right, father."

"How not?"

"I am sure you are right, though there are many in Roussignac who are a little suspicious of so much generosity. Why, they ask, after Pierre had quarrelled with him about the incident in the prison, did Barbet give him a different job, take the prison into his own hands, produce a dowry, a cottage—anything to have the place to himself? That," Victor concluded with a wave of his hand in discredit of so

uncharitable a rumour, "is what they say. But, after all, when emotion is aroused, people will say anything!"

The priest was already tired of the subject. It presented itself to
him as a quarrel between the Vincents and the Hazards, the details
of which were no concern of his, and he pressed his hands to his eyes
as he often did when he was tired.

"Of course," said Victor, "if it weren't for the claim, the whole
thing would be of no consequence."

"You attach importance to that?"

"I? I personally? Neither I nor you, father, but among ignorant
people superstition grows like a weed. Will you believe that there are
some in Roussignac who cross the street rather than let Barbet's
shadow fall on them, and others who say that, if he touched them,
they would be cured of their rheumatism? His own mother says
that, when she dies, her son will raise her from the dead."

Lancret heard this with reluctance. Himself a man in whom
passion was imprisoned but alive, he dreaded enthusiasm in others.
It fired his trail; it endangered his self-discipline. If only mankind,
and particularly his parishioners, would obey the simple rules of
conduct and faith, how much easier life would be! He had known
that there was scandal brewing but had shut his eyes to it. In the
confessional he had received evidence of it and still had done nothing. The claim that Barbet had worked a miracle was preposterous,
and yet—and yet Victor's grave words, his correct manner, his whole
air of giving the alarm without being himself alarmed, worked on
the priest like a crumb in his shirt. He distrusted Victor; he was too
smooth, too humble, too discreet; but, in face of a man so reasonable
and so orthodox, he had not the courage of his own distrust.

"As always," Victor continued, choosing his words as a woman
chooses the silks for her embroidery, "as always on these occasions,
when the religious sense overflows its permitted channels, it becomes
an emotional flood. Women—young women particularly—fear or
hate or worship Barbet. I have heard you say yourself, father, that
heresy is often rooted in sex."

Lancret was trapped. He recognized the saying as his own. All
that he loved least in himself fiercely endorsed it.

"Barbet," he remarked, controlling himself and speaking as coolly as possible, "seems to be very little touched by it all."

"Little touched?" said Victor. "I hope so. How often do you see Thérèse Despreux?"

The effect of these words on the priest was to fill him with the kind of madness that, in other men, is induced by physical jealousy. Thereafter, as long as he remained in Victor's presence, he believed whatever he was told. When Victor was gone, he was exhausted, and sat for a long time in his chair, his mouth dry, his eyes hot as though he had been weeping. He looked at the chair that Victor had occupied and remembered with disgust the limp drooping of his pointed boot. To-morrow, he said to himself, I will go to the Cheval Pie, but, when the morning came, he knew that, in his present mood, he must not encounter Thérèse, and went instead to the Maison Hazard, intending to say that he had come to make final arrangements for Renée's wedding.

He found her and Pierre outside the stables in the west courtyard. They were unable to talk quietly even of their own business, and interrupted each other continually in their eagerness to tell, for the hundredth time, what had happened *that* evening. Pierre had not been a coward! Renée had never accused him of it! And as for Barbet—whatever he had done or not done, let it be clearly understood that they had no part in it, none. Lancret watched them closely—the flaunting haphazard girl now shrill and fierce against all his knowledge of her character; the slow, inarticulate man spurting a fool's eloquence; and he said to himself: They are like people who have seen a ghost and are afraid to admit it.

When Madame Hazard came from the house and joined them, he saw in her a change so remarkable and subtle that he felt almost the panic of a dream. This garrulous, downright, pettish old woman was outwardly as she had been, but, in the presence of Renée and Pierre, a defiant exaltation, an air of martyrdom, a pride of Sinai entered into her, so that the priest said: This is the spiritual pride that makes repentance impossible; in this mood, even if she were still Catholic, she would throw off the Church. But he knew that nine-tenths of human folly consists in playing a part before an audience, and he sent Renée and Pierre about their business. "Now," he said to Madame Hazard, "what have you on your mind? I came as a friend to talk to you of Barbet, but I'd rather listen than talk." At this the old lady became quiet at once. Looking straight at Lancret out of unblinking eyes, she answered: "He is good, monsieur le curé; he is good—that is all."

There was such a finality in this reply that the priest would gladly have put no more questions to her, but he explained that he felt it to be his duty, for the sake of his own flock and to prevent scandal in his parish, to ask whether she did indeed claim for her son miraculous powers and whether she believed, as some had told him, that, when she died, Barbet would raise her from the dead. She said, as if she were speaking to a dressmaker about a ribbon, "It isn't important," and added "He is good," as though, in the three words, were all the gospels.

There is nothing more she will say, the priest thought, than those three words; certainly she is mad; but as the word "mad" formed in his mind he looked into her face and remembered what had been said of heretics before her. Never in any face had he seen a more unassailable, a more aggressive happiness. It enraged him with envy and righteousness. Aggressive, aggressive, he repeated, gazing at the serenity of this petulant, foolish, ignorant woman; and to break her quiet as his was broken, he asked her whether she supposed that Thérèse also was "good."

"Thérèse? But why? . . . There are two sorts of people," she said, patting the priest on the shoulder as though he were a schoolboy who asked a silly but forgivable question, "there are two sorts of people who will always be afraid of Thérèse Despreux: women who aren't tempted and priests who are. And there is one sort who will always loathe her—such men as Victor Vincent who cannot enjoy women. O la! la! she has her faults! But at any rate she hasn't the face of a horse and the body of a camel."

This oblique reference to Madame Vincent so delighted the old lady that she laughed and flapped her hands until water came into her eyes. Lancret, confused and indignant, stood before her with fists clenched.

"I asked you—and we were talking of your son—whether you considered that Thérèse was good?"

Madame Hazard ceased to laugh. She stooped to the ground for a stone and put it into his hand.

"There is Barbet, working at his barrels," she said, looking across the courtyard to where Barbet and Quessot were to be seen through an open door. "Ask him, monsieur le curé," and the priest, clutching the stone, made off. There was no way by which he might go home without passing the cooper's shed, but he intended to go by with no more than a nod—perhaps without turning his head. An angry bitterness entangled him—the bitterness of having seen with his own eyes the power that Barbet had upon the people with whom he lived. His own mind was divided; he had no power to strike a spark from the world or to affect men and women as Barbet affected them; he had failed as man and as priest. Barbet might be a simpleton, but for him the spark flew! Madame Hazard had become another being. He would not forget the happiness, like a reflected light, on that crumpled, ridiculous face. When he had asked whether she condemned Thérèse, first she had laughed at him, then had given him a stone. Why? What did the stone mean? He held it out. "Qui sine peccato est vestrum, primus in illam lapidem mittat." He spoke the words aloud, then tilted his hand and let the stone fall.

Barbet called out to him from the shed: "Come in for a moment, and Renée shall bring us a glass of wine." The priest's anger left him; he felt happy again and smiled and went into the great shed. After he had spoken to Quessot, who was one of his flock, and had refused the offer of wine, he was given a stool, and sat down with his feet among the shavings of Limousin oak. Quessot was binding hoops at the farther end of the shed; Barbet was swinging the chip-axe in short, even arcs, and Lancret, soothed by the craftsmanship that could command to accuracy so awkward a tool, was content to watch silently.

"You're not ill?" Barbet asked.

"Ill?"

"Out there you looked wretched. You looked what I felt when I was a boy at school and was behind with my lessons. 'I'll never catch up! I'll never catch up! I'm in a tangle and can't get out! I shall never understand anything again as long as I live!' "

"Tell me," the priest said, "what is your own opinion about what is called the 'incident in the prison'?"

"I think," Barbet answered, "people bother their heads too much with 'why?' and 'how?' and 'what will the consequence be?' I have no more *opinion* about it than I have about the grapes on a vine."

"But was it a miracle?"

"Are the grapes?"

"But people are saying that it was, and you don't deny it."

"Ah well," said Barbet, "if it was a miracle, it wasn't mine. . . . Nor are the grapes, though I grow them."

Lancret was delighted to watch Barbet at work. His own angers were appeased in this tranquil, unprovocative company. A stave was held out for his inspection when Barbet had finished paring it.

"Why do you ask me?" Lancret asked with a smile.

"I've always shown things to you. I can't do it as Quesnot does, you know. Oak is like cheese to him."

The priest nodded. "Will you answer another question? What do you feel about Thérèse?"

"I love her," Barbet replied.

Lancret had expected any answer but this, but it appeared now to have been the only possible and complete answer, so full of truth that there was no room in it for evil.

"I shall not trouble you with questions," he said, "or interrupt your work, but I should like, if I may, to sit here a little while."

Barbet put down his chip-axe, momentarily surprised. "But certainly."

"You see," the priest continued, "you have a way of making a man feel that he is not his own enemy. A woman too, perhaps. . . . Is that, I wonder, what happened in the prison? . . . No, I would rather you didn't stop. I should like you to go on with your work."

Chapter 10

ON THE DAY OF PIERRE AND RENÉE'S MARRIAGE, all Roussignac went to drink their health at the Maison Hazard, but Thérèse did not go. In the late afternoon, the company streamed out across Barbet's vineyards, followed the bride and bridegroom to the cottage in which henceforth they would live. Frédéric, forgetting that he was an invalid, joined in the songs, and returned to the Cheval Pie happy and full of news. But Thérèse did not wish to hear it; she felt herself excluded from local festivities by her father's presence, the impossibility that he should acknowledge her, his frozen greetings that struck at the root of her life. "Did the priest sing?" she demanded with a fierceness that Frédéric did not understand. "Did he join in the dances? . . . Now, listen. I am going to give a performance in the prison. Have you forgotten that? There are things to be done. Get a pencil and write them down."

Frédéric had never found life more difficult than on the day chosen for this performance. There could be no concert at the Cheval Pie that evening, but all the thirst of Roussignac would not transfer itself to the Lion Rouge; customers would come and must be served, and Frédéric had found an old man and a lanky boy to serve them. During the day he had laboured to show these understudies how everything was to be managed while he and Thérèse were absent. Thérèse disliked them instantly, or swore she did. If no one better could be found, she herself would stay; she would not go to the prison at all! "Then Monsieur Barbet must be warned," said Frédéric to test her. "Shall I go at once to the Maison Hazard and tell them you won't come? What excuse shall I give?"

"Excuse? None."

But she did not tell him to go. Instead, she looked away from

Frédéric and said: "I'm sorry. I'm making everything harder for you. . . . But the old man is like a moth-eaten blackbird and that boy you've found has crawled out from under a stone. . . . I'm sorry." Then she threw up her head. "Why do I always find myself doing things I don't want to do? Monsieur Barbet! Monsieur Barbet! There's too much Barbet. His songs, his music—now, his audience! Nothing is *mine*."

"I think he's kind," Frédéric said. "And patient. You are glad at first to have new songs written for you."

"So I am. Of course I am. I know which side my bread is buttered. It's not that."

"Well, what is it?" asked Frédéric.

"Oh, I'll go," she exclaimed. "I always do what I don't want. Don't you worry."

Frédéric put down the last of the glasses he had been wiping and shook out his dish-cloth.

"That's how you make yourself unhappy," he said. "That's how you wear yourself out—and everyone else too. I shall die soon," he added with the bleak solemnity of a youth old before his time, "and when I'm dead you'll never be really great—you mark my words— you'll never have peace until—"

"I don't want peace!"

"You want it more than anyone I have ever known. You want it so much that you are afraid of it." He flung himself at her feet, seized her hand and rubbed his cheek against it. Then, as she moved in response, he looked up at her like a dog and shouted with a fierceness made ridiculous by his sobs: "And now all you are thinking is: 'Shall I be gracious to this grovelling fool or shall I jump up like an angry queen and send him sprawling? Which part shall I play?' You ask yourself that," he continued, "because I don't exist for you. No one does. You think of everyone on earth as someone watching you. And then you say you aren't selfish! You think you're generous! In a way, it's true. But you give what you want to give and when it amuses you to give it."

She made him stand up and gazed at him with admiration. His

anger subdued and warmed her. Instead of flying into an opposite
rage, she submitted herself to this pale, blubbering prophet.

"You said I should never be really great until—until what?"

"O God," said Frédéric, "until you can be ordinary and kind.
Until someone who is in trouble comes to you tired and dull, useless
to you, and you give him safety, and put him into your own bed and
let him sleep."

What did he mean? she asked herself, as she and Frédéric walked
up through the woods to the Maison Hazard. Give him safety . . .
let him sleep.

"Frédéric, what did you mean?"

Though she did her best to recall it to him, Frédéric had forgotten
this part of their conversation.

"Did I say that?"

"Of course you did! About someone who came to me in trouble.
Who? It doesn't make sense."

"I don't know. Whatever it was, it seemed to make sense at the
time."

"Heavens above!" Thérèse exclaimed. "Do you live in a trance?
Who are you? Ezekiel?"

Frédéric shouldered the mandolin and went forward. She could
call him what she liked—Ezekiel, if it pleased her, though what she
meant by this he hadn't an idea. He was listening to her footsteps in
the dark wood behind him. She was alive and near him. He drew on
to his palate the cool evening air which told him that he also was
alive.

In Madame Hazard's parlour, Thérèse's heart failed her. She
had imagined that she would sing to the prisoners only, but others
had been allowed to come. She felt that they were hostile to her
and that only at Barbet's insistence had she been admitted to the
house. Pierre and Renée she had expected to find, but Madame
Vincent was there, forbidding and monumental, and among the
faces in the room Thérèse saw those of Victor and Hurtaux and of

the priest, her father. At once, she was at bay. Madame Hazard's chattering kindliness presented itself to her as patronage; she froze and snapped back, gripping her hands together so tightly that the muscles of her upper arms began to tremble like taut wire. Her mouth was set, the lower lip a little protruded; her face grew pale, her eyes startled and defensive. Suddenly she felt cold and sick, and sat in an upright chair, her body stiffly erect.

"If you will come now, I will take you into the courtyard."

She followed Barbet along the covered way and through the passage with two doors, Frédéric trailing behind her.

"Why have you brought me here now?" she said. "Before the others come?"

"I wanted you to see how everything was arranged. We brought your platform up safely but the grass of the courtyard isn't very smooth. We had to pack one corner with a piece of wood. Will you try it? Make sure it's firm. Dance on it."

Frédéric seated himself at the piano that stood beside the platform. She danced a few steps.

"It will do."

"And here's a tent we have rigged up for you out of an old sail. A dressing-room—if you need one. Not very grand. Table, mirror, chair, lamp. I thought it would be better than a spare cell—nearer to the stage."

"Thank you." She leaned on the back of the chair. "I suppose the prisoners have been watching us from their cells?"

"Why?"

"I thought I saw faces."

"Probably. As soon as I have brought in the others from the house, I shall let them out. There are chairs for them under the ilex."

"Let them out now."

"You would be alone with them while I was away—you and Frédéric."

"You are afraid of that?"

"I? No."

"Let them out, then."

"What is it? Do you want to talk to them?"

"I shall stay in this tent. I shan't say a word."

Without pressing for a reason, he did as she wished. From within the tent, she heard the prisoners' voices as they came across the dusky courtyard and settled in their places under the tree. It was dark in the tent; she needed the lamp to arrange the half-dozen shawls and aprons that were her wardrobe and to prepare her face. "And you had better make sure," she said to Frédéric, "that the lamps on the platform will burn."

"They will burn all right."

"Well, try them. Why so sure?"

"Monsieur Barbet has his head screwed on. There are extra lamps as well as our own—better than ours, with ribbed reflectors."

"I want them all tested," said Thérèse. "If you don't do a thing yourself, it is never done."

Frédéric raised his eyebrows and obeyed. When he was gone, Thérèse had no more commands to give, and, her face being finished, nothing to do but wait. Loneliness fell upon her like an icy mist, as it had long ago when she overheard her mother say, not angrily but with careful meaning: "The child ought not to have been born." She felt again, now, that she was outcast from the world, disinherited of its natural affections, a bastard, a priest's daughter—anyone's woman, the music-master's, Hurtaux's if he could get her—above all, a fighter against odds; and her spirit flew to her bitterness as a fighter's hand to his weapon. Mankind was a pack from which she was excluded, a vast audience of strangers hungry for her downfall. She would fight and enslave them; she would not play down to them or be pretty for their sakes. The mirror gave back rosy cheeks under the eyes' fierceness. She wiped the colour away, even from her lips, and with two upward strokes enlarged her eyes.

Barbet looked into her tent to say that all was ready.

"Tell Frédéric to begin."

"What shall you sing?"

"He knows."

Barbet stood still. "What have you done, Thérèse?"

"Done? Taken off some of my make-up." She was standing.

The shadow of a tent cord lay across her cheek and forehead like the scar of a whip, and her hands were clasped behind her.

"It's as though you had a knife hidden there," Barbet said.

She raised her shoulders and thrust her lips forward. "I'll do my job," she said. "Do I get a drink when it's over?"

She began with the fiercest of all her songs:

> *"As I was walking up the street*
> *Under the lamps, under the sky,"*

—a song that Barbet had composed of the loneliness of great cities and that she had converted to her own use. It had become for her the story not of a countrywoman remembering the earth's fruitfulness and the little incidents and festivals of her home, but a recognition, at once embittered and lascivious, of the greed and barren profit of a town. Praises of the country she twisted to ridicule, recollections of childhood to hypocrisies that were to be laughed at. The song had an edge of cruelty, of scorn for mankind and for herself, which, when it was sung as she sang it now—with a mask-like face and an insatiable hunger in the wide, penetrating eyes—made her rhythm the rhythm of a lash; and, feeling her audience, made raw by imprisonment, quiver beneath her attack, she allowed a delight of power to appear in the cumulative gesture of her body, her whole being to take light. She flashed herself into these men's eyes, estimating her strength by their excitement and by the provoked pleasure which, in them, was indistinguishable from suffering. Never had an audience been so vulnerable. Their applause was a cackle, a scream, a prolonged turbulence like the boiling of a cauldron, and often, during the songs that followed, she heard them shudder and sigh as though collectively they were her lover and were spent in her seizure of them. The women gazed at her stupefied, except Madame Vincent who, to prove that she was incapable of a boor's astonishment, nodded her great head, and beat time with her left hand, and continued to nod and beat until the movement of hand and head became the beat and nod of an automaton. Victor hugged his sides, determined to give no visible response to Thérèse, but now and then the thin, pale wedge of his face shifted and his hand went up to it and wiped it; a sweat had broken out upon his skin. Her father, Lancret, had curved his arms over the back of the chair he sat in; his wrists hung loose; his chin was down, she saw only his forehead, and a body crumpled like a sack; and yet knew that under his brows his upturned eyes were watching her as they might have watched her at the stake.

She did not look at Barbet, but shut him out from her knowledge, for this was the moment of her pride, she felt the devil's endowment upon her, and it was of all things necessary that she should despise and make negligible in her heart the man who had surrendered his work to her. That this might be certain, she needed, in so visible an audience, a point of focus for eyes and mind, and chose Blachère, swinging her regard across the others—across the abject stare of old Marcotte, whose saliva hung string-like from a sagging jaw, across the agonized and perverted idealism of Fontan's drifting eyes—sweeping them inward and inward to the centre that was Blachère. With him she had established so intimate a contact that she was able to draw that bladder of a face through the distance of tree from platform and to make him feel that she was leaning over him, her breath upon him, her scent in his nostrils.

There could be no interval. In the need to exhaust herself she sang on and on, to piano and to mandolin, aware increasingly that the night sky, the ilex, the courtyard were an ever-shrinking frame and that in the concentration of her own mind her hearers were trapped. She despised them for their submission as though they were dogs fawning upon her for the meat she threw; and suddenly pitied them because their submission was to the animalism in herself. She pitied and, in the instant, could no longer command them. Her concentration broke. She saw for the first time Barbet's eyes; they looked at her, seemingly, through Blachère's head. She stopped singing. Frédéric at the piano faltered, repeating his music. She dragged at her memory of the tune that it might give the words to her and drove the song to its end.

The audience shifted. She had lost them and lost even the will to recapture them by the means she had hitherto employed. Her being had turned over in its sleep and awakened. She was aware of the footlights shining up into her face and that some of the reflectors were ribbed, the others plain. The scene extended before her, not only to the gleam of Frédéric's white notes and the point of fire in Madame Hazard's amethyst, but to the woods, and the long, rambling path to Roussignac and the river. In all these things she herself had no part. They were not, as they had been, a setting for her emotion, nor was the audience a market for her talent. The desire to fight, to rule, to assert and magnify her individuality was gone. She did not understand the change in her, nor its origin. With a gesture that Hurtaux mistook for a struggle to remember her words, she covered her face, imagining that she lay in a remote part of the Long Wood, as once she had when a child, the earth and the charity of life enfolding her, the stress and agony of her inescapable self annihilated at last in a breathless quiet and in her hands' darkness.

"Look," said Victor, "she's played herself to a finish."

"Do you think so?" Hurtaux replied. "Unless I'm mistaken there's more in her than that."

Her fingers opened. She observed them nodding together, examined her attitude with their eyes, and dropped her hands.

Seeing below her Frédéric's drawn face and the audience like boles of wood, she compelled the muscles of her body to relax, drew breath and prepared to sing. A compassionate desire was in her to affect her audience in a new way, but it was unfamiliar and she fought against it. What are you, Thérèse Despreux? Are you mad? A saint? A nun? Who is to be in the cage—you or they? If you do not dominate them, they will trample you, and if, now, you sing with compassion for mankind it is a trick you play on them—not softness in you, not a denial of the saving hatreds, but a trick, a new beguilement of the hated, a new trap laid against fear! She raised her eyes in challenge and prepared her lips for bitterness, but, when she had begun to sing, the nature of her singing was changed.

It was a song, recalled from Barbet's experience as a soldier, of a man who went into battle full of pride and fear, determined to take vengeance of blood upon the world that had brought him to this pass. It was his fear that gave him courage, and, when he knew this,

his determination failed, but he made virtue of the failure and would have laid down his arms in the extreme piety of non-resistance. Then, looking about him, he saw that whatever part of nature man had not defiled—the birds, the sky, the undamaged crops—were continuous and unswerving in their lives, and he said: How to kill is not the question nor how not to kill, but how to live simply and with acceptance so that no work of man shall have power to separate me from the peace of God, nor the peace of God to withdraw me from the joy and suffering of man. And he continued in arms, neither as martyr nor as rebel, as he would have continued in peace if that had been his destiny.

Barbet had written this song in short rhyming verses, roughly shaped, as a colloquial ballad. Sometimes the soldier spoke his own thoughts, sometimes to others; the progress of his march was implied in the changing incidents and encounters of the roadside; and it was possible to sing the song to give an impression either that he was a chattering yokel, confused in mind, the butt of his companions, or that he was a countryman, expelled from the province of his content, but of natural gaiety and courage. Thérèse sang it now with compassion for him, as though his life were her own. The trudging agony of the march was in the sag of her body as she began, and his tormented revolt against his condition in her haunted and sullen tone. When even his hatred forsook him and he would have thrown away his arms in despair of fate, her dulled insistence on a failing rhythm carried in it the footfall of a man doomed and his sense of being herded into exile from sanity and justice. But when she lifted her head and saw the birds in their independence and touched the arm of the next man in the column so that he also lifted his head and saw, then her audience drew breath, and she put away all gesture, presenting herself, with the final art of communicative repose that none can learn, as the voice and hearing of the soldier and his companions, as a mediator between him and those natural endurances by which acceptance comes to mankind. While she sang, she knew for the first time—not what Barbet had intended by the song, for this she had long known and in her arrogance perverted—but the spontaneous bliss in him that the song expressed, and she drew the prisoners into her lightness of heart and sang many songs and danced for them so that now they were in awe, now laughing, now rapt in her adventure, until at last she sang again the song with which she had begun :

> *As I was walking up the street*
> *Under the lamps, under the sky,*

but plainly, without bitterness or sentiment, with no accent of opinion, as though she were singing to children a song that they had heard a thousand times before.

She was gone from the platform before their silence broke, and would not return. In her dressing-tent, she sat before her mirror, her hands on her knees, her nostrils distended by her breathing.

Frédéric came. "Monsieur Barbet asks if he may see you."

She shook her head. "Not yet." But Hurtaux thrust away the flap. Victor was at his side.

"I want to say—" Hurtaux began.

Victor seized his arm. "You're mad, Hurtaux! You will give everything away. You are not intelligent."

"Mademoiselle," said Hurtaux, disregarding his companion, "you are—you could become a great diseuse. I offer you a contract."

Thérèse did not answer.

"Did you hear me? What are you doing, mademoiselle?"

"My breathing exercises."

"Now?"

"Now."

"I offer you a contract."

She threw back at him her old challenge. "Not for money. Not for a contract."

"I tell you, I offer you a contract."

"For services within the contract?"

He smiled. "For services within the contract."

"No more?"

"None."

"Why?" she said. "You astonish me. Am I so ugly?"

He patted her shoulder. "I will tell you," he answered. "Because I shall make money out of you."

"You mean that?"

"Firmly."

"Where?"

"Bordeaux. Lyons. Paris."

"Ah!" she said. "You think you mean it to-night. We will talk of it in the morning."

They hesitated. She said again in a tone of dismissal: "We will talk of it in the morning."

When they were gone, she cried: "Frédéric! Frédéric! Where is Monsieur Barbet now?"

But it was the priest who entered.

"Tell me, my child. Something changed you. Something happened."

She would admit nothing. "I'm learning my job," she said.

Chapter 11

WHAT VICTOR COULD NOT HAVE IN ONE WAY, HE
would have in another. As soon as he knew certainly that
Thérèse intended a contract with Hurtaux and to leave the Cheval
Pie, he consulted with his sister, Bette. Thérèse's going by her own
choice must weaken their hand. Scandal would die away; they could
not now so easily drive Barbet from his home.

"The Maison Hazard, I am afraid, is in the future, my dear
Bette," Victor said, "but the Cheval Pie is yours for the asking."

It was true. Faced by the prospect of Thérèse's going, Madame
Sernet knew that she could no longer run the inn and was glad to
sell. It was Thérèse herself who, by delaying the signature of her
contract with Hurtaux, enabled the old woman to hold out for a
price. "Pay what I ask or I shall stay where I am," said Thérèse, and
Victor believed her because one believes what one most fears to
believe. The price was low and Anton paid it, consenting also to
maintain Frédéric in his employment. "After all," said Victor, "he
will soon be dead. Meanwhile he can play the piano."

On the evening of the day on which her contract with Hurtaux
was signed, Thérèse, after her concert, made a speech to her audience.

"Mesdames, Messieurs. I shall not sing here again. To-morrow
I prepare for my journey. On the next day I go to Bordeaux. Soon
I shall be in Paris. Come to see me there. Perhaps I shall need an
audience. Do not stare at the posters and say: 'Thérèse Despreux.
She is the girl who sang at Roussignac!' and turn away. Perhaps I
shall be poor, very poor, poorer than I am here. Paris is a great city.
Perhaps by then I shall be lonely. In any case, you are the only
friends I have in the world. It will be you who have given me Paris.
Mesdames, Messieurs, I shall be glad to see you. Bring me a little

of the earth of Roussignac and—bring me camellias when I die."

After this oration of which, at the time, she was extremely proud, they gathered about her, shook her hand, laughed and kissed her. In the more susceptible eyes there were tears, and she persuaded herself that there could be no audience on earth so understanding as this. Was she a fool to leave them? Her confidence was shaken as it always was by the taking of any decisive step. She felt that her contract with Hurtaux, which an hour ago she had considered a masterpiece of negotiation, was less good than it should have been. She had been cheated; she wished to retract. Why had she no man who would act for her—no agent to make bargains as other women had? But when she imagined such an agent, she instantly distrusted him, and was sure that she could do her business better herself.

Not until the courtyard was emptied and she saw Barbet approaching across the square did she remember that she had promised to go out with him that night in his boat, and at once she had no thought but of how she might avoid her promise. He would be kind to her and forbearing; at long intervals he would say things that enchanted her by their straightforwardness; but to-night he would certainly talk about her work. This she dreaded, for she was fond of him, and she knew that, whenever he spoke of her work, she intuitively, and against her will, ranged herself for battle, saying at random, and in a tone of angry conviction, things which she ceased to believe when they had passed her lips. She could force herself to agree with him, but there was a devil in her by which it was made impossible that she should equably discuss with him any subject arising from her own art, and necessary that she should spurn every suggestion of his. He had a habit of penetrating too far, of disturbing her assurances. The truth came from him with an inward authority that would have subjugated her if she had not instantly defied it, and she defied it against friendship and reason as a fierce and timid cat strikes at the gentlest of hands.

"Barbet," she said as he came up to her, "I'm tired to-night. I didn't know I should be. I'm sorry I brought you so far."

"Then I'll leave this song," he answered calmly, taking a roll of paper from under his arm. "Put it in your trunk. You can look at it when you are settled in Bordeaux."

"And you?"—for she was never able to credit his acceptances.

"I shall go on the river for a little while."

"Even if I'm not there?"

"You will be," he said, "in one way or another. You have often been there when you didn't know it, and in the vineyards—even in the prison. Now I won't keep you. You are tired. Good night, Thérèse. You have signed with Hurtaux?"

"This afternoon."

"I hope it turns out to be a fortunate day for you."

"It is the twenty-fifth of July. Twenty-five is my lucky number."

She turned into the house and, going to her room, said half-seriously to herself: If I don't go with him to-night, shall I be unlucky at Bordeaux? He is my mascot, perhaps.

Then, as a penance for so much egoism, she knelt at her bedside in the position of one about to repeat her prayers.

"Pater noster . . ." she began, but her eye fell on a pattern of the quilt that reminded her of an albatross. An albatross was not a good omen. She rose quickly and kicked off her shoes. Her candle was set down on the wooden chair beside her bed and she undid the neck of her dress. Suddenly she was still and cold.

If I don't see him to-night, I shall not see him again. Now or never. That was the Albatross!

She ran downstairs and into the wood at the back of the house. He was leaning on one of the bridges that spanned the stream, and seemed to have been waiting for her.

The path was so dark among the trees—a thin moon and the stars being overclouded—that they had difficulty in making their way. Neither had brought a lamp, and on the rough ground Barbet stumbled and had to seize a branch to steady himself. "I know the path," Thérèse said. "Let me go in front." She slid past him in the darkness and he felt her hand close over his. At the edge of the little wood they could see more easily and soon were in the open. She released his hand and walked beside him along the tow-path. He had turned up-river away from the town and she said: "Where's your boat? Isn't she with the others by the bridge wharf?"

"I brought her up to the deep pool," Barbet said. "The birds roost there."

The boat was drawn up in a shallow creek. They pushed her out with oars driven into the ground. Reeds scraped against her sides and bent stubbornly in the crutches, but at last she made her way through them and swam clear with so sudden a movement that Barbet was thrown off his balance. A stumble against the thwart knocked away his feet; the oar he held with his left hand twisted its blade in the boat's under-suck and dragged him outward. He would have been in the water if Thérèse had not with both hands grasped his struggling forearm and wrenched him out of the air.

The starlings asleep among the reeds near by rose with a whirl and clatter of wings, a multitudinous shriek of wings and voices as though the air were calico and they tearing it.

"It's not often," said Barbet, "that I can get clear without disturbing them. I had to-night, until that happened. . . . Thank you, Thérèse. Have we lost an oar?"

"I caught that too." She was breathless and frightened. "You would have been drowned," she said.

"It's not deep yet."

"That's why. You'd have been caught in the weeds and the mud. I should have been waiting for you to come up. But you wouldn't have come. You'd have been stifling now in the mud and the reeds, and I should have been kneeling in the boat, peering out —nothing to see, only ripples close in—it's too dark—and everyone would have said —"

"What?"

"They couldn't prove it but they'd think it. No one gives me the benefit of the doubt."

"Why should anyone suppose you wished to kill me? Aren't we known to be friends?"

"That isn't the word Victor uses, or Renée and Pierre, or Bette—"

"Victor," Barbet answered, "is the unhappiest man I know. Unhappier even than Blachère." He began to row into lighter water, beyond the shadow of the trees.

"If I hadn't come, you'd have been dead," said Thérèse.

"But I can swim!"

She was furious. "I tell you you'd have been dead! I saw an albatross. That was why I came."

This had no meaning for him and he made no answer.

"Well," she exclaimed, "don't you want to *know* about my albatross? You ought to want to know about my albatross when I've saved your life." And after a pause she said, quietly and seriously: "I believe I did, you know."

"What?"

"Save your life."

He pulled on cheerfully. Then, resting on his oars: "I think you did. Thank you, Thérèse."

"Oh, well," she said with a sigh, "you don't really believe it and never will; I know that . . . I wish you believed me. I wish people gave me credit for the real things I do and not for the things they pretend about me. I'm not a good woman. I'm no use to any man. I *use* them. I can't be trusted. I lie and lie. I always shall. . . . But I'm quick. I don't stand about wringing my hands. I pulled you out of the air. I have strong fingers and wrists. . . . Feel them. . . . Now may I lie down in the bottom of the boat and go to sleep if I want to? . . . Oh, I'm so glad I came. I'm so glad. I'm glad I saved your life too or you wouldn't be here to row the boat."

"I believe I amuse you," said Barbet.

"Do you mind?"

"I like it. You are gentle when people amuse you in that way— when you feel you're older than they are."

"Am I so fierce?"

"Listen," he said. "Don't talk for a while. I want to go up to the deep pool and nose in among the reeds very quietly without putting up the birds. Some of them are restless now. Listen."

"Starlings?"

"Swallows. Starlings live next door."

She crawled into the bows, lay upon her face and looked out over the stem of the boat. By her guess in the darkness, they were still far from the shore. Barbet judged his distance and gave four powerful strokes; then ceased, and boated his oars that there might be no sound of their feather on the surface. The boat glided in under its own way. The chuckle ceased under the quarters, the bow wave dropped, the gleam of water fell more and more slowly astern. There was a creaking of reeds; against them, the boat brought up.

"Pull her in a little by hand," Barbet whispered. And when he had been obeyed: "Enough. Let her swing to the gap."

They were enclosed by reeds, the sky clear above them, the stars weakening. The nearest swallows awoke but gave no alarm; there was a shifting of wings, a brief, inquiring conversation, then silence again.

Barbet pointed upwards. "Day coming," he said.

Thérèse opened her eyes, which she had closed at the flutter of wings. Beside her a reed was curved against the sky by the weight of roosting swallows. The line of illumination, which alone at first defined it, broadened as the light grew; the whole reed became visible, and the swallows changed from iron to bronze. In two nights she would be at Bordeaux; she let her hand sink until the water was a bracelet about her wrist. A swallow left the reed on which he was perched and dropped upon another nearer to her, disturbing its occupants and bringing up all their heads in protest. She and he watched each other until her hand was cold and she withdrew it from the water to dry in the warm air, and fell asleep.

When she awoke, the swallows too were astir. They preened themselves and chattered before setting out on their voyage. As they took flight, reed after reed swayed up against the sky, and suddenly, screaming to one another, the starlings were away. Company after company of birds rose into the air. Thérèse, watching them, heard in imagination the early traffic of Bordeaux under her window and the clash of pails in the courtyard of the unknown house where she would lodge, and, though she wished to see the sky only and the tranquil expectancy of Barbet's shoulders and his tufted head, she saw the flaked plaster of a ceiling and the rusted knob of an iron bed. One morning soon there would be the unshaven chin of a stranger on her pillow and an open mouth. She would hesitate to wake him; while he gaped there, she would not have to pretend, even to herself, that she had any interest in him. He was a man, and she needed men. At night she could be selective; but in the morning they were chin and mouth.

"Shall you come here often in the mornings?" she asked. "I wish . . . I can't help it. It's like drink, I suppose."

This also had no meaning for him. "I think," he said, "it's time we were starting back."

"That always comes. . . . The odd thing is, it needn't."

When they were clear of the reeds and on the open river, she said: "I want half an hour."

For an instant he hesitated, then turned the bows against the stream and used the oars only to check the drift.

"Barbet," she said, "that night at the prison, when I was singing, what did you do?"

"Do? Nothing."

"But I sang differently. I felt different. I was different. I didn't fight any more. And now, with you, I don't want to. . . . Was what you did to me what you did to the prisoners that evening when they went back to their cells—was it?"

"Whatever was done, you did inside yourself, Thérèse. I didn't do it. Have you got it in your head that I'm a miracle-worker?"

"But you were there."

"Yes. I was there."

"Well!"

"If I'm of any use to you, Thérèse, I expect it's because I love you."

"*And* the prisoners?" she cried. "Oh, it's the old story, I suppose. Everyone who says they love you wants to change you. And if they succeed, they don't love you any more. Are you reforming a tart?"

"Whoever loves you wants you not to hate yourself. That's all, I think."

"You say you love me. How do you love me? As you love the prisoners? I believe you love all mankind!" she continued with irony and tenderness. "Is that how you love me?" She looked at him for a long time. "O my God," she said at last. "I believe it's true. I don't want to believe it. I believe you do love me. What's the good of your loving me? I'm no good to any man except as—"

"That's not the point," said Barbet.

"Have you never lain with a woman?"

"Oh yes. I'm a very ordinary man. . . . And I love you—you yourself—"

"That's what I'm asking," she said. "Why me in particular?"

"You open windows for me."

"Is that true?" she said. "Is it?"

After an interval Barbet continued: "Just now you said something that puzzled me. When I wanted to go back, you said: 'That always comes. . . . The odd thing is, it needn't.' What did you mean?"

She stretched her arms above her head and yawned. "I had been thinking of Bordeaux, and of your prison. I *must* go there; you *must* go to the Maison Hazard. Must! Why—must? If you had been drowned, what then? And if I disappeared, who would be a sou the worse? Suppose to-night we didn't go back, but landed on the other bank and walked across the hill there, and never came back; suppose—"

"That's what I call making voyages," he said.

"Well?"

"Until this moment, had you imagined it?"

"No."

"Then it's fancy. It's not imagination. It doesn't mean anything. It would be just running away," Barbet said.

"Acting," said Thérèse. "For me. Not for you."

"Yes," he answered. "At this moment it would be acting—even for me."

"Then I have no power over you. What you said isn't true—that I can open windows for you! But I saved your life," she cried.

"That was because I saw an albatross. Let me row back. . . . No, I *want* to row. . . . O God," she said, "now it's the end. I've been happy to-night. What a fool I am. Have you been happy too?"

"Yes, I've been happy too."

"And you might have been drowned," she said. "The person you have to thank is my *al*batross."

Chapter 12

EVEN IN THE VINEYARDS THAT ESCAPED THE PHYL-
loxera, there was a poor vintage that year, but from one source or
another the shippers still contrived to supply their customers and the
house of Hazard and Vincent prospered. To their annoyance, Barbet
seldom sold his brandy to them or to any firm in Roussignac. He had
a connexion in Paris and preferred to sell direct to merchants there.
Often he acted for a group of the smaller proprietors in his neighbourhood, selling their product with his own, charging them no commission and saving them the profits of the Roussignac middlemen. For
this reason, as the phylloxera spread and the supplies of genuine cognac fell away, it became increasingly important for Anton to gain
control of the Maison Hazard, for this would carry with it indirectly
control of the smaller producers for whom Barbet was accustomed to
act. But for the time being Anton was content. What cognac he
had to sell he could sell at good prices and his other interests served
him well. With Thérèse's going, the business of the Cheval Pie slackened, but it yielded Anton a moderate interest on its cost, and tak-
ings at the Lion Rouge returned to their former health. In any
case, the life—one might almost have said the parliament—of the
town was drawn back again to his own inn, and Anton, who cared
for power more even than for wealth, was satisfied. Indeed, during
the autumn he became so benign that he contemplated making up
his quarrel with his mother, but she disliked more and more any in-
trusion into her home and did not encourage him. He and Bette
called on her birthday and on other formal occasions. They went
for the credit of the family and were received for the same reason.
Barbet and his brother seldom met except during these visits or when
Barbet called at the mayor's office to collect the money due for his

prisoners' upkeep. Sometimes Anton appeared at the Maison Hazard as local deputy for the inspector of prisons who came seldom, but though he glanced at the accounts and signed them, he had never thought it necessary, under Barbet's eye, to visit the prisoners themselves. Barbet gave him a glass of wine and they discussed the death of Gambetta.

"Do you wish to visit the prisoners?" Barbet asked.

Anton shrugged his shoulders. "I'll take your word for them. And it's my opinion," he added, "that you treat them too well. How much are you out of pocket by them?"

"Not much. Chiefly at piquet. They can't pay their losses, you see."

Anton frowned. "I suppose none of them has asked to see me?"

"Oh no," Barbet admitted with a smile. "But you know that strictly you oughtn't to ask me that."

"Now, now, now!" Anton exclaimed heartily, slapping him on the back, "you leave me to know my own business! There's no need for me to be poking my nose into their cells, asking for trouble. I hate whining. I hate complaints. It's pleasant here in the sun. The end of autumn's the best time of the year. Anyone due for release?"

"Autun before long."

"You will notify me of that."

"But certainly."

"Good," said Anton, and added abruptly: "What has happened to that girl?"

"Thérèse? She was still at Bordeaux when last I heard."

"She writes to you?"

"Two letters. The last was some time ago. She's not a prolific writer. She prefers talking."

With his little finger Anton hoisted a fly out of his wine and flicked it on to the grass. "A good riddance if you ask me. Is she doing well, did you gather?"

"She said: 'well enough.' . . . But I wonder a little."

"You may. If there'd been success to report, she would have told us about it. Such a flourish of trumpets! Hurtaux wasn't good enough for her. Wasn't she going to conquer Paris? She'd have done better to stay at the Cheval Pie where someone would listen to her."

"Did you ever listen to her, Anton?"

"Yes."

"And what did you think? What did you honestly think—you yourself?"

Anton considered. "Oh, she has a figure, but I like them blonde, with more flesh on them."

"I meant—as a diseuse."

"Talent," said Anton, "but too—"

"Too what?"

"Too—unexpected. I like to know what's coming. I like to know where I am. She's uncomfortable, that girl. . . ." He looked at Barbet without turning his head. "I hear she has a new lover—so Victor says."

"It didn't need the système Vincent to tell you that," Barbet replied. "She has been months away. I hear she has had a meal."

The time for Autun's release fell in mid-winter and he was reluctant to go. Work would be hard to come by; this wasn't a season to turn a man into the streets; and Barbet was sorry to lose him, for he had taught Autun piquet, a game for which it appeared that he had a natural aptitude. "The odd thing about Autun," Barbet told his mother, "is that he sheds his vices when he plays piquet. It puts a ring round him; he forgets all his complaints against the world, and inside the ring he's extraordinarily skilful."

"I think you ought to give up cards," said Madame Hazard.

"I give up piquet!"

"It isn't consistent."

"With what?"

"With what you are," said his mother solemnly.

"You mean—with your idea of me, mother. First you make me a saint. Now you want me to be a martyr. That will never do."

She consented to smile because he laughed, but she was not satisfied.

"You know," he continued, "it's not only Autun. Everyone has something they can be single-minded about. Often it's a trivial thing like piquet—a game of some kind. With Fontan it's music. With Thérèse—"

"You are still thinking about her?"

This conversation alarmed Madame Hazard, but her alarm was short-lived, for afterwards, when Barbet spoke of Thérèse, he spoke so calmly that his mother's anxiety was appeased, but she began to be a little disappointed that he worked no more miracles.

"Nevertheless, my dear Emilie, he has the power," she told Madame Vincent. "That I know. And when the time comes, he will manifest it."

"And when will that be?" Madame Vincent demanded.

But Madame Hazard had grown cautious and would not say what was in her mind—that when she died Barbet would raise her from the dead. Her eyes glittered; she saw herself sitting up among the candles, and a picture of the scene in the following number of *L'Illustration*. She would be the heroine of France, and, imagining herself so, she looked pityingly at Madame Vincent, who, for pride's sake, would toss up her great nose as if she were a horse with an emptying food-bag, and say that her dear friend Chouquette hadn't been dead at all.

"That is what is infuriating about you, Emilie," said Madame Hazard aloud.

"And what may that be?" asked Madame Vincent, innocent of offence.

"That you never will admit anything!" cried Madame Hazard. "If Voltaire rose from the dead before your eyes, you would only quote Voltaire to prove that it was impossible."

"That is unfair, Chouquette!" Madame Vincent exclaimed, aware that she had done nothing to provoke this attack. "You know quite well that I do not quote to prove things. I am not so stupid. Nothing worth proving can be proved. God, for example. I quote because the lines run in my head."

Chapter 13

IN THE EARLY MONTHS OF 1884, BARBET SPENT more and more of his time with the prisoners.

"You have not brought me any more tunes lately," said Fontan, and Barbet answered that perhaps they would come with the spring.

"And the girl?" Fontan asked.

"There is no news of her except that she has left Bordeaux."

"At the inn where she lived—don't they know about her there?"

"While she was in Bordeaux, she used to send money at intervals —sometimes more, sometimes less—what she could afford, I suppose—sometimes to the old woman Sernet, more often to Frédéric. It comes no more."

Barbet did not wish to talk of Thérèse. Victor said she had quarrelled with Hurtaux and gone to Paris in a huff. "She scrambled into the night train as it was going out of the station," was Victor's end to the story, and when Barbet himself made a journey to Angoulême, having heard that Thérèse's employer was to be found there, Hurtaux would at first tell nothing except that his clients at Bordeaux had not liked her style and that she had refused to change it. "But I will say this for her," he added in a burst of confidence, a wide grin spreading over his face. "From Paris she sent me the penalty on her contract. Not a large sum. Notes in an envelope with a scribble on a piece of paper, but more than I ever thought to recover."

"I should like to see the scribble," said Barbet politely, "—if you will allow me?"

Hurtaux produced it from the portfolio he carried in his breast pocket. A large sheet of hand-made paper was spread on the table between them. "I can see her," said Hurtaux, "going into a stationer's shop to buy that singly—to show me how prosperous she was."

On the paper was written:

Not for money. Not for a contract. Penalty enclosed.

THÉRÈSE DESPREUX

Keep this paper. You will be able to sell it some day for more than the notes.

THÉRÈSE DESPREUX

"No address," said Barbet.

"The post-mark was Paris. . . . She likes signing her name, that young woman."

"And you did keep the paper?"

"A memento," said Hurtaux with a flourish. "Besides, she may be right. I may be able to sell it some day for more than the notes."

"What were the notes?"

"A hundred and twenty."

"I will give you a hundred and fifty." Barbet put down the notes on the table between them.

"It is yours, Monsieur Hazard. But why?"

"It pleases me," said Barbet. "But I am surprised," he added, folding Thérèse's letter and tucking it into his pocket, "that, if you believe in Thérèse Despreux, you should have let her go."

Recollection of the scene made Hurtaux's eyes dance and the creases about his nostrils twitch. "I didn't let her go. She went. Bless my soul, I ran after her to the station and caught at her petticoat as she was climbing into the train."

"That was a stupid thing to do, if the train was moving," Barbet interposed. "You might have pulled her back on the platform and killed her."

"Yes," said Hurtaux who was too interested in his memories to hear what Barbet was saying, "the train was moving all right. Off she went—and she waved to me, too. I don't think she bore me any ill-will. She's a professional, and what legs she has! She'd have been insulted if I hadn't admired them. We may have disagreed, but we understood each other. And that wasn't the only difference

between us. About some things—even strictly professional things—
she could be stubborn. There was no reason in it."

"In what?"

"Well," said Hurtaux, "some of her songs she sang in costume,
some in her own dress, and some she stripped for."

"Stripped?" said Barbet.

"More or less—on special evenings. For one song she wouldn't.
If she'd said, 'No, I won't do that at all,' I would have understood
it. There are women like that. Usually they have flat chests but
sometimes they are religious. One recognizes that; one allows for it
in their salary. But why—I ask you—why for one song and not for
another?"

"It may have been inappropriate to the song in question," Barbet
suggested.

"Isn't that for me to judge?"

"No," said Barbet, "it is for her to judge."

"Then you shall judge," said Hurtaux, spreading out magnani-
mous hands. "It was a song about a tart from the country walking
through the streets of Paris. In the end she goes to her room with a
man and there—"

"Looks out of her window on to the roofs. That's where it ends,"
and Barbet began to murmur it:

> *"As I was walking up the street,*
> *Under the lamps, under the sky—*

Is that the song you mean?"

"And wasn't I right?" Hurtaux exclaimed. "Wouldn't it give
point to the end if the girl, when she reached her room, began—"

"Well," said Barbet, "we won't dispute about it. But I thought it
was a hymn."

His companion regarded such ignorance with tolerant pity. Then
a light of suspicion dawned in his eye.

"Didn't you write some of her songs? I seem to remember her
telling me—"

Barbet admitted that he had given her an idea for one or two.

He ceased his inquiries, for he had no wish to interfere in her life.

He was neither tolerant nor intolerant of the flesh. He happened to have won mastery over it; Thérése evidently had not. This was not a reason to condemn or to forgive her. A special link existed between them, and for him it was enough.

There was a time, soon after her going, when he felt the physical grief of loneliness. The sentiment of place did not at once leave him. He shunned the river because of her and chose a new mooring for his boat; but the mood passed; he grew to accept her absence without personal rebellion against it.

BOOK TWO

The River Below Paris

Bon, bon,
Napoléon
Va rentrer dans sa maison.
OLD SONG

Chapter 1

IN THE SPRING OF '84, BARBET WENT TO LYONS TO
visit merchants and afterwards to Paris. From the station, where
he arrived at eight in the morning, he walked across the Pont d'Austerlitz, carrying his bag. He had intended to go at once to the Hôtel
Bagnolet, where Madame Bagnolet would be expecting him, but by
the time he reached the quays the handle of his bag was cutting his
fingers and at a café in the Rue de l'Hôpital he seated himself at a
table and ordered coffee and bread.

It is at such a moment as this that she might pass by, he thought,
though he had supposed his mind to be occupied by the appointments he must keep in Paris; that, precisely, is how things happen in
this world! But as he looked into the faces of the girls who were
hurrying to their work, and the noise of shunting and the shriek of
an engine's whistle came to him from the Gare d'Orléans behind his
back, the notion that Thérèse might appear at that hour in the Rue
de l'Hôpital presented itself as a silly fancy, not as an imagining of
the kind that falls like the touch of a hand on one's shoulder and is
certainly fulfilled. A set of newspapers in wooden clips was hanging
within his reach. He took one down and searched for the list of
theatres and music-halls. What a fool! She wasn't a star. Her name
wouldn't be there. His coffee was cold. He paid and left it.

A turning out of the Rue Poliveau brought him into the Impasse
Marcel, which had the form of a knobbed cane, narrow at the entrance but broadening at its inner end into a circular courtyard,
where stood the Hôtel Bagnolet. Madame Bagnolet appeared in a
black stuff-gown, which smelt of peppermint, and a pair of black
slippers with felt soles. She took Barbet's hand between her own, and
assured him, as she did always, that nothing was changed. What

would happen when she was dead, who could say? Certainly while she lived he would always find, when he came to Paris, that everything was as it had been in his father's day. Then, leading him up the passage, she made her established joke—even Mademoiselle was not changed—and this immortal and nameless creature, whom Julien Hazard had christened Mademoiselle d'Austerlitz, emerged from her shadowy desk at the foot of the stairs. She was, and had always been, forty-three years of age—forty-three because, as Julien had said, one must fix the age of a woman somewhere, and, in the case of Mademoiselle d'Austerlitz, the age of forty-three would do as well as another. Her hair, a natural yellow, was piled high on her head, and if ever the colour of it paled one would not notice it in the coloured beams that fell through the stained glass of the fanlight. To any greeting she responded with agitated joy, like a canary when you whistle. When one of Madame Bagnolet's guests said good morning to her or asked, as he retired for the night, that a hot-brick might be put in his bed, she answered as though his voice were the fulfilment of some girlish dream, and when Barbet said how-d'you-do and offered her his hand, she came to him with little steps that hissed on the tiled floor and opened her eyes very wide and exclaimed, as though he had inquired into the state of her soul: "Mais, ça va bien comme toujours! Suis toujours contente de la vie." All the silver bangles she was wearing shot down her wrists, to slide up her arms again as she clasped her hands at her breast and said that the train from Lyons must have been very late. Her preserved enthusiasms, which she called son cœur de jeune fille, did not impair her efficiency. She forgot nothing. No bill scratched in her angular writing had ever been inaccurate. No guest who had once asked for an extra pillow was ever allowed to find his head too low again, though a year or more should separate his visits. When she was at her desk, none had need of a time-table. Sometimes the bangles danced and the pages flickered, but one had always the impression that she was answering out of her head.

It was she who led Barbet upstairs to the rooms—a communicating bedroom and sitting-room—that were the perquisite of the

Hazard family when they came to Paris. Barbet had shared them with his father and had been to them ever since, firmly resisting his mother's suggestion that he should keep his money in the family by staying with relations of hers at Vanves. "People know where to find me at the Hôtel Bagnolet. Besides, it is convenient for the Jardin des Plantes"—reasons that were indeed good reasons but not the reason that weighed chiefly with him. He stayed with Madame Bagnolet because to have gone elsewhere would have required of him questions and explanations and decisions that were a waste of thought. In the Impasse Marcel, the merchants whom he visited and who sometimes visited him were well known to Mademoiselle. She welcomed each by name, knew what refreshment he would take and what aspect of politics or finance or horse-racing would interest him as he followed her upstairs. She knew at what hour to call Barbet in the morning and she knew that at all other times it was her duty to leave him alone and not to feel slighted if he passed her desk without speaking to her. In his eyes, the virtue of the Hôtel Bagnolet was that they had learned how little he wanted and took him as a matter of course.

But even Mademoiselle had her ritual. She showed him the rooms as if he were a newcomer, patting the bed, shaking the curtains, making sure that the windows would open and shut, even inviting him to share with her the view of the tree-tops of the Jardin des Plantes which appeared as a thin panel of sky and foliage between the walls of the Impasse. Meanwhile he had opened his bag and begun to take from it the smaller samples of brandy that he carried in it.

"The rest," he said, "will come from the station."

"To be sure. I shall be expecting it. The testing glasses are on the top shelf, as usual."

"Thank you, mademoiselle."

"And on the bottom shelf there is your cheese, and bread, and your bordeaux in half-bottles."

"Thank you, mademoiselle."

"Then have you everything, Monsieur Hazard?"

"Everything, mademoiselle."

"And in case, as you did last year, you should lose your pencil, there are three, ready sharpened, in the vase on the mantelpiece."

"Thank you, mademoiselle. And you yourself? You are looking very well."

"Ah, monsieur, you understand me. None better. You know how it is possible, in the midst of a life that few would envy, to be always happy."

She had said this on a dozen like occasions, standing in the doorway, her hand on the knob, her silver bangles fallen to her knuckles in a cascade. Two phrases of their ritual remained to be spoken. "Then there is nothing more I can do for you?" she would ask, turning the knob. "Nothing, mademoiselle," he would answer. "You have already done everything to make me at home."

She said her part.

"Then there is nothing more I can do to make you comfortable, Monsieur Hazard?"

To her astonishment he looked round from the mantelpiece, where he had been arranging his brandy flasks like a file of soldiers, and said:

"There is something, mademoiselle. You know Paris well. You have many acquaintances. I am looking for a young girl."

An exclamation of surprise moved her lips but she did not utter it. Her hand went to her brooch, her finger-nail scraping the cameo at her breast, her bangles clicked to her elbow in a sheath of silver, but she said only: "In the hotel?"

"I am looking," Barbet continued, "for a girl called Thérèse Despreux. The name doesn't happen to be familiar to you? Probably she is working in a music-hall or a café concert. She comes from our part of the world, but we have lost track of her."

Mademoiselle breathed steadily again. She was anxious now only that Monsieur Hazard should not perceive in what way she had misunderstood him. To her the finding of Thérèse had become a professional duty like the working out of a journey in her time-table. There were, she said, ways of finding anyone in Paris. She would employ them.

"Monsieur Mouche will be able to help me no doubt. I expect him in at noon. His brother keeps a shop in Montmartre. I will inquire from him."

"That is very kind of you. One does not like to lose touch with old friends."

"No," said Mademoiselle d'Austerlitz, opening her eyes to the full extent of their romance. "It is sometimes as if the earth had swallowed them up," and she looked not at Barbet but through the space he occupied, as though she were alone in the room and expected to see rise up from the carpet those young men of the 'sixties who, if they had not been swallowed up, might have allowed her to dedicate herself to them.

Chapter 2

O N HIS SECOND NIGHT IN PARIS, BARBET WENT
alone to Montmartre by omnibus. Monsieur Mouche had been
unproductive; neither he nor his brother, Aristide, had heard of the
young woman in question; but Aristide, who sold their material to
painters and had, by his brother's report, an acquaintance with artists
and poets that was "tout ce qu'il y a d'intime," suggested that Monsieur Hazard would at any rate not waste his time if he visited the
Écurie Plence which, in the past year, had become famous, and was,
in Aristide's opinion, a centre of life.

Barbet had had a strenuous and successful day. The merchants
he visited at Bercy had treated him with friendly hospitality, and his
notebook, which he studied over a solitary meal in the square of
St. Germain des Prés, contained entries of which his father would
have been proud. He would have liked to wander up the Rue Bonaparte when his coffee was done and perhaps look into St. Sulpice on
his way home. Once in the Hôtel Bagnolet, he would have sat in his
chair, preferring the adventure of thought to the book on his knee;
then have slept, glad that the contacts of the day, friendly though
they had been, were over. Instead, he took the omnibus to Montmartre. The Écurie Plence was found sooner than he wished; he
turned a corner and it was staring at him.

In spite of the place's name, it had not occurred to him that he
would find himself in a stable. A floor of paving-stones sloped towards what had once been a central drain, now boarded over. At
the end of the room was a stage enclosed within a proscenium arch
painted crimson and decorated with horses' heads in gilt. The curtains were apart and the scene lighted. The middle of the room,
empty as a ballroom between dances, was flanked by crowded tables

and by old stable fittings ingeniously converted. All the tables were tilted a little inwards by the slope of the floor, their white discs lay up in what appeared to be a distorted perspective, the customers held their bodies against the slope of their chairs as though they were inclined against a wind, and wine slanted in the glass. The horses' stalls had been reduced in height; they served now as the backs of benches; heads and shoulders appeared over them; and on the mangers, covered in, were perched, against either wall, a row of young men and women who preferred to dangle their legs or could find no place elsewhere. At their backs were long gilded mirrors which, facing each other across the room, held, in unending repetition, the white discs, the inclined heads, the flickering hands and faces, the hot blaze of unshaded gas. As Barbet entered, eyes were turned to recognize the newcomer and, discovering a stranger, remained to stare.

The idea that he had entered what was, in effect, a club did not arise in his mind. There was no reason that these, or any human beings, should be hostile to him and he did not suppose that they were. On his way up the room, he encountered a boy wearing an apron and carrying a tray. He asked for a glass of brandy, then looked calmly about him to decide where he should sit.

Every chair was full, but on one of the mangers, between two girls, a place was vacant. Putting his hands behind him on to the ledge, he hoisted himself on to it, then looked out. The room broke into a shout of laughter, for now, standing before Barbet, was the man whose place and whose two women he had unwittingly usurped, a young man, tall and thin and shaggy, Quixote and a wolf-hound, with eyes to which absinthe, before it dulled them, could still give, and had now given, a dazzling lucidity. This extraordinary being, to whom Barbet would have instantly apologized for having taken his seat, had evidently no thought that his seat had been taken, no sense of claim on it or on the women. His mind had cleared itself, as if by an explosion, and had gathered itself again upon the apparition of Barbet. He stretched his hands into the air and cried out:

"No. No. No. Do not laugh, my friends. This man has come out of the mirror. He is making a journey. He is more realist than

us all. He is happy. He has such eyes in his head that he has no
need to pretend that the world is vile. He perceives that you,
Madeleine, are an angel, and that I, Sébastien Cugnot, am not, when
drunk, a fool. Look at the eyes in his head!"

To this oration, so passionately begun and ended in a voice stran-
gled by its own irony, the audience responded at first by rapt attention, then by mocking applause. Cugnot took the glass that the girl
on Barbet's right had been holding for him, emptied it, and turning
again to face the room, leaned back between her knees.

"And after all, who are you?"

"My name is Hazard. I am called Barbet Hazard. I come from
Roussignac. I am selling my brandy in Paris."

"I am Sébastien—Sébastien Cugnot. I paint and I make marionettes. I am a greater painter than the world will ever know. Unfortunately I am also a greater painter than I myself shall ever believe. That is why everything I do ends badly. I am a tight-rope
walker who loses his nerve half-way across. My vice is—what is my
vice, Madeleine?"

"Ah," said the girl who had held his glass—a girl with deep violet
eyes, a full mouth and the high, rounded cheeks of a child, "your
vice, Cugnot, is that you make speeches. You make a speech when I
am taking off your shoes. My vice is that I take them off."

"Why do you?" said Barbet.

"And why shouldn't I?"

"There is no reason that you shouldn't, mademoiselle. There are
a dozen that you should. I was asking which of them—"

"It's simple enough," Madeleine said. She ran her fingers over
Cugnot's head, thrusting his hair forward over his eyes, and would
say no more of the subject. "And now," she continued at last, "what
do you say now, Monsieur du Miroir?"

"I am very grateful to you, mademoiselle, for his sake. But it has
always seemed strange to me—in women, I mean, in women more
often than in men—that they will not admit their virtues to themselves, but call them vices and think of them in that way."

The girl on his left, who had remained hitherto averted and sullen while she twisted and twisted a great carbuncle ring that she wore on her left thumb, now turned her eyes on Barbet, and Cugnot's face came up and the group at the nearest table set down their glasses.

"For example?" said Madeleine.

"But this will never do," exclaimed a middle-aged Jew, rising from the table with an air of authority. Before continuing to speak, he ran his fingers outward across his eyes and down his cheeks as though he were drawing pain out of his head. "I must interrupt you, Madeleine. Cugnot, you have not introduced your friend."

"He introduces himself. He is the fool. But this, my dear Barbet," Cugnot continued, bowing at the Jew, "is a Great Man in whose court we must all sing for our supper. He is Plence. He has genius —the genius, peculiar to his race, of a connoisseur. He owns this stable. We are his horses, we are his mares. He chooses us, he rides us, he enters us for races, he pats us and feeds us and buries us. Is there one in this room—perhaps not one—who will survive him and of whom posterity will say: 'Plence was his groom'? The rest of us, certainly, will wear his racing colours in the grave. 'Sébastien Cugnot? Sébastien Cugnot?' Ah yes, he was John the Baptist in the Écurie Plence. He stood up and prophesied. Sometimes he brought two women with him, like dogs on a string; it was his way of advertising himself.' That is what they will say, fifty years hence. 'In Paris of the 'eighties, L'Écurie Plence—L'Écurie Plence—L'Écurie Plence!' You see, he is smiling. It charms him. It is true. He will bury us all. You understand, of course, that I am paid to insult him. To-night I have made my speech. I shall pay nothing." He turned on Plence with the scream of a child. "Nothing. Nothing at all."

"Entendu," said Plence. "Now let us talk the language of civilized men."

When there was room at Plence's table, Barbet and Cugnot, with the girl called Madeleine, were brought to it. The girl with the ring remained on the ledge, Cugnot having forgotten her. From time to time a man stood up on the stage, demanded audience, and recited his own poems, or a girl sang fierce verses with rhymes like the clash of knives thrown on an iron table, or a group of students, setting up an apparatus like the box of Punch and Judy, crouched behind it to give voices to a piece they had written for marionettes.

"They told me," said Barbet to Cugnot, "that from here singers and dancers are sometimes recruited for the music-halls?"

"They told you that! Did you hear, Plence? They told him that."

"They told him the truth," Plence answered.

Cugnot tipped back his chair. "Once this was a charming place. We talked, we sang, we amused ourselves, we heard verses. Do we now exist to recruit the music-halls and to entertain le déluge?"

"Le déluge?" said Barbet.

"It is Cugnot's word for the aristocracy of the Third Republic. At any rate our ark is beginning to float on it. As you see"—and Plence pointed to the stage—"I have founded a theatre—"

"Le Théâtre Plence!" Cugnot exclaimed. "Is it possible that you have not heard of it?"

"I am from the provinces," Barbet answered in order that Monsieur Plence should not feel hurt, but Plence seemed not to care.

"It is a theatre," he explained, "chiefly for silhouettes or marionettes. But there are variety turns as well. Le déluge has heard of it. On Saturday and Sunday nights they come here. You shall come as my guest."

"Soon," said Cugnot, "it will be Monday and Tuesday and Wednesday—and Thursday and Friday as well. L'Écurie is finished. It will appear in the guide-books. Americans will describe it in their diaries of travel. The English will sit at this table and expect us to throw knives for them."

"Then," said Plence, "we will throw knives for them. It is a livelihood like another. We can continue our civilization elsewhere—"

He stopped abruptly. A grave young man had mounted the platform and come forward to recite his verses. The room was at once silent, and, when the verses were spoken, they were eagerly applauded and discussed. The poet came to Plence's table and smouldered there, forgetting the drink given him, his hands clasped together and clipped between his knees. "He has never dared to recite before," Madeleine whispered. "This, for him, is success. He hasn't said twenty words. What do you suppose he's thinking about? The Academy?"

"That he has no one to share it with," Barbet answered at once.

"Ah!" the girl exclaimed. "It is true, of course. He lives alone. None of us knows him. He belongs to no one," but she forgot the young poet; Cugnot had begun to speak; her eyes returned to him. Whoever was singing or reciting, whatever the conversation at the table, even when she was looking elsewhere or speaking to others, she seemed to have Cugnot in her charge, as though he were a blind man whom she was leading.

Barbet watched the scene and heard the conversation around him with lively interest. He was particularly interested when Plence, after listening to a girl who had sung and recited at the piano, began to criticize the art of a diseuse, saying that no art was less considered as an art, that the women chose their songs from the music shops with the idea always of placating their audience—never of challenging them to the appreciation of a new style. "The music-halls bully the girls into behaving as if they were clowns," he said. "Now clowning *is* traditional and even a clown of genius must work within the tradition. So must an actor to a great extent. Even if he's not using classical material, even if the play's modern, he must always use a convention. He has a choice of conventions, certainly, but he must use one of the conventions that his audience recognizes. For him it is a necessary code between stage and audience. It carries its meaning because its origins are in the past and because every playgoer, as he enters a theatre, adjusts his mind to it. A painter, if he's a revolutionary, can create a new convention of his own and hope that people will become accustomed to it some day. He can wait—though he may have to wait until he's dead and rotten. But an actor can't wait. There's no posterity for him. He must use a convention his audience accepts to-night or can be persuaded to accept pretty soon. And even a writer," Plence continued, wishing to draw the young poet into his argument, "even a writer is to some extent bound by the past. Isn't that true, Casimir? Like a painter, he can afford to wait; he can rebel and wait; but literature has an inescapable past; he is held by it as he is by heredity. There are, for example, a hundred forms of verse but there is a perceptible general convention governing them all—how shall I put it?—a convention which—"

"Which tells the listener that what he's listening to isn't prose," Cugnot put in, "which enables him to make an adjustment to the intensity of poetry. A modern poet, until he learns better, speaks of defying the past or of breaking away from it. He wants to march into exile with all the brass bands playing. In fact, he can't. The most he can do is to move house into a different part of the country from that in which Corneille lived; still he remains in the same kingdom with him. There is a rule of poetry wider than Corneille's rule or any particular rule of verse—a wider rule or, as you say, convention that includes him and all French poets. The man who thinks that, when he has mocked at Lamartine and called himself a realist, he has created a new world is like a man who moves from Paris to Senlis and says that he has discovered a continent."

"And yet," said Casimir, wrenching up his head, "it is necessary to rebel."

"It is sometimes necessary to move from Paris to Senlis."

"It is sometimes necessary to believe that Senlis is a new continent," Casimir replied. "If not, no one would move."

"Certainly," said Cugnot, "it is necessary to move, but to understand also that, having moved, one is still in France."

Plence had listened to this dialogue with darting satisfaction, his lips parted, his eyes moving from face to face. Now he began to pat the table with a soft, emphatic hand.

"And the art of the diseuse," he said, "lies outside all that. That is my point. The great art of poetry, the secondary art of acting, the strange, specialized art of clowning, each is held—or, more accurately, each moves and changes and grows—within a great convention that is—if one may put it so—the language of the art—a language which, in each instance, the world has learned to understand. But the art of the diseuse has no Corneille, no Mozart, no Michael

Angelo—even no Ingres. It has no Paris from which to move to Senlis. It has no including France. And yet the diseuses we have work always as if they were bound by a tradition that does not, in their case, exist."

"I know one who doesn't," said Barbet.

They had altogether forgotten him, and came up, visibly surprised, out of the waters of their own controversy to find him quietly regarding them from the bank.

"But that can be of no interest to you," he added hastily. "I'm sorry. After all, you do not teach me how to make cognac," and he folded his hands, prepared to listen again.

For a moment, Plence seemed willing to accept this, to allow Barbet to retire into silence, and to plunge again into the pleasures of his own discourse.

"A diseuse—" he began.

"Plence," cried Cugnot. "Look at our friend. Look at his eyes. In this instant, while you tip the wine in your glass, you are throwing a fortune away."

Plence blinked at him. "Why?"

"Why do you think our friend came out of the mirror? Why did he hoist himself into *my* place? How does it happen that he, who has never been to the Écurie before, is sitting at your table? These things do not happen without a reason. I was listening while you said that our diseuses work always as if they were bound by a false tradition, and suddenly, at my elbow, I heard him say: 'I know one who doesn't.' It is quite simple. What he says is true. He knows one who doesn't. Who is she?"

"Her name is Thérèse Despreux."

Plence once more ran his hands outward over his eyes and down his cheeks. "I never heard of her," he answered in a tone of irritation and finality.

Cugnot imitated his gesture. "Plence! Plence! You who know so much! You who are so astute! You who have a nose for the truffles! You keep a stable. You are offered the winner of the Grand Prix. You wipe your brilliant eyes and you say: 'I never heard of her!'"

"Well," Plence cried, "have you?"

"Certainly."

"That is a lie. When?"

"To-night. Didn't you hear him say the name? Thérèse Despreux. Thérèse Despreux. Thérèse Despreux. At ten o'clock in any music-hall in the world."

Barbet was at a loss. He did not understand why, or in what way, these two men were quarrelling, nor did he understand with how great an effort of self-control Plence compelled himself to reach out for the declamatory hand that Cugnot had raised in the air, and draw it to the table, and say:

"When you speak like this, Cugnot, you drive me mad, but, when you speak like this, I listen to you. I am Plence. I keep the stable. I have judgment but I do not see visions. You are without judgment when you are sane, but when you are mad—"

"Visions?" said Cugnot, suddenly docile. "Have you never known, quite certainly, where you must put your money en plein?"

After a moment's consideration, Plence interlaced his fingers and leaned across the table towards Barbet.

"Tell me, my friend, who is this girl?"

"She is a local girl. She sang and danced in the Cheval Pie at Roussignac."

"And afterwards?"

"At Bordeaux. A man named Hurtaux—"

"Hurtaux? He has her? Under contract?"

"She ran away from Bordeaux. He caught at her skirt while the train was moving. But she paid the penalty on her contract," Barbet explained anxiously. "She sent him this," and he produced from his pocketbook the sheet of hand-made paper he had bought from Hurtaux. He cleared a space among the saucers and laid it on the table before Plence.

"Why do you show me this?"

"I thought," said Barbet, "that you seemed to doubt her existence."

"And where is she now?"

"Where? That is what I am trying to find out."

"But have you news of her?"

"Unfortunately none."

"Good God," Plence exclaimed, "she may be in Marseilles by now."

"No," Barbet answered. "She is in Paris."

Madeleine's fingers closed on Cugnot's wrist. She threw back her head and laughed and sighed and said to Barbet, secretly under her breath, so that none but Cugnot heard her: "Que Dieu te garde. Que Dieu te bénisse. Tu la verras demain," and Cugnot, leaning forward, intervened suddenly:

"You have asked every question, Plence, except the one that matters. I will ask it. Tell me," he continued, returning to Barbet the paper Thérèse had written, "in what way is she different from other diseuses?"

Barbet did not answer.

"Has she a better voice?"

"She has a good voice."

"Is she more beautiful?"

Barbet shook his head.

"You said she was independent of the false tradition which—"

"Did I say that?" said Barbet with a smile. "It doesn't sound like me." He looked round the room over the heads of those who, at the table, were gazing at him, and he said: "It's very hot in here. I have had a long day. I think I will go home." But he did not rise. Instead, taking the stem of a glass between his finger and thumb, he twisted it to and fro, edging its base further and further up the table along a rivulet of spilled wine, and Cugnot, to recall him, laid his palm upon the glass. Barbet, surprised, looked straight into his face and said:

"You see, while she tells a story it is true."

It was evident that he had more to say, and they waited.

"That's what's so odd. You'd think that there'd be nothing to stop her. But there is. Monsieur Plence will understand. She's like a race-horse which—"

"You leave her to me," said Plence. "I'll train her, if that's the trouble. What does she do—bite or swerve?"

"Well, you see," Barbet continued, "it isn't so simple as that. At first, she always thinks that she is right and that whoever criticizes her is a blind fool. Not that she can't criticize herself; she can—she can be fierce against her own mistakes, but only after a long, bitter struggle. But no one can help her. She won't let them. If anyone offers her an idea—I mean, an idea about her own performance—she becomes angry, as though she were being invaded, and until she has got over it and stopped being suspicious, really there's nothing that even Monsieur Plence could do."

Plence smiled. "There are ways, I assure you, of dealing with any actress. You bully one, you flatter another, you make love to a third. Or, if she's genuinely intelligent, you give her your reasons —one, two, three—and then—"

"Yes, that is all very well," Barbet interrupted, "but in any discussion with her the important sentences have to be spoken at intervals of at least a week. It isn't a question of persuading her that an idea is valuable but of giving her time to forget that it was not originally her own. She isn't slow; she's extremely quick; she knows in a flash the value of an idea, but, if it was not she who thought of it, she resists and resists it, until at last her resistance snaps, and to save her egotism she gives the idea a new dress and wakes up one morning to find that it is her own."

Barbet paused, smiling; then continued to himself: "The time has then come to speak the second sentence of the argument and to watch the process repeat itself. And now," he went on, "you will think she is a very stubborn and foolish girl, but it is not so; she is a brilliant one, and this everlasting resistance to other people's ideas isn't stupid rebellion. It isn't rebellion at all. It's self-discipline. *Self*-discipline," he repeated. "You see this match-box? This resistance is the box on which to strike her own match. She has arrogance but never, never complacency. She is always fighting a battle and never winning it. But she must fight by herself. And that means—"

Barbet stopped and began once more to push his glass up the rivulet of wine. Cugnot again put his hand upon it.

"It means," Barbet exclaimed with energy, dragging back the

glass and gripping it to him, "that the work she does is done with blood. That is all. That is all. Take it or leave it."

No one had expected him to speak so freely or with so much precision, and he, awaking from his own eloquence and seeing the close-regarding astonishment of the faces surrounding him, said to himself: I must have talked a lot. What made me let myself go like that? But to them he said nothing.

Plence declared that he was extremely interested by Barbet's account of Thérèse and added, in a lordly way, that the finding of her might be left to him. He would send out his scouts; if she was in Montmartre, if she was in Paris, he would find her—and Plence dropped the subject, summoned to his table the students who had experimented with marionettes and pointed out their errors to them.

"You are wasting your time," said Cugnot, putting his hand under Barbet's arm and lifting him from his chair. "Plence is a man who believes nothing until he has seen it. That is why he makes money—and makes nothing else. If you think he will stir a finger to find your Thérèse Despreux, you are mistaken; though, if she is found, he will know how to bring her to market. . . . Come, we will find her ourselves."

But they did not find her. They went from place to place. Each to Barbet was like the last—a clash of voices and glass and crockery, a desert of tables, rubbed plush and squeaking chairs; but he was happy in their intervening walks on narrow pavements where Cugnot and Madeleine and he had often to go in single file, among lean cats that came up from the gutters. Looking at Madeleine's back, he became aware of the extraordinary patience of this girl who could have no interest in the search and might well have said that they were looking for a needle in a haystack. Instead she took it for granted that, if Cugnot had set out to find Thérèse Despreux, it was necessary to find her, and when Barbet said "You must be tired, mademoiselle, why should you be dragged farther?" she smiled over her shoulder and answered: "You are good for Cugnot. He will be able to paint to-morrow."

At last, seated at a café table, Cugnot fell asleep—not with slow, drowsy nodding, but suddenly, as if, while walking at full speed along a path, he had come to a crevasse and disappeared into it. Madeleine wrote his address on an envelope that she took from his pocket and handed it to Barbet.

"He will let you know at your Hôtel Bagnolet," she said. "He won't forget. He will find her."

"Why he should take so much trouble for me, I don't understand," Barbet answered.

Madeleine made a movement of her shoulders that, in another woman, would have been a shrug, but in her was a contraction of them, a pressing of them forward—one of her many smooth and gentle movements that gave an impression of graciousness; a graciousness of the body that belongs to coloured peoples and to certain great animals. "Perhaps to annoy Plence," she answered, then raised her eyebrows, took breath and smiled. "No. He despises Plence. . . . Perhaps because he likes you." Then she looked at Cugnot, who slept without sagging, alert, like a blind man erect in his chair. "I expect it's because he wants to see her face."

"Her face?"

"You made him imagine it, you know. You made me imagine it—though you didn't describe a feature."

Barbet was silent, and she said after a little while: "There's not another man on earth who wouldn't have asked me then what I imagined. All the others would have asked that."

"Would they?" said Barbet. "It's no merit in me that I didn't. I wasn't being polite, you know. I supposed that you had imagined her as she is."

She smiled. "It's simple, isn't it?" and she inclined her head towards Cugnot. "He's like that. But in other ways he's complicated. When he's painting, when I'm sitting for him—" She broke off. "I'm his model, you know, as well as his mistress."

"But you have not always been a model?" Barbet said.

"Certainly I wasn't born one," she replied. "Now, shall I wake him?"

Cugnot believed that he had not been asleep.

"It is too late for you to go back across the river," he said to Barbet. "You will sleep in my studio. To-morrow I shall find the girl. Am I allowed to paint her?"

"Why not?" said Barbet, "if you can make her keep still."

They walked together until Cugnot halted. "This is my door. Come in. You go first, Madeleine. Here are the matches."

But Barbet said he must return to the Hôtel Bagnolet; he had business to do there at ten in the morning.

"How shall you go?" Madeleine asked.

"Walk," said Barbet, "unless someone drives me."

He had not left them five minutes when a cart of vegetables passed him. A basket fell into the street.

"Hé, hé," he cried, "here's a basket of yours."

He lifted it on to the tail of the cart and made fast the cord. The boy who had been driving leaned against the wheel.

"That was lucky," he said. "I should have been beaten for that," and he was glad of Barbet's company on his journey. The horse knew his own way, and turned from the Rue La Bruyère into the Place St. Georges with no more guidance than a shake of the reins. The boy was ill and tired, and Barbet, at the sight of the Hôtel Thiers, which had been burned in '71, bestirred himself to tell stories of those days, to which the boy responded at first with sullen grunts, then with eyes turning and watchful, then with laughter. All the way down the Rue Montmartre the stories continued until, as they approached the vegetable market, the boy began to tell in his turn of his daily adventures and of his hope that he might before long escape from work in the Halles and go, as his elder brother had done, to a farm in Normandy. Last year, when he had been very ill, he had visited the farm on which his brother was employed, and he exchanged tales of it for Barbet's tales of Roussignac and the Charente. When the cart drew up near to the church of St. Eustache, the boy's face was happy and alive; he would not willingly allow Barbet to go. "I'm early this morning. There's ten minutes to spare." He gave a friend charge of his cart and walked with Barbet, saying he would put him on his way; there was a short cut he knew of to the east of the Halles. "You pass the Tour St. Jacques and keep on until you come to the Hôtel de Ville; then you can cross the river at Notre-Dame." They went together no further than the square of the Innocents. There Barbet found in his pocket three francs and some smaller money and said good-bye. The boy returned to his work, and Barbet, looking up beyond the bas-reliefs of the fountain to the white morning sky, thought that he had been foolish to wander about all night in quest of Thérèse. By now, she had another life and would have forgotten him. He had assumed that she needed him, but now, as he came to the river, the simplicity of his mind was crossed, his confidence failed him, and he paused to watch a string of barges go down stream. I've lost sight of her, that's all, he said to himself. If ever she knew how I have spent to-night, she'd think I was a pretty fool. His eye followed the barges and the slow, bulging swirl of their wake. For a moment his mind was emptied of her. And yet, he thought, she isn't vanished. She isn't in Marseilles. She's in Paris. To-night I have been close to her. While we were wandering from café to café, if I had turned in suddenly at—but he could not see the turning; only the staircase, the first landing and the second and the third, and the room with three beds on one of which she was sitting, a coat wrapped round her and a bare foot thrust out with a mule dangling from the toe. The barges had turned out of sight and Barbet walked on across the river. Madame Bagnolet had given him a key and he let himself in. While he was winding his watch, he looked at his list of engagements for the day, then said his prayers. I shall be saying them again in three hours, he thought. That's what comes of staying out all night, and he tucked his head into his pillow, curled himself into a ball, and went to sleep.

Chapter 3

NEXT DAY, WHEN AT NOON HE CAME IN FROM HIS work, Mademoiselle d'Austerlitz rose from her desk to say that a lady had called upon him and left a note.

Will you come to Cugnot's studio any time before six? I think we have news of her.

MADELEINE VAUTHIER.

He had a second appointment in the afternoon and came to Montmartre soon after five. Madeleine was alone.

"Cugnot is at the Gare du Nord."

"The Gare du Nord?"

"He is painting it." She looked at a clock that had pheasants engraved on its face. "He ought to have been back by now."

"You have news of Thérèse?"

"Sit down," she said, "and I will tell you about it. Do you mind if I try to draw you while we talk?"

"Not at all," he answered. "I ought to be a good model. Thérèse used to laugh at me because I have a habit of sitting still."

Madeleine was sharpening pencils. She's very slow, Barbet thought, to give me her news, whatever it is. Is she frightened of it? Has she heard that Thérèse is dead?"

"If you have heard that she is dead, that will be wrong," he said.

The pencil clicked into the ledge of the easel. "You are so sure?"

"Oh yes, quite sure. She is alive and in Paris."

"Yes," Madeleine answered, "she is alive and in Paris. At least she was until very lately. This morning, early, a girl came to the door and insisted on seeing Cugnot. An odd girl. If she had been prosperous, she might have had a swagger of her own. Not by nature a cringer or a tart, but now both; very poor and with a way of looking at you as if she expected you to hit her. I thought she'd come for money. So she had—but I thought she meant to black-mail Cugnot about something, and it wasn't that. . . . Do you remember, last night, we went to the Deux Lapins?"

"I'm vague about the names," said Barbet.

"It was one of the first places we went to after leaving Plence. There were four girls sitting together in a corner—one with a black veil. This girl came in and joined them after we had gone. She heard we had been asking for Thérèse Despreux and she knew her address. She came here this morning to sell it."

"To sell it," Barbet repeated. "Well, poor girl. . . . How much do I owe Monsieur Cugnot?"

"Five francs. She wanted ten."

On this Barbet made no comment except: "Did she give you her own address?"

"Of course she did. . . . I should leave her alone if I were you."

"Oh," said Barbet with a smile, "I don't think I have anything to fear."

"You may think not, but that kind bites."

"Not me," Barbet answered. "They laugh at me, you know. So do you and Monsieur Cugnot. That's why you're so kind to me. . . . But that's no matter. What did she say?"

Madeleine did not answer at once; her pencil moved firmly on her paper; and Barbet, without shifting his head, let his eyes travel about the room. "Well," Madeleine said at last, "it's not easy. I don't know what your interest may be in Thérèse Despreux, and—"

"That is simple, mademoiselle. I love her. She thinks that I— if she thinks of me at all, she thinks that I'm a kind, comic fellow— the sort of provincial, you understand, who is completely ignorant of the world. I amuse her for that reason. That is all."

"And are you ignorant of the world?"

"Not in the least. I have been a soldier."

"That's just as well in the circumstances. It makes it less hard to say what I have to say. This woman told us—"

"Why do you speak of her so harshly, mademoiselle? After all—"

"After all—what?"

"Not long ago she was a very small child."

"Was she? I promise you she's forgotten it by now. Don't you understand? She came here for money. She wouldn't write down the address until we gave it her."

"I expect she needed it," said Barbet. "And please," he continued, speaking with gentleness and consideration, "please believe that, whatever has happened to Thérèse, you need not hesitate to tell me. Whatever she had done, she remains the same human being."

The sheet of paper was tugged away from the drawing-pins. "I'm sorry. I'm wasting your time. I can't draw you now."

Last night Barbet had not been aware of the streak of hardness in Madeleine that she had exhibited in talking of the girl who had brought news of Thérèse, and he kept his eyes on her. She stood at the window, looking out, her arms straight behind her, her fingers interlocked, her shoulders forced back; she spoke across her shoulder. The girl, who was known as Annette, had lived with Thérèse on the third floor of a lodging-house. Formerly Thérèse had been employed in several café-concerts and petty music-halls, sometimes in the programme, sometimes as a dresser or odd-job woman on the side of the stage, sometimes as waitress or ouvreuse. Annette, too, had done work of the same kind when she could get it, but whether her job was or was not connected with the stage made no odds to her; there had been a dressmaker who employed her and she earned, on the side, at a maison de passe. Thérèse clung to the stage at all costs. Annette had told her she'd get ill and die, but she said: "Leave me alone! I'll live in my *own* way and my way is *in* the theatre. The rest isn't real."

"And what did she live on meanwhile?" Barbet asked. "I suppose she put by a little to tide her over between jobs?"

"Perhaps." Madeleine raised incredulous eyebrows. "But it is as well to face the probabilities. You know how Annette earned her pocket-money."

Barbet was silent. Then he asked whether Annette was still living with Thérèse.

"She was until six weeks ago. Then she was offered four weeks as a dancer in a touring chorus."

"And since she came back?"

"She hasn't seen Thérèse."

"Why not?"

"I asked that. She said: 'She was ill when I left.' "

"Is that a reason?"

"She said," Madeleine answered, with her eyes on Barbet's face, "that she thought Thérèse might be dead."

"Still," said Barbet, "I don't understand."

"Don't you? Annette deserted her. And that's not all."

"What more?" Barbet asked steadily.

"She had money that belonged to Thérèse."

"Did she admit that?"

"When I guessed it, she did. She howled like a coward, then admitted it. All the pleasures of confession! Forty-one francs. She said it was borrowed. . . . And now, I suppose, you will still say that it's not long since that woman was a very small child!"

"Oddly enough," said Barbet, "I don't think Thérèse would hate or despise her. Why do you smile?"

"You endow your Thérèse with your own qualities, Monsieur Hazard. Do you really imagine for example that this girl you love has been living in chastity since you last saw her?"

"Good heavens, no," said Barbet. "But that doesn't say she'd despise or hate a woman for stealing forty-one francs. . . . Or that she sold herself."

"And if you found that she had sold herself—that she went to the same house as Annette—"

"Did Annette say that?"

"On the contrary, she said that Thérèse had a catchword—"

" 'Not for money. Not for a contract,' " said Barbet. "It's an interesting rule, isn't it?"

"And suppose she broke it? What effect would it have on you?"

"On me? That isn't the question. And yet," he added, "perhaps it is. Perhaps it is a question I may have to answer. You see, mademoiselle, I am not at all a saint; certainly not an ascetic, though I live plainly enough as a matter of taste; but I try to take the simplest possible view of everything and not to be shocked by myself or by anyone else." He picked up from the floor the piece of paper on which the drawing of him had been begun. "It is true, then—I do look like a water-spaniel. Finish it some day, mademoiselle." He put the paper into her hands. "You think that Monsieur Cugnot will be in before long?"

"Are you waiting for him?"

"I thought I should like to thank him."

"Is that why you have been talking to me all this time?" Madeleine smiled. "Good heavens, I shall never understand you! Look, here is your Thérèse's address, Rue Lilas—somewhere between the Rue La Bruyère and the Rue Notre-Dame de Lorette. You must ask."

"Did you say the Rue La Bruyère?"

"Why does that surprise you?"

"It doesn't. I must have passed very close to the Rue Lilas last night. . . . And may I have the other address?"

"Annette?"

"Please, if I may. Here are the five francs."

She took from his hand the piece of paper she had given him and wrote on it again.

"God protect you," she said. "I expect He will."

When Annette heard that he had come from Cugnot's studio, she was frightened into a stream of words.

"She's no better than I am. It's she who says I stole the money, but it's not true. It's not true. You have no proof."

"Were you fond of Thérèse?" Barbet asked.

"Of Thérèse? I wasn't speaking of her. I meant Cugnot's girl."

"I know. Shall we forget her? Tell me about Thérèse."

"What do you want to know?"

"Was she ever hungry?"

"We both were."

"Any friends?"

"Oh, she had friends. They weren't any good though. She wouldn't take anything except a meal now and then. And she always made herself out worse than she was. Just when a fellow was beginning to feel responsible for her, she'd go off with another —and say so, too. . . . And often," Annette added, "when they wanted her to come to a meal, she'd make them ask me too. That was generally the end of it. What's more, she meant it to be."

"But you were fond of her?"

"Fond of her? What a queer chap you are. 'Fond'—what d'you think I am—her sister? I was mad about her if that's what you mean." Annette paused, picked up a stocking she had been darning and laid it down again. "So you see," she went on, "after the affair with the money, I had to go. I thought I could pay it back. I spent part of it on things for her—I swear I did. That made it worse; she thought I was giving her a present and I let her. So, when I couldn't pay back, I had to go, hadn't I? I suppose she found afterwards that it was gone. There was a loose tile. 'That's the last to fall back on,' she'd say. I suppose she went for the money after I'd gone."

"There it is," Barbet said, counting it out on to the seat of a wooden chair. "Forty-one francs."

"But I can't take it to her now!" said Annette.

"Yes, you can."

"I can't. What should I say?"

"Talk to her about other things and leave the money."

"But she'd ask. First thing she'd say—"

"No," Barbet answered, "you know that's not true. You forget, I've known Thérèse since she was a child. She has no malice. It's almost a fault in her. And anyhow," he added with a smile, "she'd be much too curious to see what *you* were going to say to help you by giving you a cue."

"You're very clever, no doubt," Annette replied. "But I warn you—you'd better put that money back into your pocket. I warn you."

"I'll take the risk," said Barbet.

He said good-bye to Annette, made his way down her stairs, and, once in the street, took off his hat and wiped his forehead. Rue Lilas. Well, he thought, it has a pretty name anyway, and set out. On the way he bought some grapes, a bottle of red wine, a corkscrew, a loaf of bread, some sausage and a basket to carry them in. And now, he said to himself, something quite useless; it will please her more than food or drink; besides, she may not need food or drink. Flowers? He had not hands enough to carry them, but he saw in a junk-shop a small box with lilies of the valley enamelled on its lid and this he could slip into his waistcoat pocket. The man in the shop said it was a patch-box. That ought to be useless enough, Barbet thought as he marched off with it; and he took it out in the street, unable to deny himself the pleasure of unwrapping it and studying the enamelled lilies, hoping they would please her.

It was almost at the spot where the vegetables had fallen from the boy's cart that he turned out of the Rue La Bruyère. Rue Lilas, Number Ten, was a tall, narrow house, very dark, that smelt of onions and wet clothes. A fat child carrying a pail told him that Despreux lived on the third landing, but was out.

"Out? She's not ill, then?"

"She's out," the child repeated and went off with her pail.

Barbet made the journey of the stairs, glad of his basket which would make their meeting easy. There would be no need for either of them to speak while she took out the contents; her head would be bent over the basket and he would stand aside saying nothing and looking at the top of her head. On the third landing he stopped. His heart was beating; there was the same tightness about his heart that there had been when his father had taken him to a bull-fight at Nîmes. In a moment, he thought, her hand will take the basket, and he held it out in the air, as though he were offering it to her. He remembered that the child had said that Despreux was out, but did not believe it. When he knocked on the door her voice would answer.

He knocked.

"Who's there?"

"Barbet."

"Who? What do you want? Why in heaven's name can't I be left alone?"

He knocked again. "Thérèse. It's me. It's Barbet—Barbet Hazard."

This time she heard. He knew that she became rigid and listened. Then she came across the room—but how slowly! The key turned in the lock, the door opened.

"You!"

"Thérèse. . . . May I come in?"

"I suppose so." She turned her back on him, advanced a few paces, and sat down clumsily on one of the three beds that the room contained.

"Well," she said, "what have you come for?"

"To see you."

"Not much worth seeing."

Her eyes moved suddenly from Barbet's face. Their gaze was directed towards the wall on his left and, having rested there a little while, moved to the tin wash-stand, then to the ripped and sagging wall-paper that surrounded a pipe to which a stove had formerly been attached, then to each of the two bedsteads, naked to their rusty springs, opposite the bed on which she herself was seated. There was nothing furtive or hasty in her gaze, nothing ashamed—only an intense and almost impersonal curiosity as though, in another self that Barbet's presence had evoked, she were watching herself in this scene, and she began to smile and said: "Well? What do you think of her? She hasn't been a success, has she? Not that it matters. But tell me," she added, "how the devil did you run me to earth?"

"I'll tell you about that if you'll come out and eat with me. Or would you rather eat here?"

"Here?"

He presented his basket and she laughed aloud. "What did you think? Did you think I was starving?" But she took the basket on to her lap and began to unpack it. He watched her hands moving and the top of her head. As soon as she came upon grapes, she laid a bunch in her left palm and began to eat. "Oh, I'm hungry!" she exclaimed. "But I'm not starving, you know. I'm sorry—but really I'm not! Just ordinary hungry. I've been out looking for a job. Couldn't we eat here? That's what I should like. I don't want to go out again yet. Let's eat here and afterwards go to a café and talk. I'm glad you came. I didn't think I was, but I am!" At this she came upon the corkscrew. "It's new. Did you buy it?"

"I thought you might not have one."

Her eyebrows went up; her lips were pressed together; she made her face of a clown. "When will you know me, I wonder?" And while both his hands were occupied with corkscrew and bottle, she put her arm round him and laid her face for a moment against the side of his head as though she were caressing a dog. "Well," she said, taking plates out of a cupboard in the wall, "your hair still grows the same way. That's something certain in a doubtful world."

They ate the food he had brought and shared the bottle of wine. Meanwhile he tried to tell her of his adventures of last night, but could not hold her attention. She wanted him to tell her of Roussignac. Did Anton take as much at the Cheval Pie as had been taken in her day? No? Good; and what had become of Frédéric? Was he still alive? Yes? Good.

"I expect they think I've gone grand and that that is why I haven't sent any money for so long? Is that what they think?"

"No, Thérèse."

She was indignant. "Oh, so they think I've failed, do they? They think that. They'll soon learn better. I've been ill, that's all. It's not easy to get started again. But once I get a start—"

"That's what I was trying to tell you about," Barbet put in. "Last night I met a man called Cugnot. Do you know him by any chance?"

"When I've made these fools listen to me," Thérèse exclaimed, "when at *last* they wake up and see me and blink their eyes to the tune of fifteen hundred francs a week, then I'll come to Roussignac— no, I won't; I'll go to Angoulême and sing there and all of you in Roussignac shall come to me. Victor will come, and I'll sing *at* him. I know the song! I'll sing at him till he wriggles in his seat, and then I'll blow him out of it."

Barbet waited patiently. "I wish you liked people. Then they'd like you."

"I? Like people? I like almost everything if it has a taste."

"I said people—not things."

"I like people too when they aren't stupid."

"Then perhaps you'd like Cugnot."

"Should I? Listen. I want to tell you something; then you'll understand what I mean by stupid. I went to a place this afternoon to try and get work. I had sung there before. They knew me. And I knew they had a gap in their programme. But it was Eve Charreton who got the job. Do you know why? Because she grovels to them. Because in all her life she has never had one idea of her own. She's polite. She's *tact*ful. She has only one word in her vocabulary and that is: 'Yes.' She sings, she dances, she thinks—she does everything like an affable, well-oiled machine—oily with compromise! Oh dear," said Thérèse, "I like the woman too. That's odd, isn't it? I'm sorry. What were you saying of Cugnot?"

What appeared chiefly to interest her in Barbet's tale was not the individuality of Cugnot, which interested him, but the idea of Barbet's being in the Écurie at all.

"How did it happen? Strangers who wander in there except on special nights are usually—well, made to know that they are strangers. What did you do? Just walk in as if the place belonged to you and order a cognac?"

"I did order a cognac," said Barbet. A swift, astonished smile spread on his face. "And, do you know, I forgot to drink it! It never entered my mind until this moment. When Cugnot appeared, waving his arms, I must have put it down somewhere, and after that—"

"Never mind. Someone else will have drunk it for you."

"But I didn't pay for it either!"

Thérèse refilled his glass. "I shall call you Daniel," she said. "You'd be at home in a lion's den. And if they put you into a burning fiery furnace, you'd stroll about like the Shadrach trio and not a tuft of your hair would be singed. And if they shut you up in a Roman prison, you'd just walk out. What is Plence like? I've never met him. It's a kind of côterie, that place—with fringes. Once I was on the fringe but I didn't get in. Has he eyes like saucers? Has he eyes like great round towers?"

"In fact," said Barbet, "he has eyes like a very small pig's."

"What did you two talk about? What could you? You don't talk the same language."

"Oh yes we do. We talked about you."

"Me? To Plence? He's never heard of me."

"He hadn't. He has now."

"Now tell me," said Thérèse, stiff with suspicion, "what have you been saying?"

Barbet thought that he had completely forgotten what he had said on the astonishing occasion when he had heard himself become eloquent in the Écurie Plence, but now he remembered not only the substance of his comment on Thérèse but a great part of the words in which it had been expressed, and he began to say them as if he were reading from a book and reading badly. Having begun, he could not stop, though the heart had gone out of his speech long before it ended. He had expected that his opinions would be violently attacked, even that he would be interrupted, but Thérèse waited until he was done; then said, in a tone of moderation: "I could tell you why you are wrong," and was surprisingly silent.

He left his argument there and was glad to leave it. She had changed and the change in her was invalidating his criticism.

"What are you thinking?" she asked. "Why are you laughing at me? Why do you always smile at me like that when I'm serious?"

Before he could answer, her head swung round. An envelope was appearing under the door. She watched it move and watched it after it was still. Footsteps retreated.

"That ought to make one curious," she said. "It doesn't though," and she stared at the envelope without moving. "Oh, Barbet," she said, "I do so want to do ordinary things again. Is the river still there?"

"Why did you say that then?"

She looked at the envelope. "Things coming in on me, I suppose."

"Are you ill, Thérèse? Really ill, I mean."

"No. I was. I'm not now. But I haven't a job and that makes me want to—"

"To—what?"

She shook her head and turned the subject. "Do you know," she said, "*why* I'm arrogant? It's because my art is a second-hand art. It isn't like writing poetry or composing music. That is going on a voyage; my job isn't and I—"

"Thérèse, do something I ask without questioning it?"

"Yes."

"Two things."

"Yes."

"Come this evening—now, I mean, and see Cugnot."

"What will happen then?"

"Plence."

"I see. Good. Yes. And the other thing?"

"One day before I leave Paris—to-morrow or the next day— come on the river with me."

She was puzzled—then understood. "For a voyage—by bateau- mouche?"

"We could go up-river to Charenton or down-river to Auteuil."

"I should like that. It would be a change." She looked slowly round the room. "You are a funny person. I talk grandly about poetry and music and voyages, and you suggest the bateaux-mouches. You are more unlike me than anyone else. More unlike than anyone in the whole world. And yet we're the same person. Why are we?"

"Well," said Barbet, "so many people stand on their dignity—like Naaman. They swear that nothing is any good to them except the rivers of Damascus. You and I both take the nearest river—the Jordan or the Seine."

"That's because I always enjoy myself wherever I am," said Thérèse defiantly.

"Does that mean that you are happy?"

"I didn't say that. I said I enjoyed myself." She walked across the room, picked up the letter and opened it. "Well, I didn't think I should ever see that again. . . . Forty-eight francs fifty."

"Forty-eight fifty?" said Barbet in surprise.

Thérèse recounted on her fingers. "With what I have. . . . This is forty-one. . . . Now let's go to Cugnot." But she sat on her bed again. "I am tired. It's true. I was hungry, you know." She gazed at him. "If I had known an hour ago that you would be perched on that chair—well . . . And forty-one francs come home like a pigeon! . . . I always thought you were my mascot." She broke off her chatter and looked at him seriously. "I was your mascot once," she said. "I fished you out of the water. Do you remember my *al*batross?"

"I didn't understand about the albatross," Barbet confessed.

"Never mind," she said, "never mind. Albatrosses are special. Albatrosses are a *thing*. On the way to Cugnot, I'll stand my mascot a drink. Where does he live—Cugnot, I mean?"

Chapter 4

IT WAS ARRANGED THAT, ON THE DAY OF THEIR voyage, Thérèse was to take a boat from the Pont d'Austerlitz on the right bank as nearly as possible at eleven o'clock; Barbet, coming from the Jardin des Plantes, would wait on the pontoon of the Pont d'Austerlitz on the left bank; when she appeared, he would join her.

Because he would wait so patiently, she was determined not to keep him waiting, and reached the Pont d'Austerlitz at twenty minutes to eleven. Should she take an earlier boat and, having crossed the river, wait, and let him find her on his own pontoon? But she decided to stay where she was. She had imagined herself, as the boat crossed the river, leaning over the rail and waving to him. She had imagined that, when he recognized her, he would clutch at the handkerchief in his breast pocket and flourish it in the air. . . . Well, so it should be. She wouldn't cross the river until eleven had struck. She would stay where she was.

And she was content. It had been a chilly Easter—or so it had seemed to her, for her illness had been lingering then—but now spring was in the chestnut-trees and small, fat clouds were floating in the sky like the puffs of a royal salute. She went down the gangway on to the pontoon, which rocked enough in the river's movement to change the pressure of her feet from right to left, from left to right, and to give a little twist now and then to the heels of her shoes. She began to smile because she couldn't prevent herself from swaying to and fro, and she said to a little girl who was leaning over the railings:

"It's like the Pacific, isn't it?"

"No," said the little girl, "it is the Mediterranean Sea."

"Well," said Thérèse, delighted to find that her own and Barbet's belief in voyages was not an isolated faith, "you can say what you like, but for me this is the Pacific Ocean."

"No," said the little girl without turning her head, "it is the Mediterranean Sea." She stretched out an arm with so much energy that the sun shook on her finger-nail. "And over there," she exclaimed, "is Fréjus."

An old gentleman, who had been standing a yard away but so still that Thérèse had not noticed him, now turned and lifted his hat. Even this was an effort to him; his fingers groped for the brim; it was as if a wax figure had come jerkily to life; and, when the hat was off, it required too much effort of him to put it on again.

"You must forgive her, mademoiselle. She is my great-grand-daughter. It is not her fault that I am so old."

"He was twenty-one," the child asserted.

"She means, mademoiselle, that I was twenty-one at that time." And before Thérèse could speak, he added: "No, no, it is not impossible. . . . And now what they are talking of is Tonkin. I ask you, what has a Republic to do in Tonkin? . . ." His bowler was in his hand and he stared at it with surprise. "On that occasion I had, of course, a white cockade in my shako. I remember tearing it out." He clasped his fingers and neatly plucked an invisible cockade out of his bowler hat.

"Wave it round your head, grandpapa! Wave it round your head!" the child commanded, and he waved it slowly, on a stiff arm, at the level of his tie. "And now? What do you say now? Say it, grandpapa!"

He shook his head.

"But you always do. Have you forgotten?"

"No," he answered, "I have not forgotten. But you see, Andrée, this lady may not agree with us." He looked at Thérèse. Something in her face encouraged him. "And yet, after all," he said, "it's a spring morning and this is still called the Pont d'Austerlitz. It pleases the child, mademoiselle, to hear me say—but you must not shout about it, Andrée, you must be quiet!"

"To hear you say what, monsieur?"

"Tell her, tell her."

"Ah, but Andrée, you have heard it so often before. You see," he added, "it happens that I was one of the Fifth. Our officer didn't know what to do. There they came round a bend in the road and our job was to stop them. We were a battalion—right across the road, too. The man next to me saw the bearskins. 'It's the Guard!' he said. A few Lancers too. But even then I didn't see the Emperor. When the Lancers came up, we were turned about and began to retreat, but the horses were clattering in our rear. Our officer kept looking behind him; he didn't like it; he didn't like it a bit—and I don't wonder; but at last he made up his mind. We halted and turned, bayonets fixed. And there we stood. Then I saw him. Not up to my shoulder—black hat and all. The Guard had reversed their arms and he came walking out of them. My uncle had told me: 'In Russia, the wounded stopped groaning when he rode past.' We were silent too. There were two birds squabbling in the road, making the dust fly. Someone shouted: 'Fire! Fire!' Twice. If it had been said *once,* some of us would have let off. Twice was too much; more a scream than an order; no one stirred. Then he stopped. 'Men of the—' "

"And what were you thinking about?" the child prompted. "You've forgotten that."

The old man was embarrassed. "Your memory is too good, Andrée. The lady wouldn't be interested in that."

"Wouldn't she? I think it's the most interesting part."

"Well," said he, "you will excuse me, mademoiselle, the child will have the whole story. But I had been marching, I had been marching a long time, and, since the child will have it, I was thinking that my breeches were too tight in the seat. They work up, you know." Then he resumed his narrative. " 'Men of the Fifth,' the Emperor said, and then some more I didn't hear. He was opening his great-coat and I saw the green one underneath. 'If there is one of you who would kill his Emperor, here I am.' That is how to talk to French-men, mademoiselle—the Guard behind you with their arms reversed. We came round him. We touched him. We touched the Emperor; we touched the Revolution, you understand. They touched his sword, his boots, and I said to myself: I will touch his hat, and I touched his hat. And I said to myself : I shall remember, and I do remember."

"And you shouted—?"

"Vive l'Empereur!"

"And that night at Grenoble? Go on, go on."

"That night at Grenoble there was a woman singing—no, no, Andrée, you must not sing it here."

But the child sang it :

> " 'Bon! Bon!
> Napoléon
> Va rentrer dans sa maison.' "

Thérèse, her eyes shining, her voice hushed and deepened by the joys of conspiracy, sang it with her. They joined hands and danced together.

"That," said Thérèse, a little breathless, "gives me an idea for a song. Thank you, monsieur. Songs are my job, you know. This is my lucky day." And she began experimentally to feel her way into a little verse with Barbet's name in it but the form and turn of the child's song. The rhymes were haphazard but they would come. "Va rentrer dans sa maison!" she concluded. "If I can get it right, that song goes everywhere. You can sing it about all the world—living or dying."

"And who is Barbet, mademoiselle?"

"You, me, everyone. What France is and what the French laugh at—at least, they will if I can make them. He can be the subject of twenty songs—all different!"

"Where is Monsieur Barbet?" asked the little girl.

"Over there. Across the river. Or he will be soon."

"Then you will be taking this boat," said the soldier of the Fifth.

"Not this one. The next. He's not there yet."

"Au revoir, then, mademoiselle. I wish you luck in the Pacific."

"And I you, monsieur, in the Mediterranean Sea."

They bowed. They smiled.

"Please, who are you?" said the little girl.

"Thérèse Despreux."

"Are you famous? May I touch you?"

The boat came and went with a great rocking of the pontoon and Thérèse was alone again. Everything is changed when one is happy, everything except the knowledge that to be happy is a kind of madness, that sanity will return as clouds return, that the instant is a gleam—you stretch out your hands to feel the sun on them and you say: there is the sun, I feel it. I am happy. I am alive. Thérèse stretched out her hands and turned them in the sun. She walked into the little shelter that stood on the pontoon. Though its sides were open, a stuffiness of old tar clung to it. She liked the smell and sniffed it. She liked the foolish, friendly advertisements with which the shelter was plastered and read them again and again as though they were personal to her and would not have been there, or would have been in some way different, if yesterday her fortunes had not suddenly taken a turn, if she had not seen Plence and captured him, if she—if to-day were not set apart for her voyage with Barbet. One of them was an omen. There were omens everywhere. The old man had been an omen—Bon! bon! Napoléon—but this placard for pianos was pointing the finger of fortune at her. "Pianos. A. Bord." A familiar piano, made by the industrious gentleman of that name. But to-day it ought to have meant, and for a fantastic instant it did mean, that there would be a piano on board the steamboat and that she and Barbet would make their voyage to music.

Other intending passengers gathered on the pontoon. When the steamer came, it had begun already to be crowded. Thérèse found a place forward on the port side, and before the river was half crossed became aware of a young man with small, fluffy whiskers who was hovering near her. He supposed that she was alone and it amused her that he should for a minute or two continue to suppose it. Therefore, when he smiled and plucked up courage to say it was a fine morning, she agreed with the utmost friendliness. To-day she was exempt from men; she liked them the better for it, and at this young man, who had elbowed his way to her side like a shy puppy determined to be noticed, she looked without any emotion except of liking for another human being with a gay voice and the sun in his eyes. What surprised her was his response. He seemed to become aware at once that the adventure he had planned with her would come to nothing. His glance came down to inquire what rings she was wearing and returned to her face, baffled by her gloves. He decided that he had made a mistake, and strove to apologize without too foolishly confessing a need for apology.

"Well," she said to help him, "why should you think you are intruding? It's your spring day as well as mine."

"Yes, madame, but you see I—"

"You wanted someone to share it with you? That isn't unpardonable."

"No, madame. You are very kind. But, you see, I—I'm afraid I—"

"I wish you'd tell me something."

"If I can, of course I—"

"Why did you hit on me? . . . No, tell me. My nose, my eyes, my hat—what was it?"

He took a breath. "It was your back, madame."

"Ah! now you're telling me the truth. And what made you change your mind? You did change your mind quite suddenly. Why did you decide that I wouldn't do?"

"Madame, it wasn't that! It was only—"

"What made you decide that I didn't *want* to do?"

He threw up his hands. "My God, you are like the Recording Angel!"

"Angel will do," she said. "Now answer my question."

"It was—it was—I don't know."

"Yes, you do. Did I look married?"

He shrugged his shoulders.

"Or betrothed?"

He smiled.

"Or a nun?"

"I will tell you," he cried. "I will tell you. It was that you were so friendly, so easy, you looked so happy, so content that I—"

"Content," she repeated. "Happy— And you are not, monsieur?"

At once he fell in love with her and began to tell her the story of his life.

"Now listen," she said. "I like you. Good-bye."

As the steamer approached the left bank, those who were waiting for it on the pontoon began to move aimlessly, a step in one direction, a step in another, and Barbet appeared among them because he was still. While they hustled their way up the gangway, he waited, then followed them.

"What are you smiling at?" Thérèse asked.

"It's in your face that you have good news."

"Good heavens, what has happened to my face? It seems to be giving everything away this morning." She looked into his eyes. "Is it really a different face from the one you found in the Rue Lilas?"

"Certainly it is. You have had a long night's sleep, and you went to sleep looking forward to to-day. Isn't that true?"

"That's because I was coming with you on a voyage," she answered. "That's because I like being taken charge of. I hope you are going to pay for everything. Are you? Then it's a real holiday. Oh, and there is good news too."

Houses, grey and dirty cream and sepia, flowed in and out of sight as the steamer plodded on down the river. The domes of Paris shone, wheeled, vanished and appeared again. The sooty arch of a bridge, blotting out the sunshine for an instant, turned all faces upward, to be dazzled, a moment later, by the keen and chalky blue of the sky. Meanwhile she told him her news. Cugnot had taken her to Plence. Plence had been tired and sceptical but had given her an audition. She had sung, told stories, performed a monologue.

"A monologue?"

"Well, a kind of play, but all the other actors are made of air. I did one about a lodging with three beds in it. I am a shop-girl. I come in very late. The other two are in bed. I begin to talk about the people who come to the shop I work in—the women, and the men they bring with them—and the others talk about men too, only you don't hear what they say—you guess that from my answers; and then—"

"Who wrote it?"

"No one wrote it. It isn't written. But I made it up. It varies a bit each time. There are dozens more—long ones, short ones—politics, tarts, mashers, washerwomen, thieves. You see, I can listen. I know how they speak. I can tell Paris things about itself. Plence asked me what I called my monologues. They hadn't a name; I had to make one up. So I said: 'They're called Petits Chevaux, after the Écurie. Anyhow they will be if you give me a job.' He didn't say anything to that. I thought he might have smiled, but he didn't. You're quite right. His eyes do *look* like a very small pig's, but they are a connoisseur's eyes. It's like the first time you strip for a painter, only for Plence you don't need to strip. He made me go on and on. 'More,' he said. 'More. . . . Another song.' Then he stood up and said to Cugnot: 'Well, the Grand Prix?' and to me he said: 'Good.' He made a little cup with his hand. 'You can have Paris,' he said and his fingers closed. Then at last he did smile. 'But no one knows it yet,' he said. 'That's where I come in. Now sit down there. You can appear at the Théâtre Plence six nights a week.' I said: 'But it's not open six nights a week.' 'It will be now,' he said. 'I'll gamble on you, young woman.' He offered me a month's engagement and twenty francs a night—his option to extend. I stuck at the option. In the end I said: 'If you want it, another two months at thirty. After that a new contract.' He grinned. 'Bon!' Then we had drinks. Cugnot's girl came in to look for him. I took fifty francs advance off Plence. He liked that. Then I paid for drinks. He liked that too. I didn't think he'd let me pay for them in his own place—but he did. Those little piggy eyes! We understand each other, Plence and I. I can work for him. He appreciates me. Are you glad?"

"I'm very proud, Thérèse."

"Proud? You do say queer things. You make me feel as if I were a schoolgirl who had come home with a prize. And yet," she added, "you're only ten years older than I am."

"Anyhow," said Barbet, "having won your prize, you can enjoy your holiday."

It was among the pleasures of their journey that it was slow and that no limit to it was prescribed. They had spoken of going to the Pont du Jour and so into the Bois de Boulogne, but before they reached the Tuileries they heard that they might without delay have another steamer there which would take them beyond Auteuil to St. Cloud or Suresnes, and at Barbet's suggestion they changed into it.

"Why did you suddenly decide against Auteuil?" Thérèse asked. "Don't you like it?"

"There's nothing against Auteuil," he answered, "but I wanted to go on. I have never been by river round the bend at Sèvres. And anyhow," he added, "I wanted to go on. Some day we'll do it differently. We will start by train and go to Bougival or St. Germain or Mantes and find a boat there. But to-day—you know, Thérèse, I was afraid you'd hate the bateaux-mouches; the crowd, the staring and stopping, and—"

"I have a friend," she said, "who owns barges. If we went in a barge and took long enough we could go by water all the way to Rouen, and then we could find a steamer and go to Le Havre, and then we could find another steamer and go to America, and when we were tired of America we should meet a magician who gave us one wish. At first nothing would happen, and then—and then we should find ourselves in this little boat opposite the Trocadéro. Why are you happy, Barbet?"

"Well," he answered with surprise, "in the first place we are in this little boat opposite the Trocadéro; in the second place, it's a fine day; in the third—"

"No," she interrupted, "I don't mean now—not *now* particularly. I mean, why are you a happy man?"

"Look," he said, pointing over the side. "Do you see that?"

"The river?"

"I mean the wake. It's all the same to me whether it's an Atlantic liner or a bateau-mouche. I like being able to leave things behind. Not to be entangled."

"By women?"

He raised his shoulders. "Or anything else. Property. Ambition—"

"I'm ambitious," she said. "I'm greedy, I suppose. You're lucky. Your life is all made for you. You haven't anything to be ambitious about. Are you celibate too?"

"For some time I have been in practice," he answered with a smile. "But I'm not in theory a celibate, if that's what you mean."

"Nor am I," she said, her eyes smiling. "You don't hate me for it?"

"No, Thérèse."

"But you'd think more of me if I were in practice? No, you needn't answer that. No! No! No!" she added when she saw his lips moving. "I don't want you to answer it. Not this morning anyway."

At St. Cloud they hesitated. The steamer would go on to Suresnes and they were sorry to leave it, but Thérèse's hunger decided them and soon they were seated in an open pergola at the riverside eating small fish from the Seine. When their meal was over and their coffee finished, they ordered more coffee as an excuse to sit longer at their pink-check tablecloth and watch the leaf-shadows flicker on their plates, but presently Thérèse stretched herself and said: "I feel well to-day. Let's walk. Can we walk? I feel so well I don't know what to do with it."

"Keep it, Thérèse."

She stood beside the table, her limbs taut, her face alight. "I don't want to *keep* anything. I want to spend it. In fifty years' time, where shall I be?"

To this he made no answer, for with the girl who waited on him he had been discussing the further reaches of the Seine—whether there were steamers to be had down-river—and she had answered that there was none until you came to Rouen whence you might go by water to Le Havre.

"Nothing between Suresnes and Rouen?" Barbet had said, and the girl had answered well, there might be an odd steamer here and there; she would ask the proprietor; and now he had come out with the bill and a piece of blue paper on which was written in a flourishing roundhand: "Horaire des Paquebots."

"Then there is a morning boat from Mantes to Vernon," Barbet said. "The question is how to get to Mantes."

"To-day?" said Thérèse. "We can't go to Mantes to-day. And anyhow this isn't the morning."

"But we could to-morrow."

"To-morrow! To-morrow! To-morrow!" she exclaimed.

"There is only one way to Mantes, monsieur. You take the train from the Gare St. Lazare," said the owner of the restaurant, gathering up Barbet's money. "Afterwards it is a charming voyage, mademoiselle, and worth the journey. I have made it myself many a time. Until two years ago—until my wife died—we lived at Mantes. She was born there. Here, yes, it is pretty, it is gay—but the river at Mantes and Vernon—ah, that is something to remember. The steamer is not large, but she is enchanting. If you are on the bank you hear her coming because the young men play their mandolins. Instead of a figure-head she has a great S with a line across it and her name is Gabrielle—Gabrielle d'Estrées. And the skipper, his name is Henri; we called him Henri Quatre. Tell him, mademoiselle, that you are a friend of mine and he will let you work the engine-room telegraph."

They made their way out of the restaurant and into the park of St. Cloud.

"Last time I was here, the château was standing," Barbet said, looking about him for remembrances of the past.

"Where has it gone?" said Thérèse, and Barbet told her that it had not been spirited away; it had been burned in '70; but she did not listen, she was living in the hour and stopped and threw up her head to sweep with her eyes the avenue of chestnuts, as though the sky were her canvas and she painting them.

"The great fountain isn't playing!" she exclaimed and turned away from it in indignation, but as they went up the path dividing the cascade, she said, from a long silence:

"I wonder whether he will?"

"Who? What?"

She was surprised that his thought had not marched with hers. "Mantes . . . Henri Quatre. . . . Do you think he will let me work the engine-room telegraph? When shall we go to Mantes, Barbet?"

"I thought you hated plans?"

"This isn't a plan—it's a resolve. It's more than a resolve—it's certain; it has almost happened. . . . Do you ever feel that? I felt it while he was talking. Sometimes people tell you about places and you know you won't ever go there and so you don't listen. That's why I could never learn geography. But sometimes you know you will. Then it becomes important. . . . I suppose I'm being selfish and arrogant? Am I?"

"Well," Barbet said, "there's a kind of genius that selects from life what it can use and spits out everything else."

She laughed at him. "Is there another kind?"

"I think there is."

After hesitation, she answered: "You mean the genius that knows how to be used, and is proud and humble at the same time."

"Do you despise it, Thérèse?"

"No," she said. "I'm not a fool. But it's not for me. Why should I let people use me—Plence, for instance? That's what I call taking it lying down. I can't take life lying down. Of course he can use me now. I don't mind. That's part of the game. But gradually, because I'm aliver than he is, I shall use him more and more, and some day—" Her mind shifted. "While the man was talking," she continued abruptly, "I saw that steamer quite clearly. I could draw the landing-stage for you and he didn't even mention that. It's no good saying we shan't go there, because we shall. When shall we?"

"Three days from now."

"But, Barbet, oughtn't you to have work to do?"

"That will be a Sunday—the day before I go south again."

Thérèse counted on her fingers. "Friday, Saturday, Sunday. When I wake up on Sunday, the first thing that will come into my head will be—do you know that too? You're just awake enough to know you're happy but not yet to know why. And I shall say to myself: Barbet's still in Paris. I have a job. And then I shall say: This morning I am going to Mantes for the first time, for the *first* time!"

"What do you mean, Thérèse?"

"Only that it's important."

"What is?"

"Mantes. Some day, when I'm very famous and dead, someone will write about me: 'That Sunday she went to Mantes for the first time.' Will you keep that piece of paper?"

"Which piece of paper?"

" 'Horaire des Paquebots.' " He took it from his pocket and offered it to her. "No," she said. "I want *you* to keep it. Keep it with that letter of mine you bought from Hurtaux. Is that arrogant too? I believe in helping one's biographer—Napoleon did. Poor boy, think of him, sitting at a table fifty years from now with a pen in his hand and maps of Paris all round him and photographs and notes and the *words* of songs and—he won't have a chance. He won't even have been to *bed* with me! He won't know what the Cheval Pie smelt like and if you don't know smells you don't really know anything. And now," she said, "I'm tired of fountains and waterworks and terraces and views of Paris. I want to go over there, beyond those trees. Do you see that copse with two poplars in the middle like a rabbit's ears? I want to go there and sleep. I'm tired."

They went to the place she had chosen and lay down there, not in the shade but in the full sun. She lay on her back, her face covered by an arm thrown up.

"Even with you," she said, "I tear myself to pieces, talking and talking. I hear myself talking. I don't really care about my biographer. But I say I do, and I hear myself say it, and I can't stop. I want you to keep the piece of paper, but not for that reason. And the bit about smells *was* true! That is why this afternoon is different from any other afternoon. There's a bonfire somewhere, and bonfires are autumn and this is spring . . . Now, you talk to me."

She lifted her head, blinked in the sun and gazed at him.

"Talk to me," she said. "You can tell me the truth if you like, though even you make me angry when you disagree with me. Tell me a story. Or tell me about birds. Or why you're not dull even when you say nothing. Or why you're not afraid and I am."

"What are you afraid of, Thérèse?"

"I'm not afraid," she cried, sitting upright. "I didn't say that. Yes, I did, I did, I did. I'm afraid because there are two of me, and they go about joined, except sometimes when I'm asleep. I shall go to sleep now."

She lay down and he was silent. When he thought that, under her covering arm, she was already asleep, she said:

"Say aloud the poem I know best in the world."

"Which, Thérèse?"

"About voyages."

He began: *"Heureux qui, comme Ulysse—"*

"But I suppose," she said sleepily, "that isn't really about a voyage. It's not about Gabrielle d'Estrées. It's about coming home again."

"That is what all voyages are about," he answered.

"Perhaps they are. Say it, then."

> *"Heureux qui, comme Ulysse, a fait un beau voyage,*
> *Ou comme cestuy là qui conquist la Toison,*
> *Et puis est retourné, plein d'usage et raison*
> *Vivre entre ses parents le reste de son aage!*
>
> *"Quand revoiray-je, hélas! de mon petit village*
> *Fumer la cheminée, et en quelle saison*
> *Revoiray-je le clos de ma pauvre maison*
> *Qui m'est une province, et beaucoup d'avantage?*
>
> *"Plus me plaist le sejour qu'ont basty mes ayeux,*
> *Que des palais romains le front audacieux:*
> *Plus que le marbre dur, me plaist l'ardoise fine.*
>
> *"Plus mon Loyre gaulois, que le Tybre latin,*
> *Plus mon petit Lyré, que le mont Palatin,*
> *Et plus que l'air marin, le doulceur angevine."*

When it was done, he believed again that she was asleep.

"You won't go?" she said, stretching out a hand to touch him.

"No."

"You will be here when I wake up?"

"Yes, Thérèse."

"Promise?"

"I promise."

"Thank you. Good night."

She took down her arm and opened her eyes. "That was pathos. I suppose you knew I was acting then? . . . Was I? I wish I knew."

She turned on to her side and pillowed her face upon her elbow.

Chapter 5

"I LIKE THE MAN," SAID MADELEINE, "AND I DON'T want the girl to make a fool of him."

Cugnot, on the edge of his model-throne, cleaning his brushes in preparation for an afternoon's work, answered that she could be at peace on Barbet's account; he was well able to take care of himself.

"There are chinks in any armour," she replied, "and if there's a man inside you can trust Thérèse to find them."

"Barbet doesn't wear armour."

"So much the worse."

"On the contrary," said Cugnot, "so much the better. He travels light. I remember once, when I was in Vienna, going to a performance of *A Midsummer-Night's Dream*. I was a boy. I had a high standard in fairies, and I thought very little of those on the stage. They skipped and jumped and floated on wires, but you knew very well that if you pinched them they'd squeal, and if you slapped them on the back, they'd gasp like mortals. But Oberon was different from the rest. He had been a dancer, I think. When the lovers were chasing one another in the wood, he was among them continually without being visible to them. And this Oberon did give an impression that he was invisible and intangible. I remember one moment in particular. There was a knot of lovers and he in the middle. I remember thinking: 'They'll bump into him and that will spoil everything.' And suddenly he glided through them as if he were made of air. Through them and back again, in and out, as if there were nothing of him they could ever touch or catch hold of—as if he really were free."

"And you think Barbet is a fairy?" she asked with irony.

"Not at all. That's why I like him. He eats and drinks and works like the rest of us, and, unless I'm mistaken, when he was a soldier, he must have been a good man to have in your company. It is possible to be free without being a fairy or a monk. Good heavens," Cugnot added, "don't I know it myself! I am a liberated being when I drink absinthe. Then I am capable at any moment of dying and being born again. That's how I know that freedom exists. The difficulty is to be free consistently, to be free when you're sober, always to be free."

"It depends on what you mean by freedom," Madeleine said.

"That at any rate is plain enough," Cugnot began, but he hesitated, squeezing out the brush he held. "It means," he said, "it means, among other things that are perhaps the concern of heaven, being able to put down this brush and walk out of this room and not to feel that I have to return—not to feel that I am on a piece of elastic that will make me want to come back."

"Not even to paint?"

"No. Nor to lie with you. Nor to bury the dead."

"Do you want that? There's no one to stop you. You aren't a prisoner."

"No," he answered. "I don't want it. Not only that—I am incapable of accepting it. I should be afraid of making a fool of myself. That's why I need you to look after me. But Barbet doesn't, I assure you."

"We shall see," said Madeleine. "It's time you began work."

"She's not here yet. She's not due for five minutes."

"Who?"

"Thérèse."

"Is she coming? For what?"

"A portrait."

"Why?"

"Because, Madeleine, in a month or two I shall be able to sell it more easily than any picture I have ever painted. And because she has screwed out of Plence all the advance she can get and needs money to tide her over. And because the head interests me. Do you object?"

"No. . . . You were painting me. It's unfinished."

"I shall finish it."

"You finish nothing. You begin and begin. Why do you finish nothing?"

"Because," he said, "though I have a pinch of salt to put on the tail of genius, I am not a great man. If I were, your occupation would be gone."

"I believe you are a great man."

"Ah!" he answered, "it is part of your occupation to say so."

Throughout the afternoon, while Cugnot was beginning his portrait of Thérèse, Madeleine sat in an upright chair, her fingers playing with the tattered fringe that hung from its upholstered arms. It was his habit to neglect her, to treat her, when it pleased him, as if she did not exist, and it was her power over him that she could without resentment, and, indeed, with a unique pride, be neglected.

Thérèse, as she entered, said at once that, when her engagement began at the Écurie, her life would begin again. She would do her hair as it was done to-day, with a plain twist low on the neck, and she would wear what she called her uniform. She had brought it with her. In it she would be painted.

"If it is what I want to paint," said Cugnot.

"No," she answered, "in that or not at all."

"Am I painting to your commission or are you a professional model?"

"I am a professional model," she replied at once. "I will do whatever else you tell me. I will sit for the figure. I will take any pose, however hard, and I'll hold it. I'm not an amateur. I'll give you your money's worth. But if you are going to paint my portrait, then you must paint *me*. And this is me!" She ripped off the string from the cardboard box in which she had brought her chosen clothes. "This is Thérèse Despreux. If you don't paint me in it, you won't be able to sell the picture when I'm famous. Why don't you want to paint me in it? You haven't seen it yet."

"My God," said Cugnot, "put it on. If I didn't like you, I should hate you."

She put on a taut black dress of wool finely woven; a pair of mittens in crimson silk—"They go," she said, "with the décor of the

Écurie"—and crimson shoes. "You see," she said, stroking the long sleeves, "I am completely covered and yet—" She stretched herself within the skin of the dress to complete the sentence. "Now, you choose the light. I will give you the pose."

She was a good model. She stood upright with a challenge in her body, as though she were about to sing, and, while she stood, she sang in her mind, song after song, her eyes quick with ideas, her lips for ever about to move under the imagined words. When she was given her first rest, she began to talk at once. They knew she had been with Barbet to St. Cloud; to-morrow she was going with him to Mantes.

"At St. Cloud," she said, "I went to sleep on the grass. Did I tell you? The sun was hot, right through my clothes, hot on my body. And when I woke up it was gone."

"Well, Thérèse, what is the point of that story?"

She looked at Cugnot with astonishment; then smiled. "I suppose there isn't a point for you. I'm sorry. I leave gaps always. What I meant was that hours had passed; everything was changed; the trees looked different, and the smell of wood-smoke—I'd smelt it before— but now it was a twilight smell; and I shuddered, everything was so altered, so new and sudden, but he was still there." She had shut her eyes while she was speaking, and now opened them.

"You are in love with him," said Madeleine.

Thérèse gazed at her. "I? With Barbet?"

And, Madeleine turning to Cugnot, said: "You didn't bargain for that. Even Oberon was caught by that."

"What do you mean? What are you talking about?" Thérèse cried.

Cugnot picked up a brush. "Why are you going to Mantes?" he said. "Take the pose again."

Chapter 6

WHETHER ON SUNDAYS OR ON WEEK-DAYS THE train that gave the best connexion with the steamer at Mantes left the Gare St. Lazare at 10:31. At half-past ten Thérèse came on to the platform and found Barbet waiting beside the compartment he had chosen.

"What should you have done if I hadn't come?"

"Waited," said Barbet.

As soon as she was in her place, the train moved out. She was wearing a pale straw hat with trailing ribbons of deep violet. This she took off and allowed her head to fall back on to the upholstery; at the same time her feet came forward a few inches and small-toed boots with uppers of violet silk appeared from under her dress. There were little crevices in the leather and over her left instep the silk was split. Remembering this, she withdrew her feet.

The noise of the train in leaving the station made it impossible to be heard, and Barbet was glad; he did not wish to speak, for her eyes had a dangerous, sullen and hostile brightness like a glaze. He felt that he was intruding upon an animal in its lair.

At last, in recollection of what she had said at St. Cloud, he asked what she had thought of when she woke this morning—had she remembered that she was going to Mantes?

"Of course I remembered. If I hadn't, I shouldn't be here, should I?"

There was so little graciousness in this, that Barbet was silent. He was in happy mood; he wished to be friendly and light-hearted; and the best thing to do with the impatiences of Thérèse was to wait until they were over. But she had no intention that this impatience should die quietly; she wished to spend it. She looked away from him, then swiftly back and away again, expectant of his questioning, and when she found that he would ask no questions, there was nothing left for her to do but to answer them.

"I had three hours' sleep last night."

"Why only three?" asked Barbet politely.

"Because I had to catch the 10:31 at the Gare St. Lazare."

Barbet looked at the back gardens which, at that moment, were passing under his window, then at her. The bones under her eyes and the sliced shadow thrown by them on to her cheeks were accentuated, as though she had a fever, and her hands could not be still. From the row of spherical buttons which ran between her waist and the spray of black lace at her breast, there sprang out a series of fine creases, like creases in the bark of a sapling, which communicated the spring and suppleness of her body.

"You must be very tired."

"Do I look tired?"

"Your eyes, yes; but not—"

"That's absinthe," she said. "With Cugnot and Philippe de Courcelet. It does me good. I'm not a bit tired by that. I'm never tired when I enjoy myself. But I sat for him yesterday—a standing pose, as if I were singing. When the sky clouded over and the light became bad, he had to stop painting. We had some coffee and afterwards he turned on the gas and said he would do a drawing of the figure." She waited for him to scold her, and, when he did not, continued as if he had.

"I went to him as a professional model. I needed the money. He paid me. I like to be given orders by people entitled to give them. There was no question of minding or not minding. I did what I was told. When I was half undressed, Courcelet came, so I covered myself up and—"

"Who is Monsieur de Courcelet?"

"Philippe de Courcelet! I thought you would at least know that. He collects pictures. He was in an embassy somewhere—Rome, I think, or Madrid. Since then he has been a politician. He has never taken office himself. He won't. For that reason, everyone eats out of his hand. They all go to him when they want to know anything.

They call him The Barometer. He amuses me." She paused again for a question and, receiving none, continued: "He must be fifty. Almost sixty, perhaps. Terribly good-looking—black hair, white streaks and edges, eyes that *look* at you, and vain—so vain it's endearing. And no conscience at all. That's a relief. Anyhow he's amusing. He looked at me as if"—and she raised her voice on the deliberate phrase—"as if I were an Ingres."

Even this did not stir Barbet to curiosity.

"I stood there with a wrap round me while we were introduced," she went on. "Courcelet and Cugnot began to talk together as if I were a part of the furniture, so I sat down and waited. Courcelet had come in to see Cugnot's canvas of the Gare du Nord and to ask him out to dinner. Then he said: 'But I won't interrupt your work. It's early. I'll smoke a cigar. Go on with your drawing.' When Cugnot said his drawing wasn't begun yet, Courcelet looked at me again and said, 'A new model?' and Cugnot stood beside his easel and picked up a piece of charcoal and nodded at me. So I showed myself, and when I had turned round and stretched and bent and taken some trial poses and stood there waiting for Cugnot to tell me what he wanted, I saw Courcelet's eyebrows go up. 'A beautiful body, if I may say so. More than a right angle under the breasts and the nipples placed high. Extremely rare.' Then he smiled at me. 'No, no, mademoiselle. I am, as it were, studying a picture. I consider you as if you were an Ingres.'"

She looked at Barbet, hoping that he would be dazzled by this remark, but it appeared to have made no effect upon him.

"Anyhow," she continued, "they took me and Madeleine out to dinner. Afterwards we went to Courcelet's rooms in the Palais Royal. I sang for them."

"Successfully?"

"Very. Why?"

"A man in Courcelet's position can do a lot to help you."

"I don't want his help. I don't want anyone's help. What I do, I will do alone."

There was a long silence.

"He is going to bring parties and parties of people when I am at the Écurie. . . . And now why don't you say that that *is* helping me? I gave you the chance. Why don't you say it?"

"Because I hoped you'd get away from the whole subject."

"From Philippe de Courcelet? Why should you object to him? Why should you?"

"I don't. I wasn't thinking of him. I meant only that there's to-day to talk about instead of last night."

At that she paused. When she continued, it was with an increased defiance.

"He took me round his rooms and showed me his books. When we were stooping over a book together, he said out of the corner of his mouth: 'Go away with the others. Shake them off. Then come back.'"

Barbet waited.

"I wanted to," she said.

"He attracted you?"

"I like him. He amuses me. He is so dignified and so vain that—" She began to laugh and laughed uncontrollably. "But I didn't. I expect I shall, but I didn't then. I stayed, but I made Cugnot and Madeleine stay too. But I shan't always. Why should I? You think that because I enjoy going on the river with you and because I *was* hungry when you found me in the Rue Lilas, and because it was through you that I got to know Plence at all—you think that it's wrong of me to—"

"Thérèse, I have said nothing."

"You think it all the same. You think I ought to live like a nun. Well, I don't and never have. Long before I left Angoulême—before I left Roussignac, if it comes to that—"

"I know."

"What do you know? You think you do, but you don't and it's just as well that you should."

All the way to Mantes she told him of the lovers she had had—how one had served for an hour, another for a fortnight, how each had believed that he possessed her, how she had adored them all while they lasted; how she despised the race of men, how she delighted in their company, their violence, their shames, their flatteries.

She repeated their long-dead conversations, and described their clothing, their nakedness, their most intimate and ridiculous habits, with
the relish of a prima donna who tells how the small fry of the stage
have existed as a background to her triumphs and humiliations. She
turned over each episode in her mind with the unresting agony of one
whose hoard is of false jewels known to be false. She jangled and
boasted them; flashed them in her own eyes and in his. She lay down
upon her past and licked it with the dreadful obsession of a cat
licking fur.

"I think this is Mantes," said Barbet as the train began to slow
down. "You will need your parasol. It's probably a little way to
the landing-stage and the sun is hot."

"I haven't a parasol. I pawned it," she answered. "It was given
to me—by the music-master in Angoulême. It had an ivory knob."
And she told again, as though she had not already told it, the story
of the music-master whose merits had been that he never disagreed
with her.

"Didn't that make it dull?"

"Dull? Why? I like people who like what I like."

In the street outside the railway station they walked in silence.
How long will this silence go on? he thought. What can I say that
will not insult her? He was watching the dust shake on the welt of
his boot, when she said: "You won't believe it now. But I am worth
loving."

He answered: "I do believe it."

"Do you? Why? You must be a fool."

On the steamer, tucking into the opening of her glove the ticket
he had bought, she remarked casually, as though it were of no consequence: "What Cugnot said is true."

"What did he say?"

"After we left Courcelet's we were drunk. We walked miles. In
the Rue de Chazelles we saw an impossible thing—an enormous
woman out of the sky looking at us over the roofs of the houses. Cugnot shouted: 'Look. It is the end of the world!' 'Nonsense,' said
Madeleine, 'it is the Statue of Liberty that they will send to America.'
Cugnot began to laugh. He laughed and laughed. He was disap-

pointed. He had thought that it really *was* the end of the world. When he found it wasn't, he became sober and said: 'That man of yours, that Barbet, he is a fool. He would take the end of the world as a matter of course—which indeed it is.' Then Cugnot turned up his coat collar, a huge brown collar. His face inside it was white and shiny like a split walnut after you've peeled it. We walked home. He took my arm and hugged it to him as if he were cold. 'Oh yes,' he said, 'he's a complete fool, he came out of the mirror. In this life some condemn and some forgive us, but it takes a fool to know that we are innocent."

"That's mostly fine talk," said Barbet. "It's simpler than that. Forgiveness after the event doesn't amount to much. Love begins at the beginning, that's all. If it didn't, you and I and Cugnot would have a poorish chance at the end of the world. But fortunately," he added, "this isn't the end of the world. To-day I'm going to Vernon for the first time."

"Happy?"

He nodded. "And you?"

"I'm never happy. But I enjoy myself!"

"Why not happy, Thérèse?"

"For the same reason that I enjoy myself: because I'm always hungry, I suppose."

In the side-pocket of his jacket, his hand closed over a small case containing two packs of cards. I wish she'd play piquet with me, he thought, but probably that would bore her. I have never played piquet with her. I don't even know whether she plays.

The paddles were beginning to turn and he did not ask. His fingers came upon another parcel which surprised him. What a fool I am, he thought, I'd clean forgotten it, and he handed it to her.

"What is it?"

"I believe it's a patch-box."

"What for?"

"For you."

She unwrapped it. "Oh," she exclaimed, "lilies of the valley! You are good to me. You are—why now? When I've been bad. You ought to have beaten me. Why do you give it to me now?"

"Well, that was luck."

"Is it really true," she said, "that you love me? You—*me*? I don't see how you can. Oh!" she exclaimed, "I'd do anything for you."

"Well," he said, "would you play piquet with me? We could play on that bench, in the lee of deck-house. Or would that bore you?"

"Bore me? I like to be asked for things. I do like people who know what they want."

Barbet was not easily surprised by the seeming inconsistencies of men and women which make their pattern; but he discovered with delight a new aspect of Thérèse in the course of that day's journey— a Thérèse whose energy of mind was gradually withdrawn from bitterness and rebellion because it was directed away from herself.

She asked again how it could be true that he loved her who had nothing, or almost nothing, in common with him, and added another question: if he had no ambition and no wish for power, what was he driving at? to what did he look forward? He tried to tell her of his feeling that his life and hers and the lives of his prisoners were parts of a single life which—

"Oh," she interrupted with her old impulse, "I was educated as a Catholic. I believe in an after-life," but he said that he wasn't speaking of an after-life only, but of a present life.

"Do you mean," she answered, "that while you and I live our separate lives here, we are at the same time—now, at this moment— living another life?"

"I think so. After all, when we sleep, we don't cease altogether to be aware of the waking life we left behind. And wherever we are— in Paris, in the vineyards, or leaning on the rail of this boat and watching that barge go up-stream, we don't forget completely the life we left behind when we were born. We are living it now, sometimes more, sometimes less, and—"

"If that were true," she said, "the differences between you and me wouldn't matter, and—what would happen to wars and poverty if that were true?"

Barbet watched her eager, changing face. There was challenge in her tone; she was sharpening her mind on him and was happy in the experiment.

"I don't suppose they'd cease," he answered. "It *is* true, and they haven't ceased; but if we could really feel that other life—I mean, feel it like a pulse beating—we should at least know from what we are cut off by the split in our life here, and in the end we might grow out of it. Children fight for toys while they are children —real battles; they value their toys, they are bound to them; and a few years later—there they all are—piled up, disused, in a cupboard."

"My trouble," said Thérèse, "is that I *like* toys. I have never had enough of them. I don't want to put them in a cupboard."

They had been passing through Vétheuil; the long, cultivated island beyond the town was falling away on their quarter; a small boy, naked to the waist, with blue breeches low on his thighs, stood to wave a glistening arm.

"If it were really true," she persisted with stubborn independence, "I mean—if you felt completely that you and I and the prisoners and the birds were all living another common life outside our separate lives here, would there be any point in keeping the prisoners shut up?"

"None," said Barbet.

"Then it's not true? You don't feel it completely?"

"It is true," Barbet said, "but I am not a complete man. You see," he added, "I am also an ignorant man. For a Frenchman, I have read very little, and I am not a Catholic. But I shall learn. The birds have taught me. And you, Thérèse, have taught me."

"I? I have taught you? How?"

"You can laugh at me," he replied, "but you have taught me as the birds have—by being so different from me. If there were only our differences, I couldn't love you, Thérèse. There's everything on earth to divide us and nothing that anyone else could see to bring us together except our songs. And perhaps I don't love you as men love women who share their lives, but I love you."

"As a lover?"

"You mean, do I desire you? Yes, very often when I am near you, but that isn't what I was thinking about."

"And yet, you know," she answered, "no one would believe that you were thinking about anything else. Cugnot thinks already that I am your mistress—or that I have been. No one ever gives me the benefit of the doubt, or would suppose that you of all men could want to be with me for any other reason. That's what will be said in Roussignac. 'Poor fool, what does he see in her? He has been bewitched by the tart from Angoulême!' And other people, I dare say, will wonder what on earth Thérèse Despreux sees in you. You will be credited with a hundred obscure vices. My poor Barbet, if you are to be seen with me at all, you might as well be hanged for a sheep as for a lamb."

They decided not to go as far as Vernon but to leave the Gabrielle d'Estrées at La Roche Guyon and wait for her return in the early evening. As they walked up from the landing-stage, Thérèse halted in the middle of the road to gaze at the castle of La Rochefoucauld. Everything they saw, a light on the trees, a gleam on the river, two pairs of initials carved on the bark of a tree, seemed to them precious and ephemeral, and in answer to the farewell that all happiness begins to whisper as soon as it is recognized, they said to each other: "We will come here again."

"But we shall come here often," she exclaimed. "For us this isn't the last time."

And suddenly their melancholy was gone.

"It's the first time. Often and often we shall say: 'Do you remember the first time we came to La Roche Guyon?'" and they treasured all they saw, the sharp, scoop-like shadows curled by sunlight under the bridge, the stone fountain at the foot of the slope from the castle, even their thirst—"a memorable thirst," Thérèse said—as they sat outside an inn near the fountain and looked up at the castle and the grass-rimmed cliff behind it and, above the cliff, trees clustering to the skyline with the tower of the donjon looking out of them. She did not then seem divided from him. The girl who had boasted of her lovers and flourished the squalors of her life as they travelled from Paris to Mantes was gone; his unease in her presence was gone;

she was no longer defiant, spectacular, clamorous for effect, nor did she talk only of herself and her achievements, but of Roussignac, of her father and of the prisoners.

"Barbet," she said, "I am happy when I am with you. It isn't the river or the holiday; it's being with you. I'm sorry Thérèse Despreux behaved vilely on the way from Paris. I have left her behind in the train." She looked at him with profound curiosity as if she were examining her face in a mirror. "Sometimes," she continued, "I think of you as if you were shut up in your own prison; and it's true—a gaoler is as much a prisoner as the prisoners themselves, just as an actress, though she may think she's ruling her audience and playing on them, is ruled by them. A great actress gives out and takes in, but in the end they suck her blood. They don't suck your blood—the world, I mean. That's why you are different from everyone else. Others are tied to something that sucks their blood—fear, money, pride—something. You are not tied to any of those things. But you are tied to your prison; I don't know why. You aren't even tied to me, though you say you love me, though you do love me. 'But not,' you said, 'as men love women with whom they share their lives.' That is right. If ever you loved me in that way, I should suck your blood, and then I shouldn't love you any more."

"Any more?" Barbet echoed.

She turned her head away, then faced him. "Oh yes," she admitted, "I love you. Didn't you know? It's only when I'm with you that I don't despise or defend myself. You have me as I am—even the foolish good in me—and, when you put your hand in your pocket, out comes a little box with lilies of the valley on it."

BOOK THREE

The Doors Are Shut

Ma chandelle est morte;
Je n'ai plus de feu.
Ouvre-moi ta porte
Pour l'amour de Dieu.

"AU CLAIRE DE LA LUNE"

Chapter 1

AFTER HIS RETURN TO THE MAISON HAZARD, Barbet was continuously and happily at work. He did not ask himself when he should see Thérèse again. Perhaps not until next spring; perhaps he would go to Paris before the vintage; certainly months would pass before he saw her, and he was not impatient. He had always loved her, though he had not always said so, even to himself, and if now she had said that she loved him, that had been, in her, a dramatic courtesy which bound her to nothing and changed nothing. He had his work to do and she hers; and when a letter came from her describing her first successes at the Écurie Plence he read it a second time in the coopers' shed and thought that, as long as they lived, he and she would be separated. We are people who are almost strangers except when we are alone together or are far apart. In company, there are only our differences; it's as if we ourselves, the selves that recognize each other, were being shouted down. I become dull and say nothing. I should always be an embarrassment to her in her world and she would soon grow tired of mine. That is the long and short of it; our lives don't run together and never will unless—

Barbet straightened his back and let the chip-axe hang idle. Unless, of course, one day, when we were alone together, at Mantes, for example, or at La Roche Guyon or on the deck of the Gabrielle d'Estrées, we should both stop arguing in our minds and forget Paris and Roussignac and the prisoners and the Écurie, and go on and go on and not look at my watch and not come back. That would be a voyage! Next day, what would happen? The skies wouldn't fall, I suppose. We should be alive and the sun would be punctual and we should wonder why we had been afraid to be together. No one would care; people would fuss because they felt they ought to fuss, but no one would care. Someone would look after the prisoners and someone else would sing at the Écurie; we should find work and our lives would go on.

To accept life in this way, not to force it, not to plan it, but to accept it, was for Barbet more real than to live by what the world considered to be its realities, but he knew that it was only within himself that such acceptances were possible, for outwardly the world's realities were kicked against in vain; they were not to be overridden or transcended by anger or rebelliousness, by any plan, by any act of will, but only by those impulses of nature which, like the touch of a wing on the surface of a pool, trouble the water and send out rings endlessly.

Lancret had come into the shed unnoticed. He stood watching Barbet for a little while, then said:

"What are you thinking of, Barbet?"

"To tell you the truth," said Barbet, surprised to find the chip-axe idle in his hand, "I was thinking about two things at the same time—the spring frosts and the pool of Bethesda. The rings on the water. You spoke of them once. Do you remember?"

"No."

"I had always imagined," Barbet answered, "that rings went out on the water—and broke in little waves on the shore, and I asked: did you think they could have been caused by the touch of a bird's wing on the surface? You said it didn't matter whether it was a bird's wing or an angel's; both were natural; both were a part of God. If the rings went out and the pool was filled with power, we needn't trouble our heads about the cause, except that it was of God."

"I am glad I said that," Lancret answered. "I must have been a younger man at the time."

"Oh yes," said Barbet. "I wasn't much more than a boy."

"I think it is true, though I couldn't now say it so simply," the priest replied, seating himself on a bench and twisting an oak-shaving round his forefinger. "The Bible isn't about conjurors. Miracles are not an arbitrary magic but a summoning of those reserves of nature which underlie common experience. They are more natural than what we call nature; that is what is exceptional about them—they are *more* natural, not less."

Lancret looked up to see how his discourse was being received.

"You are not of my flock," he continued with nervous defiance. "If you were, I'd be more cautious. As it is, I'll say what I have to say. The skeptical and the credulous—your brother, Anton, for example, and your poor mother—in certain ways they are very alike. It's as if they were living in an enclosed harbour and had forgotten the sea outside. One day the sea flows in strongly; there is an exceptional tide; and one says that it's impossible, that it isn't true, and the other throws up her hands and says it's a stroke of magic. Both forget the sea outside and that it is always there and always connected with the water in the harbour; and some try to shut out the sea and to pretend that there is only the harbour; and it is God's mercy that the sea breaks in or the water in the harbour would stagnate. Whatever is not included in their experience—the rings on the water of the pool, the communion of saints, even the love of men and women that does not conform to their pattern of match-making —the sceptics and the credulous consider unreal. Causeless, magical, bewitched, impossible, absurd—a hundred conflicting names, but always unreal."

Lancret had twisted the oak-shaving round his finger until the flesh below it was white.

"Yes. Even the love of men and women that doesn't answer their formula they say is not love. I know they said it of me. It is wickedness or infatuation or madness or plain folly, but for them it is not love. They are always wiser than those who love, and often, to their own satisfaction, they are proved to be right. The world justifies the world in its own eyes. The harbour pollutes its water."

"And yet," said Barbet, "one can't go outside the harbour while one is alive. The harbour is the world in which we live."

"No," the priest answered, "one can't go outside the harbour but one can be aware of the sea, one can admit the natural power of God. You can't guide the flight of birds or angels, but when the rings go out, when the waters are touched, you can enter into them."

"Meanwhile," said Barbet, "one goes on with one's work."

"Meanwhile," said the priest, "one goes on with one's work." He strode away a few paces. "I must visit Madame Sernet this evening."

"Worse?" said Barbet.

"Dying, I think. . . . I must go. But she doesn't want me. She only sends for me because she hates me."

"If she dies, what will happen to Frédéric?"

Lancret shrugged his shoulders. "The less work for him," he said.

There was much to do at that season outside the prison and the coopers' shed. In the north courtyard itself Barbet had established a workshop, and there he taught his prisoners to carpenter or make barrels, and often worked with them instead of at Quessot's side. But for many hours of each day he was absent from the prison. Weeds were growing fast among the vines, and the soil had to be broken with the hoe and broken again that it might be clean always and freshened by the spring air. The young shoots were lengthening —some were almost as long as his hand—and the vine-stems appeared now to be darker than at any other time of the year—black and crusted against the lower surface of the leaves. Soon the leaves would grow and the bistre-green of their upper surfaces conceal the form of the vine-stems, but in mid-May there was no saying whether the vines were green or grey; they were so pale that when the skies were heavy with rain and the lustre went out of the air and all deep colour was deepened and pallor faded, there was ivory in the leaves of the vines and the stems were a pattern of iron. After rain had fallen, Pierre and Barbet watched with anxiety the movement of the wind for three or four days. If while the soil was still moist the wind moved to the north-west, there was danger of frost, and in the evenings Barbet would come out and sit on his low wall, which was protected by prison and house from north-westerly winds, and hope for a breeze off the river. When there was none and a clear sky, he walked through the house into the west courtyard, and old Quessot would look out from the coopers' shed and wait until his return.

"A north-wester to-night, Quessot!"

"Even so," Quessot would answer, "who's lucky with the phylloxera may be lucky with the frosts."

In that month Barbet's fortune held. There was a frost in the third week and Pierre was out early to see the damage—"Too early," said Madame Hazard, "nothing shows until the sun is well up. You think you've escaped, but at ten o'clock—" It was soon after ten that Barbet himself went out to find many shoots burnt and hanging down, the crispness gone out of them, and Renée crying disaster. There was no reason in a frost! she exclaimed. Other vineyards had escaped; the Maison Hazard had been bitten; there was no reason or justice in the frost! But Barbet found that the frost had been capricious among his own vines; many were untouched; and even on those affected the secondary bud, the contre-bouton, had not been destroyed and would replace the first.

Chapter 2

I T WAS VICTOR WHO MADE BARBET UNDERSTAND
what had become of Thérèse. He had been to Paris. On his return
in mid-July, he and his mother came to supper at the Maison Hazard.
Pierre and Renée were at table. Victor said that he had seen Thérèse's
performance at the Écurie.

"And was it good?" Madame Vincent asked.

Victor pressed his finger-tips together. "Shall we say, mother,
that it was at any rate extremely successful." Then he shook himself
and, with an eye on Barbet, added: "No! No! We must not be
ungenerous. It was—how shall I put it?—it was altogether original.
Of course upon others the name wouldn't have the same effect."

"What name?" said Madame Hazard.

"Barbet's name. Didn't you know that? Half her songs are about
him. Funny songs and solemn songs; country songs and town songs;
political skits and—"

"But what does she find to say about Barbet?" Renée inquired.

"Enough," said Victor, "more than enough, I assure you. She
has really been very clever about it. She has set him up as a type—
a man who finds himself in the midst of the most ordinary adventures, who does all the day-to-day things that are done by thousands
of Frenchmen and who behaves always unexpectedly. He never says
or thinks what others would say or think. He is a kind of simpleton
whose comments on everything that happens are satire without his
knowing it. So there you are, Barbet—a famous man! I hope you
like it. The point is—she can use you as a kind of newspaper. You
can go to the races, you can go to the salon or attend a debate in the
Chamber; you can wander through Montmartre, and there is one
very popular sketch in which she points to an empty place at one

of the tables and pretends that you are sitting there. All Paris, as far as I can make out, is talking of Barbet. You have made her fortune."

"Well," said Barbet, "I must say I think she deserves it. It takes some doing to make me into a figure of satire and romance. Besides, it isn't me, you know; it's someone she has invented. There was a lady who wrote to a great novelist claiming that she was the original of one of his characters, and he said—"

" 'My dear Princess,' " Madame Vincent intervened, " 'my dear Princess,' Balzac replied, 'you deceive yourself. Since I created the original, you have become one of ten thousand copies.' "

"Mother," said Victor severely, "you have quoted that before and quoted it differently. And it wasn't Balzac."

The old lady looked at him in alarm. She was losing confidence in herself and feared that her memory might be failing her. He had found that he could always frighten her in this way.

"Nonsense," said Barbet firmly. "Certainly it was Balzac."

He felt that it was worth a lie to see Madame Vincent happy again. Having contented her, he rose from the table and went out to visit the prisoners.

They also had finished supper, but were free in their courtyard, for the heat of the year had come and the cells were intolerable until the sun had been off them for several hours. Fontan was under the ilex, the mandolin beside him unused; his feet were crossed, his wrists were supported by his knees and his hands hung slack; he seemed never to blink but to be always watching some distant object that puzzled him. Marcotte had perched himself on a stool at the entrance of the shed used by the prisoners for cooperage and was engaged in his everlasting task of building a model ship.

"Something to do. I can sell it when I'm out."

He disparaged his ship and grumbled at it, but he clutched it to him whenever Blachère approached and would take it with him into his cell at night. At his feet, while he worked, Balze and Heim were seated on the ground, playing a game with pebbles, and at the farther end of the courtyard Blachère stood alone, his hands clasped behind him, staring at the walls. He advanced three paces, halted and stared, advanced, halted and stared again. When he saw Barbet, he lowered his head and began to rub the seams of his trousers with flat palms. No one knew why he did this and no one except Barbet paid any attention to him, but Barbet knew it to be a signal of approach; soon Blachère's feet would move forward; he would come very close, his head on one side, his thick lips open, his breathing audible, and would be still with a sidling stillness, like a deformed tree.

This evening Barbet passed by the others and went to Blachère, who said:

"What do you want with me?"

"I want an understanding with you," Barbet answered, and sat on the burned grass. "Sit down and talk." Blachère remained standing.

"You are my enemy," Barbet continued. "Will you tell me why? The others are not."

"That is why," said Blachère. "And because you keep me shut up."

"What do you expect me to do—let you out?"

"As for that, I expect nothing."

"And if you went out—what then?"

"I was an animal-tamer."

"You enjoyed that?"

"Ah! Enjoyed? Well, it was something. To make a bear turn a somersault is something."

"Why does a bear turn a somersault?"

"Because he finds it is a thing he can do better than other bears. You see," said Blachère, dropping to his knees in sudden eagerness and thrusting his face towards Barbet's, "they are vain—animals. That's what people don't understand. It's not food and it's not the whip that tames them; it's not kindness and it's not fear; it's vanity. You can play on it. It's like playing on a man's conscience. I remember a woman who said to me once: 'You haven't got a conscience, Blachère, that's why you are my master. I can do anything with a man by playing on his conscience. . . .' Now, what was I talking about?" Blachère said.

"You were telling me how to train animals," Barbet answered steadily.

"Ah, yes," said Blachère, "animals. How did I come to be telling you of animals?"

"I asked you about them."

Blachère nodded. "You have a conscience?" he said with a glance like the snatch of a claw.

"Yes."

"Then why do you keep me shut up? Would you keep an animal in a cage?"

"No."

"Then why do you keep me shut up? There are men who'd turn the key and shoot the bolts as easy as a cook slams an oven. Not you. They'd keep a prison because they were paid for it; they'd keep it without a thought; no conscience in them. But you—you have a conscience—you're in the cage yourself."

"Someone else said that to me not long ago," Barbet replied.

Blachère came nearer, as though he were about to say more; then refrained. The seed was planted.

"My God," he said, "I should like the smell of a bear again— and look out if they begin to dribble from the upper jaw. Look out then, I warn you!"

He leaned on the ground in silence, his eyes narrow, his nostrils moving, and Barbet found that afterwards, when he was talking to Marcotte of the harvest or to Fontan of the celebrations there had been in Roussignac on the Fourteenth of July, Blachère still had power to visit him and would not be cast out. Even when the prisoners were returned to their cells, he was unwilling to share the company in his mother's parlour, and went out into the fields. All the barley was not yet harvested; oats and wheat were to come. Rains in June had delayed the haymaking; in a few days, with more than one crop to take in, there would be great pressure of work on the farm, and Barbet recalled a project he had had—to release the prisoners on parole that they might work in the fields. Perhaps it would have been, in any case, impossible; Victor and Anton would have resisted it and the regulations have been enforced; nevertheless, the thought of it tempted him. But he himself would not have dared to release Blachère. Like the prison itself, the man had power over him. To be rid of his prisoners had been a desire long present in his mind. So long as the idea had been his own, it had appeared simple and good. Now Blachère had, by his prompting, robbed it of naturalness and made of it a temptation to be resisted. He was hedged in by Blachère, and he turned away from the fields into the darkening vineyard and went to the edge of the falling ground from which the river could be seen. The water had no gloss; it was a chalky mist appearing among the blackened trees; and on the marshes the great sheets of wild valerian, light pink in the daytime, were no more now than a pale rubbing of the darkness.

He felt a touch on his arm. His mother said: "What is on your mind, Barbet?"

"Have they gone?"

"Everyone's gone. . . . Are you thinking of Thérèse? Why do you think of her, Barbet? She is another man's mistress—so Victor says. He says she is moving from Montmartre, from—what was the street?"

"Rue Lilas."

"From the Rue Lilas to a flat in the Île St. Louis. And she is the mistress of—I forget the name—"

"Courcelet."

"Then you knew?"

"That isn't the point, mother."

"Then what?"

"You remember that evening in the prison—when the prisoners were ugly, and then were quiet? I don't think I could do that now. I have begun to argue with myself. Nothing tells me what to do or what to be."

"It will come back, my son, if you rest. Sometimes, you know, I begin to argue about God. That shuts him out. But he is there. He comes back if you rest."

"Blachère troubles me."

"Ah!" Madame Hazard exclaimed, "that man is the devil. Don't listen to him."

Barbet took her arm. "That sounds easy. But to believe that a man is the devil is to make him so. . . . I saw the first families of swallows to-day."

"I saw none. Where?"

"On the telegraph wires."

Early next morning, before great heat had come to the day, Barbet left the labourers in the fields, climbed his tilbury and trotted into Roussignac to collect from Anton money for the prisoners' upkeep and do other business there. Anton's room at the Lion Rouge was empty but a message told him to go to the Hôtel de Ville. Anton had been there and left. Would Barbet please follow him to his private house? Barbet smiled: "My brother's flitting this morning?"

"I think," said the clerk, "that he was a little disturbed."

In the house with the gargoyles Barbet found Anton, Bette and Victor assembled. They were seated in Bette's parlour, evidently waiting.

"Did you know of this?" said Anton, taking up a roll of paper from the floor and extending it before Barbet's eyes. It was a placard announcing that Thérèse Despreux, from the Êucrie Plence in Paris, would appear in Angoulême for three nights on Thursday, Friday and Saturday, the 7th, 8th and 9th of August.

"No," said Barbet. "How did you get it?"

"It came to me by post," Bette answered.

"From Angoulême?"

"From Paris. She must have sent it herself."

"Well," said Barbet, "you can't stop her, you know. If she wishes to come to Angoulême, she will come to Angoulême. What harm does it do you?"

Victor intervened. "Do you suppose she will stop at Angoulême? She will come here."

"And why not? I don't understand, Anton. I don't see what's troubling you."

Anton rose.

"I am not," he said, "a squeamish man. I am not, I hope, a proud one. I am not one to grudge success to any poor girl who goes out from Roussignac to conquer a greater world. But Victor has pointed out to me that, from the political point of view, there may be a certain embarrassment in—" He sat down suddenly. "You, Victor, you explain to Barbet what we mean."

"I will explain," said Bette. "It doesn't need an oration. Within less than a week of her coming, it will be the Fifteenth of August. You know well enough though it's the Virgin's fête, it is also the Emperor's, and, though it may be true that the Bonapartists don't dare to come into the open, they use the day, under cover, as an answer to the Fourteenth of July. Anton serves the Republic. But your family—his family—is known to be Bonapartist. Your mother is mad about it—a regular badinguet. That has always made it difficult for Anton with the Comités Républicains. And it isn't Anton only. She sings—"

"She sings," Victor exclaimed, "about anything on earth—the more topical, the more personal the better. Or she might, as Bette suggests, kick up her Bonapartist heels. There is no limit to what she may say."

"Not," said Bette, "that we have anything to conceal, but naturally one wishes to avoid unpleasantness."

"Naturally," Barbet replied. "Then be pleasant to her."

"She shall not come into Roussignac."

Barbet shrugged his shoulders. "God bless my soul, you can't prevent it."

"And where is she to stay? At the Lion Rouge? At the Cheval Pie? Anton owns them both."

"Now listen, Bette. She's a determined girl. If she has made up her mind to come, you will only make a fool of yourself if you try to shut her out."

"I know, I know," cried Anton in exasperation. "That's what I say. If only she could be *persuaded* not to come."

"By me? Is that why I am summoned?"

"Half the songs are about you by name," said Victor. "What happens if she uses Barbet to attack Anton?"

"Well, if she does, one laughs and gets over it. But she may be coming for a holiday or she may not come here at all."

"Let us hope so," Bette replied, "but, if I know her, she has come to show off. The question is, Barbet, if we keep her out of the Lion Rouge and the Cheval Pie, will you undertake not to invite her to the Maison Hazard?"

"No," said Barbet.

"You are mad!" She turned to the others. "I told you it was useless! He is besotted."

"My dear Bette," her brother put in, "you are not a diplomat. You should never ask a saint a direct question about a harlot. He always gives the wrong answer."

At this moment a servant entered to say that Frédéric was at the door.

"Bring him in," said Anton.

He was brought in. He held a letter in his hand. After a bewildered glance from face to face, he swerved to Barbet. "She is coming back!" he cried, his face alight. "She is coming back! She has ordered rooms for Sunday the 10th. Two rooms—a bedroom *and* a salon. She asks the price."

"Give me that letter," said Bette, but Anton stretched out his hand for it.

"The usual price. . . . Well, go, boy! Take the letter. It stinks of scent."

Victor intercepted it and sniffed. "Good scent but too much of it. That is Thérèse all over."

Frédéric held out his two hands for it. It was laid on them flat, as if it were a brimming dish. He crunched it, held it to him, turned and fled.

Chapter 3

A LITTLE TO HIS SURPRISE, ANTON FOUND THAT
he was greatly tempted to see one of Thérèse's performances in
Angoulême. It was in his nature to give credit to success and he was
annoyed by his wife's bitterness. Bless my soul, he said to himself, the
girl has courage—and she may be dangerous. His instinct was to
conciliate her. "Be nice to her," Barbet had said, and Barbet was
less of a fool than Bette and Victor supposed.

But to go to Angoulême needed an independence of others' opinion that Anton did not possess. He found that he was expected to
disapprove of Thérèse, and his reputation in Roussignac was that of
a sound man, a man who did what was expected of him. His sub-
stantial friends who gathered at the Lion Rouge agreed with him
that Thérèse had come to flaunt herself—or was it that he agreed
with them or that they and he were echoing their wives? The
women of Roussignac were hot against her. No doubt she imagined
that, because she had had a little success in Paris, every house in the
district would be thrown open at her knock! She would soon find
out her mistake.

"It astonishes me," said Anton to Victor, "that no one gives her
credit for wanting to come home with her triumph. Even a dog
runs back wagging his tail when he has done something he's proud
of. And yet if I refused her rooms in the Cheval Pie, I should have
local opinion behind me!"

"You were wise not to do that," Victor replied. "As long as
Courcelet has the ear of the Ministry of the Interior, neither you nor
I can afford to slap her in the face."

"Do you want to?" Anton demanded.

"N-no. She is not now in my way. But she's excessive, that girl.

Good or bad, she overflows. Have you ever known a relationship between her and anyone else, man or woman, that hadn't an element of sex in it? Even her father's afraid of her—and he's a priest."

"Do you know what Barbet once said to me about you and Thérèse?" Anton inquired. "Shall I tell you what he said? He said you were her enemy because you would rather be admired by her than by anyone on earth."

Victor drew his hand slowly across his lips. There was a long pause, after which Anton said in a loud, hearty voice: "You are probably right. She must be good in bed."

"I didn't say so," Victor answered.

"That's why the women hate her," said Anton, pursuing his own thought, "but they'll go to see her on the sly."

"And you?"

Anton pursed his lips over a breath sharply indrawn. "I don't see how I can."

Victor too withheld himself because he knew that it would give her satisfaction to find him in the audience. Pierre and Renée could not afford the journey. Barbet was held to the prison. But on Wednesday Madame Hazard said firmly what she intended to do next day. If no one would come with her, she would go alone. Madame Vincent shrugged her shoulders. Chouquette was mad; she must be humoured. "Very well, Chouquette, I will look after you."

The two old ladies set out together by the afternoon train. They found at the station many inhabitants of Roussignac who, as far as possible, chose separate compartments and advanced good reasons for going to Angoulême not connected with Thérèse Despreux. They might or might not, they said, look in on her performance. "Nonsense," said Madame Hazard. "They'll all be there. They are like me. They can't keep away." She looked out of the window as the train started and slapped her knees. "I confess, my dear Emilie, this is a treat for me. As one gets old, one needs to see a little life now and then." Madame Vincent showed her teeth indulgently. "There, there, Chouquette, you mustn't get excited. It is a hot day and you will tire yourself."

They went shopping in Angoulême and, as if the town were foreign to them, visited the cathedral and cooled themselves on the ramparts. At dinner Madame Hazard insisted upon eating grillon, a fat pâté against which she had been warned; they went to Thérèse's performance in a mood to be pleased and were excited beyond their expectation. They were to spend the night in Angoulême and Madame Vincent came into Madame Hazard's bedroom and sat upon her bed to discuss the experiences of the day.

"Some day," said Madame Hazard with generous enthusiasm, "there'll be a statue to that girl in the square outside the Cheval Pie. She will become the head of her profession."

"She has talent enough," Madame Vincent replied in a guarded tone. "But I doubt the statue."

"Nonsense, Emilie, if she has talent enough—"

"But one must know how to apply talent in this world, and you know, Chouquette, in many ways the poor girl is such a fool. You and I, we have enjoyed ourselves. Your round cheeks are still burning with the excitement of it. But, admit it—we are tired out, we are exhausted. It's as if she had seized us by the wrists and pushed her face into ours and shone her eyes into ours and cried: 'Listen to me! Listen to me! You *shall* listen to me. I am Thérèse Despreux.' And she succeeds. It is magnificent. But you come away dizzy, as if you had drunk too much—as if she had forced the wine down your throat. She is a pitiless actress, and in the end— . . . Besides," Madame Vincent continued without pausing to describe the fate of pitiless actresses, "to become the head of any profession needs undying patience, and she hasn't got it. I am told she behaved very badly to that fellow Hurtaux. I dare say he deserved it, but what's the good of working for months and months and then spoiling it all by flying off for a whim? The girl's too high-and-mighty. She doesn't really value any opinion but her own, and she's as suspicious as a street urchin."

"You are quoting Victor," Madame Hazard interrupted. "It isn't fair to quote Victor."

Madame Vincent considered this accusation and honestly rejected it. "No," she said. "Victor may share my opinion but my opinion is my own. I have known the girl as long as you have, Chouquette, and I remember she used always to say: 'I hate people who take offence.' But she takes offence quicker than anyone I've ever known if she isn't what she calls 'appreciated.' Not so much because she appreciates herself. Rather because she doesn't. She needs to be everlastingly patted on the back. 'Say nice things to me, Madame Vincent. Say them, even if they're not true.' I used to tell her she had a beautiful nose—I used to *say* it because I couldn't believe she would do anything except laugh—but, no; she was as happy as if she believed it. She was so starving for flattery that she did believe it. And it's an appetite that grows. She may advance but she will always leave enemies in her rear."

Madame Hazard was for a moment without a reply. To gain time she said: "I disagree."

"You can disagree or not, my dear Chouquette. It is what the world says."

"Ah, that may be, that may be, but it is not what Barbet would say. He would not condemn her. No, no," said Madame Hazard, lying down in bed and pulling the sheet over her nose with a decisive and final gesture, "that would not be Barbet's opinion."

Madame Vincent gazed at her and hesitated. "No," she said in a deep voice, "perhaps not. All the same, Chouquette, it is the world's view of her, and it's the world that puts up statues."

Whoever saw Thérèse brought home praise or controversy. By Friday evening, she was famous in Roussignac, and not in Roussignac only. On Saturday the whole countryside—Saintes, Cognac, Segonzac, Châteauneuf—flocked to Angoulême and returned quoting her and talking like Parisians. On Sunday morning she sent on her maid to Royan where she had taken a villa by the sea, and herself came to Roussignac almost in tears of joy because, she was sure, her past had been redeemed. She would no longer be thought of as "the tart from Angoulême"—it was, indeed, for this reason that she had chosen Angoulême and rejected the richer but to her meaningless promises of Bordeaux and Limoges—and she would be free to do what she loved more than anything on earth: throw her arms round

everyone's neck, forgive her enemies, feel innocent and happy and
stand the world a drink.

The world did not come for its drink. She had hired two carriages
to meet her at the station, one for herself, the other for a mountain
of luggage. She had imagined that this procession would be a joke;
she would make the most of it and laugh back and wave her handkerchief and stop her carriage to talk to people who waved to her.
But no one waved. They were coming out of church and eyed her
as though she were part of a circus. And Frédéric treated her with a
secret, slavish devotion, as though he were harbouring a refugee.
His instinct was that she should not show herself and he had laid
her midday meal indoors. A battle was needed to have it moved into
the garden under the plane-trees.

"What is it, Frédéric? What have I done? Didn't they like my
performance?"

"Oh yes, oh yes, they liked *that*," he answered, delighted to be
able to give her this much good news. "Everyone is saying how good
it was—how very Parisian and—"

"It's not Parisian! Anyhow, it's not what they mean by Parisian!
It's my own. The whole point is that Paris has never seen anything
at all like it before."

Frédéric was silent. When one tried to say anything to please
Thérèse, she would always fling off into argument against the form
in which it was said. Whether she was Parisian or not Parisian
mattered nothing to him, but it was her vanity to be precise; given a
chance, she would torment the word with her emphasis until, forgetting the compliment, she would persuade herself that she had been
insulted.

"They said that too," said Frédéric humbly and for the sake of
peace. "They said they had never seen anything like it before."

"Oh, they did, did they? Then why aren't they nice to me? Is
the Cheval Pie always empty on Sundays at this time?"

"It's fuller in the evening," Frédéric replied.

She turned on him. "That isn't what I asked!" Then, seeing his
white face, understanding at last a little of the patience of his goodwill, she said, "But you are kind. You don't hate me," in a voice of

such tenderness that, when the words were said, she couldn't help being proud of the way in which she had spoken them, and though, in truth, her words had sprung from a genuine impulse of gratitude, she now observed the rush of tears to Frédéric's eyes as she might have observed an effect upon an audience. He tried to conceal his tears. Against her will, she pursued him.

"Why are you crying?"

"Because—because you said it so beautifully!"—a reply that so amused her at her own expense that her face lighted up, all her angers were suddenly thrown off, she laughed and seized Frédéric's hands and dragged him down to the chair beside her and to his astonishment rubbed her face against his shoulder. Now, why on earth had that pleased her? He didn't know. He had never known what would please her. He gazed at her radiant face. Anyhow, it was radiant, and Thérèse, happy, was an intoxication to him. The whole world changed its colour. He was alive; he smelt the trees, he saw the serrated shadow cast upon her flesh by the ring she wore. He could chaff her and feel that all privilege was at his feet. He rose, made her a waiter's bow, and asked what apéritif mademoiselle would take before luncheon.

A few customers appeared at the Cheval Pie while she was eating —an old, solitary man who was past caring for anyone's opinion of him, three youths who were already so far out of Anton's good graces that they had nothing to lose, and a group of four men whom she knew to be dependents of Bette's and who were, she supposed, her scouts. None approached her. They stared, nodded half-heartedly and became engrossed in their drink. The boycott was plain. Thérèse's principle was to attack. I will go over and make them talk to me, she thought, but she was too unhappy to stir. When Frédéric brought her coffee, her mind flashed to a resolve to call at the house with the gargoyles, but rain began to fall and she went upstairs and lay upon her bed. During the afternoon, Barbet came to the Cheval Pie. She returned a message that she could not see him; then, at the sound of his footsteps in retreat, kneeled upon her bed and looked out through the curtains. She called Frédéric.

"This bed creaks."

"Oh no, mademoiselle, I—"

"Don't call me 'mademoiselle.' Call me Thérèse. I say this bed creaks. It always did. My God, I ought to know! Get some oil."

She oiled the springs herself while Frédéric watched. She asked him for his news and about the girl who did the cooking and about Madame Sernet's funeral, but always cut short his answers by a more exciting narrative of her own. She began by describing her new flat in the Île St. Louis and the bed she would have there, shaped like a swan; and when details of the furniture had been described, she related her triumphs at the Écurie and told him by what numbers the audiences had increased, and how they applauded, and what Monsieur de Courcelet had said, and how much more she valued the opinion of the girls who thronged the pavement each night when she came out.

"But why do you value their opinion more than his?"

"Well, you see," she said, "they're nicer!"

"But do you think they are when you're not there?"

"I expect so. Why not? And even if they aren't, it's what they *say* matters to me."

"I see," said Frédéric.

In his company she could enjoy all her successes again. He was a fresh audience and she recovered her spirits.

"What did you say to Monsieur Barbet?"

"That you were resting. He will return in an hour."

"Good."

"When he comes, will you go down to the garden?"

"Not at first," said Thérèse. She had a salon and would receive him there. "Now I shall change my dress." Frédéric took the oil-can and moved towards the door. "Sit there," she commanded, "and talk to me." He was silent. "*Talk* to me! Very well, if you're dumb, you can help me. This unhooks at the back. . . . But wash your hands first. They are covered with oil."

Chapter 4

S HE WONDERED IF HER DRESS, WHICH WAS DE-
signed for company she would have at Royan, was too spectacular
to please Barbet, and walked to and fro between bedroom and sitting-room, gazing at the piles of luggage and trying to think of something she might wear that he would not notice at all. The sitting-
room had formerly been her aunt's bedroom, and she remembered
that she had never been allowed to move the bed when the old woman
was in it but had been made to crawl under it with cloth and pail. A
sofa stood in that corner now. Thérèse lay upon it and stroked her
lilac dress and looked down between the wall and the sofa's edge to
see whether the crack in the floor had been repaired. It had the shape
of a lizard—a rounded head, a long body, a thin, pointed tail. She
put down her hand and touched it and shovelled dust over its rim;
then rose and put on her gloves.

This time Barbet drove his tilbury into the square of the Cheval
Pie. At the sound of his wheels she felt she had been rescued and
all her resolves of dignity forsook her. She ran on to the balcony
of Madame Sernet's room, intending to call and wave, and there
suddenly, at the sight of Barbet climbing out—the active figure, the
square shoulders, the brown hand that gave a standing twist to the
reins—a current of tenderness ran down her body and her eyes
closed. When she looked again, his face was towards her; a moment
later he was hidden by a plane-tree, then in the open, talking to
Frédéric; and it pleased her to watch him, who had not seen her.
She went downstairs slowly, afraid that, when she appeared in the
garden, he might, in his wish to be kind, speak of the failure of her
coming to Roussignac and try to console her with little lies, and she
did not wish to be consoled, her desire for local triumph no longer

existed; it seemed never to have existed, the subject was dead in her mind, she had passed beyond it and wanted only to be near Barbet and feel his eyes upon her. At the foot of the stairs she heard Frédéric say: "She said she would receive you in her salon, Monsieur Barbet," and guessed Barbet's smile as he answered: "Well, Frédéric, I can't pretend not to know my way, but I think you had better go up first and announce me."

"No you needn't," Thérèse cried. Then, face to face with Barbet: "You did climb three flights of stairs to me once. Do you remember?"

"Rue Lilas," said he.

"And what was the first thing we did?"

He looked at her, puzzled. "We talked a bit and then—"

"No," she interrupted, "the *first* thing we did was to have a drink. . . . Frédéric!" In a moment she was sitting at the table at which she had eaten her solitary meal, but now Barbet was opposite her and she his hostess. When Frédéric brought a carafe of wine, her hand went to it before Barbet's; it was she who filled the glasses, and, as she set down the carafe, her hand rested an instant on the table; she had thought, not that he would touch her, but that she might, for that instant, permit herself the imagination of his touch. Instead he drew back and her heart was chilled by ridiculous disappointment; he drew away with a grinding of his chair in the dust, and she followed him with her eyes, possessed by a superstition that, if he went from her now, though it were but to call Frédéric or to find a thicker shade from the plane-tree, he would be irretrievably gone, and when she saw that he was lifting his chair and moving it to the end of the table so that he might be nearer to her, when he was seated again and reached for his glass and touched hers with it, the clink of the glasses ran down to her elbow; it seemed to her that a miracle had happened, she smiled and closed her eyes and said her prayer to St. Antoine, then opened her eyes and looked at Barbet as though she had been blind and were now seeing him for the first time.

"Why, Thérèse?"

She answered his question with questioning eyes, then put away pretence of not having understood it. "Only that I'm happy," she said. "Are you going to Royan for the Quinze Août?"

"No."

"But everybody does. Anton will go and Bette and the Vincents —everyone. Why not you?"

"Pierre and Renée are going."

"But you could go too. There's no work in the vineyards."

"I have my prisoners."

She let this go unanswered, having begun to speak of Royan only because Courcelet had appeared in her mind. He and Cugnot and Madeleine—perhaps Plence also—would be her guests at Royan; it was possible because, though life at Royan during August was very gay, it was also very simple, and a few weeks ago, when the plan was made, nothing had seemed to her more delightful than to spend her savings in this way and in this place where the wealthy shippers would send their sons with a fine horse and a buggy, where the solid proprietors would go in the hope of mixing socially with these grand gentlemen of Cognac, and where the whole countryside would pour in by the excursion trains on the 14th August to sleep where they could—at inns, in the woods, on the beach—and play cards and eat in the open and make love and make music and stare at M. Zola's villa, Paradou, as if it were the house of an ogre. Thérèse had been there once when she was a child; her mother had taken her and she had made friends on the beach with strange children who knew nothing against her. When she had fallen on her face while paddling, no one had been angry; she had sat naked inside her mother's coat while her own clothes were dried in the sun. She had pulled up the coat like a hood over her head; inside was the smell of her mother and through the collar the sunlit beach had appeared in a frame. In other years they had been too poor to go to Royan, and Thérèse had held it in her heart. To have a villa of her own there, if only for a fortnight, to entertain her friends from Paris, to be seen and recognized by everyone—in a word, to promote herself visibly from the beach to a phaeton and a pair of horses had seemed to her the surest of all proofs that Thérèse, the priest's daughter, had indeed become Thérèse Despreux; and now she told Barbet of her plans with a child's pride but with a child's fear that he might discover a flaw in them. If he had said that she was being ostentatious or foolishly extravagant, she would have flared against him. A thousand eloquent defences were ready on her tongue. But she had use for none of them. He asked only where her villa stood and whether it had a garden and what was the colour of the horses she had hired, and when she said that they were white, he answered: "White horses and your lilac dress."

"But you won't be there?"

"No," he said, "I must stay with my prisoners. . . . And now, if you're ready, shall we drive home? My mother is expecting you to supper, and the prisoners are expecting theirs."

She looked at him in mock indignation and made one of her faces of despair. "You too!" she exclaimed.

"I too? What have I done?"

"What have you *done!* I have a song about that.

" '*Stay at table till* I've *finished*
Stay in bed till I'm *awake.* . . .'

Sometimes I think I must be the only person in the world who knows how to live in the moment. Everyone else is always thinking of the *next* thing. Templéraud does. Templéraud is a young man I've discovered to write tunes for me. While I want him to work at one, he begins to whistle the next. Courcelet's as bad. He discusses the Chambertin while we are drinking the Pouilly, and as soon as his head is on the pillow he begins to wonder about his engagements for the next morning." She began to sing quietly the tune that Templéraud had written for her—a gay tune with a mock-melancholy and a sudden twist in its last verse:

"*Stay at table till I've finished*
Unless thou art the angel Death.
None but he shall steal my pleasure,
None but he shall stop my breath.

Do not forsake this moment
For the doubtful years to come;
Who looks beyond his instant
Enters his tomb.

And there," she cried, "they think it's ended. They begin to applaud. And then I turn on them—

"Do not applaud my singing
Till I myself am dumb!

You see? That shows them! . . . Now, if you are ready, shall we drive home to supper?"

Courcelet and the white horses were still in her mind as she sat back, erect, under the hood of the tilbury and waved to Frédéric. She did not repudiate the expected delights of Royan because she was differently happy in Barbet's company, and it was part of the pleasure of being with him to know that he was not shocked by aspects of her life in which he had no share. With him she felt no need either for defensive boasting or for concealment, and, as they drove out of Roussignac by the road bordering the Long Wood, there came to her a sense of confidence and well-being, of not being alone in the world. All her bitterness against Roussignac and her disappointment left her and she touched Barbet's arm and said:

"Thank you."

"For what, Thérèse?"

"For making me feel as I do."

"How is that?"

She hesitated for a moment. "You make me feel you are glad to be with me. You did in the Gabrielle d'Estrées. You do always."

"I have often imagined you on that seat beside me," he answered, "so clearly that it has seemed possible to put out my hand and touch your arm as I touch it now."

Though the sun was aslant and long bars of shadow lay across the dust, the great heat of August hung in the air and when the road inclined upward, the curve at the level of their eyes shimmered and

broke. The pony drooped his head and trudged forward on a slackened rein.

"Could we get out and walk for a little while?" said Thérèse.
"Perhaps to the top of the hill." They climbed down on the springy
step and walked at the roadside, where the blue of the lucern-flower
appeared among the dark green of its shoots. Thérèse stooped to
turn the flowers with both her hands, and, as she did so, a grass-snake
came out of cover and began its journey across the road, leaving a
zigzag trail in the dust.

"He has a long way to go before he reaches the meadows," she
said, and was still, her eyes fixed, following the snake in her mind,
how he would go through sun and darkness until he came to the
river. While she stood, Barbet came to her and took her in his arms.
The pony had halted at a distance, and Thérèse, as her eyes closed,
saw the radial shadows of the wheel-spokes lie across the dust like the
ribs of a fan. An instant later, when he had kissed her, she opened
her eyes and recognized them again. Her hand was in his hand, she
was at peace, not greedy for time, without fear even of its passing;
and it was without anguish that she saw that time had passed; the
grass-snake was gone, its track only remained. As she and Barbet
approached the tilbury, the pony began to move forward. Barbet
called to him to stand; they climbed again into their seats. For the
rest of their journey to the Maison Hazard, they talked at ease but
seldom, there being a natural repose in the cooling sky and in their
nearness to each other.

Madame Hazard had heard the sound of their wheels and was
at the gateway of the south-east courtyard to welcome them. The
deaf woman, the widow Garbut, looked out from the door under
the vine to say that the prisoners' supper was cooked, and Barbet,
leaving Thérèse with his mother, remounted the tilbury and drove
it round the house to the stables in the west courtyard.

"We shan't see him again for a little while," said Madame
Hazard. "The men must be fed, and ten to one he'll stay and talk
to them. Our own supper must wait."

Before their coming she had been sitting in the wall-shade near the pomegranate-tree and thither she now returned, offering Thérèse a straight wooden chair beside her.

"There is something I have to say to you," she began at once. "I was thinking of it as I sat here. When Thérèse comes, I said to myself—and now your coming has put it clean out of my mind."

"It will come back," said Thérèse, "if we talk of something else," and she asked how the harvest had been and whether the Hazard vineyards had still escaped the phylloxera.

"Of course they have," said Madame Hazard. Then, recalling that the family miracle had not been complete, she added: "There was a patch on the high ground. Barbet dug up the vines and burned them and burned every vine within twenty-five metres. There has been no more." She looked at Thérèse in troubled silence, unable to remember the subject on which she had wished to speak. At last she attempted another. "Madame Vincent and I saw your performance in Angoulême. For my own part, I enjoyed it without reserve— without reserve," she repeated in an emphatic, querulous tone as if her opinion were being challenged. "How you remember the words is what puzzles me. So many words! So many words! Do you know, I could often have thought you were making them up as you went along. I suppose you weren't? Is that a silly question?"

"I wasn't making them up," Thérèse answered. "But I'm glad you thought I was."

Madame Hazard sighed. "I can remember singers who sounded like a musical box. I can remember actresses who seemed always to be acting to the wall behind me. But you, Thérèse, you made me laugh and cry inside myself because you were whispering into my own ear." She began to chuckle and silently to clap her hands. "I expect it was that which upset Madame Vincent."

"Oh, was she upset?"

"She is very dignified," said Madame Hazard. "She don't like anyone to come too close. She don't like anyone to tickle her ear. . . . Of course one or two of your songs were Barbet's own songs; I've heard him sing them about the house; and you've changed 'em. All except one."

"Which?"

" 'As I was going up the street.' You sang that *his* way."

"I never change that," said Thérèse. "From the very beginning, I have never changed that. That was why I quarrelled with Hurtaux."

"Good," said Madame Hazard, "I like them better as they were. But I'm out of date, perhaps, and perhaps I'm a silly old woman." She stared at Thérèse with wide, unblinking eyes and said: "They think, of course, that I am sometimes a little mad?"

It was almost an interrogation. Thérèse felt that a reply was expected of her. "The world is so sane," she answered, "that sometimes it is necessary to be a little mad."

"Poor Emilie is sane," Madame Hazard said gravely and with the compassionate emphasis she would have used in speaking of a disease. "She believes nothing she has not been taught, and if anything from outside, anything unexpected, your performance, for example, makes a strong impression on her, she at once begins to explain it away. My poor husband was like that. When he was a little drunk, instead of enjoying it, he would always explain that it was not so. He would say there was a rim of pressure above his eyes, and soon he would take out his watch and show it to me and ask whether I knew that in 1836 it had cost eleven hundred and twenty francs. . . . Now, what was I saying? Ah, yes, poor Emilie!" But she could not remember what she had been saying about Emilie. Small grunting noises of irritation came out of her silence. "Bless my soul!" she exclaimed, "there was something I had to say to you and certainly it wasn't about Emilie."

Thérèse tried to help her. "Was it about my coming to Roussignac?"

"No," Madame Hazard replied, "it was about the kingdom of God." She was on the scent, her voice rose, her face brightened— then clouded again. "But there are so many things to say about the kingdom of God," she continued sadly, "one hardly knows where to begin. If only Barbet were here—" and suddenly she threw up her head in joy, sniffing the air. "Of course," she said, "it was of Barbet I wished to speak." She looked into Thérèse's eyes.

"I think you are a young woman capable of telling the truth. Answer this : Do you intend to marry Barbet?"

Thérèse looked at her incredulously. "Marry!" The question was fantastically opposed to her own idea of her life in Paris but it made her catch her breath. "Do not fear," she exclaimed. "We shall not. We shall not. We shall not." She felt a pulse stir in her throat as though there were wings in her blood, and she held her body against the throb of pain within her. "What on earth put that idea into your head?"

Madame Hazard rose to her feet. "Now there are a few things I must attend to before supper. Will you stay here or come into the house?"

Thérèse chose to stay and, when she was alone, seated herself on the low wall by which the courtyard was enclosed. A mewing cry drew her gaze upward to a family of buzzards circling above the vines. As she watched their smooth, grave flight, and felt the heat of the stone wall under her hands, she remembered the words she had spoken to Madame Hazard and tried to interpret them. No man was freer than Barbet; he was freer than the rich or the ambitious or the hungry or the timid ; neither possessions nor desire nor fear for the future imprisoned him; yet she had said that he was a prisoner and, in speaking, had felt it to be true. A prisoner of what? She shrugged her shoulders in attempted indifference. She wasn't his keeper, she had troubles enough of her own, but she knew that he also suffered, though his expression was normally that of a happy and unburdened man, and her question persisted. If I were near him, she thought, I should know what it is that holds him; if I were near him, I—and she put her hand to her throat, she saw again the shadow of the wheel-spokes lie upon the road like a fan. Good God, she said, when will you learn, Thérèse Despreux? Are you fallen in love again? The buzzards' mounting circles had carried them out of sight. Over the empty cornfields, in the direction of Pierre and Renée's cottage, a troop of grey-brown corn-bunting swept low, crying "quit . . . quit" and a loud "quit." When they were gone, there was unbroken silence, the deep, torpid silence of an end of an August afternoon, until four little birds of olive brown with white bands across their wings appeared on a branch within a few yards of Thérèse, carrying her mind back to a day of her childhood on which she had been standing at the edge of the Long Wood with her mother and Barbet and the priest. They had been talking together and she listening to the migration-call of these little birds, who passed in great numbers. Sometimes they had come to rest near her ; she had pointed and asked their name. Her mother had shushed her, the priest had not heard, and it was Barbet who had told her that they were pied flycatchers and, taking her hand in one of his, had stooped quickly down and pointed from the level of her eyes to another bird, perched high on the yellow flower of the Jerusalem artichoke, which, he had said, was a whinchat. The name she remembered and the excitement of watching the sway of the yellow flower, but the bird itself she had forgotten.

There was a sound of footsteps behind her. She turned, expecting to ask Barbet what a whinchat was like, but it was the priest, her father, who had entered by the gateway, and she was suddenly hot, the colour high in her cheeks. He had followed her to the Maison Hazard, but to encounter her alone was unexpected, and he stood before her like a guilty child, unable to take her hand until she moved forward and gave it to him. Thérèse had no small-talk ; it was her way to break silence by an abrupt plunge into the subject of her own thought, and now she surprised the priest and herself by saying :

"He has gone to feed his prisoners."

The priest nodded. "You passed me on the way—in the tilbury."

"Passed you ? Not on the road ?"

"I was on the path, inside the edge of the wood."

"Where ?"

"You stopped soon after."

She considered this : "The grass-snake must have passed at your feet."

And he answered : "I didn't see a grass-snake."

She smiled and turned with him to the chairs under the pomegranate tree. "His mother was here with me. She has gone in to see to supper. Are you staying to supper ?"

"If I am asked."

"Then she had better be told you are here."

He put a hand on her arm. "No. Stay. I have a standing invitation. Stay a little while."

She leaned back in her chair and waited.

"Then it is true, Thérèse?"

"What is true?"

"What they say."

"What do they say?"

"That he visits you in Paris. That you and Barbet——"

"Are you blind?" she exclaimed. "You saw with your own eyes! It was the first time he had ever held me in his arms. . . . Do you believe me?"

"Yes," said Lancret. "And what does it lead to?"

"The old question: what does it lead to? Can no one live in the moment?"

"No one can stay in the moment, Thérèse. It is already past."

She shook her head. "There's this evening. There's still supper to come. Hours and hours and hours. All of this evening is one moment."

"Are you as unhappy as that?" he asked.

"I? Unhappy?"

"If a few hours this evening mean so much to you——"

"Not unhappy. Lonely," she said. "This is a special place. It isn't Paris. It isn't Roussignac. It's a special place."

He insisted no further and folded his hands.

"When you are sitting beside me, as you are now, which do you feel," she asked, "my father or my priest?" and Lancret knew that the opportunity to serve her, for which he had prayed so long, was coming to him; the test of his capacity was coming, in what form he did not know; and, without unfolding his hands, he made in his mind the sign of the cross, and prayed silently: Give me wisdom. Give me charity. Give me words.

"Why do you ask that?" he said. "To provoke me?"

"Oh no, oh no," she cried. "Why should I wish to provoke you or anyone? I am not a wild beast. I have a question to ask.

I don't want your prejudice as a man. I want your answer as a priest."

"You wish to confess."

"If I did I should have said so. I want what I say I want, an answer to a question. . . . I'm sorry, I'm sorry," she added. "I sound impatient, I know."

Lancret controlled himself. He put irritation from him and calmed himself. "I will answer as a priest," he said. "Ask what you will."

"It is this," Thérèse replied. "Barbet is a good man, innocent—innocent," she repeated, "almost a sinless man."

"Let us say that he is good," Lancret intervened. "The word may be allowed to explain itself."

"And he is happy," Thérèse continued. "That is why it is peace to be near him—because he is at peace himself, and, in that way, happy. It's in his face. And yet, sometimes—I saw it just now as he went off to feed his prisoners—sometimes his face darkens. The creases at his eyes tighten, his look goes away from you—back into his own mind—the look on other men's faces. Shut in. Held. What is it? What holds him—him of all men?"

"Modesty of spirit," the priest answered. "Shyness before God."

He heard his own voice say these words instantly as though his answer had been long prepared, but when Thérèse asked what he meant by them he could not at first reply. It was as if he had opened a book at hazard and read these words aloud and must now seek their context. He stood up and, to steady his mind, walked away from Thérèse to the low wall, where he stood, looking across the river to the hills of the Grande Champagne, striving to interpret the words which, he believed, had been given him. This belief he recognized as a temptation to his pride; he had prayed for words, they had been put into his mouth; he might now, if he would, turn them to his own purposes and twist them with intellectual subtleties, for he was envious of a spiritual quality in Barbet that he himself was without and to reveal a flaw in that quality would compensate him. Therefore, when Thérèse had followed him and stood at his side, to protect himself against this temptation and put envy behind him he said: "I love the man. He is nearer God than I. I will not speak against him." But as he said this, it entered his mind that he might speak of Barbet in terms of his own defect, and he continued: "Every sin has its opposite. Even spiritual arrogance has its opposite in an excessive modesty of spirit; the remedy for one is humility, for the other exaltation. Barbet is limited—or, as you say, imprisoned —by his refusal to recognize anything exceptional—any exceptional power and therefore any exceptional duty in himself. He is like a man fitted to command who wishes always to remain a private soldier, or like a child of rare talent who says always, 'I am not different from the others in my class.' There was an evening when his prisoners were dangerous and he went in to them unarmed and quieted them and they obeyed him. But you were there, Thérèse, you saw it."

"Yes," she answered. "There was nothing spectacular in that. It happened quite naturally."

"That is why it happened at all," the priest answered, spreading out his hands. "Barbet did not guess that he was doing anything exceptional. If he had known that he was doing what credulous fools might call a miracle, he would have shrunk from it. All his life is a refusal to be conspicuous—I do not mean conspicuous to others; he is not afraid of opinion; he is scarcely aware of opinion; I mean a refusal to be conspicuous in his own eyes, to claim any exemption for himself, even to think of himself as different from others. He retreats so far from the introspection by which the rest of us are flattered, from all the sins of intellectual or spiritual pride which beset us, that he is bound by his own simplicity. He cultivates his vines, makes his barrels, looks after his prisoners. All these things his father did and it is not enough. Barbet is not his father, but he makes his life conform to the outline of his father's as if it were in some way presumptuous to excel him, even to differ from him. He compels his spirit to inhabit too small a house, Thérèse."

"Have you told him so?"

"Never, I am not his priest."

"But as a man, a friend."

Lancret hesitated. "Until you asked your question," he replied,

"I did not know what I have just said. 'Modesty of spirit. . . . Shyness before God.' I have never used such phrases or heard them used to describe an error. But it is true—he inhabits a house too small for him. If, as you say, he is sometimes unhappy, it is because he is beginning to know it. Perhaps it is you, not I, who can help him."

Barbet came from the house carrying a tray on which were plums preserved in cognac and a bottle of pineau. Thérèse disliked pineau ; the mixture of cognac and unfermented wine was too sweet for her taste ; but this evening she accepted and enjoyed it. Madame Hazard followed her son. Supper had long been ready. She scolded him for having delayed with his prisoners and at once there came into his eyes that expression of confinement and battle of which Thérèse had spoken. She looked into the priest's face, wondering whether he had recognized it, but he was supping the juice of his plums.

They sat down to their meal in the old kitchen now no longer used for cooking. In the fireplace was an iron backing with a figure of Bonaparte mounted, and above the mantelshelf a gun supported upon a rack of goat-horns. The walls were thick, having deep cupboards built into them, and the room was cool. Over their food they talked of food, then of Blachère and Fontan—a subject from which Barbet turned away ; then of the experiments that were being made in grafted vines, then of Paris, of Royan, of the whinchat and the pied flycatcher—a roving conversation skimming the surface of all their minds. Daylight fell into this room through narrow, embrasured windows. Its shafts wheeled and faded on the brick floor. When darkness was near and Madame Hazard would have had them move into the parlor, Barbet said : "Shall we stay here, mother ? Thérèse and I will clear the table. You can have your game in here." To be so little a stranger that she might carry dishes and bring cards and candles delighted Thérèse. She and Barbet played piquet at one end of the table, Lancret and Madame Hazard at the other. Their voices, falling upon the silence, seemed not to break but to accent it, and she said :

"Do you always play in the evenings with your mother ? At this time, I am at the Écurie."

Barbet held his cards against him and listened, then continued his game. Thérèse knew that his imagination had carried him into the cells with his prisoners, and when their game was done, the players at the other end of the table still continuing, she was content to sit opposite him, wordless, and to watch his face. As long as he and she might sit thus and the priest and Madame Hazard mutter and exclaim over the slap and patter of their cards, so long would this stage of the evening last, and Thérèse found rest in it; she did not want time to move forward into questions and action; she wanted to be as she now was, near to him and silent, still living in the very evening in which he had first taken her in his arms, not looking back upon it as she would to-morrow look back out of her own separated experience, but lodged in his life, a part of his actual recognitions. Nevertheless she began soon to try to engrave upon her memory his face as she now saw it, and the attempt, because it was a clinging to time, frightened her; she lost her hold, her mind leapt forward, she wondered whether Plence would travel to Royan with Cugnot and Madeleine and whether the wine she had ordered a month ago would have resettled well enough for Courcelet to drink it. Madame Hazard's game was done and Thérèse said to herself: The evening is over! It is all over! While the others were putting away the cards and Madame Hazard bringing out a bottle of wine with which, she said, to crown the evening, Thérèse went from the room across the covered way and into the west courtyard, wishing to loiter, to waste time like a child whose bedtime is come. Perhaps, if she went away, the glasses of wine, when poured out, would prove not to be, after all, a farewell; perhaps they would all sit down again and begin to talk. In the courtyard, under a deep, starry sky, she wandered, stood, looked up, wandered again. She counted seven stars. Never had she achieved the counting of seven stars on seven successive nights; if she did, her wish would be fulfilled; but now she had no heart for her habitual wish, which was for herself, and no language to wish for him. Instead she remembered the evening on which she had sung in the other, the prisoners' courtyard, and imagined herself again on that platform with the ribbed reflectors, and felt again the impact which had quelled the defiance in her and converted her song. She shut her eyes, struggling for the words of her song as she had done formerly, but now, when she opened them, there were no prisoners. She felt her hand taken and heard Barbet say: "What are you doing, Thérèse? Counting the stars?" She was glad to go indoors with him and drink the wine that Madame Hazard put into her hand.

"I will drive you and Thérèse into Roussignac," he said to Lancret. "It will be time enough to go the rounds when I come back."

The three of them were pressed together in the tilbury. The evening was already ended. Little was said.

"That is where we saw the grass-snake," said Thérèse.

Lancret was put down at his house. At the Cheval Pie, Thérèse would not allow Barbet to leave the tilbury. She was exhausted and feared that they might stand opposite each other, trying to say good night, trying to prolong what could not be prolonged.

"No. Stay where you are. Please stay where you are." With sudden resolution, she added: "To-morrow I shall go to Royan. Good-bye."

"Good night, Thérèse."

She had turned away when his voice followed her.

"Thérèse, tell me something. When I came out into the court-yard, what were you doing? Your lips were moving."

"Oh," she said in an abrupt, hard voice, as if she were mocking him, as if she wished to sting and hurt him, "I was emptying your prison for you."

"You can't do that. Only I could do that."

"That is true."

She thought he would say more, but after a moment's hesitation he said good night, gathered the reins and drove away.

Chapter 5

THÉRÈSE OBEYED HER IMPULSE TO LEAVE ROUS-signac next morning and so came to Royan before the house was prepared for her. Her maid, Charlotte, and Bridier, a cook of Courcelet's who had been sent in advance of his master, occupied it, and, as soon as they perceived that Thérèse was in an undemanding, almost a submissive mood, and had not the energy to quell them, they made her unexpected coming an excuse for serving her as little as possible. Rooms that might have been uncovered were left under dust-sheets, her meals were "simplified," even the milk for her morning coffee was brought without a strainer until, in a flash of rage, she sprang out of bed, seized a hair-brush and would evidently have used it if Charlotte had not fled from the room. The girl returned with the strainer and began to make excuses: there was so much to do in the house before the guests came; she and Bridier had expected to have no one to wait on until Thursday. Thérèse, in bed again, did not raise her eyes. She poured out her coffee and seemed not to be listening. "Go away," she said.

That day, her third at Royan, she spent in a mood of despondency. When the carriage and the white horses she had hired were brought for her inspection, they neither pleased nor displeased her; they were part of the conversation she had had with Barbet, and, after her eyes had fixed upon them, she wrenched herself away without giving the coachman orders. He waited half an hour before driving them back to the stables.

In the afternoon she went on to the beach with a rug over her arm and writing materials in her hand. She would not write to Barbet, but she might at any rate send a letter to Frédéric, and she wrote the envelope first because her pencil was eager for the word

"Roussignac." Then she looked at the sea and tried to think of the sea, but she felt nothing, not even the pleasant melancholy she had hoped for, nothing except the bleakness of knowing that, though she and Barbet loved each other, their lives lay apart. Even if he were to ask it, she must never allow herself to become his wife, trying to live at the Maison Hazard, nor must he, whose whole virtue was of tranquillity, be dragged at her heels through Paris, a lost man, patted or despised as the husband of Thérèse Despreux. The simple escape from paradox would have been to say that, since it was so evidently impracticable that her life should be joined with his or his with hers, their love itself was a delusion, a sentimentality of opposites, and she asked herself seriously and honestly whether this was so. Was she thinking as she thought now only because she was alone? When Cugnot and Madeleine came to-morrow, would her memory of Barbet be submerged in the news of Paris, in the saving rashness of their company, in her own passion to entertain? And if Philippe de Courcelet came with them, and to-morrow night—as was likely at the outset of a holiday—made his infrequent claim upon her, would she refuse for Barbet's sake? He amused her; she liked his leisurely and assured appreciation; his eyes would compel response in her, arousing desire the more certainly because, with him, it might be satisfied without commitment. All this she faced and accepted, no longer, as in the past, boasting to herself of her independence in morals, nor, with any reversion of sentiment, blaming herself. She recognized that others would blame her and say that her preparedness to receive Courcelet was proof that what she felt for Barbet was not love but a desire to play another part, this time a romantic one. In face of this recognition and this self-knowledge stood her innermost sense that she did indeed love him and that, though the outward conduct of her life might be unchanged, she would continue to love him. Others might prove their love by fidelity of body; she also if he demanded and valued it; but he did not; and to herself the proof of her love for him and of its difference from what else she had known was precisely that she did not wish him to be jealous. Jealousy was a cord by which men were bound and she would not bind him by jealousy, or by marriage, or by any submission of his life to hers—a heroic resolve, so improbable in its self-abnegation that she curled her lip at it. She knew what would have been said of it by the girl who had travelled with Barbet in the train to Mantes or by the Thérèse to whom, in Paris, Courcelet had been so skilfully applying the brilliant varnish of his own indifferentism. I can't help it, she thought; I change, that's all, and I change so fast that no varnish will stick. The resolve was a true resolve—truer than her attempt to sneer at it.

DEAR FRÉDÉRIC,

I left so hurriedly, there were so many things to do at the last moment, that I didn't properly say good-bye to you. You must have thought me a pig, particularly after your waiting up for me on Sunday night. I didn't properly thank you for that either. The door was open, it was dark inside—as it used to be when I lived there—and when you came out of the little room on the right, the piano-room—it was a shock. I didn't say much. I couldn't. I didn't mean to be unkind. Please forgive me. What had you been doing? Sitting there in the dark all that time?

The people from Paris haven't come yet. I'm all alone. This is written on the beach. I remember sitting here with my mother. The paper has been lying face downwards, I suppose it has got damp and that's why the pencil writes so smudgily. Do you often see Barbet? I suppose not. Do something for me—or don't if you'd rather not; I shall understand; anyhow I shan't know. Tell him you have had a letter from me and thank him for Sunday. Say I won't write from here as everyone will be fussing, but I will write from Paris . . .

A little boy came to retrieve his ball which had rolled to Thérèse's feet. She might have tossed it to him, but held it out so that he must come near to take it.

"Play with me," he said.

"Are you alone?"

"No."

"Then why am I to play with you?"

He had not taken his eyes from her. "I like you," he said.

There could not be a better reason. She rose and played with him. When he had had enough, he turned his back on her abruptly and ran full tilt towards his own people.

"Oh, well!" She sat down again. Bon, bon, Napoléon, va rentrer dans sa maison.

". . . but I will write from Paris or from La Roche Guyon."

But perhaps she wouldn't. She tore up her letter, returned to the villa, sent for Charlotte, Bridier and the coachman, reasserted discipline, put her house in order. Next day, when Cugnot and Madeleine arrived, she found that they had brought Templéraud with them. He had written music for some of her songs and wished to write more. No shadow of embarrassment touched him in coming to Royan uninvited. Last night Cugnot had said, "Why don't you come too? She'll be idle there; you can try your tunes on her," and he had come, sure of Thérèse's welcome, as he was of a welcome from all women, old or young. His golden hair and full lips gave him a childlike appearance which a square jawbone and lean, sculptured cheeks saved from childishness; he had learned how to open his eyes, which were glistening and heavily lashed, in such a way as surrounded the iris with white and gave an effect of vagueness, of dreamy intensity, of "not being there," and this effect was used, in its turn, to foster the idea of a charming irresponsibility so that it was a solecism to expect him to be punctual or pay his debts or remember at what girl's expense he supped last night. In this useful affectation there was an element of truth; he was naturally head-in-air, good-humoured and spendthrift; and was a little distinguished among Thérèse's male and female adorers at the Écurie by his ability sometimes to produce work that others would buy and by his quality of not being slavish, of expecting to be courted—his attitude of take-it-or-leave-it even towards Thérèse herself. She was never in his company without a desire for self-abasement, a wish to drown herself in his casualness. To drown herself—not to dip into it. It was this that surprised her. Whenever he had suggested that she should be his mistress, she had passionately resisted the temptation of her senses, for the reason, astonishing in her later self-analysis, that in

his instance, she was by the casual pass romantically dissatisfied—
and dissatisfied not because he was offering too little but because he
demanded of her less than she might, some day, have to give. She
said, for her pride: I shall have him when it suits me, and, though
she would not admit it even to herself, she often listened with contempt to the beautiful voice with which he spoke to women as if he
were stroking a cat. He strokes and purrs at the same time, she said,
but in public she praised his voice, and had long known, within her
secret criticism, that of all the mauvais-sujets who attracted her
there was none in whom she was more likely to discover some day a
romantic and disastrous oblivion. Some day! It was not her habit
to trouble her head about the future, and their relationship had become one of light-hearted postponements which gave an edge to
their encounters. At the station she was kissed by him with just
enough excitement to make easy for her any response she chose; she
made none, but put her arm in his as they walked out, with Cugnot
and Madeleine, to the waiting carriage.

In the company of these three her spirits rose. Cugnot, who was
wearing yellow gloves, took off one of them to hold her hand and
elaborately took it off again to pat her white horses—a politeness
which, when they laughed at him for it, he defended with such seriousness and so good a pretence of having been wounded by their
laughter that at first they laughed the more, then stopped, for one
never knew at what point Cugnot made—it was Madeleine's phrase
—"his transition" and included himself in his own hoodwinking.
What were the tunes? Thérèse demanded. Templéraud hummed
the first, she picked it up, Cugnot beat time with a cane thrust into
his empty glove. As yet there were no words.

"I'm not a poet but I will write a new Barbet song for you,"
Cugnot exclaimed. "Only give me a title and I will write the
words!"

Thérèse looked from face to face.

"You, Thérèse, you always have a title up your sleeve!"

She was silent and stared out of the carriage towards the sea, but
at that moment she became aware of Madeleine's discerning eye upon

her and threw herself upon their gaiety. She began to sing the tune
again. "What is it like? What is it like, Etienne? Not the tune, but
the rhythm—it's a travesty of something?"

"I wondered how long it would take you to find that out. Listen.
It's a variant of a very old song," said Templéraud in the caressing
voice of an actor about to make a declaration of love. He sang the
tune again with a different stress. Instantly they perceived the original and began to sing it. Four lines they sang together; then, at
Cugnot's signal, he and Madeleine and Templéraud abandoned to
Thérèse the falling cadence:

> "*Ma chandelle est morte,*
> *Je n'ai plus de feu.*
> *Ouvre-moi ta porte*
> *Pour l'amour de Dieu.*"

She sang again:

> "*Ouvre-lui sa porte*
> *Pour l'amour de Dieu.*"

She pulled down her veil and said: "There's your title, Cugnot:
'Ouvre-lui.'"

"To Templéraud's tune?"

"What? No. No, my God. To the old tune."

"But, Thérèse, however you change the words, you can't make
an up-to-date music-hall song out of 'Au Clair de la Lune.'"

"Can't I! Why not?"

Cugnot shrugged his shoulders. "It is tender. It is sad. It is
romantic. It is dead against the fashion."

"That's why I chose it. That is why I can make it succeed," said
Thérèse. ". . . This is the house. Be nice to Charlotte. She's in a
temper."

But Charlotte was sulky no longer. She enjoyed gay company
and Templéraud kissed her soundly at the carriage door.

Chapter 6

"MY DEAR THÉRÈSE," SAID CUGNOT, A WEEK later, "you are bored."

She was sitting to him for a portrait-drawing. "No," she answered, "why should I be? I haven't been sitting half an hour."

"I didn't mean bored by this sitting. I meant—"

"Nonsense," said Thérèse. "If one is alive, one is never bored!"

It was an article of faith, and she determinedly filled her days. She sat to Cugnot; she worked with Templéraud at her songs, refused him, desired him, laughed at him and at herself as though this were Paris and Roussignac did not exist. She drove, played cards and submitted herself to Courcelet's latest vanity—to improve her mind by teaching her history. Fortunately he had wit, knowledge and a roving mind which could be led easily into divagation, and Thérèse, who did not believe in missing chances, learned all she could of what happened to interest her in Periclean Athens and Florence of the sixteenth century. These were Courcelet's subjects. Being no fool, he introduced them opportunely, so that his teaching was less a lecture than a conversation, and Thérèse enjoyed being taught. "Men ought always to teach women," she told him to his delight. "If ever I had had a tutor, I should certainly have fallen in love with him."

But though she did not permit herself the crime of being bored, her mind needed holding. She was more critical than she had been of Templéraud's songs because she herself brought to them a less concentrated enthusiasm; she was not carried away by them or, even for a moment, intoxicated by the idea of singing them in Paris; none of them seemed the best in the world because it was hers, because she had discovered it; she did not wake up with its tune in her blood but had, each morning, to lead her intelligence back to an analysis of it and its treatment. When she wrote words to fit the tunes, or collaborated with Cugnot or Madeleine, or produced a group of verses for Templéraud to set to music, what she produced was, she believed, good, but she had little joy in producing it or even in contemplating the surprise, the applause with which it would be received. Paris seemed far away; even Royan was sometimes far away, though she was in it. She wrote a long serial letter to Barbet which she did not send. I am a professional diseuse, she said to herself. That's my job and always will be.

One afternoon, while walking with Madeleine in the woods, she said these words aloud. Madeleine looked at her and answered: "You said that twice yesterday. You have said it three times to-day," and because Thérèse was afraid to speak at once of Barbet to Madeleine, she gave no reply but walked ahead in silence before looking over her shoulder to speak of Cugnot as a prelude to Barbet. Madeleine loved Cugnot; her eyes continually rested on him as if they had neither rest nor pleasure elsewhere, as if only to see him were the beat of her heart; she touched him often as though he were magnet to her steel, and, when she did not, even her holding back was touch to one who saw it; and Thérèse knew that though, upon many aspects of life, Madeleine's point of view was different from her own, she might speak to her of Barbet without fear to encounter the chill of the unloving. She approached her own subject by way of Madeleine's. "You are lucky," she said. "You come out for this walk with me and you have him to go back to. When we return and come nearer the house and walk up the steps, the house will be alive for you because, suddenly, you may hear his voice. At dinner, the wine won't be just wine—it will be the taste of that instant in which you see him over the rim of the wineglass. And when this time ends, there's Paris. You'll go back with him. In the train, near him. In the studio, his things, your own."

"He may turn me out. He does, you know, when he wants to live alone for a time."

"Does that matter? You come back."

"Is Courcelet nothing?"

"Oh yes," said Thérèse, "he's my depravity. And someone to dine with. . . . Do you think it is possible to change one's whole way of life?"

"Certainly. It has been done."

"I mean—possible for me?"

"If you wanted to. If you wanted to enough, it would in fact be already changed. The old way would have become valueless."

"You mean," said Thérèse, "that if I loved Barbet enough to change my life for him, I should drop Courcelet?"

"Oh no. I'm not a fool. I mean much more than that. In the end, Courcelet would go with the rest. In himself, he's not important."

"That's something," Thérèse answered. "Only you would see that. If you had another man while loving Cugnot, would that be important?"

"Bless you," said Madeleine, "when I'm away from him, do you suppose I'm chaste for his sake? I'm chaste for my own sake. I don't make sacrifices for him. If I did, I should think I was ceasing to love him. What others, outside, would call sacrifices are nothing of the kind. They are a part of loving him. Listen," she said. "This is the point. They are a part of my own converted will. So I believe. So I feel. For him—no, not even 'for' him—*in* him, I have become what I am."

A narrowing of the path gave Thérèse a reason to fall behind into single file. At last she said:

"You aren't an actress."

"No."

"I am. I am a professional diseuse."

"How much does that mean to you? As much as it did?"

"Yes."

"You say it doubtfully. What is it, Thérèse? Are you contemplating giving up the stage for him?"

"Why should I?" Her voice quickened to an agitated defiance. "Why shouldn't I? Do you suppose I'm incapable of it? You make me speak as if I didn't love him. Why do you do that? You are happy. It's easy for you. You are like a married woman. You have only to trail round after Cugnot and live in his studio when he'll let you. 'In him I have become what I am!'—God, what a phrase! You read metaphysics, you have a phrase for everything. I have my life to live and it's my own life. That doesn't say I'm incapable of— Don't you understand? I have nothing of Barbet. *He* won't be in the house when we get back. We have never been lovers. You tell Cugnot that. He thinks we have. You tell him that. I should like him to know."

She sat down on a bank, her fists clenched, her shoulders trembling, and when Madeleine turned back and came near, she burst out:

"All right, I know it! I know it! If it comes to the point, I shall know whether I'm acting or not!" Then she stood up and began to walk again at Madeleine's side and said in an even and quiet voice: "I'm sorry I was vehement. I have a pretty steady mind; I can see myself. In emergency, I always behave well. I know inside me that our love can never have the ordinary, natural fulfilments. Not only because he lives in the Charente and my work is in Paris. It isn't a question of one of us being noble and giving up a career for love. We should do no good if we did. And it isn't even a question of our being different kinds of human being; none of the clichés apply; and, what's more, we aren't so different—anyhow our fires glow to the same bellows. What I think is true is that most people ask too much of love. They ask everything all the time. They ask the things that don't belong to their particular kind of love. And what Barbet and I can't ask is to be lastingly together—a rooted happiness, home, children. We might have the rest if we could forgo that. I see that now—clearly enough—talking to you. And I've had experience enough to know the difference between—oh, what I've had a score of times and the enduring love, however separated, that there might be between him and me. But always one wants more. I say now that I don't. I say most people want too much and I imagine that I'm wiser than they are. But soon, perhaps to-night, I shall want more. I shall say: 'Why is it wrong, why should it be impossible that he and I should be together?' I shall want a home—or think I do. I shall want children. I shall imagine that kind of life with him;

it will seem real; what I have been saying now to you will seem a sneer at a kind of life that, in fact, I want and envy. Do you see that? I'm not dramatizing myself. If I am, I can at any rate see myself in both parts, and I swear I can hiss myself off the stage if I begin to sentimentalize either." She turned down the corners of her mouth. "And I know," she said, "which I shall play when it comes to the point."

"Which, Thérèse?"

"Not the clinging woman. . . . Oh," she added in reply to Madeleine's glance, "it won't be a noble renunciation for his sake! And I shan't even pretend to myself that it was. I've outgrown *La Dame aux Camélias,* I promise you. Anyhow it wasn't really for *his* sake that Marguerite Gautier let Armand go; and if it was, it would have been better if Dumas fils hadn't said so. Besides, Barbet isn't Armand. I couldn't cage him if I wanted to. When he knocks, the door opens."

Madeleine cut the air with the switch she was carrying. "According to the Gospels," she answered, "that applies to all of us."

"Except that we don't knock," said Thérèse. "I signed the Plence contract this morning."

Chapter 7

WHEN SHE WAS RETURNED TO PARIS, THÉRÈSE set her face against the weakness that had come so near to capturing her at Roussignac. That she and Barbet should be lastingly together was impracticable; that she should take to herself the credit of "renouncing" him was a sentimentality of Dumas fils. She was a professional diseuse; in becoming one, she had unfitted herself to be anything else. Of this she was by turns proud, ashamed and disbelieving, but it was a formula to which she clung during that autumn.

Having, as she then supposed, reached a decision which excluded a major change in her way of life, Thérèse, after her manner, which was as drastic and imperious in thought as in action, variously supported it, seeking desperately by every means in her power to prove to herself that it was right. Her support was sometimes a plain acceptance, which lent her a new quietness of demeanour; sometimes an irony at the expense of this very quietness which, when Cugnot praised it, she swore was a pose, suggested by the demure bonnets with which she had decided "to contradict the fashion"; and sometimes by a stormy revulsion from everything that Barbet stood for in her mind. Then she would resume her old, scalding habit of claiming for herself a virtue of unsentimental honesty, tell lie after lie for no other purpose than to proclaim herself a liar, and lash Courcelet into bitter frenzy by glorifying whatever was weak or vicious in her camp followers at the Écurie. So rapid were her twists of motive that all Courcelet's subtlety did not enable him to perceive how it came about that, by agonized contraries, she praised these sycophants because she loved Barbet and wished to drown the impulse in herself to love him. In these moods, she would hear no criticism of them, who by their flatteries eased her from self-criticism, and when Courcelet said she was mad, that she must at all costs free herself of the Écurie, she answered that these people understood her and were not for ever asking her to become different from what she was. "They appreciate me!" she declared. "You hate them because you are rich. You don't love the theatre."

But she had, in truth, outgrown them. The comfort she gained in their company was brief; the drug no longer worked, for they did not, in fact, fool her; she despised them while they petted her and the more for being blind to her contempt. Her integrity could be overlaid but not killed, and often, returning alone in high excitement from the Écurie or from a party at which, made drunk by noise and adulation, she had betrayed herself in the wildest extravagances of mood, she would gaze blank-eyed, as though it were a dead house in Pompeii, at the flat of the Île St. Louis upon which she had spent so much care, and, because there was nothing she wished to do, kick off her shoes and sit upright on the arm of a chair or on the edge of her bed in that bitter chill of lucidity which a critical intelligence creates for itself amid the heat of wine.

One night in early October, as she let herself into the flat, she saw, on the floor of the entrance passage, a letter addressed in Barbet's hand. She stooped, touched it, then, in sickness of heart, let it lie. She passed through the sitting-room, lighted a hand-lamp, looked into her mirror and sat down on her bed, thinking that she did not wish to fall asleep fully dressed, but without initiative to move. The dress she wore, that had been a delight and a challenge earlier in the evening, filled her now with distaste. Remembering the praises she had heard of it and the hands that had touched it, she felt only that she had exposed herself in a cattle market.

After half an hour, her head nodded; she wrenched it up and turned it. That's something, she said, looking through the communicating door into her sitting-room. Her rooms still pleased her when she remembered that they were hers; she had made them, she possessed them, she was no more a lodger in the Rue Lilas. But I was happier in the Rue Lilas! Nevertheless she surveyed her possessions. They pleased her, not now by those peculiarities, those special accents of taste which the camp followers delighted in and called

"Despreux," but rather by those plainnesses which were the choice of an earlier Thérèse—the window of her sitting-room that gave upon the river and what she called the back-garden of Notre-Dame, or the flowers she had cultivated outside her bedroom window, or her stove, which had pictures of Dutch country scenes on blue-and-white tiles and was called Het Vaderland (which she pronounced fantastically) and was, in effect, not an enclosed stove but an open grate with a tubular flue. She rose from her bed and walked from one room to the other, comforting herself with these possessions, thinking of them by the names she had given them that they might not remain inanimate.

While she knelt on her window-seat, the door of her flat opened. She did not move but allowed Courcelet the pleasure of surprising her by putting his arms about her waist.

"I thought I should find you asleep."

"Then you'd have wakened me."

"Not necessarily."

"What do you want? A warm bed for the night?"

"Then get into it, my dear. How can you work if you never sleep?"

She undressed obediently and gave him wine. "I have no supper laid. I wasn't expecting you to-night. I can get you some."

"Dearest, Thérèse, go to bed. You are exhausted. I have supped. I didn't expect myself."

"Thank God you came. I can't sleep. I'm not in the least tired. I want to talk." She added suddenly: "I've made plans."

"Look," he said, holding out Barbet's letter. "I found this in the passage."

She took it and laid it on a table, face downwards.

"Don't you want to read it?"

"No."

He looked at it and hesitated. "Well," he said, "what plans?"

"You are right, Philippe, I need another string to my bow than the Écurie."

"And what about the rabble?"

"You mean?"

"Your hangers-on. They won't like it."

In a passion of resentful loyalty, she cancelled her plans, and sprang to defence of the party from which she had come. Courcelet lay back in his chair and waited. She would return to her "plan," and he had a scientific interest in the process. In the end what he called her "delayed wisdom" always prevailed; perhaps because she was country-bred or because she had been educated by the priest, Lancret, she always permitted her sense of ultimate advantage to prevail, in the nick of time, over her follies. When her flood of words ceased and he judged that she was at last finally prepared to surrender, Courcelet began:

"May I speak now?"

"Certainly, if you don't attack my friends."

"Dear Thérèse, I shall not attack them. I shall tell you how, in my view, your own mind works. You must not interrupt me in order to make a display of loyalty; you must contradict me only if something that I say is untrue. Is that agreed?"

"I shall not interrupt," Thérèse answered. "I like you when you are playing your own game. Besides, you will be talking about me. That is always interesting."

"Very well," Courcelet continued. "What at root you are proud of is your French country stock and your power to live by your own work, by what you yourself do or make or invent. You are a self-reliant animal. That distinguished you from a harlot even in your most promiscuous days. It distinguishes you now from all parasites. Others are parasites on you. And in your heart you despise them. Myself, for example. I earn my place by amusing and educating you and by my supreme negative virtue of not bothering you, but you are much less attached to me than you are to Het Vaderland, an old stove that you found for yourself in a remote ironmonger's, which is yours—bought with money you yourself earned—and—"

"All right," said Thérèse, "but leave Het Vaderland alone. He's special. I don't want him talked about."

Courcelet refilled his glass and, as he did so, pressed her hand. "I appreciate that. Children are often very secretive about their dolls. I won't invade your territory."

"You haven't hit on the real reason that I despise you," Thérèse said, "—if 'despise' is the word."

"Haven't I?" But he scented diversion and refused the trail. "I will return to that. Meanwhile, what you despise more than me—"

"I don't despise!" she exclaimed. "It is you who despise. I love people. I love anyone who does a job of work well. I—"

"There speaks Michael Angelo! Do you remember what he said on the subject? I told you at Royan. 'I am of all men the most inclined to love people. Whenever I see one who can do or say something better than the rest of the world, I can't help loving him; and then I give myself up to him and am his rather than my own.' Roughly that."

"Well?"

"Only that Michael Angelo—"

"I thought this conversation was to be about me?"

"Very well, as you please," Courcelet replied, straightening himself to the challenge. "What, at root, you despise are the Hurtaux and Plences of this world, the men who don't produce but live by what others have produced, the tradesmen of the arts who are not content to be tradesmen but give themselves the airs of artists. And even more, in your heart—for Plence and Hurtaux do at any rate shoulder a little commercial risk when they fail to pass it on to dupes and backers—even more you despise the wild, excitable neurotics, without my detachment or your saving, country-bred sanity, who cover their failures by pretending that they don't want to succeed and that anyone who works outside a coterie—at the Divertissements or at the Variétés for example instead of at the Écurie—has sold his precious self to the Philistines. They would have formed a club to sneer at Michael Angelo when they heard that he was employed by the Vatican. How can you enjoy the company of these people, and listen to their prattle as if it had value, and say you love them and let them hold you prisoner? Do you suppose that Michael Angelo would have given himself up to them and become theirs rather than his own?"

Thérèse tightened her lips but made no answer.

"They have affected your legend, Thérèse."

At that she was instantly alarmed.

"Every woman, certainly every actress, has a legend," Courcelet said, "and she is happy and successful whose legend is, as it were, a projection—perhaps an enlargement, an exaggeration, but still a projection—of her own nature. If her legend becomes distorted, if others make it for her—advertising touts or managers or newspapers or stupid friends and it becomes a contradiction of her nature, then she is divided against herself, her energies are split between two lives, she becomes barren and lost. As an actress, a diseuse, you were entitled to make your own legend. What was it? An egoist. An individualist, self-reliant, not clinging, contemptuous of patronage, a rebel against the big battalions. A girl who didn't bargain with her sex, who admitted her own pleasure and indulged it, but would cut out her own pleasure and anyone else's for the sake of her job. As an artist, unrelenting and unswerving, never complacent, never satisfied; as a woman generous, a giver-out, a good loser sans rancune—all that, Thérèse, is what you designed, and it was possible—a legend you could hold together—because inside yourself you knew yourself to be—what?—a quietist amid the din?"

She flinched, recovered and said firmly: "That is completely untrue. Why did you say it?"

"The man you love is a quietist?"

"Ah! . . . So you said it to test me. . . . You are cruel."

"To test your realism, Thérèse."

"Then I have survived the test. And if I'm not a quietist, which certainly I am not, what am I? You are so wise and so foolish that you interest me, Philippe."

"Then you shall tell me. If you aren't a quietist within the din, what is it that was to hold the legend together? What are you, Thérèse?"

"Natural," she answered, "within the legend."

"Ah, that will serve!" he cried. "That will serve! Now do you understand what I mean when I say that your rabble have distorted your legend? Put it no higher than professional advantage. I won't say that they have corrupted you; I don't think they have; in any case, I am not concerned with your morals. What they have done is to give the impression that your whole legend is a pretence, that there is no naturalness within it, no stability or endurance, that you are one of themselves—living emotionally from hand to mouth, even your vitality a whipped-up vitality, the effect of a drug."

At this Thérèse moved in her chair, but he cried: "Wait. I will give you an instance. You can't deny it; you have acknowledged to me that your tongue is your enemy. Why has it become so? Isn't it part of your nature—isn't it the life-blood of your whole legend, your image of yourself—that you don't hedge or pander to convention but speak with absolute directness?"

"But moods change," she answered. "What is true now isn't necessarily true to-morrow!"

"I didn't say 'speak with final truth,'" he answered, in the tone of an exacting but patient schoolmaster; "I said 'with directness.' It was so, even when I first came to know you. You were extravagant then; thank God, you always will be; you are not replying for a Government but for yourself; but then you were also naturally direct. They applauded you; it was new to them; they were stung and exhilarated by it; then they wanted it, like a drug, stronger and stronger. You gave it them. Led on and led on by their flashy response, your tongue has acquired a habit of violence that has made a vice of your virtue. . . . Not that only. You are naturally a realist. You would have been one if Monsieur Zola had never been born. You are so true a realist that, though you have long ceased to be a practising Catholic, I have never heard you make a sentimental denial of God; you do not suppose, as your rabble do, that, where you or they can see nothing, nothing exists. That," Courcelet added in parenthesis, "is why I love you in so far as I am capable of loving anyone; you are a more realistic sceptic than I am myself; you are not credulous, you believe very little, but you are not barren and indifferent as I am; there is nothing you are incapable of believing. That is your nature—again the core of your legend, its link with what is great in the romantics—and yet you identify yourself with these little men who are 'realists' by fashion and formula. Their arid fear of being called sentimental has confined them in the pose that we ought to cast off, if we have ever assumed it, when our beard begins to grow—a preserved and aging callowness, an effete immaturity. They are tolerant of nothing but their own failures. They treat everyone with whom they disagree as dishonest and fortify their ignorance with their sneers, like a frightened cur snarling to encourage himself. They sneer indiscriminately and always in the same tone—at Musset, at Chopin, at governments, at rich men, powerful men, men who believe, soldiers who die—at everyone who accepts responsibility, above all the responsibility of greatness that they so easily evade. I am not speaking of the artists who go to the Écurie—men such as Cugnot—or of the people who drive out from my wicked world to gape at you and the artists; I am speaking of the gossips and hysterics of the place—Plence's slaves, your slaves for the time being—who have no place in life at all except in this coterie. It is their whole importance to feed Plence's importance or treat you as a goddess—for the time being. But you are their slave, Thérèse, not they yours, for they have nothing to lose except their appetites and you have put your legend in their power. You are isolated. Your whole professional reputation rests on the Écurie. If for a moment you offended the rabble, if they shrieked a little less hysterically on Tuesday than on Monday, Plence's brain would begin to wonder how soonest to be rid of you, and, as things stand, you would go elsewhere as a suppliant. You must go elsewhere at your time, not at his. Your time is now. Then you can return at your price, not his. He must become not what he now thinks he is— your patron, almost your collaborator—but a middleman who, like other middlemen, competes for his goods in an open market."

"No," said Thérèse, "I shall always ask less from Plence than from anyone else in Paris. I like him. He understands me. The Écurie is my place."

"So be it," said Courcelet. "I am not worrying about your salary."

"And I shall come back to the Écurie!"

"Then you will leave it?" he cried instantly.

She had said more than she had intended, but not more than her resolve. Should she give him the satisfaction of supposing that he had persuaded her?

"You have been knocking at an open door, Philippe. . . . No, not always, I know. To-night you have; I told you I had made plans—"

"When does your contract end?" Courcelet interrupted. She would go; he had gained his purpose and would clinch it; he was indifferent to the credit, as yet. His intelligence preceded his vanity.

"The third week of November."

"To-morrow, then, you will send out scouts."

"No," said Thérèse. "None of your diplomacy! I will go to the Divertissements and ask for work. . . . No, no, leave me alone. I will do things in my own way. It is part of my legend. Now I am going to bed."

"Thank you," said Courcelet. "I ask no other reward for my sermon. You have a faultless intuition. But there is one question I should like to ask," he added. "What decided you 'to make plans'?"

"Your wisdom," she said.

"What decided you to make plans?" he repeated.

She jerked out the bow of his tie.

"When other women are miserable," he said, "they go out and spend money. When Thérèse is desperate, she sets out to make it. Both motives lead to the grands boulevards."

"Don't talk to me," she answered. "I am tired. Is the bottle empty? Give me some wine." She looked at the table.

"Read that letter, Thérèse."

She did not move.

"It has the Charente postmark. Read it."

She turned it over and looked at the handwriting, the corners of her mouth falling.

"Do you love him, Thérèse?"

"I don't know. . . . Yes. . . . Why?"

"Then you don't want me?"

"For God's sake don't talk," she said. "Everything is killed by talk."

Was the man jealous—he, the indifferentist? He was no longer smiling. His face was gravely sensual as she had seen it sometimes when he slept, when he dreamed. Even of jealousy he was a con-

noisseur. He was tasting it and it tasted sweetly of rejuvena-
tion.

"Very well, you shall have it," she said, coldly emphatic. "I will
read it. I will read it aloud to you, whatever it is."

He blinked and ran his tongue slowly across his upper lip; then,
when she sat down, seated himself opposite her. He took the kettle
from the stove and let it dangle from his wrist, jigging it and sliding it.

"You are like Victor."

He opened his mouth.

"Victor Vincent," she said.

She broke the envelope and began to read:

DEAREST THÉRÈSE,

Though I expect you do not wish to be bothered with many
letters, I have been promising myself to-day that I would write
to you this evening. As I told you once, you open doors for me,
and it does me good to remember that Roussignac is not all the
world. At present, as you can imagine, it is nearly all the world.
We have been sniffing our casks and tightening our hoops, and
two days ago grape-picking began. The rest you can imagine.
We—I mean our own vineyards—have done what would be considered moderately well in normal times; now, with the rest of
the country so badly hit by the phylloxera, even that much prosperity is remarkable. Anton can't understand why we are more
or less immune.

I had thought I might have been coming to Paris before the
vintage began. Now I expect I shall not see you until after the
distillation. I wish you could be here again some autumn. It is
the time of year I love best, except that people go out shooting.
The swallows and martins will soon be off for the South. There
was an army of them on the roof early this morning. Thrushes
and redwing are coming from the north and, as I said, the guns
are out but the thrushes know about them and take cover under
the vines.

Now I seem to have written very little of you, and you will be saying: why does he write only of the vines and the birds? what a provincial he is! But I can promise you I think often of the bonfire at St. Cloud, and of how thirsty we were at La Roche Guyon. The other day there was a Paris newspaper on Anton's table when I was in his room, and I saw a caricature of you. What big eyes! I am always a bit alarmed if I see the name of anyone I love in a newspaper and if I saw a caricature of myself I should feel that the world had turned upside-down. But I expect you are accustomed to it—or will be soon—and, when you are very famous, you will take no more notice of it than I do of my own face when I shave.

As I must be up early, I shall now go to bed. The prisoners often ask about you. I tore out the caricature, meaning to show it to Fontan, but until this moment I have thought no more about it. I have just found it in my pocket and am thoroughly ashamed of myself. Good night, dear Thérèse.

BARBET.

When the letter was done, she waited, not looking into Courcelet's face. His arm reached forward across her sight. The kettle was set down.

"The vintage," he said. "The phylloxera. Yes."

"Are you dumb?"

"What do you expect me to say?"

"Anything. You are naturally eloquent."

"My dear Thérèse!"

Anger stirred in her again. She saw ahead a scene in which, for Barbet's sake, she would stormily reject him, and the scene disgusted her. "For Barbet's sake!" Dumas fils! She was a sane woman. Courcelet's right was established. He amused her. He was her depravity. He would serve. She put Barbet's letter into its envelope, tossed it on to her desk and rose, intending to stretch out her hand to Courcelet. At the same time he too rose and his feet shifted on the carpet. When she looked at him, she found him breathless.

"You are enchanting," he said, "enchanting. Like a girl."

She replied: "I want to sleep alone."

"Why?"

"Why? Because I want to sleep."

"For his sake?"

Never quarrel. Never quarrel with a hungry man. Cover his vanity. But she said:

"For my own. I want to sprawl."

"I am to go then?"

"Listen—" she began.

"I will go," he said. His recovery was admirable. "Will you please re-knot my tie? It was you who undid it."

She obeyed. He took her hand and kissed it. At the door, he turned:

"Nevertheless, you go to the Divertissements?"

"All the more, I go to the Divertissements."

When the outer door had shut, she went to bed and turned upon her face and sprawled her limbs and slept.

Chapter 8

NEXT MORNING PHILIPPE DE COURCELET SENT
her flowers, this promptness being, she supposed, a sign of peace
—a sign, at any rate, that after so unaccustomed a ruffling of emotion,
he had resumed his habit of indifference and wished to announce it.
He rarely quarrelled; if he did permit himself so warm a lapse, he
would not add to it the emotional discomfort of a reconciliation, but
forget silently. She was willing to be thus discreetly reconciled; it
amused her to watch herself respond to his urbane good-breeding as
it would have amused her to prove, in his company, that one need not
be an aristocrat to dance a minuet. But it disconcerted her when she
found that, though he attended the Écurie, he was never alone; there
were always friends at his table, he welcomed her but hedged himself
in, and she did not know what was required of her. Supposing herself
to be still nominally his mistress, she accepted his invitations to supper, but at these suppers she was one among his many guests; he
treated her with charming intimacy but without confidence; when
he drove her home, he avoided any question of breach by walking
up to her flat and talking to her as he had a hundred times and leaving as he had a hundred times; it was impossible to ask: "Have we
quarrelled or have we not?" Nevertheless she asked it. "Quarrelled? What on earth is there to quarrel about? My dearest
Thérèse, surely we understand each other perfectly?" She did not
understand. She felt that she was being outmanœuvred, that she
was lonely and without friends.

The inner circle of the Écurie, which Courcelet called the rabble,
was, as he had foretold, chilled against her, when, having secured
her engagement for the winter, she allowed it to be known that she

was going to the Divertissements. Plence, having something to lose,
was more guarded. His resentment would not strike unless she failed
at the Divertissements, and he professed to be delighted by the news
for her sake; she had taken, he said, a necessary professional step;
he was glad to have been useful in launching a great artist who had
now outgrown him; he would watch her future with affectionate
sympathy, and hope that some day he would be able to buy her back
for the Écurie. She needed friendship so passionately that she flung
her arms round his neck. Of course she would come back! She
would never be happy anywhere but at the Écurie. It was *her* place
—or was it his? She laughed and cried. "Oh, thank you, thank you
for being so kind. I knew you would be! We do understand each
other? We do understand each other, dear Plence, don't we? It
isn't a *ques*tion of money. I'll come back for almost nothing if you
want me. I'll do anything for people if only they're *nice* to me."

"Entendu," said Plence.

She told Courcelet that he had been wrong about Plence. "I
don't care what people say. I adore him. I have always found him
honest."

Courcelet's eyebrows went up. It was in his mind to say that, in
less dubious men than Plence, honesty did not need to be proclaimed
so vehemently and that, in any case, it wasn't reason enough for
adoring a tradesman, but he denied himself the retort. Suddenly
he was sorry for Thérèse. She had promoted herself from Montmartre to the fashionable splendours of the Théâtre des Divertissements Lyriques and the triumph was empty if none would rejoice
with her. Anyone would do, even Plence—anyone who didn't argue
or reprove or advise but would let her throw her arms round his neck.
It was for this reason that she needed the rabble at the Écurie; having no volition of their own, they would, like dolls, dance to any
string she pulled. When she was lonely, she had a habit of going to
them, as a child to its toy cupboard.

"Poor Thérèse," he said, delighted to find in himself that imaginative sympathy with a woman different from him in kind which
he had often said was the hall-mark of an artist. "Poor Thérèse!"
but as he said it and put out his hand to touch her affectionately, he

asked himself—just as the rabble asked themselves!—whether he was not being sentimental, and a look of patronage came into his face which he felt upon it and could not banish in time. Fear succeeded it. He thought she would strike him.

"You are pitying me," she said.

He answered, awkwardly and stupidly: "Is that a crime?"

"It is worse than a crime. It is a blunder."

Now what is one to do with a girl who, when you expect her to slap your face, whips out a saying of Fouché? Courcelet glowed with admiration. His guard was down. He seized her hand with the impetuousness of a lover and kissed it in delight. She responded instantly. This at any rate was enthusiasm. It puzzled her; she didn't understand it; but it moved her heart. For its sake, she would forgive anything. If he would be glad, no matter why, she would be glad with him.

"You are funny!" she said.

"I will give you a present to celebrate that," he exclaimed. "I have had my eye on it a long time. The very thing! I know where we'll go! I know the place!"

Without waiting for his own carriage, he put her into a cab and gave the driver precise instructions. When they reached their destination, a street to the south of the river behind the Quai Voltaire, he commanded her to wait, climbed out and vanished through a doorway. She thought: in Roussignac the distillation has begun, and put the thought from her. "What street are we in?" she asked the cabman. He told her. A moment later she could not remember the name and dared not ask for it. Why had she asked at all? I like Philippe, she thought, he's dry; he plays by the rules; but when she leaned out of the cab she found herself looking into the face of a girl who was happy. The girl didn't see her. She was looking beyond the tail of the cab into the street. A man, who had crossed the street, came round the wheel and joined her. They walked away, their smiles alight with the joy of being together, he with the heavy basket she had been carrying. Courcelet so nearly collided with them that he took off his hat and apologized.

"The Palais Royal," he said to the cabman.

"Look," he said to Thérèse. "Undo it."

She undid the packet he had placed in her hands. It contained a small enamelled box on one side of which was the letter T in diamonds and the other letter F.

"Is it a patch-box? Have you ever seen my patch-box with the lilies of the valley? It was given to me in the Rue Lilas."

"It's a snuff-box," said Courcelet.

"No, not the Rue Lilas!" exclaimed Thérèse. "It was given to me at Mantes."

"It belonged to Fouché," said Courcelet. "That is his F. Inside, you will find an inscription. There's no doubt of it. The T, I'm afraid, was added by the second owner, an Austrian, who bought it in '21, after Fouché's death. When I first saw it, I hoped the T might have been Talleyrand's—but no such luck. We have the whole pedigree."

"It's lovely," she said. "But why Fouché?"

"Because—" He stared. Then, guarding himself with a smile from being fooled, quoted her own quotation.

"But why Fouché?"

"He said it."

"He didn't! I did!"

Courcelet laughed aloud as he laughed seldom. This, he thought, is admirable fooling; then wondered—was it possible? Hadn't she known?

"Anyhow," she said, turning the box over, "T stands for Thérèse."

She remembered that, on this occasion, he would wish to be spontaneously kissed, and turned her head. But not in the cab—it rocked on the cobbles; at the Palais Royal.

In Courcelet's rooms, she again thanked him for Fouché's snuff-box and kissed him, but his arms did not move upon her or her body slacken within them. She looked at him kindly, for she was fond of him, and thought: such as it was, it is over.

"Well?" she said.

Not pretending to misunderstand her, he smiled an old smile, considerate and patient. "After all, if one doesn't make a tragedy of it, there are still good wine and good talk."

"As bad as that?"

"As intelligent as that."

"Too intelligent," she answered. "I am tired of being moderate. If one is young, to be moderate is a torment unless one is also happy. I want to lose my head. I want to drown myself. . . . Dear Philippe, you needn't look so alarmed—I don't mean in the Seine."

"Well, certainly," he said, "I am not the appropriate person in whom to drown yourself."

She looked at him and answered slowly: "When you and I are together, each of us is always alone."

"Isn't that the charm and the convenience—"

"Yes," she interrupted. "It was. I'm grateful. You have been—"

"Thérèse, you are committing a cardinal error. You are about to say good-bye."

"Wouldn't that be honest?"

"Yes, yes," he said with good-humoured impatience. "If I were a young man wishing to drown himself in you, then it would save us both from the humiliation of bobbing heroically in the shallows. As it is—"

But he would not say "go and drown yourself in whom you please." A twinge of jealousy checked the words. He wished to retain, if not absolute possession, a suzerainty over her, and a reversion. Postpone, postpone. Anything, when one is growing old, is better than finality.

"As it is," he went on, "I understand you better, perhaps, than you wish to understand yourself. At the customary time, when you were green, you missed your experience of love. I and others have been substitutes. You produced a philosophy to explain us—a philosophy of casualness and indifference tenable by me because, in me, it is founded on disillusionment, but not by you—you are not disillusioned because until now you have never loved. Now, already sensually mature, you have fallen in love with a wine-grower. The heavens have opened to you when you are equipped to appreciate them. I envy you the experience. I fell deeply in love before I was a man. The heavens opened before I had ever watched a lady brush her hair. As a result, the two things have been for me always separate—then separate hopes, now separate despairs. It is the fate of most women who are well brought up, but, unlike me, they do not acknowledge this separateness; they hanker for a romantic unity which their own experience—the fact that their minds began to dream of raptures before their bodies had taught them how to select and fulfil their dreams—has made, for them, impossible. I am not the materialist you suppose, Thérèse; nor the dry sceptic. I know that men and women can love. But to love is an art like another; an amateur does not produce an enduring masterpiece."

"Thank you," said Thérèse. "Then I am fortunate."

"So is Barbet Hazard."

She drew breath at the name. "When I spoke of drowning myself, I wasn't thinking of him. That wouldn't be drowning."

He had been aware of this, and he said: "Of whom, then?"

She threw up her arms and stretched and smiled. "No one. I don't know. Another substitute, perhaps. This time without moderation."

"Is that a reason that you shouldn't sometimes dine with me here or at Larue?"

"None, unless you consider it a reason. Are you proof against jealousy?"

"No," said Courcelet, "I should be sorry if I were. But I do not allow jealousy to turn my wine to vinegar."

From that time onward she saw little of him. He did not surrender his key to her flat but seldom used it; his attendance on her was chiefly in public; and she understood that what he required of her was that she should not spectacularly cease to be his mistress. He would not be driven by jealousy or desire to force an issue with her; he preferred suspense to an end, being capable of putting sections of life into brackets; his vanity enabled him to hope, perhaps to believe, that she would not be unfaithful to him; he would besiege her with his detachment and patience; he would starve her of his company, which she enjoyed. In the end, if he did not formally abandon them, he might recover his privileges.

Indeed, she missed him, and missed even more that steely casualness in herself which had formerly made him sufficient to her. Until the evening on which she had driven with Barbet to supper at the Maison Hazard she had been able to sustain herself by reserved and bracketed pleasures; and now she could not. She was unarmoured and lonely. The proudest boast of her egoism—that she was clear-minded and conscienceless, that she knew precisely what she wanted —was no longer valid; if it had been, she would not have left Roussignac instantly or have forbidden herself to write to Barbet, but have stayed and used her power upon him. This weakness alarmed her; she was changing and drifting. She wished still to desire Courcelet's company, remembering what pleasure it had given her, but, in his company, found that she had lost her taste for it; her attention wandered; she smelt the hot, leathery smell of the tilbury hood or saw the swallows on the reeds or counted seven stars in the western courtyard or, striving to turn away from vain imagining of Barbet, was driven back to the moment in which, as she watched his face while his mother and the priest continued their game of cards, she had thought: this happiness is with me now, he is near me now, and had dreaded the future time when the present would have become a memory.

Sometimes during that November, when she was alone, or with Courcelet at a restaurant, or working with Templéraud at the new songs they were preparing for the Divertissements, her sense of isolation, of being rootless and out-of-touch, became so urgent that her hand, for an instant, moved in the air as though she were groping for physical contact. Courcelet watched this gesture with amiable curiosity. "You have a new mannerism," he said, "and a very becoming one. You have a beautiful left hand." Templéraud also observed it. What it meant he did not know except that she was unhappy and therefore vulnerable. One evening in his own rooms in the Rue du Paon, as he twisted on the piano-stool to speak to her, he found that her back was towards him and her hand extended, the fingers closing on the air, and he put his own hand in hers, so that, as her fingers closed, her body was shaken by the surprise and joy of a human contact. He drew her down instantly and she came to him not only without resistance but with extreme impulse, as though a dam were broken and her whole being were released and poured out. On her knees before him, she lifted a face so transfigured that he had not the courage of it and put his hand over her head and pressed it against him that her face might be hidden. He supposed, nevertheless, that what she felt was the lust to which he was accustomed and when she spoke he did not understand that she was expressing more than this. She said: "Why didn't you tell me that it was you I loved? It is you. I love you," and she continued in this way until he silenced her. He said that he loved her; the word "love" came to him out of the past as if it were the "good morning, sir" of a tradesman when a customer enters his shop; and it was not until he had lain with her that he began to understand that she was using the word as something else than common form. He looked down at her face, at once startled and appeased; he stroked her forehead and was appalled by the expression of rapturous peace in the eyes that opened and regarded him. Wishing to return to the piano, he moved his left foot towards the edge of the bed, but covered his retreat by smiling at her with that soft upward curling of the mouth-corners which gave to his lips an expression of great tenderness. Her eyes filled with tears; she put her arms round him with the passionate confidence of a terrified child whose safety was in him.

A harder man than Templéraud could not long have deluded her; because, in fact, he did not love her, her eye, which was still shrewd, must have seen through him; but Templéraud was malleable by devotion, and, when he had ceased to be astonished, he began to live the part for which her passion cast him, to feel and breathe it. As Christmas passed and the new year came, he learned even to say to himself when he woke in the morning: I love her, and to believe that this was true.

To this seeming romance, circumstances contributed—first of all that his fame sprang up with her new fame at the Divertissements. By Courcelet's contrivance—because to be her patron was his dearest vanity and because he felt that Templéraud was not at the level of his jealousy—Thérèse was launched upon certain drawing-rooms where, at that time, journalism, politics, finance and that florid aristocracy of the Third Republic which Plence had called le déluge, used artists and singers as a kind of rococo decoration. Wherever Thérèse went, Templéraud, with his mop of golden hair, his lifted eyebrows, his slow, vague, enchanted smile, gave her his arm. Every compliment paid her, she shared with him, looking into his face, laying her hand on his when others appreciated him, flaring to indignation if any omitted him from her honours. Her honours were great. The "uniform" in which Cugnot had been compelled to paint her on the day of her first meeting with Courcelet—the black dress, the crimson mittens and shoes—became a mark for caricaturists as early as January '85; her dramatic monologues, the Petits Chevaux, drew not the fashionable only but the painters and writers of Paris to the Divertissements at the hour of her appearance there; and it was by members of her audience that she was given new subjects for brief Barbet songs and sketches which, topical as a newspaper, would often disappear from her programme after a single night. It was a time of social and political disquiet. The ministry of Jules Ferry was felt to be near its fall; the senatorial elections at the end of January gave it an appearance of renewed strength, but Courcelet was not deceived by them; "It's not the Ministry only, it's the Republic that is in difficulties," he said, "and Ferry is worn out." Paris was insecure; Royalism and Bonapartism were renewing their hopes; the Extreme Left, the surviving Communards, were resharpening their weapons; on all these things and on the trifling incidents of each day the fictitious character to whom the name of Barbet had been given was called upon to make his comment. Even in these topical fragments Thérèse jealously preserved his individuality, the plainness, the directness, the absence of spite that was the essence of his own songs, and because the tone of Paris was bitter and uneasy he became a unique legend precisely because his political comment was not. Her Barbet songs had for a Paris surfeited with shrewdness and intrigue the delight of something fresh, incongruous, holding the challenge of truth in its innocence, and they became a fantastic oracle, to be quoted with the affectionate laughter that abides in nursery tales and endorses the truth in them.

Thérèse would not eat before her performance. When it was over she went out to supper, seldom with Templéraud alone but always with him among her escort unless Courcelet was her host, for Courcelet, as he himself would say with a reserved and patient smile, still had the privilege of private audience. "But why?" said Templéraud. "Why that old man?" "Because I *like* him," Thérèse answered. "Because he is a barometer!" She knew that she had lost her head; she liked to be told so, but only from Courcelet could she endure the telling. He was her life-line to sanity; as long as she held it, she could go out of her depth as far as she pleased, she could, so to speak, drown with assurance of recovery.

"But life-lines snap," said he.

If she was not invited to a private house, she supped often at an L-shaped table set in a corner of the large room at Maubant's. What pleased her there was that, instead of ordinary wine-glasses, there were red goblets on spiral stems, and that the table-cloths had long silk fringes that she could twine over her wrist, and that the gas-lights were shaded by enormous tulips of red silk. It gave her a sense of establishment to go continually to the same place—to feel, when a good evening came to an end, that it was one of a series, part of a routine, and that to-morrow, at the same hour, she would come to the same table. There was variety enough in the company; her table became a club; whoever took her there must expect others to join them; four became a dozen, a dozen fifteen, fifteen overflowed on to little tables drawn into the L. Drinking coffee herself, she would talk of cognac, of the vines, of Roussignac and the Charente, of the music that Templéraud had composed for her at Royan. "We," she would say always of him and herself—a strange form of egoism, Courcelet observed, that converts itself into the plural.

It was the excitement of her company that all her opinions came from her own mint. They came with an unexpectedness that seemed at first extravagantly inconsistent because it was without party in morals, in art, in politics, in anything, but which, springing always from her passionate and improvising spirit, had the consistency, not indeed of any system or external loyalty, but of her generosity, her happiness in loving and praising, her gratitude for all boldness. Ferry she admired, though her sentiment was in the First Empire; she admired him because he stood to his guns and, according to his lights, for France; but his friends were baulked in their attempt to make her his adherent in her songs. "Why, if you admire him?" "Because," she said, "I don't want to," and would give no reason less imperious. Nevertheless, when it amused her and she found a good rhyme, she would sometimes give the President of the Council a pat on the back from the stage of the Divertissements.

Never had money flowed for her as it flowed now—for her, not to her. Her salary was high and would increase; it dazzled her country memories, yet was not wealth. But outside her flat in the Île St. Louis, she spent little, and lived at the world's expense as though money were endless, investing her savings meanwhile as Courcelet directed her, selling at his command and begging him for permission, which for a long time he refused, to buy a carriage and pair of her own. She slipped his guard to buy pictures—her own portrait from Cugnot, a red-chalk from Madeleine, pen-drawings of Caran d'Ache, paintings and drawings by young men of the open-air and, to everyone's astonishment, a tiny sketch of Meissonier's. The naturalists had supposed her to be an adherent of theirs. They bombarded her with their indignation when, one evening at Maubant's, she brought Meissonier out of her card-case. Plence was there. He dragged his finger-tips across his eyes and began to lecture her on the demerits of Meissonier with the moral fervour of a Communard on the subject of Thiers. At last he threw up his hands and cried: "Twelve hundred francs for a visiting-card! Twelve hundred francs for the Old Guard!" And three times, in sepulchral despair: "Why Meissonier? Meissonier? Meissonier?" "Because," said Thérèse to prick his rhetoric, "he was born in the year of Waterloo." Then, when Plence was being laughed at, she added: "And because he can draw! And because he pleases me! Is that enough?"

"You will say next that Hugo is your poet. He is near enough to the grave."

"Thank you," said Thérèse, "you have given me an idea. I will recite Hugo to-morrow night. It will astonish the Divertissements.

Why are you intolerant of old men? Why must I pretend to despise Hugo because I can read Mallarmé?"

She had bought the Meissonier because Templéraud had admired it as they walked together through the auction rooms in the Rue Drouot, and she gave it him in a silver case, asking that he would carry it with him. Whenever she saw it in his possession she was happy; it seemed to her a miracle that she should have become rich enough to buy Meissonier; and because Templéraud was by nature vague, elusive, unseizable, she began, by a rule of contraries, to search her life for signs that her relationship with him was permanent. She gave him little gifts of the kind that a wife gives to a husband, not a mistress to her lover; she changed the habit of her life because his digestion required a morning walk on the quays; she began to wonder whether, in encouraging his partnership with her and persuading him to write new songs, she was standing between him and his development as a composer. Her admiration had the same impact as her passion; Templéraud was converted to ambition as he had been to love, and to the same extent—that is to say, he began to play the part of a young composer, he found reason to despise the masters of the generation that had preceded his own, and believed in his heart that, when his absent-mindedness made him forget his appointments with Thérèse, he had been occupied in the design of a symphony. Nevertheless there was in her a saving energy; she believed in his symphony when he was absent from her; when he was present, she made sure that he produced what tunes she needed at the Divertissements.

Sometimes she would break away from Templéraud, from Courcelet, from her company at Maubant's, and visit Cugnot and Madeleine in their studio, because it was unchanged and because nothing in their manner bowed down to her new fame. To them it was an unimportant toy. They did not despise it or blame her for enjoying it, but assumed that when she came to them she had put it away in a cupboard and wished to think and speak of other things. Once she took Templéraud with her, wishing him to share with her the pleasure, the sense of security, she had in Madeleine and Cugnot's relationship, but the evening was a failure; Templéraud was more than ever elusive; he seemed to "go away" from her. "Why did you 'go away' from me to-night?" she had asked as they drove home. "Don't you like Cugnot and Madeleine?" He had smiled and left her answerless. "Did I 'go away'? My darling, you imagined it. At any rate, I didn't know that I had." She made excuses for him. Perhaps he had been thinking about his symphony, perhaps he had been shy because Cugnot and Madeleine had not been alone; Annette had been there, Plence and two young dancers had come in during the evening.

"What did you think of Annette?"

"Which was she?"

"Annette? The dark girl who was there all the time. Not one of those who came in with Plence. You were talking to her when they came. You were charming to her; I thought you must have known who she is. She's a part of my history, Etienne. I have told you about her. Don't you remember? She was the girl who shared my room in the Rue Lilas."

"And cheated you?"

"Oh no; she didn't mean to cheat; she paid back in the end."

"And now you have been helping her?"

"A little," Thérèse admitted. "And I wanted her to meet Plence to-night; nowadays Plence will do a great deal that I ask; he wants me back at the Écurie, you see."

As they climbed the stairs to her flat, Thérèse continued to chatter of Annette, describing their adventures together when they were out of work and poor. "Often we were hungry, and she's poor still. But it's not charity, Etienne; I like bad hats. I lost touch with her for a time, but I was glad, really glad, when she turned up again. She'll never be first-rate—on the stage, I mean; she doesn't care enough; but she has talent; I expect she'll marry and be happy. Be nice to her, Etienne."

Thérèse did not tell him that it was through Annette that Barbet had found her in the Rue Lilas. She herself had not forgotten it, but had put it a little way from her, out of the focus of memory, among the shadows which half-conceal those moments of the past that by their happiness, or by their misery, are unbearably contrasted with the present. It reappeared for an instant as she opened her flat, for there was a letter on the carpet and she remembered how Annette's envelope containing forty-one francs had been slid under her door while she was talking to Barbet. The whole scene returned, the new corkscrew, the tuft of Barbet's hair, the weight of the grapes on her palm, and the recollection was so vivid, so deep a stab, that she might have taken relief in speaking of it to Templéraud; but as she stooped for the letter, he had walked beyond her into the sitting-room, his back was towards her, and, after a glance in his direction, she closed her lips. The letter was addressed in Barbet's writing. She held it between her hands; then, in the sitting-room, put it away in the drawer of a walnut desk. Templéraud swung on his heel.

"What did you put in there, Thérèse?"

"A letter."

"But you didn't read it?"

"No."

"Or open it?"

"No."

"You have put other letters in that drawer?"

"Yes. Unread. Unopened."

He smiled indulgently. "The little wine-grower? Why do you keep his letters if you don't open them?"

She was silent.

"Some day, you know, you will have to burn them," he said.

"Perhaps." She made a movement towards him. For his sake she would have burned them. She lowered her head and pressed the backs of her hands against her dress, longing that this abject obedience, this surrender of her innermost fortress, should be demanded of her by him. But Templéraud's mind had drifted from the subject; he took her into his arms and kissed her. For an instant, and for the first time, response was absent in her; she thought: I have not burned them, he is still alive, he is asleep now in his bed; then she felt Templéraud's lips upon her eyelids, desire grew upon her like a fungus on the brain, Cugnot and Madeleine and Annette were forgotten, the pile of letters in the drawer behind her fell from her mind, the delight of subjection to Templéraud rose about her, overwhelming her in a darkness against the world.

"Do you see much of her?" he said.

"Who?"

"That girl."

She opened her eyes, struggling back to recognition and understanding: "What girl? Darling, what girl?"

"Annette."

"Oh, Annette! I asked her to supper at Maubant's. Thursday, I think."

He released her and warmed his hands at the stove.

"Come on Thursday," she said. "You might be able to help her. She has a better voice than mine. A better singing voice, I mean."

He stretched himself. "Sleepy? It's a cold night. I think I'll bring my things and undress by the fire."

She was always on her guard against allowing herself to cling to Templéraud. Their partnership must be free; they must not be answerable to each other; and sometimes, that he might do likewise, she would refuse to tell him where she would be at a given time. Afterwards, without seeming to inform him, she would let him know where she had been, but so drifting were his moods that she was never sure that he remembered the truancy she was trying to explain.

He preferred always that their conversation should slide away from facts and decisions, and she found it hard to discover even what his judgment was on her interpretation of his music. As professional partners, they ought, she said to Annette, to have gone regularly "into committee. Then he could tell me," she added, "line by line what he really thinks."

"Well," said Annette, "that's all very well for you and me, but I don't think Etienne is that kind of artist. He isn't just efficient; he's intuitive."

"And where did you pick up that jargon?" Thérèse demanded. "It has been the excuse of everyone who has been too lazy to do his job since the beginning of time. No. Make no mistake. Etienne is efficient, all right. When it's a question of new work, he's efficient. But he isn't patient about going back over old work—repairs and maintenance. In a partnership like ours there must be repairs and maintenance."

The renewal of her friendship with Annette was a sauce with a sharp flavour that pleased her. She could persuade herself that after their experience of poverty, they stood together in the world, and that Annette, because superficially a wastrel, had a kinship with her that only they could recognize. How happy I am! she told herself continually. She was satisfied in body; the foundations of life had become firm under her feet because she was loyal, and content to be loyal, to one man. Not to have to lie to anyone was a peaceful experience which she enjoyed, and it surprised her that sometimes, when Templéraud asked where she had been or what she had said, the answer that sprang to her lips was not the innocent truth but a lie without cause or purpose. She would speak it and he believe her; two or three days later, when he had forgotten the incident, she would recall it and tell him that she had lied, delighted to observe that he was greatly flattered by these confessions, though they confused his brain and he did not know whether they were true or false. She explained this to Courcelet. "Why do I lie? Is it just a habit?" Before he could reply, she continued: "That is what is so extraordinary! Men are so easy to deceive that it seems a waste of time to be true to them. They don't really appreciate it. They don't know the difference. If you make a habit of confessing to lies that were obviously pointless, a man becomes so entangled that he ceases to have the least idea whether you are lying or not. It's too easy."

"Dear Thérèse," Courcelet answered, narrowing his eyes in affectionate derision, "why are you talking like a milliner's assistant in a cheap play? It's not your custom. It is true that you can so confuse a man that he doesn't know whether you are lying, but that, if I may say so with discretion, is proof of your stupidity and shallowness, not of his. To kick over a chess-table does not prove that you can play chess. I have always supposed it to be one of the profoundest honours that one human being can pay another—to care and know when he is telling the truth. If you destroy the knowledge, in the end you destroy the care."

Thérèse began to laugh. "All right. All right," she said. "Don't be angry with me. It's not true."

"What is not true?"

"That I lie to Templéraud. Why should I? I love him. I have nothing to lie about."

"No," said Courcelet, "and yet you do lie."

"Sometimes, perhaps, for the fun of it."

Courcelet walked away from her and looked out through his window over the arcades of the Palais Royal.

"Rain," he said with a sigh, "I am tired of it. I am growing old. I want the sun to shine." Then he turned to her and said in a flat voice without emotion: "Isn't it the whole problem of existence to overcome the difficulty of communication between one human being and another? Without lucidity nothing is workable. It is the virtue without which women are dull and art meaningless. And yet, loving this man as you say, you deliberately confuse your relationship with him by lying 'for the fun of it'! That seems to me an odd habit in an actress who doesn't mumble on the stage. As I am your audience and not at present your lover, could you give me a true answer to one question?"

"Yes."

"Would you lie to your vine-grower?"

She did not answer.

"When does he appear in Paris again?"

"I don't know."

"Doesn't he write to you?"

"Yes, he writes."

"Well?"

She shook her head. Even to Courcelet, she would not confess to her hoard of unopened letters.

How happy I am! she told herself, for gradually Templéraud was persuaded into a partnership as she understood it, and would often "go into committee on repairs and maintenance." What had produced this docility in him she did not know or stay to ask. It consisted in his noticing with precision any change she had made in her performance. If he was opposed to it, she countered his opposition fiercely, saying that criticism of detail made her self-conscious and that several of her admirers had particularly applauded the passage he criticized; but more often he praised the change she had made, and she felt that he was not only a vague and beautiful lover but a constructive partner, greatly more intelligent than a jealous world supposed him to be. Then she would throw her arms round his neck and they would talk of the house they would have in Burgundy. They would go there between her engagements in Paris and would live in the utmost simplicity, for, if you were happy, what need was there to be extravagant? He would suggest details of this establishment—his room must be on the ground floor with steps into the garden so that, when he was composing, he could take the air without walking through the house, or there must be a canopy to her bed with stars on it—and she would feel that the house was real and that they would grow old in it together and were capable of making each other lastingly and quietly happy. "You know, Etienne," she said, "I suppose people would have thought it fantastic that you and I should live peacefully together. But it isn't. Oh, my darling, I love you! I want no one else."

But she could not help being a little surprised as well as gratified that he, the least observant of men, should have become capable of noticing every change of timing or attack, every detailed twist of her performance in which she happened, at the moment, to be particularly interested. She had decided that an improvement might be made in the way she took a curtain-call. She would be moving towards the audience, so that the curtain should seem to fall between her admirers and their expectation and provoke them to more applause. The forward movement, she explained to Annette, would have to be judged with the utmost precision; if it were too slight, it would seem hesitant and miss its effect, if it were advanced too far down-stage, the curtain would seem to have fallen clumsily in her face. She had shown Annette what she intended, the inclination of her body and the angle at which she would place her forward foot. "Like a mouse," Annette had said stupidly.

At the Divertissements, she used this method with success, winning for herself, even on Monday night, two more curtains than were customary on Monday nights. When next Templéraud "went into committee" with her, he asked if he was not right in thinking that she had changed her method of taking a curtain-call, and praised her skill.

"Of course," he said with an air of wisdom that she found enchanting, "it may be dangerous, Thérèse. You can't afford to be a fraction of a second wrong. If you didn't move far enough, the thing would miss its effect. If you are even a few inches too far down-stage—"

She smiled with delight. "You are a darling, Etienne, to care so much. You have thought it out as if it were your own performance, not mine."

"Naturally. But you know, Thérèse, there's one thing—"

"Now," she cried, "don't spoil it all. What?"

"No, I'm not criticizing. One thing that I particularly admired. The angle of your foot—looking out from under your dress like a mouse."

Words leapt to her mind. It was Annette who told you that! she would have said, but was silent. Everything you have said was told you by her! but the words had no sound except in her brain. She looked at his smiling mouth, the wide eyes expectant of her customary praise for the acuteness of his observation, the golden hair that grew away from his forehead like the flick of a pennon in the wind, and she thought that it was, after all, natural that he should have noticed how important it was to time that curtain-call accurately. The likening of the tip of a woman's shoe to a mouse looking out from under her petticoat was common stock; there was no reason to assume that it had been borrowed from Annette. She decided to say to Etienne, quietly and without emphasis, that Annette also had happened to speak of a mouse, and see what reply he made. But she said nothing and turned her mind away.

Afterwards her memory called up from the past the many conversations in which she had analysed her work to Annette and Templéraud's repetitions of them. How was it possible that, until the word "mouse" had forced the connexion upon her, she had not suspected it? The connexion was evident, but she would not allow herself to blame Etienne. Soon, she thought, he and I will laugh together over it, and was glad that she had not embarrassed him by at once blurting out her discovery. Time enough, time enough! There was no harm in his foolish trick—nothing to blame him for, nothing to fear. Nothing to fear, she repeated. Was it not charming and childish in him to want so much to please her that he cheated for her sake, like a boy using a crib at school? She felt no resentment against him or against Annette, said nothing on the subject to either of them, and relapsed into the joy of having two friends who conspired to flatter her work and evidently discussed it when absent from her. Nevertheless, she decided to give Annette no more material for conspiracy. The decision stood for a week. After that Annette's purring adoration of her proved irresistible; she poured out her plans, her amendments, her triumphs and misgivings. It amused her to count the days until Etienne dutifully repeated them. She gave him a new nickname.

"My little parrot!"

"But why parrot?" he asked, examining himself in her long mirror. He had been trying on for a second time the renaissance costume he was to wear when he and she went together to a ball at Monsieur Gaillard's house—a fantastic house, "un château de Blois nouveau modèle" wrote a polite journalist celebrating the approaching festivity, but Thérèse was pleased by her invitation to it and by having secured one for Templéraud. How handsome he looked! She turned him about and gave a twist to his cloak as though she were dressing a child for a party, and kissed him suddenly with tears in her eyes. Why? Because he was hers; because, whatever happened between them, she would never again be able to look into her long mirror without remembering that it had held his reflection in this costume which her hands were now touching and from which there came to her nostrils the thick, exciting smell of a costumier's wardrobe.

"But this," he said taking the head-dress in his hands. "Is it right? I mean, does it belong to the rest?"

She had to confess that it did not. Courcelet had suggested their

wearing renaissance costume and had approved her choice for
Etienne, but the head-dress, a velvet cap with a fall of velvet at the
side, she had chosen afterwards. "Give it to me," she said. "I will
make sure. I will show it to Philippe."

An appointment with Courcelet was made. She would have
lunch with him on Thursday, bringing the cap with her, and she
looked forward to the discussion of renaissance dress that the cap
would provoke, to being shown the new Tissot Courcelet had
bought, and to leading him into one of those shrewd commentaries
on public affairs which gave fresh material for her performances. It
was his pride to give her, whenever they met, at least one idea on
which to build a topical verse; he delighted in an opportunity to
display his knowledge of the by-ways of history; and when she
invited herself to lunch with him on the pretext of Templéraud's
head-dress, she had no sense that she was wasting his time. But
before the day of their meeting came everything was changed. On
Sunday the 29th General Brière de l'Isle's despatch from Hanoi
threw the city into alarm and Thérèse contrived for the Divertissements a new verse, bidding her audience

> "Be at ease,
> The bad Chinese
> Are not at the gates of Paris."

But she was too late. Jules Ferry could not weather the storm. His
majority, seeing the elections a few months ahead, deserted him; on
Monday the Government fell; a scramble for office began, an inele-
gant scramble above all for the Ministry of the Interior which would
control the official candidatures, and Courcelet, himself independent
of office, a broker between all parties, the man above all others who
was believed to have his ear to the ground, received a stream of
callers at his rooms in the Palais Royal. On Thursday, a note from
him said: "Noon impossible. Forgive me—impossible all day.
Please come very late—after your supper at Maubant's."

Afraid of disappointing Templéraud, she showed him the message. If, after supper, he would go straight to her flat, she would
follow him there when she left the Palais Royal. "You always come

first," she said, "and if you'd rather I didn't go to Philippe, I can easily get out of it. After all, it is he who has changed our appointment. I can easily say no?"

She said this with eager questioning, but he replied that Courcelet must not be disappointed. "He must be desperately busy. If he makes time to see you in the middle of the night, it wouldn't be courteous—"

"Then you mustn't stay awake for me. Go to bed and go to sleep. I have never come in and found you in my bed, asleep."

Templéraud put his arm round her. "As if we were married?"

She took breath.

"But in fact," he continued, "I think I won't go to your flat to-night. I have work to do in the morning. I must be up early, and it would do me no harm to work late."

"You mean you won't come to Maubant's?"

"I think not, Thérèse. Not to-night. I'll go home and have some supper on a tray. Then I can work on steadily."

"Of course," she said. "You must always do that independently of me. What is the work to be? My songs or the symphony?"

He replied that he would work on the symphony; he had found that it was always best to do so in long stretches, late at night.

"I'm glad," she said. "I like to think of you working in that way. I shall think of you as I come home from Philippe's. Shall you be working then, I wonder?"

"That depends on what time you leave him."

She put her hand on his arm. "You're not jealous? You don't mind?"

"But, my darling, why should I be jealous?"

She enjoyed her visit to Courcelet. It renewed the spirit in her to observe the gallant detachment of this man whose worldliness was the armour of his acceptances. He was capable of acerbity, of an ironic lightness at her expense, of an extreme vanity; yet in all things he was temperate, a possessor of himself who chose even his faults as a man chooses a vintage, and in whom, it seemed, anger and self-pity and jealousy, all the resentments of life, had, like once-jagged stones, been worn smooth by the drip of experience. Even in his dressing-gown and slippers he preserved the effect of one who had been a young dandy under Louis-Philippe and who had spent his life in cultivating a sense of proportion. In the past, in this room, she had come to him as his mistress. Any but he might now have appeared to suffer or have fallen into a mood of romantic melancholy. Courcelet, instead, when he had shown her his Tissot, talked eagerly and at once of the costume of the Renaissance, pulled out books from his shelves and spread their illustrations before her on the hearth-rug; he settled the problem of Templéraud's cap with authority but not in haste, and, when she thanked him, replied simply that everyone liked being consulted on his own subject.

"But you have others," she said, running her hand over a pile of newspapers that lay on a stool beside his chair.

"Politics?" he answered. "Ah, that reminds me. I have an idea for you. You may know—or indeed you may not—that the Gambettists are hanging on Freycinet's doorbell. They think that, when the smoke clears away, they will find him at the head of the Government. Probably they are wrong. He will be a member of the Government, but what he wants is the Foreign Office for the time being. I wish you'd chip the Gambettists a little; they're a good target for a verse. Would this do—or something like it?"

She took the piece of paper he handed to her and tried the words silently with her lips. "Yes," she said, "it's good—and it's in character for Barbet. It's the angle from which he'd look at the thing."

"Who?"

"Barbet," she answered in surprise. "I said Barbet."

"You did, Thérèse, I know. But which Barbet? I gave you that scrap of paper, you read it, you used his name. Which was on your mind—your own vine-grower or the fictitious character you have created in your songs?"

"Oh, I was thinking of the songs."

"I see. That was what I wanted to know. Is the man forgotten?"

"No," she answered, "but why do you speak of him?"

"Because it's so long since you spoke of him, Thérèse."

She answered with fire: "I was a fool about him long enough. Nothing could ever have come of it. I am happy now. Why spoil that?"

Tolerance and good manners were always stronger in Courcelet than a desire to press for the truth. Intellectual curiosity would tempt him to probe into the minds of others, but, unless they were politicians, he would cease instantly if they winced. Now he turned up the collar of his dressing-gown and settled more deeply into his chair, allowing his thought, as he watched her troubled face, to proceed unexpressed. No mistress of his had given him so much pleasure, and none stirred in him so profound a compassion.

"You and I, Thérèse," he said at last, "we dramatize ourselves. For years I cast myself for the wrong part. At root I am a historian, as you know, a historian of the past or the present—it makes no odds; but I saw myself as a statesman without having the capacity, the bluntness, the thickness of skin, without having even the taste for it. For a time diplomacy was a substitute, but still I was cast for the wrong part. And now, this room. People say I'm mad to live here. 'Above the arcades of the Palais Royal,' they say, 'how do you hear yourself speak?' And it is true that a military band in the garden can be irksome on a summer's evening when it is too hot to shut the windows and you aren't in the mood for it. But the other side is quiet as the grave and I don't want both sides to be quiet as the grave —that is to be premature. I like my Palais Royal and the glitter of the arcades and the foolish pop-gun they fire at noon. This is my setting, Thérèse—books, pictures, you at near two in the morning to ask about a renaissance cap, and all day the would-be statesmen— the great men whom everyone will forget—have been coming to me. Why? Because I don't compete. Because I don't want office. Because I'm no one. And because I know. I am the barometer. And why, do you suppose, I know? Because they tell me. I am the best informed newspaper in Paris. Why? Because I don't publish my information. I have power. Under any government I can have what little things I want—any *little* thing, a post for one man, a privilege for another, any *little* thing because all I want is little things. Oh yes, still I am dramatizing myself. I love to sit here and watch them come to me. I take care that, in going, they shan't meet on the stairs, as if this were a well-regulated brothel, and I remark with interest the weakness of human nature which, having come with such secrecy and gone with such discretion, so often leaves its gloves behind. Those are young Monsieur Clemenceau's gloves on the marble table. He was my last caller. I haven't put them away. The gloves of Waldeck-Rousseau are already safely in the drawer. I keep them all as Lord Byron, I am told, collected locks of hair from each of his mistresses. . . . You see? Yes, I am dramatizing myself still. But in my true rôle at last. I sit here. History and beauty come to me. And you? But that, you will say, is not my concern—and indeed it is not."

"I have often wondered," she said, wishing to avoid the discussion of Barbet to which, she feared, he might return, "why you bother your head with Clemenceau and Waldeck-Rousseau and the rest."

"Because, Thérèse, I do not wish to be ambitious, and there is no surer corrective to ambition than to watch politicians scrambling for the boats when the ship is sinking. And in any case I am sometimes given an opportunity to serve France, though, if one is mixed in politics, one must do that by stealth. But what the world will remember me for—if it remembers me at all—is that I bought Manet when others didn't and was your lover for a little while when others weren't. And I shall be remembered for that collection of gloves. How strange it is," he added, his eyes on the ceiling, "I have been talking for the sake of talking and you have been silent for the sake of being silent, and the little vine-grower, whom we have been so considerately avoiding, has been present in both our minds." He leaned forward now, the cord of his dressing-gown dangling from his extended hands. "I assure you: if that door were to open and he to walk into the room, it would seem to me the most natural thing in the world."

Thérèse looked at the door. "I must go," she said. "Before I go, may I write a letter at your table?"

"So late? But certainly."

"I shall deliver it on the way home."

She wrote to Templéraud:

My Darling,

I want to think of no one but you. I have been talking to
Philippe—I am in his rooms now, just going—but I have been
thinking of you at work. No one wishes to be disturbed at work,
but I know that if I had been working alone for hours with no
prospect of seeing you, and suddenly a note from you tumbled
through my letter-box, I should be happy and work better because
I wasn't lonely any more. So I shall drop this in at your door on
the way home to say I love you.

Thérèse.

When she had finished this, she found that there were tears in
her eyes, and she turned abruptly to Courcelet, intending to say:
"Oh, that is nothing—tears. It means nothing, they come so easily.
I can turn them on," but she had taken longer to write than she had
known, and Courcelet, when she looked at him, was asleep. An idea
that amused her came into her mind. She was wearing long kid
gloves which she had turned back at the wrist. Now she drew them
off and laid them across Courcelet's knee. As she stooped, a tear,
the existence of which she had forgotten, ran down her cheek.
When she stood up, her great eyes were sparkling, and the temptation to disturb Templéraud at his work and go in to him fell upon
her with the force, the delight, the quickening of mortality remembered. To go to him now, contrary to her expectation or his, would
have the joy of being given a present for no reason or of sitting down
at a café and sharing a bottle of champagne in the middle of a hot
summer's morning. The taste of that champagne was on her lips
and the chill of the glass under her fingers as she walked cautiously
down the stairs of Courcelet's lodging and, with a hug of her cloak
round her shoulders, let herself out into the Rue Montpensier.

It was dark and silent, but there was spring in the darkness. Near
the Français a cab was standing; she hesitated, but the cabman
was asleep; the horse rolled his eye at her; the white of his eye swam
gigantically in the beam of a street lamp, and she laughed aloud as he
turned his head to stare after her—he was a horse by Caran d'Ache.
And on the way here, my darling, I met a horse by Caran d'Ache!

Should she go in to see Templéraud or drop the letter and be gone before he opened his door? Perhaps he had done his work and was already asleep. Perhaps he was working still and her coming would be an interruption. I ought not to stay! I will slide the letter in quietly, so quietly that he will not even come to the door. As she walked down the Rue de Rivoli, past the Oratoire, her mind was so firm against temptation that she was able to enjoy the virtue of having resisted it, but when she turned into the Rue des Bourdonnais and knew that one lamp only divided her from the little street that she called the Rue Etienne, though its name was Rue du Paon, it seemed to her foolish to have walked nearly a kilometre, to be almost on his doorstep and to run away.

The winter is really over, she thought; next Sunday will be Easter Day; and the long spring and summer flowed into her blood, the warm nights that were coming, the drives out of Paris to drink milk in the Bois at five in the morning, the scent of trees at daybreak when the sun was slanting up into their branches. Soon the vine-buds would be opening at Roussignac, swelling through their woolly covers, and showing the crimson points of their tiny leaves. On the edge of the vineyards, the cherry-trees would blossom, the Guigne de la Maurie which was her own cherry-tree because she remembered her mother telling her its name nearly twenty years ago at St. Brice. There was a stinging in her throat because she was so happy, and she longed to sing, to dance, to stand on tiptoe and stretch out her arms as though she were awaking from a rapturous sleep. She stood still, raised herself on tiptoe and parted her cloak that the air might be on her throat and breast; then, hearing footsteps in the Rue des Bourdonnais approach from the direction of the river, she said to herself: They'd think me mad! and turned rapidly into the side-street.

She had her own key to the building in which Templéraud lived. His lodgings were on the top floor. Far above her there was a gleam of illumination, perhaps from the little wall lamp on the third landing, but the lower flights were in darkness. She began to climb slowly, her hand on the rail.

The woodwork gave out a musty smell as though it were sodden, but it was a smell that pleased her because it was in coming to Etienne that she had grown familiar with it. She moved quickly and with her eyes fast shut.

As her fingers were turned by the first bend of the hand-rail, she heard the street door close. Whoever had entered began at once to climb the stairs and Thérèse advanced more quickly; if she were overtaken she would have to make her presence known in the darkness, but if she kept her distance ahead, the new-comer would turn aside into a flat on one of the landings below Etienne's. The new-comer did not turn aside. The footsteps passed the first landing and the second. Their advance was regular and assured. Thérèse thought suddenly: This is a visitor for Etienne.

There was a remaining possibility that this might not be so: a third landing on which lived two families, a young student with his father and mother, and, opposite them, a widower with two small daughters. The student might be returning late. Thérèse hesitated. If she went on, he might vanish behind her and the footsteps cease. She wished to believe this but could not. The footsteps were a woman's. They were drawing nearer; soon Thérèse would be visible from below; and she wished only to be hidden. A weak oil lamp was burning in a wall-bracket. It illumined a curtain, hung on a semi-circular rail, which was used to conceal an earthenware sink, now partly exposed. The tap was thinly running. Behind this curtain Thérèse hid herself.

When she saw Annette's face rise above the stairs, she remembered that Templéraud had once said of her: "She is like you," and her left arm and her leg and the whole of her left side began to ache; the pain ran up to the base of her skull and she closed her eyes, hearing the footsteps pass and go upward; then a tapping on his door, a signal, the door opening, their voices, the door shut. It was she who had entered; she felt his arm about her and the warmth of his lamp; she was beginning to hold out to him the letter she had written at Courcelet's and to say, as she had imagined herself saying, "You see, I am my own postman," when she found the letter in her hand; it was wet and her hand was wet; she must have held them near the tap, and she opened her eyes.

Except the trickle of water, there was no sound in the building. She seized the tap, but the brass was hard on the bone of her thumb. When she looked at the stair-head, where Annette's face had been, there was no face. So she is in his room. She has kicked off her shoes and is on his sofa; he is taking the lobe of her ear between his lips. But it is not true. He was surprised by her coming. She came with a message. I will go up and knock. But Annette must have had the key to the outer door.

Thérèse began then to remember the many assurances and tokens of love that she had given Templéraud and the happiness they had shared and the work they had done together. What had been became merged in what would have been, so that all her life appeared to be found and lost in him, and this spring and summer were cut off, and time was drained away like water from a basin. I will go away, I will go away, she thought, but she dreaded the street, the Rue Etienne, where she had been happy, and she listened and listened, saying to herself that truth would turn suddenly as a dream turns; his door would open, Annette come out; the spring and the summer and the pulse in her blood return. She listened, but heard only the thin trickle of water in the sink.

There is no one belonging to me. It is a long way to the Île St. Louis; the flat will be empty, letters on the floor. On my dressing-table in the theatre I left my brooch. In his pocket, on the chair beside his bed, within reach of her hand, is the card-case; if she stretches out her hand she can take it and open it and see my Meissonier, which I gave him. And he will say "Thérèse gave it me." But not so; they are asleep; hours have passed; light through the slats is crawling on his arm. He will say "Thérèse gave it me," but she will be clever; she won't laugh; she will say it is beautiful and yawn and stretch herself.

Thérèse moved on to the landing and looked about her. There was a window on the staircase which she had not seen before; a streak of oily smoke blackened the chimney of the wall lamp, which was dying. Soon the caretaker will go down and open the door, she thought, and steadied herself on the hand-rail of the stairs. She was glad of the smell of the lamp because it was outside her brain and called her out, away from nothingness, to touch and smell and thirst. After two flights she could not hear the water; it was gone; but two flights lower she heard it again.

It was morning in the streets. Soon she saw under her eyes the stone steps of a church; people in black were going and coming; she went in and found that it was Good Friday. She wanted only to sit down but when she sat the pain in her head returned, and she said: I am not waiting for anything. Why am I here? I don't know this church. She started up. I am in evening dress. I have nothing on my head. She drew the hood of her cloak over her head and thrust her cheek into the cold silk. Outside, a cab was standing. The man, who had driven her before, smiled and recognized her, and she asked him gratefully what news he had of his son in Tonkin.

Chapter 9

WHEN NEXT TEMPLÉRAUD WISHED TO COME TO her flat in the Île St. Louis, she did not refuse, nor, when he took her in his arms, did she resist, but she told him that he must no longer think of himself as her lover.

"Why, Thérèse?"

"Because it is over."

He did not argue or protest. A smile moved on his face. He looked at her with a moment's curiosity, but was careful to ask only:

"Have we quarrelled?"

"No. We shall work together unless you are a fool."

At supper at Maubant's she stretched her arm across the table. "Etienne, please give me my Meissonier." She did not return it or he ask that it should be returned.

Never by any word of hers should he be allowed to guess the reason for her having rejected him. She must have some part to sustain her, and the discipline of continued intimacy with him and Annette gave her strength; it demanded a continual effort, a fierce pride, to behave in their company as if she were blind to their desire for each other.

With Templéraud, she went in her renaissance dress to the bal Gaillard. As they arrived, the painter Jacquet swaggered into the Place Malesherbes on horseback, wearing a costume of the period of Henri III, a white pourpoint embroidered with gold, a sweeping plume to his hat, a sword at his side; and the crowd waved and laughed and shouted "Vive le Roy!" Her hand tightened on Templéraud's arm. She was delighted by Jacquet; his was an absurdity after her own heart; in a moment, she too would have been waving;

she and Templéraud would have been gay together. But suddenly
she was lonely and the more lonely because he was near her.

April and May were hard months, the harder because she would
not permit herself the relaxation of sorrow, which she condemned as
self-pity. She drove herself to work and pleasure, and permitted herself no slackening in the pace of her life. Her table at Maubant's
began to change its character; it became harsher, more strident,
richer, conforming more nearly to fashion, less to personal taste.
Men came there, and attached themselves to Thérèse, men whom
she despised but now invented reasons to admire. "Why these?"
asked Courcelet. "The poor rabble of adorers at the Écurie was better
than these! And you take them home with you and sit up all night?
Is it true?"

"Yes."

"Why?"

"Because there are some miseries that make one fastidious,
Philippe—so fastidious *inside* that what happens outside doesn't matter a damn. I could go to bed with all of them in turn and make each
believe it was an adventure and that I hadn't a trouble in the world!"

"In fact, you don't?"

"In fact, not yet. You had better be the first if it pleases you."

He smiled the insult away, and tried both to draw the truth from
her and to steady her, not by sympathy but by a deliberately incurious
lightness of heart. It was his attitude to all suffering bound in by
silences; in the end, he had found, the silence broke, the story poured
out; but now his method was unavailing—she was an actress who
could play comedy the better when her world was in ruins.

And how closely she was bound to her comedy, her tragedy, her
seemingly brilliant and various life! The theatre, the restaurant,
her flat on the Quai d'Orléans—her flat, the restaurant, the theatre!
"But you," she said, "you and your politics—your circle is as narrow!" He examined himself; it was far from being true; he could
shut out politics to-morrow and still have a full life. History, the
theatre, a little racing, friends—friends whose lives and whose
families interested and amused him apart from any bearing they

might have on his own fortunes. "Ah," she said, "that is because everything has come easily to you. You have a family and a back- ground. You have never had to fight. Or at worst you fight with your back against a comfortable, reassuring wall. I have no wall. I fight in the open. I am surrounded."

It had long been his purpose to draw her out of this desperate encirclement, but whatever diversions he planned, whatever invita- tions he contrived, she took her encirclement with her and could sus- tain interest in nothing that was not, directly or indirectly, a battle for or against Thérèse Despreux. Now more than ever was this true. She seemed scarcely to listen to news he brought her from a world outside her own unless it was news that could be turned to a verse. Even Victor Hugo, he found, was grist to her mill.

On a Sunday morning, with his carriage at her door to drive her into the May sunshine, he stood in her sitting-room beside her walnut desk, looking sometimes with critical approval at the reflection in her mirror of the upward wave of silver above his ears, and sometimes at the clear sky above Notre-Dame.

"Notre-Dame de Paris!"

She too was beside the desk, going through her strange ritual, into which he had long ceased to inquire, of dropping into it yet another unopened letter from her vine-grower of Roussignac.

"Why do you say that?"

"Have you ever read the book?"

"What book?"

"Victor Hugo: *Notre-Dame de Paris*. Victor Hugo is dying," he said, rolling the head of his tie-pin between forefinger and thumb and stretching his neck which, though a trifle loose in the collar, was still, he decided, not the neck of an old man.

"Dying?" she exclaimed. "Are you sure? Is that true?"

The note of personal alarm in her voice surprised and gratified him.

"That touches you, my dear? It will touch all France."

She locked the walnut drawer; the key clicked into a porcelain vase. "You see, I use verses of his. I shall have to change them."

"Bless you," he said, "so you will. The choice of new ones ought not to be hard. 'Sombre' was a favourite word of his." And having summoned her interest, he persisted; he would enjoy a discussion of Hugo as they drove out together; and he told her that on Thursday, after a dinner in honour of de Lesseps, Hugo had been taken ill. Slow heart, congestion of the lungs. Yesterday no worse, but no better.

"Oh, the old fellow is a lion. He will fight on, but he knows where he is going. He said to Lockroy: 'My friend, it is a dead man who is talking to you.' "

By this time Thérèse was ready to set out.

"We will drive to his house and drop a card," Courcelet said.

They were not the only visitors. In front of the little house a carriage was already drawn up when they arrived; two others awaited their turn.

"There will be a book. I will write my name and return to you."

"Can I write my name?"

"Certainly." He was glad not to have hesitated.

By the time Thérèse had stood under the scalloped canopy that stretched out over the door, and had examined the lamps set in the wall, and had waited until outgoing callers had squeezed past her, and had written her name in the book, she had acquired a personal, an almost possessive, interest in the poet lying upstairs. Beside the house, tall trees looked out over his garden wall.

"I hope his room is on the garden?"

Courcelet nodded.

"Then he's quiet," she said. "I'm glad. . . . You know, he might recover, even though he is so old."

She was silent as they drove on.

"If not," she said unexpectedly, "it will be history. Wouldn't it be strange to know, when you were dying, that that day would be remembered because it was the day on which *you*, Victor Hugo, died?"

Courcelet patted her hand. "I doubt whether he cares."

"I should!" said Thérèse. Then she sighed: "Oh dear, do you ever have your feelings hopelessly mixed! At one moment I feel like all the poems ever written about ambition, and I wish I could die in a small house with a garden, and people near me who love me and prop themselves against walls with handkerchiefs to their eyes or kneel at the bedside and hold my hand. And that seems much better than being famous. Then I think: suppose they *did* love me and hold my hand and dangled wet handkerchiefs, and I *wasn't* famous —I should have failed, and I should say: 'I'm dying, there isn't time to make good.' And I should sit up in bed and say: 'I can't die yet. I'm not ready. I can't die a failure. I'm not ready. Bring me some soup! Bring me some *strong* soup!' When I die, come to my bed and tell me I am famous, Philippe. If you tell me I have succeeded, I shall believe you. . . . I suppose," she added, staring at the coachman's back, "Victor Hugo has it every way—fame and love as well, a home and the Panthéon. Will they give him the Panthéon?"

"This Government?" said Courcelet. "I wonder. It would be almost too much to ask them to make up their minds. They might offend some part of their majority. . . . But he ought to have the Panthéon."

Thérèse meditated in silence, the taut silence in which her plots were hatched.

"Now listen," she said. "I like Victor Hugo. I have recited his poems often and often since Plence scoffed at him, and now I have written my name in his book. I am sure there's a poem of his about the Panthéon?"

"There is. Alphonse Nourrit sang it in the Panthéon in '31. Five hundred choristers, my father told me. The Marseillaise, the Parisienne of Casimir Delavigne, and then the Hymne of Victor Hugo. He can't have been thirty."

"Yes, yes," said Thérèse impatiently, "but how does it go?"

"I can manage the first lines. I haven't your memory, Thérèse:

> *"Ceux qui pieusement sont morts pour la patrie*
> *Ont droit qu'à leur cercueil—"*

" 'La foule vienne et prie!' " cried Thérèse. She ran through the stanza at high speed but did not find what her memory echoed.

"Somewhere is the *word* 'Panthéon'! That is what I want!" She shut her eyes and clasped her hands. Then at last—

> *"C'est pour ces morts, dont l'ombre est ici bienvenue,*
> *Que le haut Panthéon élève dans la nue,*
> *Au-dessus de Paris, la ville aux mille tours,*
> *La reine de nos Tyrs et de nos Babylones,*
>   *Cette couronne de colonnes*
> *Que le soleil levant redore tous les jours!"*

She put up her parasol with a click. " 'La ville aux mille tours . . . le soleil levant redore tous les jours!' More inspired lines have been written. Still, there he is in that little house waiting for the Panthéon, and he shall have it. You must pull strings too."

"Does it matter, Thérèse?"

"Well," she said, "the Panthéon may not matter to him, and it may not matter in itself, but it does matter if I am going to sing about it!"

He smiled, for he knew that she was trailing the coat of her own egotism; he smiled then, but afterwards his lips set. How impossible it was to draw her out of her own encirclement! Hugo had interested and touched her, and yet, in jest or in earnest, her thoughts were back to the Divertissements within a quarter of an hour.

He wished to help her, but it was easier to let her have her head. It touched his vanity to know that what he thought of as his privileges were restored, though he did not avail himself of them except in allowing the world to believe that Thérèse Despreux was his mistress, and it was a part of his dandyism, a part indeed of his fear of old age, not to preach to ladies. Preaching, he thought, is a privilege of romantic youths who can't be suspected—or suspect themselves—of being capable of nothing else. But he remained unquiet; he could not hide from himself the bleak and barren desperation of her mood, and one evening, more than a week later, he insisted unexpectedly on returning with her after her performance.

"No, Philippe, not to-night."

He was tired. On Friday Hugo had died; on Sunday there had been bloodshed over the Red Flag in the cemetery of Père-Lachaise;

the Government was fluttered and politicians were running hither and thither. Courcelet had little energy left to struggle with a woman, but he was stubborn, her refusal piqued him, he insisted. "You have always told me that at least I have first claim on you."

"You are content on those terms?"

"That is not the point. They are the best I can get until you sicken of the others."

"I have sickened long ago."

"Well?"

"They are—oh!" she cried, "what do you mean by talking of them to me? They are not things to be talked about. You who are discreet, who are not a jealous boy, once you knew when to be silent! And now . . ." She clenched her fists in the effort of control. "Philippe, I'm sorry," she continued when she could allow herself to speak again, "I'm truly sorry; you are kind and generous; you have a right to think what you please and do what you please, but, for a little while, do not always say what you think."

But Courcelet would not be led from his purpose, though it was against his nature and his breeding to be importunate.

"Listen, Thérèse. I am not asking to be your lover to-night. I want to talk."

"Why to-night? Why at all? What use is there in talking?"

"Because," he said, "I choose to-night."

"You are being a fool. Very well. As you choose. I was trying to save you from humiliation. Someone else will come."

"Then, Thérèse, you will send him away."

"Ah," she said with a smile, "that hadn't occurred to me. How clever you are! You have provided my entertainment for the evening."

In her sitting-room, she gave him wine, sat down and waited. This was her rigid defence and he admired it. She knows as well as I do, he thought, that it's not in my part to lecture actresses for the good of their souls, and, though I wait all night, she'll not give me a cue or take one. He smiled at his own discomfiture and looked at her over the edge of his glass, hoping that she too would smile, accepting his surrender, and that their conversation would flow on with its accustomed ease. But her lips did not move or her eyes answer. She regarded him fixedly, with expectation and, he thought, with fear. Her body had slackened; he saw her as she might be when she was an old woman, and he said to himself : What the girl needs is a priest.

"Now that you are here—" she began. "I am listening. Have you anything to say worth saying?"

"No, Thérèse. I beg your pardon. I haven't the character. You need—"

"What?"

"A priest."

"Because I am dying?"

He turned from the truth in that, rose, clasped his hands behind him and walked across the room to the window. "I beg your pardon, Thérèse. I am of no use to you. It makes me ridiculous, and it's my special folly that I'm afraid of being ridiculous. I wasn't born to play in tragedy."

"Weren't you? I have never known you play in anything else. Isn't it tragedy never to be simple, to be always afraid that you are 'playing the wrong part,' to be everlastingly bargaining with yourself and cheating yourself—to be incapable of loving?"

"All that is true," he answered. "I said: 'I haven't the character.'"

She followed him to the window and put her hand in his. "Poor Philippe! Poor Philippe!"

He turned swiftly. "I came here to comfort *you*!"

"Poor Philippe! You hadn't a chance. I have played you clean off the stage."

Seeing the trap and delighting in the skill with which she had baited it, he struggled yet: "That is why I said you needed a priest."

"Oh, my father is a priest. A priest is a man."

"That isn't true."

"No," she answered, "it isn't, but it was something to say."

"You despise men?"

"Not more than a good barmaid despises humanity. But one ob-

serves that they all come for the same thing. . . . You know,
Philippe, it's interesting—they don't all begin like that, but with me
they all come to it. It's something in me, I suppose; it's my fault; I
can't resist it—at some point I turn on the current, just to see the
manikin hop and make sure that he hops like all the other man-
ikins. Then I pay for it. To him it becomes more and more important. All the men who appear at my bar become drunkards—except
you."

"I—"

"Ah, you are different, of course!"

"To how many others have you said that?"

"How many, do you think, have asked me that question? But you
are different, Philippe. Do you know why?"

"Yes," he answered. "I know why. Because I am old."

"Because you do love me—in so far as you are capable of it. Or
the fault may be mine. Perhaps I should say: 'so far as *I* am capable
of allowing any man to love me.' Oh, that wouldn't be true if the
man were my equal or if he were *more* than I am, but no man ever
is. They are all like actors who don't know their parts. I have to
carry the scene—I have to; it's true; they are so little."

"Even Templéraud?"

She would say nothing against Templéraud. "He was a baby,"
she said. "Rather a greedy baby. Do you remember that night—I
suppose it was only two months ago—when I came to talk to you
about his costume for the bal Gaillard? That night I—"

"What happened, Thérèse?"

She shook her head. "I was only going to say that I remember he
tried the costume on in front of the long mirror in my bedroom."

There was a quiet, secretive knocking on the outer door. Thérèse
stiffened, and Courcelet put his hand over her wrist.

"Let him knock, child, whoever he is. We understand each other,
you and I. Don't be frightened. Don't be ashamed."

She whispered: "I will tell him that—"

"No, let him knock."

The knocking was repeated.

"From the street he may have seen the light in my window."

"And if so?"

"I mean, he won't go away."

The knocking was repeated.

"For him," she said, "it may be like the tap running."

What she meant, Courcelet had not an idea, but he answered, "Not in the least; that is altogether different," and tightened his hold on her and forced her to sit down, seating himself on the sofa beside her.

There was one more knocking, loud, abrupt, angry, then a long silence.

"Go to the door and look."

She obeyed, returned, stood before him like a child that is come into a strange room.

"He is gone," she said and, falling on her knees beside the sofa, clutched her face in her arms and began to cry wtih hard sobs, rending and slow, as though her body would break.

"It was not Templéraud at the door," Courcelet said. "You have forgotten, Thérèse, my dear. It wasn't Templéraud."

"What was it, then? You see, you see, you don't know."

She sat back, shameless of her distorted face.

"It wasn't he, Thérèse."

So sure was he of his cleverness in having discerned the twist of her mind and the substitution it had made that he repeated like an old nurse: "It wasn't he at the door, it wasn't Etienne."

"Oh no," she answered, "certainly it was not Etienne."

The need to take charge of her, to command her without regard for her resistances, appeared to Courcelet. He had lost his bearings and feared that, if she were left to kneel in mid-floor, she might break into ungovernable hysteria. No tears were on her face; her sobs came singly and at long intervals. He stared at her, his action paralysed, some echo in his brain uselessly telling him that, if a woman became hysterical, the way to shock her out of it was to slap her face. I couldn't, he said to himself, I couldn't; she is too lonely. Why did I come here? And now, how the devil do I go away? He decided that, if she were in bed, then he could safely leave her.

"Thérèse," he said, "drink this." He gave her the wine in his own glass. She swallowed it and held out the glass, which he refilled; she drank again—the glassful—without pause for breath.

"The music-master in Angoulême," she said, "threw his glass against the wall. I wonder what has become of—"

"Go to bed, Thérèse."

"Yes." But she did not move. "Don't be frightened, Philippe. I shall be sane again in the morning. I'm only acting. I'm lonely. I want to be sure you don't go away."

But Courcelet had heard that mad people were so adroit that they would pretend to be sane to elude the watchfulness of others and he said stubbornly:

"Get up and undress and go to bed, Thérèse."

The corners of her mouth went down but she obeyed at once. He waited until there was silence in her bedroom, then entered. The bedclothes were drawn high; he could not see her face, but knew from her breathing that she was asleep. He blew out her candle, returned to the sitting-room, cautiously gathered his hat, his cloak, his stick, walking on tiptoe, extinguished the lamp and went out.

No sooner had the outer door closed behind him than she leaned up into the darkness and felt for matches. She was careful to do all that she did without haste, noticing everything, feeling everything, the gilt on her swan's high wings, the cool linen under her leg as she slid forward, the down in her slippers as her feet entered them. Candle in hand, she went to the walnut desk, shook out a key from a high porcelain jar that stood on it, unlocked a drawer and, with a swift movement of her hand, gathered to her the bundle of letters it contained. Then, as though she had committed a theft, she ran to her bed, the candle-flame flat and streaming, and lay on her back, her breath audible, her heart apace.

When her breath was quiet, she turned on her side, intending to read the letters in the order of their dates. She had a simple hunger for the news they would contain of men and places familiar to her but external to her present life, and she began to read with the undivided joy of rediscovering a story not forgotten though put away. But before the first page was turned, she became aware of herself reading, her fingers released the paper, her eyes came up as though she were being watched. Even to read these letters seemed false to her now.

Her fear of sentimentality, her abiding distrust of whatever gentleness of motive in herself threatened to loose the armour she wore against the world, suggested to her that the intuitive tenderness with which she had safeguarded these letters was a lie, and that she had deliberately hoarded them so that, in such a mood as this, she might dramatize the reading of them. Her memory, seeking the instant in which the decision to read them had been made, drove her back and back, mercilessly pursuing, beyond her pretence of sleep while Courcelet was blowing out her candle, beyond what appeared now as her pretence of suffering and her pretence of madness while Theuriet was knocking at the outer door, to the spectacular and designed candour of her likening herself to a barmaid and saying, with the dagger of Templéraud's indifference twisting in its wound, that men became drunkards who— She tossed in her bed and sat erect, her hands pressing upward the flesh of her cheeks. It had been then, in the midst of the contrived brutality of that speech, that Barbet had appeared in her mind; her imagination had swept her on until she had believed, and not believed, that it was he at the door, until she had known that to-night, when she was alone, a fascinated spectator of her own repentances, she would fall into a luxury of self-accusation, and at last, dragged upon the in-turning spiral of her self-criticism, sleep.

She lay down on her side again, supported on her elbow, restless and confused, scorning her confusion—a stupidity, she had always said, of idle women who made pets of their consciences, and took them out and combed and frizzed and wept over them and put them away again. Her remedy was in her job, in action, in the challenge of a new task, a new struggle, a new appetite that summoned the decisive energies of her mind. In action, she knew, she was swift and fearless, robust in the whole experience of the senses—hungry with joy, thirsty with joy, a tigress for work, undaunted, unfailing. And now she lay here without the will to read the letters or to put them away, between night and morning, fingering the candle-wax, without appetite even for sleep. She jerked herself upright in the bed.

Thérèse Despreux, you are a professional diseuse! But she could not rally, the old incantation was dead. Thérèse Despreux! Thérèse Despreux! She slid down on to her pillow, sick at heart of this stale trick of calling herself by name. If only there were a being on earth to whom it was not a name on a placard, to whom she belonged, who would seize and hold her, whose faith in her was stronger than her own distrust! Since her mother died, she had not known any such reassurance. Her father had not recognized her. Learning to shrink from his timid approaches, she had fallen away from the Church. All her nightmares had been of isolation, and she had fought them by her genius to compel the attention of strangers to herself, by the challenge with which she cried her wares, by her boldness, her humour and anger, her refusal to be put down. She had not dared be tired lest her protective self-reliance should fail her; but she had learned to mock, that she might not pity, herself, and this mocking voice, her own, turned to ridicule the impulse she now felt to surrender, to abdicate her prides and powers. It seemed to her that, in remembering her father and mother and the unconsoled nightmares from which she had awakened, screaming, in the Cheval Pie, she was only playing the part of a little girl, and playing it because to do so put a gloss of pathos on her failure to hold Templéraud. Was even her desire to read Barbet's letters a sop thrown into the same tawdry drama? She raised the letters by thrusting her hand under a pile of them, and with indifference, almost with contempt, allowed them to slide from her palm. She stared at them, yellow on the sheet.

One night at Royan, the night after her walk through the woods with Madeleine, Courcelet had spoken of George Sand, the conversation had run to music and to Chopin, and Templéraud, echoing Plence as Thérèse now perceived, had attacked the Romantics, saying that they were sentimental, that they lied. Cugnot had taken fire, not in defence of the Romantics, but in counter-attack upon those whose catchword for all feeling but hatred was "sentimentality." He had asked which was the greater lie—to be sentimental or to be paralysed by the fear of sentimentality? Was it not better, in art, to be wrong in boldness than wrong in fear? And Courcelet had said: "If I may be allowed to speak with authority, as one whose whole life is a lie and certainly not a romantic one, I suggest that the greatest of lies is by self-consciousness to freeze the heart. To be incapable of surrender is the final cowardice. The priests call it spiritual pride."

He is clever, my poor Philippe, Thérèse thought, there is point in everything he says, but it takes you no further. What he said then is true—perhaps it is true—it seemed true and I remember it, but, though it sounds like an answer, it is, like the answers of all clever men, only the question repeated; it is a phrase he has made, it goes on in the head. "To be incapable of surrender is the final cowardice." Poor Philippe! . . . Poor Thérèse! You are pitying him because you dare not pity yourself. If for a moment you were to cease to deafen yourself with your own name, you could not endure the silence.

Thérèse Despreux! Thérèse Despreux! The name written on schoolbooks. The name she had given to Plence when she was unknown: What is your name? Thérèse Despreux. The name, on the hoardings, of the woman they paid to see at the Divertissements. Her own name and yet not hers. The name on the envelopes. "To be incapable of self-surrender is the final cowardice." Poor Philippe! The name of the girl lying in the great bed. A name to freeze the heart.

"If only I could stop arguing," Barbet had said, "then I should know what to do."

When did he say that? Perhaps at some time when he had been speaking to her about the glow-worms in the prison. She could not remember. It is almost morning, she thought; the candle is down. There was another beside it, partly burned; she lighted it and extinguished the first.

From the envelopes the plain handwriting looked up at her—her own name, the heavy Q of the Quai d'Orléans, the word "Paris" in great capitals, as though it were the name of a foreign country. The thought of his undemanding patience in writing, week after week, to her who did not answer, quieted her. She began to read. No letter was of great length, for Barbet kept near to his observation, the birds he saw and heard, the changes of river and hedgerow, the progress of the fields, the vintage, the distillation. Against this background the familiar figures appeared—his mother, "who becomes more gay as she grows older, and happier too, I think"; Anton, who "isn't such a villain as you suppose, Thérèse. It's a bad day if I can't make him laugh at his own bluster"; and "your father, who calls on me more often than a heretic has any right to expect, wanting news of you but never asking for it. I would volunteer it if I had any." There was never a stronger hint than this that he required an answer. "You have your own reasons for not writing; some day you will tell me what they were and I shall seem foolish not to have understood."

Though he wrote seldom of himself, his letters produced in her a feeling of his presence in the flowers, the animals and even in the people he spoke of, for he recognized no division between himself and them. His mind was neither self-abnegating nor self-assertive. He did not think: the Others and I; he did not think: I and the Others; but seemed to be unaware of any opposition or boundary between himself and what he perceived. To follow with him, page by page, the movement of the year brought to Thérèse a peace that she might not have known if she had read each letter when it came, for their continuity included her; even when he spoke of himself and her, one in Charente, the other in Paris, their separation was of place only and accidental; when he said that he loved her, his love was not an intensification of their two separated individualities, there was no stress in it or crying out against the distance between them or possessive jealousy of her life remote from his; and she, who had believed a loving covetousness to be a sign and part of love itself, saw for the first time that there was an alternative to it that was not indifference—a fullness of recognition, a calm and passionate acceptance of unity within the ultimate unity of all sentient creatures.

Understanding of these ideas came to her slowly as she read. They were nowhere expressed in what he wrote but were instinct in the warmth and modesty of his writing. His descriptions were not of external things towards which he looked outward, but rather of a natural and, because natural, a miraculous world of which he and she were a part. He told her in January how on New Year's Day the children had followed the custom she knew well, going from door to

door in Roussignac for pennies, and in his writing he himself seemed
to be one of the children—"Each door has an expression," he said.
"Some are wolves' doors and frown, and you have to be brave to
knock." He told how the fire brigade, in uniform and brass helmets,
had come out even to the Maison Hazard to serenade him with bugles
and drums; how, when all the men had received their five-franc
pieces and their glasses of wine, he and they and his mother and old
Quessot had clinked glasses together—

> *Bonne année, bonne santé*
> *Et le paradis à la fin de vos jours*

—"the old greeting," he said, "which I knew you wouldn't forget
to give to your audience at the Divertissements. It would be good
and please them and draw them in. Some people in an audience
seem to need a lot of drawing in; just because they have paid and sit
where they do, they behave as if the footlights were a wall." "I know
that! I feel that!" Thérèse exclaimed under her breath as she read,
for he spoke in terms of her experience as though it were his own, as
though he also had stood on a stage and felt the tug of an audience
like the tug of a fish on a line, and her heart beat faster as she turned
the page, for had it not been on the morning of New Year's Day itself that she had remembered the old greeting and resolved to use
it, proud then of so apt a trick of showmanship?

As his letters passed on through the winter into the spring, her
sense of isolation fell away from her, her heart lightened, but, when
her eye fell upon the page he had dated Easter, 1885, the venom and
anguish of those days struck at her afresh. "I feel separated from my
prisoners," he wrote. "I am ashamed that it is so and feel it to be
wrong. You told me once that, in my relation to them, I seemed to
you to be a prisoner myself, and I am sure that is true and that it is
wrong. But I feel that, since they are condemned and must be prisoners somewhere, I should be only a coward and do no good by
washing my hands of them. Can I not help them and be of some
use? That is my dilemma. I am hedged in, I argue, I think too much
about myself—whether I should be doing right or doing wrong to
give up the prison—and so I make myself important and separate,

from which nothing good can come. Now if you were in a prison I should let you out if I could, and if a wild bird were in a cage I should open the door, and if an animal were in a trap I should release it. That is simple enough. But I can't stop arguing about the prisoners because, even if I were to give up the prison, that wouldn't set them free. . . ."

When she had done reading this, she put down the letter and looked at the envelopes that were as yet unopened. Thérèse Despreux. Thérèse Despreux. It was no longer an isolated and warring name; an insane emphasis had been lifted from it. She read it tranquilly as she might have read a name not hers. I will read the others in the morning, she said to herself, and knew, as she lay down to sleep, that her first waking thought would be of gladness that she had still to hear of Roussignac in April and May. In the darkness she remembered that more than a week, perhaps a fortnight, had passed since a letter came from him. Her memory was accurate; at will, she could turn it backwards, day by day, like the pages of a book; and she remembered that, as she was putting away the last letter she had received, Courcelet, beside her at the walnut desk, had been saying to her that Hugo was dying. "And to Lockroy he said: 'My friend, it is a dead man who speaks to you.'" It was on a Sunday; it was two Sundays ago. To-day was Wednesday, the 27th. She counted on her fingers: ten days. Sometimes there were intervals of more than ten days between Barbet's letters, but she sat up in bed again and relighted her candle. She would read the last.

It was dated Thursday May 14. It told of buttercups in the meadows and of the little green bunches of the montpellier maple "full of bees." "I went to see your father as I came home from Roussignac. The wallflower on the church is out. I told him I should soon be in Paris so that he might send a message if he wished. He said: 'Ask her, if she has a holiday, to come here in the summer.' I shall see him again before I leave, but I expect I shall not write again. There is always much to be arranged before I go on these journeys, particularly now that Pierre dislikes so much coming near the prison. It is not only that it takes him away from other work but that he positively dislikes it. He has to be persuaded. He seldom comes even into the house if he can avoid it, except on special occasions when we invite him, though he and Renée are always glad to see me if I visit them. I shall go to the Hôtel Bagnolet as usual, arriving probably during the afternoon of Thursday 28."

She imagined him in his corner, his head on one side, asleep in the train.

Chapter 10

THÉRÈSE WALKED ACROSS THE RIVER NEXT morning to the Hôtel Bagnolet and left there a note asking Barbet to come to her theatre if he reached Paris in time. She gave it into the hands of the lady with yellow hair whom she found at a desk near the foot of the stairs. At her question, this lady flicked the pages of a time-table and replied without looking at them that Monsieur Hazard was expected at three o'clock. His room was prepared.

"Every gentleman," she said, "has his own little ways. No doubt you have observed that, madame?"

"Yes," Thérèse answered with a smile that the shadows of the passage concealed, "that is very true. I have often observed it. And yet," she added, unable to resist the temptation to argument with one whose knowledge of men was probably as extensive as her own, "and yet I have observed also that, from another point of view, there is a remarkable sameness in gentlemen."

The time-table was put down and patted. The silver bangles tinkled merrily. "That may be. That may be. But in a hotel at any rate their differences are more important—for example, Monsieur Hazard likes his bordeaux in half bottles, and, on the mantelpiece, pencils sharpened, and, in the cupboard, bread and cheese. And, do you know, madame, I have always a feeling that he is a very happy gentleman. That, you will agree, is rare. Whatever happens, he is always pleasantly surprised. For example, the pencils. Always I put them there, but he is always pleasantly surprised as though I were giving him a present. But you know him well, madame?"

"All my life," said Thérèse. "Perhaps you will tell him I brought the note myself. Mademoiselle Thérèse Despreux."

"Ah, yes! Now, let me think. Surely I have heard that name before?"

"I sing and dance," said Thérèse. "Perhaps you have seen the name on placards."

The lady at the desk evidently had not. She shook her head and pursed her lips. "No. . . . No," she said, "it was—it was in some connexion with Monsieur Barbet—it was—ah, yes, one day he asked me—" She threw a wild glance at Thérèse and broke off, blushing in hot confusion. "Oh dear, oh dear, I was very foolish that day! Let it pass, let it pass, we are all foolish sometimes." She mustered her control. "I beg your pardon. It is an honour to know Mademoiselle Thérèse Despreux."

"And you?" said Thérèse.

"And I, mademoiselle?"

"You are not Madame Bagnolet?"

"Ah no, indeed no! . . . There! As you are a friend of Monsieur Barbet's, and as it was his father who gave me the name, you will not think it wrong if I tell you that I am always called Mademoiselle d'Austerlitz." She sighed and clasped her hands. "It is strange. Gentlemen forget that I am Mademoiselle Plon. I have had letters addressed to Mademoiselle d'Austerlitz."

"It is a gallant name," said Thérèse. "And I notice that you speak of him as Monsieur Barbet?"

"Did I do that? Well, I must be forgiven. I have known the family so long. But I am afraid," she added, with that unexpectedness which Thérèse had come to expect in her, "that Monsieur Barbet will never marry and have children. It would have been a pleasure to prepare a room for his son when he himself is gone."

"Gone!" Thérèse exclaimed. "He must be less than thirty-five."

Mademoiselle d'Austerlitz smiled pleasantly. "Yes, indeed," said she. "I suppose I must be very foolish. I forget that even I shall not live for ever. And now Victor Hugo is dead."

"You will go to the funeral?"

"Ah no, mademoiselle. The hotel is full. They say that there are three hundred thousand visitors in Paris. Some say even more. We have people who are not our clients, people we have never seen before."

"Then Monsieur Barbet was lucky to get his room."

"Ah no, mademoiselle, that is understood."

Thérèse held out her hand to say good-bye. "Tell me, why are you so devoted to him?"

Mademoiselle d'Austerlitz emerged from her shadows and her little feet hissed down the passage towards the door. "Devoted? Yes. Are you surprised? It is—now, how shall I put it?—it is that he and I, Monsieur Barbet and I—" She broke off, smiling in defeat and took Thérèse's hand between her own. "Voyons. Il est toujours content de la vie."

It had so delighted Thérèse to come upon someone who knew Barbet and would talk of him that she at once allowed her imagination to transform Mademoiselle d'Austerlitz into a fantastic and legendary creature, who had known all the generations of Hazard and who would live for ever under her pile of yellow hair. I will send her tickets for the theatre—but does she ever come out? Thérèse wondered. Does she ever sleep or eat? Or does she live always at that desk with the colours of the fanlight on the tiles at her feet? At a florist's she bought two bouquets of roses and addressed them to the Hôtel Bagnolet—one "For Mademoiselle d'Austerlitz," and the other "For Monsieur Barbet's room."

She cancelled an engagement for supper and that night refused all invitations.

"Thérèse," said Cugnot, seated beside her dressing-table while she made up for the stage, "what has happened to you? Your eyes are shining. Are you up to mischief or have you been making good resolutions?"

"No mischief," she said, "and no good resolutions; I don't believe in binding the future. But I feel like the New Year!"

"In May?"

"If you kiss my hand, I'll sing to you." She stretched out her hand. "Now come close. I'll sing in your ear.

"Bonne année, bonne santé
Et le paradis à la fin de vos jours.

Is that a good song?"

"My God," he said, kissing her hand again, "what *has* happened to you, Thérèse? When you're in this mood, you would enchant the rebel angels. And look at your eyes!"

She examined them in her mirror. "Yes, they are good to-night. They always become larger when I'm very happy or very unhappy."

"And at the moment?"

She jumped up and threw her arms round his neck. "Darling Cugnot! You must go now. Come back at the end. You'll know why."

But Barbet did not appear. Late in the evening she sent a boy to the front of the house; he returned to say that the ticket she had left at the box-office in the name of Monsieur Hazard had not been called for. Cugnot and Plence being in her dressing-room, she said that after all she would sup with them. Because, throughout the evening, she had declared consistently that she would not be supping at Maubant's, no one followed her there, but in the restaurant itself there were enough who knew her; they stopped at her table on their way to their own; they broke off from their parties to visit her; they loitered, sat down, lighted cigarettes, beckoned their companions over; and soon her table was full—ten men and two of their mistresses— the talk mounting like the stakes at a gambling table, voices and emphasis increasing, and Thérèse found herself holding the bank with the same heady excitement that would have gripped her if the table had been glittering with gold pieces. The room was hot, and heavy with smoke and the scent of flowers. She threw off a black lace wrap and felt a new heat of the air on her bare shoulders. On the bald head of the banker Schnetz little beads of sweat were forming; she watched them gather and run like raindrops on a window-pane, saw his silk handkerchief stick on his forehead and his lips suck at his champagne. He and Eugène de Quérignon, a young man with a long, pale moustache who had the interesting ambition to make

Thérèse a royal mistress as soon as the Bourbons could be restored and whose attitude towards life was, in all other things, at once as solemn ánd as frivolous, were debating with Plence, who had thrown the subject across the table as a handful of coins to be scrambled for, the value of continence and its opposite as an incentive to endeavour. The coins bounced; the company fell upon them. History, scandal, reminiscence were called in evidence. Plence recited an elaborately detailed form-book of the Écurie in which his leading performers were considered in the language of Auteuil; Quérignon's reigning mistress, Suzanne Druat, contributed an aphorism on convents; Quérignon himself drew his cuffs down over his long, thin wrists, took a deep breath and began an oration by Bossuet on the death of Thérèse Despreux. As his eloquence approached its climax, he rose in his place, stretched out his arms and was about to address all Maubant's on the perils of chastity when old Schnetz leaned across the table to pull him down, lost his feet, floundered and could not return. There he lay among the fruit and glasses, rolling on his belly, vainly slapping the table-cloth with hands too weak to raise him. Quérignon instantly leapt on to a sofa and, supporting himself on one foot, put the other neatly on Schnetz's shoulder. "You see before you," he cried, "one whom virtue has brought low, and on whom this epitaph shall be written: For him a bed was a place of pilgrimage and a supper-table his grave. For him—"

His sentence was broken by a roar of laughter. Thérèse removed his foot and rescued his victim. Poor Schnetz was so near to crying that she kissed him; his gallantry responded; he began to laugh breathlessly, then stopped: "Good God, look at Plence!" he cried.

Plence was standing in his place, his arm raised, his forefinger extended:

"Behold," he said, "the man who came out of the mirror!"

Those whose backs were to the door turned in their chairs. All Thérèse's company, and indeed the whole company of Maubant's, gazed at the man who now stood, hat in hand, momentarily dazzled by the blaze of light. He stood firmly, moving neither hand nor foot, and turned his head. He was neatly dressed in grey trousers and a square-cut jacket buttoned high. At recognition of Plence his mouth

broadened into a smile. As though no one was staring at him, he
reached for Plence's hand and shook it warmly:

"Bon soir, monsieur. Enchanté de vous revoir."

At this moment he saw Thérèse. His face lighted, but he moved
towards her without haste, a little bow to right and left asking first
that his interruption might be pardoned. Then he took her hand,
drew up a chair between her and Schnetz. As he did so, he saw Cugnot, leaned over the table again and shook his hand as he had shaken
Plence's, then sat down, unembarrassed and unruffled, taking stock
of those around him.

"I am sorry, Thérèse, not to have come to your theatre. I found
your note but I had an evening appointment with a merchant from
Bercy—rather important as he is leaving Paris to-morrow morning.
He was surprised, I can tell you, to find flowers in my room. Such
beautiful flowers too. Thank you, Thérèse. And Mademoiselle
d'Austerlitz asked me to convey her thanks—and her apologies for
not having known who you were."

"And who is it that doesn't know Thérèse Despreux?" Quérignon
interjected.

"A friend of mine," Barbet answered. "You see, she works in
my hotel. She seldom comes out—but there's a great deal she does
know, I assure you." He turned again to Thérèse. "My visitor
stayed. I came late to the theatre. You had already gone. But they
told me you were often to be found at Maubant's."

A waiter asked him what he would drink.

"Thank you," he said. "I am not thirsty," but, when Schnetz
poured him out a glass of champagne, he raised it politely and drank
a mouthful. Thérèse went through a form of introducing him, casually waving her hand and murmuring a name here and there. Carefully observant, he bowed courteously to each. His eyes were clear;
his hands on the table-cloth had the cool brown of long exposure to
weather; and he held his body erect and at ease.

"I hope I haven't interrupted an interesting conversation," he
said. "Everyone seemed to be enjoying themselves."

The interesting conversation was resumed. The wind was out of
Quérignon's oration and he started on a new tack. But his invention

failed; he lost the table; and at the farther end of it, a thin man like a white ferret raised his head to say that he knew a woman who went three times a year to Père-Lachaise where she laid flowers on the tomb of Abélard and Héloïse because she regarded it as a monument to disappointed love.

"Héloïse and Abélard, my dear friend," Schnetz cried, eager to dispute which of the two should be given precedence, but the discussion swept past him; the old story was embellished, as an example of chastity enforced, with modern instances from the drawing-room and the coulisses, the Church was criticized, the virtue of Héloïse suspected, her competence examined, her love doubted, and Abélard was considered as a schoolmaster, a prig, a fool, a coward, a hero, a hypocrite—all this in a gay, cruel dialogue that ran from tongue to tongue like flame over dry sticks until the whole table crackled with the lies of wit. Thérèse, taking her part in it, accepting each challenge as it came, parrying it, turning it to her profit, became aware that Cugnot had contributed nothing and was not listening to her. He was watching Barbet; she also turned to look at him; as she did so Quérignon said with malice, so that the provincial who had interrupted his oration should be embarrassed and befooled: "But you, sir, have said nothing!" A silence fell; Suzanne Druat began to titter; Schnetz rolled his eyes. "What would you say," Quérignon persisted, "—that chastity is productive or barren? And if it is not voluntary but enforced—what then? What do you say of Abélard and Héloïse?"

"Only that they were happy and that they suffered," Barbet answered.

"No more than that?"

"And that they were brave," Barbet said, as though he were answering questions in school.

"But all that is obvious," cried Quérignon. "You needn't be so cautious, my friend. You may speak openly. We swear to keep your secret. . . . Come, they are safely dead."

"Oh no," said Barbet, "for a long time they have been standing behind your chair."

Quérignon's shoulders twitched; he cast a swift, fluttering glance

down the table as though to beg from his own kind the support of
their ridicule; then, throwing up his head, let out a solitary and shrill
laugh like a cry, and gulped and was silent.

Barbet was astonished. His words had sprung naturally from the
impression, which had gathered in his mind while the others were
talking, that they considered Héloïse and Abélard to be divided from
themselves by impassable barriers of time and individuality—barriers
that for him had no existence, and what he had said was not a reproof
to them but a spontaneous expression of his own feeling, a short cut
to his long silence. But having alarmed Quérignon, he at once did
what he could to put him in countenance again.

"Do not misunderstand me," he said. "I did not mean that I
had seen their ghosts—only that while you were speaking—while you
were all speaking and I was listening—I thought that, when they
were in Paris, we were less real to them than they are to us, and that
nevertheless— But there, I feel that I have upset Monsieur de
Quérignon by what I said."

"Not at all, not at all," said old Schnetz, "I'd have said it myself
if I'd thought of it."

What precisely he meant by this remark no one knew, but everyone felt that there was something absurd and childlike in it. Schnetz
found himself being laughed at without hostility and was as pleased
as a boy when the world encourages him. Now, what *did* you mean?
he was asked, and replied with a seriousness which, as he was a little
drunk, set them laughing again: "Really, bless me, I'm not sure that
I know. But the world grows over one like a crust. The English
have a rhyme about blackbirds who were shut in a pie under a crust
of pastry. And then, you know, there comes a moment when the
crust breaks and the birds begin to sing!"

The tension was slackened and Quérignon given time to recover
his poise. He looked at Barbet without resentment but with curiosity and said: "I understand. Yes, I understand very well. But
you also must understand something: we talk for the sake of talking. While I talk, there is always something quite different going on
in my mind. For example, if I were to tell the truth I should confess
that ever since I first read the letters of Héloïse—ever since then I

have felt that she and I—no, let me finish, Suzanne, let me finish—
that she and I had a secret in common. I mean," he continued with
an unarmoured simplicity that Thérèse had never before known in
him, "that the book became more than a book to me. I used to turn
back to her letters as if they were my own and I used to judge others
by their appreciation of them. And every word I have said against
her to-night—" He looked round as though seeking refuge from the
necessity to say what he was about to say. Then his eyes returned
to Barbet's and he continued: "Every word was a denial of—of—
I heard myself speaking them you know—a denial of—not of her,
but of myself."

"And then, bless me, the cock crew three times!" said Schnetz.
"It is always crowing, that's the devil of it. Now if you could tell us,
Monsieur Hazard, how to wring the neck of that cock, you'd make
life a deal easier."

Thérèse had been content to be silent. She had been watching
the faces of those before her, and feeling the presence of Barbet at
her side. Conversation had become eager again, but its temper was
changed. The white ferret was describing a great disused granary
among the outbuildings of the country house in which he had been
brought up—a room, he said, that had seemed to him as large as a
cathedral. "I used to creep out of the house at night and creep back
in the morning before anyone was awake. There was no adventure
to compare with sleeping among the straw. My father sold the house
and when I went back there the granary had been pulled down and
something else had been built in its place." "What had been built
in its place?" Plence asked. "That is what is so extraordinary, I can't
remember what had been built in its place. I can see myself standing there and deciding precisely where the granary had been and
thinking: if only the place had been left vacant it would be better.
But I can't remember the new building." "You could go and look,"
said Plence. "Oh no, oh no, I shall not go there again. It makes the
cock crow, my dear Plence." And this tale of the granary was capped
by other tales of times past which revealed the tellers to themselves
as they had forgotten that they were. Old Schnetz cocked his eye
at Thérèse and said: "When the pie was opened the birds began

to sing" He touched Barbet on the arm and continued: "You know, my dear friend, it was you who broke the crust. Can you tell us why blackbirds sing?"

"Certainly," Barbet answered obligingly. "That is my own subject. Certainly I can tell you why birds sing." Then he smiled a wide, easy smile. "But I won't begin at this time of night."

Schnetz nodded with sleepy affability. Except Thérèse's table, Maubant's was empty.

"Thérèse, my dear, we have said so many foolish things to-night. And the cock is crowing. Sing us a song to make us forget them."

Often she had sung to them at the end of an evening. Now she was frightened and said: "What shall I sing?"

Cugnot leaned up the table. "Thérèse! Thérèse, you have been given your cue!"

She did not understand, smiled, shook her head. He whispered soundlessly, making with his mouth words for her to read.

"Ah yes! Ah yes!" she exclaimed. "But that is Barbet's own song!" And she turned to him.

"What song, Thérèse?"

She put her lips to his ear; then asked: "May I sing that?"

"But certainly."

"Here? Now?"

Schnetz came suddenly to life. "Is your name Barbet, sir?"

"Yes," said Barbet.

"Bless me," said Schnetz, "and it is to you we owe her songs. Barbet this and Barbet that! Barbet at the races. Barbet at the Elysée. Barbet at the Salon. Barbet in the Chamber. Barbet in the country. And we thought you were a stranger. My dear sir, you are as famous as the Eiffel tower."

"But less conspicuous," said Barbet.

Schnetz struggled for the bottle, splashed champagne from glass to glass, then forgot the toast he had intended.

"Sing, Thérèse," Cugnot said.

Thérèse straightened herself and laid her fingers on the table's edge. She sang to Barbet's own tune as Fontan had written it down.

"I said a stupid thing. I wish I could unsay it. But you alone can unsay it by not remembering my foolishness when you remember me."

"Odd," said Schnetz, eyeing Barbet as if he were a museum-piece. "Don't know how you think of it. Not sure I understand it either. The way to prove whether you understand a thing or not is to give it a title." His gaze travelled solemnly from face to face. "Now what do you say that song is about? Three words, mind you. Not more than three words."

"I will tell you what it is about," said Quérignon, jerking his head as though he had already been contradicted. "It is about the forgiveness of sins."

"Nonsense," said Schnetz. "I beg your pardon, Eugène. I don't wish to insult you. But I have always said it is a love song. Now, which of us is right?"

Barbet looked at them with surprise. "Both," he said. "But how could it be otherwise?"

Thérèse and Barbet drove together as far as the Quai d'Orléans. When he was silent and she saw his face turned to her in the darkness of the cab, she asked what he was thinking. "That I shall see you to-morrow," he said.

They knew by mutual touch that in the mind of each was the desire not to part now, but she said only: "Last night you were in the train. Did you sleep?"

"Now and then. It wasn't that I was uncomfortable. I can sleep anywhere. I was worrying my head."

"About what, Barbet?"

"You," he said, "and—"

"And?"

He did not answer, and because she could not see his eyes clearly or interpret his hesitation, Thérèse continued: "I was awake too. I was trying—" But she was too tired to explain to him about the reading of his letters. She hoped that he would not ask now why she had not replied to them. "How long are you here?"

"Tuesday or Wednesday."

"Must you go then?"

"I promised Pierre."

She listened to the small, clipped phrases. This is Barbet, she thought. This all we say. Soon I shall be alone in my flat; we shall have said good night and he will be driving on to the Hôtel Bagnolet. But she began to smile in the darkness, for the phrases pleased her by their plainness and brevity.

"Four whole days," he said, "five perhaps."

"But one night nearly gone."

He came near, wishing to kiss her. Because the cab was rocking, he had first to steady her face between his hands, and she smiled at his unpractised care and delighted in it. "We don't have to count hours, Thérèse."

"You make me feel that's true," she answered. "That's why I love you."

They were crossing a bridge and, in reply to Barbet's question, she said: "He's taking us by the Île de la Cité. We are very near. Look—look up through the little window at his side!" But the cab turned left into the Quai aux Fleurs; houses shut out the towers of the cathedral and the high stars; in a moment, they had crossed another bridge—her own bridge, Thérèse said, the Pont St. Louis —and were drawn up at the corner where the Quai d'Orléans sloped up to Thérèse's door.

"Different from the Rue Lilas," he said, looking up from the pavement.

"Less than you think."

"You were hungry then, Thérèse. It was like a fairy-tale to watch you eat food and to take you out on the river and lie about on the grass at St. Cloud, and now—"

"Barbet, dear, I can't be permanently hungry—though it's almost true that I am."

He hesitated still. "I want to go on steamboats," he said. "I want to go to Mantes and find the Gabrielle d'Estrées. She still starts at the same time."

"Did you find that out this afternoon?"

"Mademoiselle d'Austerlitz did."

"Bless her," said Thérèse. "I love routine." She began to laugh at herself, because only in his company did she observe her own contradictions. "I hope the time of the train hasn't changed. What time is it from St. Lazare?"

"Ten thirty-one."

"I shall remember."

"And not be late?"

"I meant: I shall always remember."

"I was afraid—"

"Of what, Barbet?"

"That you might not want to come."

"With you?"

"Dearest Thérèse!" he said gratefully. "But the Gare St. Lazare at ten in the morning and the Gabrielle d'Estrées . . . You are a famous star, Thérèse. You aren't a hungry rascal any more."

"I am," she said, and took his arm. "Don't say good-bye yet. You are quite near home—over the next bridge and you're at the end of the Boulevard St. Germain. Come to the edge of the river. Oh, Barbet, I'm happy. We are planning what we are *going* to do. It's still ahead. Shall we go to La Roche Guyon? When shall we go?"

"Sunday? Monday?"

"Both." Then she added: "I was doing something on Monday. What on earth was it? I know: I was burying Victor Hugo. Philippe has a window in the Rue Soufflot."

"Sunday then."

She nodded. "When we come back we can dine in peace. I have no performance. It would be no good anyway. The whole of Paris will be at the Arc de Triomphe for the lying in state. . . . And no performance on Monday."

"Are you dining with Monsieur de Courcelet after the funeral?"

"I was. . . . I'm not. . . . But Sunday," she added, "that's far away. Look!" She turned him round so that his back was to the river. "At the corner, just beside my outer door, do you see—a restaurant? To-morrow? Noon?"

Next day and on Saturday, when they met briefly in the intervals of their work, the strangeness of their separation was gone. They

talked at ease, their intimacy being the closer because it was of the
kind that no one, considering them in their separate lives, could
suspect. Even Courcelet wondered at it. After his first meeting with
Barbet, he said to Thérèse: "It is even odder than I had believed.
I had thought that to you he was a kind of toy, a pet animal, a pet
sentiment—what you will; but that man is no one's pet animal. I
suppose I am as near to being a complete materialist as any intelligent man can be and you are as near to being a complete egocentric
as any intelligent woman can be, and in both respects he is at the
opposite pole, and yet I like him and you love him, and he loves you,
Thérèse. He talked to me of you. There again I was wrong. I had
expected a virtuous provincial rescuing you from perdition. But
not at all. He isn't aware of your perdition."

"Oh yes," she said, "he is."

"He appears not to mind."

"Oh yes," she repeated, "he does."

Courcelet spread out his hands to protest against these interrup-
tions. "At any rate," he said, "he doesn't condemn you and he isn't
jealous of you. And he isn't resigned and, above all, he's not indifferent. That's what fascinates me. A tolerance that fails to distinguish between one way of living and another is only a form of laziness. It's not a virtue of the soul but a vice of the intellect—and one
that I indulge in. But to see a distinction and to see through it;
to see that I am an old dandy who wastes his life and that you—
well, my dear Thérèse, you shall write your own label—to read
the label, and understand it as he does, and not to stop there but to
say 'No. I can see through the label. I can see through the bottle.
I know that the wine—' And the odd thing is," Courcelet continued
after a pause, "that in fact he *says* nothing of the sort. He has no
theories. Most of what he told me about you was told in the process
of saying that he was going to take you down the river. Again I had
thought: this little provincial imagines that he's taking a girl from
his village inn out for a treat. But not at all. He's fully aware of
who you are and what you are. He's by no means an ingenuous
fool. . . . And then, do you know, Thérèse, I took upon myself the
delicious rôle of a father of a family. I asked him what his intentions were."

"What right had you to do that?"

"None. Curiosity. Plain wickedness."

"And all this talk, all that you have been saying," Thérèse exclaimed, "has been leading up to the pleasure you will now have—My God! Why won't people leave Barbet and me alone? Why did he walk into Maubant's? Why did I introduce him to you or leave you alone with him? No one now ever stops talking about him. 'The original of the Barbet songs!' He isn't the original of the Barbet songs. He is Barbet. He is himself. He and I—we belong to each other in our own way. It is no one else's way. It affects no one else. Certainly not you. I like you. You amuse me. You can have me when you please. You were much more affected by Templéraud than by Barbet. That makes no difference to your 'plain wickedness.' You ask him what his intentions are!"

She was on a tide of bitter anger, her cheeks flushed, her body trembling.

"Magnificent," said Courcelet. "I'm glad."

"Of what?"

"That you love him so deeply." He put his arm through hers and took her cold hand in his. "Have you ever spoken of the future to Barbet?"

"No."

"Do so, Thérèse."

As she hesitated, he watched her with eager attention, thinking that he had implanted a new idea in her, and curious for the result. But she was carefully guarded.

"No," she said at last. "Everything comes naturally with Barbet. I argue with you. Not with him."

"If he wished to marry you, Thérèse, what would you do?"

She did not answer and their conversation seemed to be ended. It was time for her to go to the theatre. Courcelet would drive her there. He went out of the room and, in the hall, picked up his hat, his gloves, his stick; then returned. Her back was to him. He would take her off her guard.

"And if he wished to lie with you, Thérèse?"

She turned slowly and smiled. "I argue with you," she said. "Not with him."

Chapter 11

"**D**O YOU REMEMBER OUR LAST JOURNEY TO Mantes?" Thérèse asked as their train moved into open country.

"I remember that you were nearly late and that you had violet tops to your boots."

Glad that he remembered, or chose to recall, no more of that bitter journey, she was content to allow the country to slide past, but at Mantes she tested his memory again. "This time," she said, "I have a parasol."

"Good," he answered. "It will be hot. But we can go leisurely. There's plenty of time between the train and the boat."

They loitered through the streets of Mantes. At the landing stage there was still time to waste; two intending passengers were sitting placidly under the awning of the Gabrielle d'Estrées, but there was no other sign of life in her except a twist of smoke rising into the windless air; and they seated themselves at a rickety table, nursing glasses of coffee on their knees. Henri, the skipper, was at a table near by, turning over a bundle of papers and checking them by a list.

"Bon jour, majesté," said Thérèse, and in a moment he was on his feet, remembering them, welcoming them, asking if they had again seen his friend at St. Cloud who first had taught them to call him Henri Quatre. He had told them more than that, Thérèse replied. He had told them that Henri Quatre would allow her to work the engine-room telegraph.

"And so you shall, mademoiselle, but not going out of harbour. How far do you go? La Roche? Good, you shall work the telegraph as we approach La Roche."

As the steamer drew away from the landing stage, Thérèse was

visited by the desire which struck her always in Barbet's company—
never to come back, the same fantastic desire, sprung seemingly from
a part of her nature ordinarily asleep, which, two years ago, when
they had watched swallows and starlings among the reeds of the
Charente, had prompted her to beg that they might not return, that
she might postpone, even by half an hour, the parting from him
which would be a re-entry to her normal life. Now she reproved
herself for idle romanticism which, if she gave rein to it, would make
her sad and poor company for him, and to give him pleasure she
said: "Do you want to play piquet? Have you brought cards with
you?"

He clapped his hand to his pocket. "How stupid! How stupid
of me! Now we shall be all day without them, unless we are able
to buy a couple of packs at La Roche. But even that will not be the
same."

"I have brought some," she said. "Clever Thérèse!"

He smiled and held out his hand.

"Say 'Clever Thérèse!'"

He repeated the words obediently and, taking the cards, began
to shuffle them.

The game was a delight to them, not for its own sake only but
because it was a ritual shared; nevertheless they did not prolong it;
the sun, the air, the excitement of each stopping place, the monot-
onous placidity of the water moving astern when the froth of their
paddles was out of it, the stump-stump of the feet of Henri Quatre
on the bridge overhead—all these were things to savour, almost to
touch as Thérèse touched the rail of the bridge-ladder with her bare
hand for the joy of feeling the sun's heat come to her from the sparkling brass. I will remember! I will remember! she said to herself,
and would have asked him if he also would remember, but forbore.
If he was living in the present, let him so live. These were their minutes together. She would not count them for him.

As they came near to La Roche, Henri Quatre remembered his
promise. His head looked down from the ladder and he called her
to the bridge. There, at once, she was intent to obey, determined
to surprise him by her competence. He began by warning her that,

when they came close to shore, he must take the telegraph himself, but, so prompt was she in obeying the orders he gave in mid-stream to test her, that he let her be, and, when the Gabrielle d'Estrées was safely alongside, he patted her shoulder and said: "A seaman, mademoiselle!"

"Oh no," she answered, "just an actress. There's no part I can't play if I give my mind to it," and, as she went ashore with Barbet, she pointed out to him with pride how clever she had been, as if Henri Quatre were Plence and had praised her performance on the stage.

"You see," Barbet said, "nothing is changed. I remember, when we were here before, you said we were here for the *first* time, and there is the tree with the initials carved on it!"

"And this," she replied, "isn't the last time. Barbet, let's make sure of it! Make up our minds now that we will come here to-morrow."

"Yes," he said, "but how you cling to time, Thérèse! How you divide it into days and hours!"

"I cling to happy things. I treasure and hoard them."

Their plan was to eat at La Roche and to spend the day there as they had done before, but first they strolled back to the landing stage and leaned against the parapet of the bridge, looking down at the Gabrielle d'Estrées. They would wave to Henri Quatre as he set out down-river. The hours lay ahead of them; it was pleasant to be idle with the warm, rough stone of the bridge under their hands.

"Thérèse!"

"What?"

"Look, she's casting off. Let's go on in her." Without waiting for answer, he hailed the skipper. "Wait! we are coming with you." They made haste over the track to the waterside and over the tufted grass. The gangway was held for them.

"But you told me," Henri Quatre called from the bridge as though they had accused him of having marooned them, "you told me that you were for La Roche."

"You are quite right," Barbet answered, a little breathless and holding up his hand as a signal of goodwill. "I am sorry. It is we who have changed our minds."

"I didn't, you know," Thérèse said. "Mine was changed for me. If I hadn't followed you at once, you would have been here now and I should still have been on that hot stone bridge. Now that I have my breath again, I shall stand up and wave to *me* on the bridge." She rose and waved. "Au revoir, Thérèse! Au revoir, La Rochefoucauld! We shall come back! . . . Now," she said, "let's eat and drink. There's food on board; I have smelt it. But first we will sit here—no, *here,* in the sun, and drink a glass of wine."

He brought her wine.

"I'm sorry for La Roche Guyon," she said, "—not to have us this afternoon. But she will wait. We will tell her about it when we come back. Where are we going, Barbet?"

"I haven't an idea," he said. "We can get off when we want to."

The small, tumpy hills by which they were passing had the glaze of the sun on their rounded slopes, a glaze broken only by blue shadows, curved on the curving earth, and, near Tripleval, by white cliffs sliced out of the hillsides with an easy knife. In contrast with the cliffs' whiteness, everything green threw up the yellow that was in it. Even in the hot stillness, the trees shone with blue and gold, glistening above their reflections which the passing of the Gabrielle d'Estrées disturbed, and as the afternoon went on and breezes began to stir, turning the poplar leaves, making all shadow and all light quiver, the yellow in the landscape deepened, the great barges themselves—Ventoux, Phébus, Paul Dermoz—running a sparkle of gold from their decks as they went by. At the locks the Gabrielle d'Estrées was given precedence; between them she was proud of her speed; but there was delay at the lock of Port-Villez. Barbet and Thérèse were drawn to the little village which they saw beyond the railway line and were in doubt whether to disembark there; but Henri Quatre would not let them go. Now that they were so near, they must come to Vernon, he said. "At Vernon one eats well but at Villez—no." He would show them where to eat; if they went where he directed them—to the inn belonging to his sister-in-law, they would have time enough to eat comfortably before the return journey began, for she lived near at hand and at this hour was always prepared for what visitors he might send; but if they went elsewhere—well, he would not be responsible. The wait at Vernon was not a long one; the Gabrielle d'Estrées must make the locks in time and be at Mantes before nightfall.

When they landed at Vernon, even Thérèse was not hungry. After the hours spent in the boat, she wished to walk, and they wandered idly through the town until they came upon a great avenue of poplars that led them back to the river not far above the bridge. Here was a stretch of grass, the little park of the town, with a few shaded benches where women sat with their sewing while children played near by. Thérèse and Barbet walked down to the water's edge and there lay on the sloping bank to watch three boys chase one another in the water and come out gasping to dry themselves in the sun.

They talked desultorily and at ease, not caring to choose or to press any subject, not observing silence when it fell—happy in the release of being together and alone. One of their silences was broken by Barbet's saying:

"Do you remember Blachère?"

"That night when I sang in the prison—I remember him then."

"He is the most intelligent of them all. Once I thought he was stupid. Then he found out my weaknesses, and now—"

"What are your weaknesses, Barbet?"

"Well," he said, "for example, if someone persuades me that I'm afraid to do something, I always want to do it to prove—perhaps to prove him wrong—more likely, to prove to myself that I'm not afraid."

"Is that a weakness?"

"Isn't it? A thing doesn't become right because I'm afraid of it."

She considered that, running her fingers through the grass. "And Blachère?" she said. "What has he told you that you are afraid to do?"

"Get rid of the prisoners."

"Are you?"

"Oh, Thérèse," he said, "I wish I could see that clearly. I feel as if I'd been puzzling over a sum for years and had become so muddled by it that—" He smiled at her. "I would push it at you and say 'Do that one for me, please,' but it happens to be a sum that one can do only for oneself. . . . You see, it doesn't become right to get rid of the prisoners because Blachère tells me I'm afraid of it."

"It doesn't become wrong."

Barbet turned over on his back, supporting his head with fingers interlaced so that he might continue to watch the river.

"Blachère can have no interest in the thing, one way or the other," he said. "Whether I rid myself of my prison or not, he will remain a prisoner until his time's up. And yet he goes on and on, tempting me to be rid of them."

"I think I know why," Thérèse answered. "I know about devils. . . . He tempts you because he knows that you will resist the temptation. The more he presses you, the more you will resist—the more you will say: 'I mustn't do this because I should be doing it to prove that I'm not afraid.' And so you'll keep your prison, and Blachère will have you imprisoned with him. That is all."

Barbet did not answer at once. After a little while, he said: "You see, more hangs to it than the plain choice between keeping prisoners or not. It's like a gate between two meadows. Do you understand?"

"What happens the other side of the gate?"

"I should have ceased to be the master of anyone whose labour I don't share. I should have ceased to use force. I shouldn't any longer be kind and patronizing as people are who go and work among the poor. To help people isn't enough. To teach prisoners how to make barrels isn't much good of itself. It leaves you separate from them and that's a kind of death. If a bird perches on my hand and I feel 'Here's a bird perching on my hand,' then I am separated from him and all the feeding and stroking in the world makes no odds; but if at that moment I feel also 'Here's a hand for me to perch on, then—"

"Then why don't you let the prisoners go, Barbet? What stops you?"

"Hand them over to another prison? Tell my own conscience to go to sleep and be comfortable? Like a man who feels that to own property is wrong and makes it over to his wife?"

"I didn't say 'hand them over.' I said 'let them go.'"

But Barbet's mind had sheered away. Though he had heard what she said, he had not received her idea. She was about to repeat it, to force it on him, but checked herself, remembering that, when she was rehearsing, people who thrust ideas upon her before she was ready for them did more harm than good. "But I haven't *come* to that yet!" she would say, and now, unpersisting because she loved him, she stretched her body on the ground and smelt the grass and turned over to spread out her arms and gaze at the sky.

"You will know what to do," she said, "when you are ready to do it."

She sat up, her arms clasped about her knees, and he beside her. Beyond the bridge heavy smoke rose against the woods of the opposite hill, the nose and the barred S of the Gabrielle d'Estrées appeared through one of the arches. Her lowered funnel swung into position again as she came upstream.

"There is Henri Quatre," said Thérèse; "do you think he will be angry with us because we didn't go to his sister-in-law's?"

She would have sprung up to wave to him.

"Don't wave," said Barbet, "he might stop for us."

They watched in silence until the Gabrielle d'Estrées had passed out of sight. By this time the swimmers had dressed and gone, the water's surface was unbroken.

Their return was made not through the avenue and the town but along the river's bank. When they left the open ground in which they had been sitting, their way narrowed, passing between a walled garden and a low parapet of stone on which men and girls were sitting in pairs, discreetly spaced; then broadened into a road, flanked on one side by houses, on the other by a broad, grassy bank, wooded at first but soon becoming open ground studded with bollards to which barges were making fast for the night. At the end of the row of houses, the road curved inland suddenly to join the main street of the town, and here, included in the curve, were the hotel and courtyard of the Trois Couronnes. Looking out over the river was a balcony on which tables were set.

Barbet and Thérèse rounded the building, for the entrance to it was from the main street. They found themselves in a dining-room which contained eight tables and was decorated with painted mirrors and artificial flowers. Two of the tables were occupied by family parties; at a third a woman in black, with a child beside her, was playing cards with an ancient and benign witch whose white head was draped in a black, woollen shawl. On the right, between a varnished staircase and a zinc bar dressed with a regiment of bottles, was a high, enclosed desk, like a pulpit, from which a stout man, with spectacles thrust up on his forehead and a blue cap on his head, gazed at the new-comers. Their entrance had set a bell jangling and all heads were turned. A baby belonging to one of the family parties climbed on to the seat of his chair that he might have an uninterrupted view of the proceedings.

On one of the mirrors, painted among festoons of roses, was the name "A. Jugiaud," and, when Barbet had said good day and the man at the desk had said good evening, Thérèse said "Monsieur Jugiaud?" a little interrogatively but with that implied recognition in her tone which, she knew, melted the ice of masculine vanity.

Monsieur Jugiaud bowed. It was, he admitted, his name. Then he lowered his spectacles on to his nose and examined Thérèse more closely. "Come, come," he said, "unless I am mistaken—"

Thérèse shut her eyes tight, frowned a little, protruded her lips; then opened her eyes and smiled. It was a signal that Monsieur Jugiaud understood; the lady did not wish to be recognized; he was silent and momentarily disappointed. Then he rubbed his cheek and entered into the conspiracy. "Bon," he said. "Parfait," and, turning to Barbet, he began to discuss with him the problem of dinner. He came down from his stool and out of his pulpit; the three of them sat down together at an empty table to drink an apéritif while the mullet was being prepared; and when Thérèse said she would like to wash and his old mother, clasping her shawl under her chin, moved to accompany her, he waved her aside, begging her not to disturb herself, and himself led the way upstairs. As soon as a turn of the stairs hid them, he seized Thérèse's hand and shook it again and again. Thérèse Despreux! Thérèse Despreux! Never had he seen such a performance, such spirit, such invention—and he a playgoer of fifty years' standing. "In Vernon they laugh at me. They say I am too old for playgoing. They say it is a waste of time and money— and it does cost money if you add the train fare! But my old mother understands. I was born in Paris, mademoiselle. It was she took me first when I was a boy, and until a few years ago she and I—off we used to go together. Now, even she is too old."

"Then she has never seen me?"

"Alas no, mademoiselle! But if mademoiselle will allow it, I should like to let her into the secret—I mean the secret that Thérèse Despreux is dining with us to-night? I have spoken of you to her so often! It would give her such pleasure!"

"But why not?" Thérèse answered. "It isn't so deep a secret. But thank you, monsieur, for your discretion. It is only that people stare and news spreads. Once, in a little restaurant very like this, when people found out, they began to sing my own songs and clapped their hands and asked me to sing to them. And then it may do harm if you refuse. They say that you are too proud, that you are un-generous."

Monsieur Jugiaud had stopped on a half-landing outside the door to which he was conducting Thérèse.

"There, mademoiselle, you will find, I think, everything you need."

When she came out, she found that he had gone up three or four stairs and waited for her. "I thought that mademoiselle might care to see—" and he went forward, assuming that she would follow him. At the end of a dark and narrow passage he threw open a door.

"It is the best we have," he said. "My wife was born in this room."

It was not large, but a sloping roof and a wall curving down a pair of steps to a second door at its farther end gave it a rambling character of its own. In the window-boxes geraniums had been planted out. Though a bed and a dressing-table occupied the greater part of the room, there was space for a sofa and a small armchair of red plush beside the broad, low windows. Kneeling on the sofa, Thérèse looked out at the barges, at the wooded island beyond, and, to her left, at the great curve of the Seine where it swept on towards Rouen.

"The Gabrielle d'Estrées left early this evening?" she suggested, turning her head to look at Monsieur Jugiaud.

"Early? I think not, mademoiselle. At about the same time as usual. Indeed, we say always that we could set our clocks by her whistle."

"Anyhow, we missed her."

"That, if I may say so, has been my good fortune, mademoiselle."

"But how do we get back?"

"Back?"

"To Mantes. To Paris."

He gazed at her, evidently doubting her intention. "There is a train in twenty minutes' time."

"I mean: after dinner."

He shook his head knowingly and rubbed his hands together. "There is no other train until four in the morning, mademoiselle."

"Mon Dieu," said Thérèse, "then we shall have to stay with you to-night."

Monsieur Jugiaud did his utmost to appear astonished. In the circumstances, did the room please mademoiselle? Thérèse surveyed it with new eyes and praised the window-boxes. It was, she said, a beautiful room; then added in a voice of alarm that Monsieur Jugiaud, as an appreciator of good acting, discreetly admired: "But I must discuss it with monsieur. And in any case we should want two rooms."

"Entendu, madame. And now I think that if madame would give herself the trouble to go downstairs, she would find the mullet awaiting her."

Barbet was already on the balcony. They sat down to their meal together, and Monsieur Jugiaud, after a little discourse on the cooking of mullet, poured out for them an open white wine from a carafe.

"Look, Thérèse," Barbet said, turning in his chair and pointing over the rail of the balcony. "Down there below the barges—do you see those boats? To-morrow, if we came straight here by train instead of taking the Gabrielle d'Estrées, we could hire one of them and be out in her all day."

Thérèse hesitated. Should she tell him now that they could not return to Paris tonight? She felt that it would trouble him, that he would hold himself responsible, that his pleasure would be spoiled, and she said only:

"If there's wind enough, we could sail."

"A whole day," said Barbet. "Then we would come back and dine here, on this balcony. . . . Thérèse?"

"Yes, Barbet."

"This, too, is a first time, not a last?"

"Why should you doubt it?"

"I don't doubt it," he answered. "But I have to be careful. You see, there's one thing in which I know I'm unusual—my surroundings make very little difference to me. Seeing what a countryman I am, you might think that Paris would get on my nerves or that I shouldn't be able to sleep or that something would go wrong; but it is not so. I seem not to have any nerves. I'm healthy anywhere and I sleep like a top. And it's the same about coming to a place like this. Maubant's and the Trois Couronnes are all the same to me. But to you—"

"Do you mean," she said, "that you think this isn't grand enough for me. Now, listen—"

"No, no," he interrupted, "I don't in the least mean that. I know that you are happy—well, because we are together, because it's a change from Paris, and the paper flowers and the painted mirrors and old Jugiaud have a taste of their own. But everyone has his own way of living. You have yours. And this—though it may be a change—doesn't fit into it. Nor do I, for that matter."

"But, Barbet, the whole basis of your life is that human beings are not separate, that you aren't separate from the birds or the vines or your prisoners or from anything in Nature. Why should you feel separated from me? Or is it that you think I feel separated from you?"

His eyes held her own steadily, but his face was troubled. "I don't muddle myself into thinking that, in this life of the senses, I am the same with the birds or the vines or with you, Thérèse. Men are not equal. Certainly they are not the same. It is—it is far back—far back behind our lives here—that the unity exists. Only there. Here you are—a famous, brilliant girl and around you there is a glitter of—"

She waited, but he did not continue. He picked up his knife and fork. "I am talking too much," he said. "We must enjoy our dinner."

"And around me," she persisted, "there is a glitter of—of what?"

"Of being courted. Of being desired."

"And spoiled?"

"Not for me. Not if I remember who I am and what I am, and what you and I really mean to each other, and am not such a fool as to play—or want to play—other men's parts."

Thérèse pressed the discussion no further, but turned it to subjects that did not disturb or trouble him. Never before had she cared deeply for the peace of any man's mind. If by giving or denying, if by any vanity of her power, she were to torment him, whom she loved selflessly as she had loved none other in her life, her anchor would be gone; and she summoned all her strength that she might be to him as, in his deep heart, he needed her to be.

That he desired her she knew. His desire was communicated in her own. Since while we talk of other things, she said to herself, and are divided by the width of this table, the evening air is yet a mutual touch between us, shall not our hands touch also? Since, in this way, we desire each other, though without the pain, without the wild avarice of extreme desire, shall he and I hold back? But she feared that, if he came to her, it might be with misgiving. He thought of her as belonging, except in the special relationship that already existed between them, to a world not his, in which, as he had said, she was "courted" and "desired." If he came to her, would it be, in part, because he felt that she expected him, in that sense, to court and desire her? And if I come to him, she asked herself suddenly, will it be, in part, because I am saying to myself that what others have had, I will not deny to him?

"What are you smiling at, Thérèse?"

"Was it a good smile?"

"I have seen happier."

She wanted to say to him: Barbet, let's be plain with each other. Let us be sure that, if ever we go to bed together, we don't do it out of politeness to each other. But at the thought of herself saying these words she burst out laughing, then suddenly was silent, afraid that he might think that she was laughing at him. Monsieur Jugiaud was coaxing the cork from a bottle of Haut Brion.

"There, madame," he said, carefully wiping the lip of the bottle, "when red wine comes with laughter there seem to be no problems any more."

" 'Seem,' " Thérèse answered, "that's an ominous word! Is that a proverb?"

"No, mademoiselle. . . . No, madame. It is only a little saying of mine. Or, rather, of my father-in-law's. You will find that we have it printed on the wine-list. I will show you."

As he was going away, Barbet exclaimed: "Bless my soul, I had forgotten to ask. What time is there a train for Paris?"

"Don't worry," said Thérèse swiftly, "I have asked about that."

From behind Barbet's back, Monsieur Jugiaud threw towards her a glance which said that in all things, to the end of his life, he was on the side of Thérèse Despreux. To prove it, he vanished. Barbet pulled out his watch.

"Oh dear," he said, "I should have liked to have time to loiter over coffee. I remember, during my military service, on the last evening of leave I used to think: suppose a miracle were to happen now, suppose a message were to come or I found that I had miscounted the days—anyhow that I didn't have to go back to-night! . . . How long have we, Thérèse? Time for coffee? When is the train?"

"The miracle *has* happened," she said. "There is no train."

"Do you mean we needn't go!"

"I thought it would worry you, Barbet."

"I suppose it ought. Isn't it strange?" he said. "Here have I been assuming quite steadily that we must go back to Paris to-night. When he brings coffee, I thought, the evening will be over. Still, I said to myself, not quite over—there'll be the train; and I had made a plan

—we were to drive a long way in Paris and sit on a pavement and drink cognac before we parted. And now—Thérèse, the evening is beginning. It is scarcely half-past eight."

Their table was lighted only through the window of the dining-room from which a wide beam fell across the balcony. As they continued their dish and drank their Haut Brion, the ancient witch, Madame Jugiaud, came out with two candlesticks. While she was fumbling for matches in the pocket of her apron, Barbet produced a box.

With the authority of age, she laid her fingers on his wrist. "No, no, monsieur. Allow me. My son has told me his secret. It will give me pleasure to light a pair of candles for Thérèse Despreux."

When it was done, Thérèse took her hand and kissed it. "Thank you, madame. They burn brighter because you lighted them."

Madame Jugiaud looked at her hand and with the other covered the place that Thérèse had kissed. "That will be something to remember," she whispered, "when I am old."

After she had gone, Thérèse said: "That was friendly. That was kind."

"Don't you expect people to be friendly and kind?"

"I'm glad when they are. . . . Barbet, why did she say that? Why did she say 'when I am old'?"

"Sometimes," he said, "just for a moment, my mother, too, thinks that she is young again."

At first they had little need of candles, but the river was becoming luminous among the meadows, and above the opposite hill, between north and east, the sky, empty now of the mirrored sunset, had that transparency of water, that low gleam of pearl, over which darkness at last suddenly flows in. On the ridge of the forest, against this sky, a detached group of trees stood out, the gleam appearing between their trunks and between their branches. Thérèse made Barbet look at them with her. "They are like—" but she wished not to liken them to anything, but to see them as they were, in their own form and endurance.

When their coffee was brought, darkness had built walls about their candles, and Barbet, as though the knowledge that they were not to return to Paris had given him release, was able to admit Thérèse to his mind more fully than ever in the past. He did so by telling her stories of her own childhood and his, of her father, of the country's battle against the phylloxera, and through them all appeared the tranquillity and the zeal of his own life.

"Does fame never tempt you, Barbet?"

"If it came, I suppose I should learn how to live in spite of it; but I would rather be without. How can a man who is very famous help feeling: 'I and the others. The others and I'? You must feel it yourself, Thérèse."

"Yes."

"And you want to feel that?"

"Should I fight for it if I didn't?"

"That," he said, "isn't an answer. Do you *want* to feel separated?"

"Yes, yes, I do," she replied. "I see life as a battle. I want to feel that I have won it. I was everyone's drudge when I was a child. 'That girl, Thérèse Despreux, will never come to any good!' I didn't believe them. I *liked* Thérèse Despreux. And I still want to prove to them that I was right and they were wrong. That's all there is to it. . . . If I were you, I should use all my brains so that I might be the one man who had overcome the phylloxera. Then I should teach others how to overcome it, and they would all say 'Clever Thérèse!' I should tell the newspapers. I should come to Paris and—"

Barbet leaned back in his chair and laughed. "Your father said to me once that, when you were a little girl, you used to tell him how you would have behaved if you had been Mary Magdalene."

"That was natural enough. That was because I am always playing parts," she exclaimed. "I can't help it. Is it wrong? Is it wrong, do you think, to be an actress at all?"

"No," he answered, "but some employments are better than others —they make it less difficult to live well. One might think the job of a soldier would make it difficult, but I found that wasn't true—anyhow," he added with a grin, "not if you are a Frenchman as well. You do what you are told, but you don't make gods of your officers or cease to have a life of your own. However keen you are as a soldier, you are still a vine-grower at heart. Soldiering has a motive while it lasts; you must see what you are driving at or you're a fool; but there's no personal design in it—unless, of course, you are a chap of the kind that collects medals."

"But don't you *want* medals?" Thérèse demanded.

"What should I do with them?" he answered. "To be a vine-grower is a good life for me, though I'd rather be a cooper and not own the place. But as I'm not a shipper as well, I couldn't make a fortune if I wanted to. Most of what I do make goes back into the land; I like that. And the work gives me a chance to see great things in little : in the bud, the grape; in the grape, the wine. The wine has the earth and the sun in it. In one of Quessot's barrels, there's the whole round of the year. And, behind the turn of the seasons, sometimes I can see a bit of the life of man, and behind that—it's hard to tell, but I do feel it, Thérèse. Not as old Quessot does, chipping away at his staves. He feels it as, perhaps, I never shall. But I too feel it. Behind the good, happy life of man with the taste of wine and the heat of a fire and the snap of cold air and the joy of being given a holiday and of putting out my hand and touching you, there is—well," he said with a shake of his head that brought his hair tumbling over his forehead, "this is where I get out of my depth." He pushed his hair back and went on: "There is an absence of all these divisions—somewhere where there aren't any. That is what makes touch exciting and real—not just the touch of something soon to be dead. That candle; I watch its light on your face, but I am not shut out by its light; I am part of it; it's as if I too were shining on your face. All the senses are lovely and happy and free; it's my fault if I let them shut me into myself; they are not prison-keepers. I can never believe that touch and taste are evil. Why are they more evil than the sight of the sky or the smell of flowers, which no one condemns? There's no need to make excuses for them; they are warm like the earth, good as a grape." He stood up and leaned out over the balcony. "That's what I want to become, not what I am, Thérèse."

"Once," she said, "I thought that you hadn't a trouble in the world. Whatever you did, you seemed to do naturally. You seemed not to plan or scheme or be in doubt about anything. Everything you did was as simple as a man's opening his eyes when daylight comes."

"That is how I should like it to be," he answered.

"But it is not?"

"Not now. Not all the time."

She asked: "Is it Blachère?"

After a long silence he said: "I ought to *know* what to do. To keep the prison or to give it up. Instead, I argue. I listen to Blachère. I try not to dislike or fear him. And I fail. I argue. It ought to be as simple as a man's opening his eyes."

"Barbet, I think it will be. Verlaine said once: 'If I go to sleep, it will come.' "

"I know," Barbet said. "But it needs faith to sleep. Quessot has it. I wonder—has Verlaine?" and, hearing a step behind him, he turned to find that Monsieur Jugiaud had come on to the balcony to ask if they had dined well. Their rooms were prepared. As they had brought no luggage, he and his mother had taken the liberty of putting into their rooms the little things they might need.

When they left the balcony, the dining-room was empty. Monsieur Jugiaud climbed into his pulpit and handed out two keys. On the ledge, candles were standing.

Thérèse began to climb the stairs. "Bon soir, monsieur. Bon soir, madame." At the turn of the staircase, she stood aside that Barbet might go ahead with the light. "Down the passage," she said. "My door has steps leading up to it."

At the steps he paused, comparing the numbers of doors and keys; then, having opened her door for her, himself went forward. She entered her room in darkness and waited. Soon a gleam of light, shining up the stairs that connected her room with his, curled upon the rounded section of her wall and threw a narrow wedge, like a sword's blade, across her ceiling. She remained silent, knowing him to be as yet unaware that a door was open between them. As her eyes became accustomed to the darkness, her mirror and bed appeared; she moved across the room and, opening her curtains on the river, sat at the window and leaned out.

She listened to Barbet's movements in the adjoining room. So quiet was the night that she heard the winding of his watch. Two nights ago, she thought, I lay in bed self-pitying, clutching his letters, making a tragedy of my life, and he was awake in the train; he has not told me the true cause of his wakefulness. This evening, when perhaps he was about to tell me, Monsieur Jugiaud came, and he accepted the interruption as patiently as he accepts all things. Searching her memory for indications of the truth, Thérèse believed suddenly that she had come upon it. "Everything you did," she had said, "was once as simple as a man's opening his eyes when daylight comes." He had answered that this was how he wished it to be. And she had asked: "But it is not?" and she had asked again: "Is it Blachère?" To this he had not replied, and it seemed to her now that he had guided their conversation away from Blachère—always, always, whenever that name had been spoken between them, it had been allowed to fall away, its challenge unanswered. At that moment she heard his door move on its hinges.

"Thérèse!"

"Barbet."

"You are in the dark."

So relieved was she by the sound of his voice, which in its calmness seemed an answer to all her fears, that she began to laugh and answered: "Of course I am in the dark. You stole my candle."

"I'm sorry. Here it is. Are you in bed?"

"How could I be in bed with no light to undress by? I have been staring out of the window."

He advanced up the stairs and stood before her, candle in hand, barefooted, wearing a great-coat of Jugiaud's—a comic figure at which she began to smile; but there are moments at which no man wishes to be thought comic, though he is loved the better for it, and she turned to the window and said:

"Look, Barbet. On the skyline. You can still see our trees."

He knelt beside her on the sofa, his hands deep in the pockets of his coat, and with a sudden, gentle movement laid his cheek against hers. She held firm, resolute to say nothing and do nothing.

"Thérèse, if I am to go away, tell me to go. . . ." But she was silent. "Thérèse!"

"What am I to you?" she said. "What can I be?" And, regarding the little scene from outside herself, she saw it as a scene of comedy and smiled at it, and saw it as a scene of tragedy and smiled at it again. It had been in her mind to ask: What can we ever be to each other, you and I? but she feared that the question was in his mind also and dared not speak it.

To-night, to-morrow and to-morrow night, she said within her. Shall we ever again be together so long? To-morrow they would cross the river and go up the hill into the forest of Vernon. To-night Hugo was lying in state under the Arc de Triomphe; to-morrow he would be buried; her place would be empty in the Rue Soufflot. It seemed that she had been many weeks absent from Paris, and she remembered from afar the day on which she had signed her name in Hugo's book. She remembered it so clearly, seeing her pen move across the page, that she felt again the solitude of Barbet's absence and suffered again that greed and pressure, that stress of the brain, which had been her passion for Templéraud. In Barbet's presence were sanity and reassurance.

"To-night, to-morrow and to-morrow night—"

"Why do you say that, Thérèse?"

"I'm sorry," she said with a smile. "My old sin—counting the hours. All to come! None yet in the past! Oh, Barbet, how little you know me! I could be faithful to you. I believe that now. I shall love you always, and be yours in my heart, but when you are gone—"

He took her hands and silenced her. "You and I will not make prisons for ourselves, Thérèse."

She shook her head. "You are strange," she said. "So be it. I love you, Barbet."

Chapter 12

THÉRÈSE HAD DRAWN BACK THE CURTAINS BE-
fore they slept and it was by the sun, flowing in over the hills
and across the river from the direction of Giverny, that she was awakened. The slope of her ceiling surprised her; she sat up, found a head
on the pillow next to hers, and saw that it was Barbet's. Now that is
very odd, she thought, and put her hand out to touch his head; then
withheld it that the daylight should awaken him also when he was
ready.

This morning, in the sunshine, the sadness and misgiving of last
night were gone; she was as light-hearted as she had been in the
Gabrielle d'Estrées and knew that, when Barbet awoke, she might,
if she did not guard her tongue, say flippant, unmeaning things that
were even now running over the surface of her mind like will-o'-the-
wisp over the surface of a lake. It had long been her intuition to play
early-morning scenes as light comedy; only thus might their monotony
be broken, and men, who would always take their tone from her, be
turned aside from embarrassing attempts to renew, when the retreat
was sounding, the passionate assurances of attack. They would say,
if they had not Courcelet's discretion, that she differed from all other
women, or even, as desire reawoke in them, would mumble into
her pillow that no experience of their lives had been equivalent with
this. Light comedy, farce, even poor farce, were, she had found,
welcome alternatives to this tarnished ritual.

She turned away from Barbet, for he was no part of these recollections and she wished to empty her mind of them. And yet, in what
other words than those she had too often heard might she express
the truth: that no experience of her life had been equivalent with
this? This had differed from other experience not in the degree of its

pleasure but in kind. . . . Poor Thérèse: has no man ever had the wit to say that to you? . . . It had differed because, now, if she dared to look over her right shoulder instead of her left, she would see the man whom she loved and whose love for her was not an undermining but a reinforcement of her citadel, which was his own, neither by his capture nor by her surrender, but in the nature of that singleness which they had last night discovered. . . . Foolish Thérèse —and yet, why foolish? It isn't foolish to be surprised, even by love. When word or fortune changes its meaning, the only folly is to cling to what is old, to turn one's head away from the changing wind. . . . She looked at him again, impatient that he should awake and speak to her, desiring that he should sleep in peace. Of course, she thought, if he stays in my shadow, he will go on sleeping, but, if I lean back, the sun will shine in his eyes.

She leaned back; he stirred and his eyes opened. He sat up, pushed the hair back from his forehead and recognized her.

"Bon jour, Barbet."

"Bon jour, Thérèse."

"Enchantée de faire votre connaissance."

He opened his eyes wide. "Honoré, mademoiselle."

A little silence followed. "I'm not used to the sun yet," he said. "Why are you looking awed, Thérèse? While I blink, you are entitled to laugh at me."

"That's all right," she said, "as long as you laugh too. You see, five minutes ago I felt like light comedy. And then I didn't. And then you woke up. And then we met, and you said: 'Honoré, mademoiselle.' Why did you say that?"

"Well, I was just awake enough to take my cue."

"And to know I was playing a scene?" Then, in a different tone, she added: "We are playing it still."

"Why are you frightened, Thérèse?"

"Because I love you." She took breath. "Because I don't know this part. It's unrehearsed. . . . And, apart from that," she added with deliberate lightness and so quickly that he could not interrupt her, "I do *like* you in the morning. Were you surprised to see me?"

He smiled. "As a matter of fact," he said, "I had seen you before.

I woke earlier. I think it was the noise of the barges getting under way."

"Didn't you notice me? I must have been on that pillow."

Again before he could answer, she continued her stream of talk, putting out a foot into the sun and letting herself down from the bed. She went about the floor barefoot, and seated herself at the mirror to brush out her hair. Barbet rose and, having stayed by her for an instant, checking her hand that held the brush and turning her face to him, went to his own room. She called to him that she had no bell; if he found one, he was to ring it. First, coffee; hot water in an hour.

"An hour? Does it take an hour to drink coffee?"

"An hour and a half," said Thérèse. "This is a holiday."

She returned to bed and propped herself with pillows. Barbet found her with the tray of coffee at her side. Everyone else, she thought, has surprised me too little.

"You surprise me," she said, "every time you walk into the room."

"But why?"

To this there was, in words, no answer but one of the many answers too often heard for her to speak them. She stretched out her hand to him and said: "Admit that it is odd, Barbet. For you too. When the barges woke you, where did you think you were?"

"The barges told me. Then I saw you."

"And you said to yourself: 'That is Thérèse.' And then? Be honest. Last night, when you came to me—before we knew, I mean, what we know now—weren't you then, in part at any rate, being kind and charming and—" She laughed into the eyes that were looking at her over the rim of the coffee-bowl he was holding in both his hands. "Like asking a lady to dance?"

"I loved her, Thérèse."

"Ah yes. Thank God. That as well. But admit that then—" She held out her bowl. "Please give me some more coffee."

With her fingers closed round the bowl, she leaned back on her pillow and smiled.

"Isn't it true," she said, "if we see it in the sunlight of morning, that we were being extremely polite to each other?"

Beyond her window-boxes a barge was making its way slowly up-river shaded by the poplars and willows of the island. "They are drinking coffee too," she said, and because there was nothing she did not wish to experience in Barbet's company she suggested that some day they should make a journey by barge from Vernon to Mantes; from Rouen to Paris, she added, her plans increasing; from Rouen to Paris would take how many days? She did not wait for the answer he could not give, for her mind had reverted to the boats they had seen from the balcony where they had dined. Was there wind enough to sail? There was no wind, not a sway in the poplar branches; even the blades of thin grass that had sprung up among the flowers in the window-boxes were still until a pair of sparrows came to peck, and flew away, and returned, and flicked their tails, and pecked and stared.

"Friends of yours, Barbet."

His eyes were already on them. She watched the quiet and gentleness of his face.

"Do you know, Thérèse," he said, as though giving answer to all she had said, an answer reserved and considered while she had been chattering, "I suppose it is, as you say, rather odd—you and I, sitting here with our coffee-cups. Look. Come nearer. You can see us in your mirror."

"A most improbable picture," she said.

"Well," he answered, "I suppose it is. I suppose we ought to consider ourselves as improbable a pair as ever awoke on the same pillow —is that what you meant by our having been 'polite' to each other?— and yet, whenever we are together, it seems to me always the most natural thing in the world."

She caught her breath; then steadied herself. His words, spoken without emotional emphasis as though he were stating a fact, plainly evident to him, which he had expected her to have recognized, filled her with such happiness that she bit her lip to drive back tears; then laughed to conceal them and pretended she was laughing—at what?

"Only your bewildered face! Do I bewilder you, Barbet?"

"Sometimes. But I catch up in the end. Or you come back to me. It's like pulling in a kite."

She looked out at the cloudless sky. "There's not enough wind."

"For what?"

"Sailing. . . . Or a kite. I should like to be a kite," she said, "though I expect I should break my string. I wonder where Mademoiselle d'Austerlitz is this morning. In that passage with the stained glass?"

At first, she had been disappointed that there had seemed not to be enough wind for sailing, but this morning disappointment could not rest upon her long. They would row, taking food and wine with them, and find a creek behind an island, or they would cross the bridge and explore the opposite hill. From among the trees on the ridge they would see the Gabrielle d'Estrées come down-river during the afternoon and that would be a time-signal to them; soon afterwards they would have to begin their walk home, the day would be drawing near its end and—

"Barbet, how shall we spend to-day—on the river? In the woods?"

"I should like the woods," he answered. "There may be birds one doesn't expect to meet. Except the swallows and starlings, you and I have never watched birds together."

"Would they come if I was there?"

"If you didn't speak or move."

"Last night," she said with a smile, "hasn't changed anything for us."

"Why should it?"

She put her hand into his. "It does, you know. People become tired or they become obsessed about each other. They don't think much about sailing or rivers or woods or birds—only about each other. I mean: to-day would be different from yesterday; we should *feel* different; we should almost be different people."

"I don't feel like that," he said. "Why should I love you differently? Or you me?"

"I know. I am glad, Barbet. I want to-day to be like yesterday—happy in the same way. Perhaps even more peaceful, not less."

She put the coffee-tray out of danger. "Come and look at the river. Then we will dress."

Below them, when they leaned out, was the roof of the balcony on which they had dined. Monsieur Jugiaud's head appeared. He hailed a man in the street who was trundling a barrow piled with vegetables, and the man looked up, called his reply and turned his barrow into a yard at the side of the Trois Couronnes. Far down-river a small boat loitered with slack sails.

"Poor Victor Hugo!"

"Well, there's fame if you like," Barbet answered.

"Still," she said, "I'm glad I'm not being buried to-day, even in the Panthéon. . . . Why are you looking at me like that? Why are you laughing at me? There should be a law. No one should be allowed to be buried on the 1st of June."

BOOK FOUR

The Doors Open

I'll walk where my own nature would be leading—
It vexes me to choose another guide—

—EMILY BRONTË.

Chapter 1

WHEN BARBET RETURNED TO THE MAISON Hazard, he found it less easy than in the past to bend his mind to the problems of farm, vineyard and prison. Pierre gave him a satisfactory report of work in progress; but said no more of the prisoners than that they had been fed and exercised. Barbet did not press him. The subject was one of which he himself had no eagerness to speak, and he took over his duties as a gaoler with an effort of will. Fontan, welcoming his return, asked if he had any fresh tunes in his head; Marcotte, with a child's pride, brought out for his admiration the new foremast he had made for his ship; Balze and Heim, still talkative and inseparable, demanded news of Paris; but Barbet knew that he disappointed them all, he had no tunes for the mandolin, and found that he praised the ship, as if it were separated from him by the glass case of a museum, without sharing its owner's delight in his craftsmanship. Blachère's critical gaze, his long silences, his sudden bursts of contempt for the small pleasures upon which the others depended found Barbet vulnerable. His relationship with his prisoners was less spontaneous than it had been. He felt that he was being cut off from them, and had deliberately to gain mastery over himself that he might not shun Blachère or be unjust to him.

In all else he was happy, but with an urgent happiness rather than the happiness of settlement and continuity. He was tempted more and more strongly to postpone what he could of his administrative work and to go into the fields and vineyards—to labour with his hands. That's natural enough, he said to himself; June is the green month; who wants to sit at a desk in June? But in other Junes the business of owning the Maison Hazard had been taken in his stride. It had been an accepted part of his existence and had not stood

359

against or impoverished his deeper, personal life of field and wood. Now he had to compel himself to its tasks. When he asked himself why, he knew that the answer was not in Vernon or in Paris but in himself. He was not hungry for Thérèse or distressed by jealousy in his absence from her. That they loved each other was a source of peace, not of disturbance in him. His feeling of increasing detachment from his ownership of the Maison Hazard was independent of Thérèse.

He had often told his mother that, if ever she saw him neglecting the place, it would be her business to keep his nose to the grindstone, and often she had twitted him for some small neglect of his father's rigid practice. It was a joke between them which gave her a privilege he valued, and he was a little surprised that she did not now exercise it. Lacking her reproof, he reproved himself, took off his jacket and settled at his desk to make up arrears.

Because he disliked account-keeping above all else, it was the wages-book that he drew towards him. In the three workings of the earth—the April digging in clumps, the June hoeing and the light hoeing in July—a labourer earned thirty-two francs for each "journal" or third part of an acre. At each working, one man did not regularly cover the same ground, and instalments of pay had to be nicely calculated. Pierre had made payments on this and other accounts during the days of Barbet's absence. His records of them were written, if written at all, on odd pieces of paper accumulated on the desk. Many of these scraps had on them a group of figures in sprawling round-hand and little else than figures; only Pierre himself could know certainly to what they referred. Though Barbet's knowledge of what business was in hand, aided by a name or a date here and there, enabled him to make sense of most of them, by some he was defeated, and these he clipped together, intending to summon Pierre and call upon his memory. But the prospect of spending even an hour of a June morning with Pierre sulkily biting a pencil among a pile of account-books was a sad one, and Barbet, knowing that he ought to stay in his chair, started up from it, and, with all the delight of a boy escaping from school, set out across the vineyards to find Pierre and tackle the job in the open.

On the way he came upon a man hoeing, and stayed to talk to him. The heavy clumps thrown up in April had become friable and were crumbling; the heaps of earth between the rows were being spread and the soil replaced at the foot of the vines; where the men had done their work the earth was again flat and evenly distributed. The vines themselves were in a condition that Barbet loved. On the main branches, the young shoots had grown fast and their green was luminous against the black of the wood. They had not yet spread horizontally and the hoeing was still easy. Tiny green flowers with yellow stamens were opening on the small bunches. From them came a gentle scent, more elusive than that of lime-trees in flower, more delicate than the sweetness of mignonette, which had for Barbet the special power to cast upon the daytime an evening enchantment, for it was on June evenings that, as a child, he had learned to know it. How often, while he lay happily awake long after he had been sent to bed, had this fragrance come in to him on the warm, light air! His room, his voyaging mind, and at last his sleep had been filled by it. Ever since, it had been for him an evening scent, and there was expectation in it—perhaps because during those nights of childhood it had been most perceptible when a breeze moved under the threat of thunder.

"What's the vintage to be?" the labourer asked, and Barbet, observing the number of flower-bunches on the vines, said he feared it would be a poor vintage. In making his estimate, he used his judgment and applied his experience as carefully as ever in the past, but his interest was professional, not personal, as if he were giving advice on property not his own.

At the edge of the vineyard, he was met by Pierre, who was in so good a humour that even the pieces of paper that came from Barbet's pocket did not cast him down. They went on together over a fold of the ground, and the cottage came suddenly into sight, set in a garden full of roses. As they walked, Barbet held out the papers one by one and Pierre instantly recognized each of them. Though he could read and write if he took pains, he had the memory of the illiterate.

"Thank you," said Barbet when he had the information he

needed, "that is clear enough. But why don't you write it down at the start? It would save trouble."

"I know. But it's dull, all that writing, for another man's accounts."

"Duller than work in another man's vineyard?"

"That's different," said Pierre. "There's pleasure in that. Besides, in the vineyards I see the thing through from beginning to end. I have as much to do with them as you do yourself—more, if it comes to that. But the accounts are yours."

"You are welcome to them, I promise you."

"That may be," said Pierre, answering Barbet's grin with his own. "But I couldn't do the accounts if I tried. Everything else I could—the vintage, the hay, the harvest, everything—"

"Distillation?"

"Well, I grant you; you're my master there; and you're a cooper and I'm not; but every vine-grower needn't be able to make his own barrels, and, as for the distillation—I learned a lot last winter. You have to set to and learn when you're a married man and a child is coming."

It was this that gave Barbet the key to Pierre's new mood. Renée had stirred ambition in him and was converting him from oaf to vine-grower; the intelligence of the Vincents, long retarded, was now emerging. And if I hadn't been so stupid as to decide that he could never be much more than an animal, Barbet thought, I might have noticed the change long ago; there have been signs enough—he has begun even to take a pride in his clothes, the cottage is neat, the garden is cultivated for flowers as well as vegetables. Pierre and Renée are on their way to becoming proprietors in spirit, though indeed there's little enough they own.

With a politeness clearly intended to mark her rise in life, Renée brought chairs into the garden and a dish of plums. She carried them past the oleanders growing in great wooden boxes against the south wall, and set them down in the shade. To explain his visit, Barbet brought out the papers from his pocket and laughed at Pierre for the excellence of his memory.

"But he oughtn't to need such a memory," Renée objected at once. "Only day labourers have such a memory as that."

"Nonsense," Barbet exclaimed. "His mother has a better memory than any woman I have ever known. He inherits it from her."

Renée was not sure whether to be pleased or displeased by this suggestion. "Still," she said, "if one is going to get on in the modern world and be a master and not a servant, one can't be afraid of pen and ink. To grow wine is one thing, but how can you market it without understanding accounts?"

"We were talking of that on the way here," Pierre put in.

"Ah," said she. "I'm glad of that. I'm not the only one to tell you."

"Come, Renée. It wasn't I," Barbet said. "It was Pierre himself who was anxious about account-keeping. He's completely in agreement with you, or I'm mistaken."

She gave her husband a vigorous glance of command and affection.

"That's true; I'm willing enough to learn," he replied, pulling at the lobe of his ear because he was embarrassed by the discovery of so much virtue in himself. "It's not only what Renée says. It's when you are away in Paris that it comes home to me. Isn't the hoeing being done as it should be? Aren't the arrangements for the haymaking made as well as you could have made them yourself? I could run this place, Victor says, if it weren't for the prison and the accounts."

At the word "Victor" Renée had frowned warningly but too late. Having stumbled on to the end of his sentence, Pierre fell into the sheepish and apologetic silence of a man whose wife's wits are readier than his own. So Victor too is behind Pierre's ambition, Barbet thought. When Anton has become owner of the Maison Hazard, Pierre is to run it—as what? as manager or as tenant? In either case, there will be good pickings for the Vincent family.

The plot ruffled him. The Maison Hazard was his home and his mother's; the système Vincent was over-reaching itself.

"Yes," he said, "but the prison and the accounts remain, Pierre.

And so, for that matter, do I. Or had Victor thought of buying a vineyard for you elsewhere? Heaven knows, they are to be had cheaply enough in the Grande Champagne—the best vineyards in France for the price of a mud-heap. I may be mad—Anton thinks I am—but I believe they will recover. It would pay a man to buy and wait."

Before he had finished saying this, his feeling of resentment against Pierre was gone, and he turned from the subject to praise the roses, Paul Meyron and La France.

"If you are going to be proprietors," he said, "you should have a pomegranate and a fig. And if you are to have a pomegranate, you must have a high stone wall for it to look over. And if you have a stone wall, you must have a gateway, Renée."

At last she saw that he was laughing at her and, because she liked Barbet and had always liked him, she smiled in return.

"To buy a place in the Grande Champagne," she said. "I wonder! We might be able to borrow the money."

This, Barbet knew, was a diversion. She had no intention of buying across the river—money or no money.

"Even there," she added, "Pierre would have to know about accounts. I think it isn't fair to shut him out from them. He ought to be given a chance to learn."

The glorious insolence of persistent women!

"Shut him out!" said Barbet. "Bless my soul, have I shut you out from them?"

"No," Pierre answered stubbornly under Renée's eye, "but now I should like to learn."

For a moment Barbet hesitated. What an innocent they must suppose me to be! he thought, and in his mind he heard Victor saying to them: You must get to understand the whole business so that when Barbet goes you can fall into his place. Renée's denial came pat.

"You mustn't suppose that we have our eye on *this* place," she said in a tone intended to comfort and disarm. "You are comfortable here and your mother too—and, of course, there are the prisoners. It is out of the question. But still—"

"But still, it is always a good thing to learn," Barbet interrupted, "and if Pierre wants to learn, I'll teach him. Anyhow, there are the books. They are all open to him. For the most part he can teach himself."

As he said this, he remembered that his mother had warned him long ago against giving Pierre access to the books. "His brother will always be looking over his shoulder," was her way of putting it. "We don't want the Vincents poking their noses into our affairs." It was just comment; his mother knew the world; there could be no greater commercial unwisdom than to contribute information to the système Vincent; perhaps it was, in a measure, true that Pierre had been deliberately discouraged from meddling at the desk. Well, thought Barbet, it shall be true no longer, and he wondered what his father would have said—what his mother would say when she knew.

"And now," he continued, "tell me. As a proprietor, Pierre— shall we need all our hay this year or can we sell some of it?"

But Pierre would not commit himself. "It looks a good crop but who can tell what we shall get in?"

If Madame Hazard noticed that Pierre now came more often to Barbet's workroom, she did not speak of it. The increasing heat made her sleepy, and often, during the period of the labourers' afternoon rest—the time chosen by Pierre for his visits, she was asleep in her bedroom. The deaf woman, Madame Garbut, nodded in a wicker chair at the kitchen door. Until Pierre rang a hand-bell at half-past two, no one stirred in field or vineyard.

The haymaking prospered. Every night the drying grass was gathered into great heaps in the meadows for protection against rain, and every morning re-spread in the sun, but the thunderstorms, when they came, were neither heavy nor prolonged and the grass dried quickly. Having time to spare, Barbet knew that, before the harvesting of barley and oats was upon him, he should take his opportunity to visit Angoulême. His annual agreement with Anton was waiting to be renewed and there was other business to be done with his lawyer. Every evening he said to himself: I must go to-morrow; but he did not go, for each hour of each day in his own country had become precious to him—so precious that he laughed at himself and thought: ordinarily I don't feel like this except when I am packing my bag.

It was the month in which the young children made their first communion. In Cognac, in Roussignac itself and in the villages, he came upon processions of boys in their best suits and little girls in their dress of a bride. He remembered Lancret's face long ago when he had heard that, as Thérèse had gone to her first communion, other children had not wished to walk with her. Nothing so powerfully evoked the past as the repetitive ceremonies that Barbet had remarked each year since he was a boy—the shrines of the Virgin set up in private gardens and sometimes in village squares; the white sheets stretched across the house-fronts with bunches of blue cornflower and daisies and forget-me-not attached to them; above all, the faces of the children, who seemed always to be the same children possessed by the same bewilderment of excitement, solemnity and exaltation. On the eve of midsummer's day, la Saint-Jean, it was a family custom that his mother should sup with Anton and Bette at their house with the gargoyles. When they had supped and the time of parting came, he put her beside him in the tilbury and set out on the road beside the Long Wood.

"You are silent, Barbet. Are you tired?"

"No, mother." And he asked whether she had enjoyed herself.

"I always enjoy supper," she said. "I always enjoy a party—even Bette's. But what I looked forward to was this—the drive home." Then she said, after a long pause: "It must have been along this road you brought Thérèse Despreux that day she came to supper?"

"Yes, mother, but that was later in the year. We met a grass-snake."

"And she is in Paris. She will miss the bonfires. Everyone who leaves the Charente misses the bonfires of Saint-Jean. I shall, I am sure."

Barbet turned to her, intending to say: You, mother? You are not going away? but said nothing. The pony had dropped to a walk.

Among the lucern at the roadside patches of ox-eye daisies shone the brighter in the fading light but the blue of the meadow clary had deepened into its own purpose and was already a ghost, receding into the darkness of the green vegetation. Barbet drew up the reins and the pony was still.

"What is it, Barbet?"

"A nightingale, I thought. Almost the last we shall hear of him. Perhaps the last."

Madame Hazard listened, but there was nothing to be heard except the reeling of a nightjar from within the wood and the noise of the field crickets. She touched her son's arm. "I should have liked to hear him," she said. "Are you sure you heard him?"

"Yes, mother."

"Quite sure?"

"Quite sure."

"That will serve," she said cheerfully. "Good-bye, nightingale. Now let us make haste home. I wouldn't miss the first gleam of the bonfires."

They sat in the garden together to watch the sky deepen over the hill of the Grande Champagne and remained for a long time silent. In the opposite villages on the ridge, points of fire appeared, at first so small that they vanished and came again as men walked across them, but steadily increasing. His mother, recognizing the villages, spoke each name quietly but made no other comment.

"Barbet," she said presently, "don't wait for me."

"But, mother, I shall go to my workroom in any case for a little while. First, I will see you to bed."

"I am not talking of bed."

"Of what, then?"

"Of this place. Home. What a fuss I made before you pulled down that wall! In your father's time, we sat outside the garden to watch the bonfires. And now the wall is gone and I don't miss it. Is that growing old?"

"Most people cling more and more to their possessions as they grow old."

"Do they?" she replied. "That is what the young think. It isn't true, Barbet. And what, may I ask, have you done this year about your agreement with Anton? Have you been to Angoulême?"

"Not yet."

"Has Victor been at you again, wanting you to sell?"

"Not at me," said Barbet, "but really Victor sometimes behaves as if I had sold already." Thinking it better that his mother should be told than that she should be made suspicious by Pierre's coming to his desk, he gave her an account of his visit to the cottage. The effect upon her surprised him.

"Well," she said calmly, "it is time he learned." She watched the fires, turning her head slowly. "Burning down. . . . I'll go upstairs now, Barbet. I like to see them from my room." He gave her his arm. "You must go your round of the walls, my son."

"Yes, mother."

At the door, under the vine, she stopped. "Do you want to sell, Barbet?"

"Why should I, mother?"

"When you were younger, I didn't know you very well," she answered. "Now you and I are closer to each other. I know when you're going on a voyage."

"And if I sold, where should we live?"

"You mean: where should I die? Is that it? I shall not die in this house. Nor you. I am becoming lighter." She put her arm round his shoulder and made him stoop down so that she might whisper in his ear. "I said good-bye to the nightingale." She began to chuckle. "Think of that! Just think of that! If I were to say 'nightingale' to Emilie Vincent, she would quote for half an hour. If I were to whisper in her ear, she would go mad. It was Thérèse Despreux who whispered in her ear. Don't wait for me. Good night, dear Barbet. Here is my candle. I shan't need it. I can find my own way to bed."

Barbet went to his workroom and turned up his lamp. On his desk were sheets of paper covered with Pierre's laborious sums. When he had corrected them, he began a letter to Thérèse in which he told her that he had driven home by the road on which they had met the grass-snake, but at first said of his mother only that she had enjoyed watching the bonfires and had now gone to bed. Then he added: "I wonder if you will understand what she meant when she said to me that she was 'becoming lighter.' I think she meant that she felt less bound—to the past, to the Maison Hazard, to everything. It must be good to grow old like that. It isn't that she's afraid of dying. I am sure she is not. On the contrary—less and less afraid. It is just that she is weighing anchor."

The next words he wrote were: "Suddenly there was a great bump and flutter against the window-pane. I thought he was gone but a moment later he found the open part of the window and was in the room. He shook the lamp and fell on this paper, a huge moth. I had to blow out the lamp. He was on the paper still. I suppose he was stunned, for he let me put him out on the sill with scarcely a flutter. I closed the shutters and pulled the curtains, as I should have done before I sat down to write. But all is well. I have just been outside and he is gone. Look how big he is. I will draw his outline on this paper where he rested. It isn't every day that a Great Night Peacock sends his visiting card to the Quai d'Orléans."

Under the heat of July, Pierre abandoned arithmetic; he would begin again, he said, after the vintage. Meanwhile, though all work but light hoeing had ceased in the vineyards, he had enough to do with the harvesting, and Renée's desire to assert her independence of the family of Hazard was satisfied by her taking a conspicuous part in the celebrations of the Fourteenth of July from which Madame Hazard, as a good Bonapartist, abstained. Anton compromised, flying the tricolour from the office of Hazard and Vincent but not from his private house. As mayor, he lent his countenance to the torchlight procession on the 13th, and next afternoon Bette gave away prizes to winners of sack-races and of competitions on the greasy pole; but it was Barbet who, by a custom of long standing, presided over the boys' swimming competitions in the Charente. The routine was invariable. His mother would enter a formal protest against his going at all, standing at his wheel as he mounted the gig, and he, as she expected, would wave his whip and drive off. Having put up his pony in a comfortable shade at the Cheval Pie and re-

cruited Frédéric as assistant timekeeper, he would march down to
the river, carrying a great watch in his hand, and start the races with
admirable dignity; but before the afternoon was over his clothes were
off, his dignity gone, and the judge became an unofficial competitor
who, having started a race, leapt into its wake and came paddling
back to start and join in the next. At night, even Madame Hazard's
Bonapartism broke down. She supped with Madame Vincent,
played piquet, quarrelled and watched the fireworks. Like bonfires,
fireworks were to her irresistible.

Having given his prisoners their meal, Barbet took his mother in
the tilbury to the Vincents' house. Victor was fortunately absent.
He had no more love of music than of any other abundant out-
pouring of human emotion, and the concert of the Philharmonic
Society was, in all conscience, abundant enough, but for his social
credit he endured its performance every Fourteenth of July. The
two ladies, therefore, sat in their garden after supper with no company but Barbet's, and disputed to their hearts' content. The roses
were spoiled and the garden very dry, but in a narrow border against
the house the Marvel of Peru had opened its flowers after the heat
of the day, and Madame Vincent had a clear advantage over her
guest in the matter of stone-crop which had never prospered at the
Maison Hazard but hung down from her tiles in cushions of bright
yellow. She did not fail to draw Madame Hazard's attention to it,
but even argument and piquet itself were abandoned when fireworks
began.

"Fireworks have improved in recent years," said Madame Vincent. "Nothing else has."

"I disagree," Madame Hazard began, but a distant fountain of
golden rain so pleased her that she clapped her hands and forgot to
speak. "Who would have thought," she said when the sky had returned to its natural colour and it was certain that the fireworks were
over, "who would have thought, in 'seventy, that we should have
fireworks again?"

"Nonsense, my dear Chouquette. It will take more than a few
Prussians to put out the French Revolution. It will take more than
guns to extinguish the liberties of France."

"Oh dear, I suppose you are right, Emilie," said Madame Hazard with a laugh and a sigh. "But I was thinking of the price of fireworks, you know. I hadn't given a thought to the liberties of France. . . . Now, Barbet, we had better be going home. Good night, dear Emilie. How noisy your swifts are!"

"But we have not finished our game," Madame Vincent objected firmly. "We were in the middle of a game when the fireworks began, and I was winning."

"I will give you the game, dear Emilie."

"To be given a game is not the same as having won it. You know that, Chouquette."

Madame Hazard knew it well. She hesitated between the joy of cheating Emilie of a victory and her private desire not to go to bed.

"We could take another glass of wine in the parlour," Madame Vincent suggested encouragingly.

Madame Hazard cast about her for an excuse to accept. "It is true," she said, "that last Monday, though it was my birthday, I went to bed at my usual time," and, putting her head on one side, she yielded to temptation.

This gave Madame Vincent so much pleasure that she generously asked the question that her guest expected of her and to which she had long known the answer:

"Of course, Chouquette. Your birthday. Were you sixty-four or sixty-five?"

"Now, Emilie, you have so good a memory, you ought to remember that. When I was born, the Emperor had not been three months in his tomb."

When the last sheaves were being taken from the cornfields and a yellowish lustre had begun to appear on the swelling grapes, Barbet had more time to spend with his prisoners. He kept pitchers of water for them in the passage leading to their courtyard, and took it to them often, fresh and cold. Once, while sitting with them under their ilex, he looked up, to find Blachère standing beside him. His first impulse was of revulsion. He turned to the other prisoners and spoke to them as if Blachère did not exist. They talked to him and among themselves, excluding Blachère, who at length walked away and sat down alone. Determined to remove a barrier for which he felt himself to be, in part, responsible, Barbet went over to Blachère and tried to talk to him, but the attempt failed.

"Why do you waste your time with me?" Blachère said at last. "You have nothing to give me. I don't want kindness from you. I want a life of my own."

Barbet knew this to be true; but, with a pride of spirit that Blachère alone could provoke, he began to justify himself. The others were by nature pacific men; there was no principle of evil in them; beneath their differences was a sense that they were part of the human community; their suffering, in imprisonment, was that it exiled them from common life. Blachère was in his own nature and by his own will an exile and a rebel, and imprisonment was to him what a cage would be to a bird of prey. I am being as great a fool as I should be if I were to set about the taming of a vulture, Barbet said to himself. I have nothing to give him because he is my enemy and hates me.

Or had he nothing to give because he was growing to hate and despise his prisoner? He came humbly to Blachère and almost begged for his friendship, but the humility was false. Even while he struggled to override the differences between them, he nursed them and became proud of them, and decided that there was a principle of evil in this man which removed him from the community of men.

Probably, Barbet decided, the truth is that certain men cannot associate together without damage to each other, and Blachère and I are two such men. Of all men on earth, I am the least fit to be his gaoler.

In the end, he left Blachère and returned to the other prisoners, but he was exhausted, as though he had lost blood, and was glad when the time came to give them their supper and leave them.

"I am going into Roussignac," he told his mother.

"For what, Barbet?"

"For the walk."

"I should wait until later in the evening. It is still hot."

"I shall go through the wood."

"It will be hot even in the wood."

But he was determined to go. He wanted to put a distance between himself and Blachère and to be possessed again of his own
mind. It was a silent and torpid day, too heavy for the song of
birds, and the night, when it came, would be blanketed by heat; even
the field crickets would have exhausted their chorus and darkness
would be scraped by the dry vibration of locusts. This afternoon
nothing was to be heard but the cirl-bunting—not a blackcap, not
a yellow-hammer; the dry-meadows and the woods seemed to be
empty; and the cirl-bunting was part of the dryness of the air. It must
be poor fun to be a bird and make a noise like a locust, Barbet thought,
and a smile broke over his face, his heart lifted, and there before him,
for once content to be visible, was a golden oriole. He sat down and
watched it.

Chapter 2

IT HAD BEEN A PECULIARITY OF THE BARREL-MAK-
ing in the prison courtyard that, though Blanchère had learned the
use of osiers and was at least as skilled as the rest in other branches of
the craft, he had not been entrusted with the chip-axe. He had not
asked for it and Barbet had not offered it to him. Each was aware,
and knew that the other was aware, of the omission, and that it was
unreasonable. The cooper's hammer, the as, was as formidable a
weapon; the chip-axe itself could have been seized from the hands
of another if Blachère had been minded to attack. Nevertheless, having felt at the outset an ill-defined reluctance to put an axe into
Blachère's hand, Barbet had never taught him the use of it. Sometimes Blachère picked it up, turned it over in his great hands and
passed it on, under Barbet's eye, to Balze or Marcotte.

One September morning, during an interval in their work, Barbet
and his prisoners were sitting together in the cover of an open shed
on the west side of the prison courtyard. As soon as tools were laid
down, Blachère had gone, as he often did, to his own cell, for it pleased
him that eyes should follow him as he went and gaze at him curiously
when he returned. Meanwhile, Fontan brought his mandolin, which
had been standing against the trunk of the ilex, and began to feel his
way into little tunes, looking to Barbet for recognitions. From his cell,
Blachère shouted to know if they were never to be free from this everlasting strumming. "He hates it," said Marcotte with relish. "It's like
a fly biting a horse." Encouraged by Balze to continue, Fontan, because he was afraid, steeled himself with the defiance of weak men
and stood up, facing the cells, and shouted his song.

Blachère slammed his door but made no further protest. Fontan's
defiance spent itself; the thrumming of his mandolin continued in a

stubborn undertone; the heart had gone from his playing but he feared that the others might despise him if he ceased. Blachère has the power to sap the pleasure from whatever a man does, Barbet thought, by planting fear in him. Marcotte was hollowing out a life-boat for his model ship and fitting into it a thwart so tiny that he could not manipulate it with his fingers but coaxed it into position with the tip of a penknife. He loved this work in miniature and had only one fear—that he might break his spectacles. Barbet had given him others, laboriously matched in Angoulême, but Marcotte had rejected them; there were not, and could not be in this world, any spectacles but his own; and now, when the time came to return to barrel-making, he looked up over them at Barbet with the expression of a man who had been disturbed in a dream. Heim shouted to Blachère that work was beginning again and Fontan laid down his mandolin.

Since he had led the riot that failed, Blachère had never refused obedience. His method of opposition to his gaoler was more subtle and personal; a slavish, inhuman docility was part of it; and he came now from his cell with a dragging submission, as though he wore chains. From the level of the courtyard two steps mounted to the floor of the shed. As he came up them, he stumbled and his right foot shattered the wood of the mandolin.

"No! No! No!" Fontan cried, his voice rising to a shriek of impotent fury.

Blachère disengaged his foot. His cheeks rose and seemed to swell under his eyes. A storm of excited comment broke out, Heim saying again and again, "I was facing him. I saw what he did," and Marcotte rubbing his hands together and uttering quick, shrill sounds like those of a frightened bird.

"I stumbled," Blachère said at last, and the cries against him were renewed. He looked at none of his accusers, but at Barbet steadfastly.

"Why did you do that?"

"I stumbled. You didn't see."

It was true that Barbet had not seen but it was necessary that he should judge. He knew the futility of punishment and, at the same time, that he must inflict it. He knew also that, if he punished Blachère, he would be submitting to Blachère's own will and design.

He said: "You will be punished. Go to your cell."

"It is unjust," Blachère replied, not in angry protest but in an even, penetrating tone. "You know it is unjust because you did not see me."

"I have no doubt of what you did."

"Nevertheless," said Blachère, "you are punishing me because you are afraid not to punish me."

Barbet again ordered him to his cell and, when he obeyed, followed him and took away his mattress, his table, his candle, and locked him in. He determined not to relax the rule of punishment, to exercise Blachère briefly and alone, to withdraw all his privileges of food and of freedom within the courtyard. As he turned away from the locked door, Blachère said:

"It is you who are inside, Monsieur Barbet."

In the time of Julien Hazard, each cell had in its door a narrow grid, normally closed, and only one other source of light and air—a window set high in the outer wall and barred. These bars were tested each night by Barbet, leaning across to them from a grassy ramp which brought him to their level and was divided from the prison wall by a deep and narrow ditch. When control of the prison passed to him from his father, he had enlarged the existing grid or spy-hole in each door to an aperture at head-level through which the cell's occupant might look out into the courtyard. These door-holes were barred and each was fitted with a glass shutter to be let down in cold weather. Through the door-holes and the external windows a draught moved that helped the prisoners during the great heats of July and August. Only one cell, set apart from the rest at the northern end of the courtyard, was not so fitted. It was less than half the size of the others; its external window was a thin slit; its door had no aperture but the old grid. Called by Julien the rat-hole, it had not been used in Barbet's time.

While under punishment, Blachère made great use of his door-hole. His face was continually and for long periods to be seen behind its bars. He appeared to have established for himself a routine which he followed strictly. When the other prisoners were at work or exercise in the courtyard, he watched them for a great part of the time and they became aware of his head always occupying the same position in the aperture, as if it were a dummy on a stake. At moments of the day which they were able to foretell, the head vanished. It was to be presumed that Blachère slept, but Barbet never found him sleeping. When he was visited, he was always in the same position, lying on his left side on the planks that were his bed, raised on his elbow, his head supported by his hand, his fingers embedded in his loose scalp, his eyes on the door. He did not stir, but allowed his food and water to be put down beside him, and did not reply if he was spoken to or himself speak until Barbet was about to go. Then he would say: "You would suffer more if you were in the rat-hole. It is hot and dark." Or he would throw out his challenge: "You can't put me in the rat-hole; I have broken no rule." At each visit, he used one of these phrases. No other words passed his lips. If another prisoner spoke to him he did not answer. During the whole daytime, no sound came from his cell.

After midnight, between one and four each morning, he kicked his door and howled at regular intervals of four minutes. Each night there were thirty-six of these outbursts—twelve to the hour. Each lasted for a minute. The kicks were slow, methodical and evenly delivered, as unemotional as the swing of a pendulum. They resounded through the courtyard and through the window of Barbet's bedroom which overlooked it. In the whole proceeding one element only was uncertain. Except by counting, it was impossible to know whether, on each occasion, the pendulum would swing thirteen or fourteen times. At their work next day, the prisoners would dispute whether thirteen or fourteen was the right number. They could not be sure even that the number varied or that they had not lost count. That he might be sure, Fontan gathered fourteen corkscrew shavings of Limousin oak and took them into his cell, but next morning fourteen had become sixteen, two of the corkscrews having broken, and his count was discredited. The prisoners pretended that the subject was of no importance to them and made a joke of the counting, but, though they laughed and spoke of other things, their conversation always returned to Blachère and his imprisonment. Holding out some pebbles in his hand, Marcotte asked: "Fourteen or thirteen?" Fontan intentionally miscounted them and passed them to Heim. The prisoners began to giggle over them like schoolgirls with a secret. The pebbles were handed to Barbet, who threw them on to the ground.

At night Barbet argued with himself in this way: Blachère is disturbing the prison so that I may be tempted to reduce his punishment to less than six nights. Blachère is disturbing the prison so that I may feel this temptation and harden myself to resist it. Blachère is disturbing the prison so that I may transfer him to the punishment cell. Blachère is disturbing the prison so that the punishment cell may enter my mind and I reject it and be conscious of weakness in having rejected it.

On the first, the second and the third nights, the kicking of the door began at one o'clock and continued three hours. Barbet did not speak of it to Blachère. After the third day, whenever he was visited and had spoken one of his two phrases, he added that he was hungry. It was true; he was accustomed to eat voraciously; low diet was a cause of suffering to him and he was tormented by need of the tobacco that was allowed to prisoners in the courtyard. On the fourth night, he preserved his routine, but on the fifth, he lost the resolution to continue his disturbance regularly. He began as before but soon after two in the morning his uproar became rapid and continuous, then ceased. On the sixth night, he steeled himself and returned to his former custom. His punishment had now run its course and on the morning of Friday the 11th of September he was given a full meal and taken out to work.

In the past Madame Hazard had had so little sympathy with Blachère that Barbet had expected her to protest long ago against this new disturbance of her nights, but she said nothing until Saturday morning when, after a quiet night, she inquired:

"Is the punishment over?"

"Yes, mother."

"What made you do it, Barbet? Were you angry with him?"

He had not yet asked himself this question and reflected before he answered it.

"No, I wasn't angry. He had broken Fontan's mandolin—I am sure deliberately. No," he repeated, "I wasn't angry with him. I punished him because what he had done was a challenge that had to be met."

"Did he suffer?"

"Yes."

"Barbet," his mother said after a moment's pause, "I wonder if it has done any good. That other night when you went in and quieted them, you didn't punish them then."

"No."

"That was a challenge."

"Yes," he said, "that was a challenge."

She went about the parlour with her feather brush as though their conversation was ended, and afterwards disappeared into the kitchen. Barbet went to his workroom and sat down to his desk. His mother presently came to his door.

"I want to ask something, Barbet."

"Yes, mother, what is it?"

"It was yesterday, Friday morning, that you let him out?"

"Yes, Friday."

"Your father would have been armed."

"I was armed."

"Is it true? You are not saying that to comfort me?"

"I was armed," he repeated.

"And now?"

"Yes, when I go into the prison."

"Does he know—Blachère?"

Though he knew that he was misunderstanding his mother, Barbet answered with a laugh not his own and in a voice not his own: "Are you afraid, mother? What are you afraid of? Do you think he will snatch the pistol and kill me?"

She sat down beside him and tried to take his hand, but he took it from the table and beyond her reach.

"Do not let him guess you are armed."

"But why? But why?" Barbet asked in the same pretence of mocking her fears, in the same tone of falseness and patronage.

"Do not let him guess, Barbet," she said. "It would please him."

When she was gone, Barbet picked up his pen and tried to work; then went into the open and sat on the bench above the pine-trees from which he could see the river. Patches of bracken had begun to rust; their yellow shone against the rosy colour of the ling in flower; and the Lombardy poplars were drawing their first golden lines in the valley. An early year, he thought; we shall have the grapes in before the month ends, and he tried to keep his mind on the vintage. But he saw Blachère lying on his side staring at the door of his cell, and his mother's words could not be driven away. He remembered the time when she had thought him foolish and impractical and there had been affection but no understanding between them. He remembered the phase of her life in which she had supposed, with a part of her mind, that she was the mother of a saint and had expected miracles of him; she had become childish, as though she were greatly older than her years, and there had seemed to be no other course than to humour and indulge her. It was with this patronizing indulgence that he had tried this morning to treat her, but he knew that it was false, that the justification of it was past, that she had outgrown it. "She is growing up," he had said to Thérèse at Vernon, and since his return from Paris in June, he had felt continually that his mother, though she preserved her little follies of manner and could be as wilful and pettish and stubborn as ever in the past, had within her a distilled and achieved wisdom which she expressed, not consecutively or in any process of argument, but seemingly in random phrases that struck to the heart of his knowledge of himself.

Then why on earth did I take my hand away? Why did I laugh and pretend I didn't understand when she said it would please Blachère to know that I was armed? It is true. I ran away from the truth. And now I sit here arguing with myself. If only I could stop arguing, then I should know what to do.

That night, when he took the prisoners their supper, he left the pistol in its niche, as he had left it when he had come in from the wood with glow-worms in his pocket, but not with the same impulse. His leaving it now was not spontaneous, but an action designed to evade Blachère's will and, therefore, conditioned by it. He was without lightness of heart; he felt that he was in a trap; and he said to his mother:

"I left the pistol behind, but I was still thinking about it."

She looked at him with so pitiful an expression that he supposed her mind to be wandering or that she had not understood him. Then she said as though she were reproving some rashness of a child:

"But that is dangerous, Barbet. Better keep the pistol. Better stay in the boat. Oh yes," she continued. "Half and half is no good. Still thinking about it is no good. That is how Saint Peter sank."

She spoke so gravely, so lightly, with such an abrupt and ludicrous leaping from idea to idea that Barbet was fascinated.

"After all," she said, "it is not surprising. A man is walking on the water and it is easy. Then the idea comes into his head—'I am not sinking,' and at once he sinks."

"I know," Barbet answered with a grin, "I tried once."

His mother was quietly interested. "When was that?"

"When I was a boy."

"You never told me."

"Well, I sank. Perhaps for the reason you suggest."

"That may be," she answered, "but of course there are other reasons for sinking."

"Anyhow," he said, "I have gone into the prison armed and I have gone in unarmed. One is as valueless as the other."

"Yes," she answered, "but when you are ready, Barbet, you will know what to do."

He heard the echo. The words had been spoken to him before, but he did not remember the circumstances. If only I could stop arguing. If only argument would sleep. But it needs faith to sleep.

"You look tired," his mother said. "Don't work tonight. Go to bed early and sleep."

It appeared to Barbet that he had been wrong in withholding the chip-axe from Blachère and he began to teach him the use of it. Blachère asked no questions—not even why now for the first time

he was given the axe, and when the others, who had already some
knowledge of it, laughed at his clumsiness, he did not reply, but applied himself to learning how to grip and how to swing it. His tend-
ency was that of all learners—to grip the handle too tightly with too
stiff a wrist and to strike instead of swinging. "The oak is cheese,"
Barbet said. "The weight of the head is almost enough. Let it fall,
let it swing. Your job is to guide it, to prevent it from striking too
deep." He tried to put his hand over Blachère's that they might
swing the axe together, but Blachère's hand was too big. The wood
came away unevenly, in little chips, until, late on the third afternoon
of experiment, the fall of the axe was lucky, and a long shaving, called
une anglaise because it was a tradition among coopers that English
ladies did their hair in corkscrew curls, fell to the ground. Marcotte
seized it and dangled it in the air. "Look what Blachère has made!
Look what the good pupil has made! That is better than kicking
one's door all night." Blachère straightened himself. The chip-axe
hung loose in his hand; his eyes narrowed and his feet shifted. Then
all of a sudden a madness of anger flowed up his body into his face,
which became suffused with blood; he threw back his head and
twisted it to and fro on its short neck as if this blood were suffocating
him; he thrust his way past Marcotte with one rolling swing of his
thighs and fell upon the model ship with axe and boot, striking and
trampling it so that the splinters crackled like a fire and jumped on
the stones. Balze, Heim and Fontan threw themselves upon him.
They wrenched at the axe; but its work was done, it came easily into
their hands. Marcotte, unaware of any danger to himself, was on
his knees among the ruins of his ship, snatching at fragments, clutching them to his belly, and crying out repeatedly: "My little ship—the
months! My little ship—the months!" In the first agony of attack,
his hand had run up his face, thrusting his spectacles back; now he
had lost them on his forehead; he could not see the fragments he
held or understand why he did not see them. He curved his back; his
head drooped downward; his spectacles slid on his sweaty temples
and fell. With a movement of extraordinary agility, Blachère
stretched out his foot and ground them into the stones.

At this, his appearance changed. An expression of sensual appeasement, almost of somnolence, appeared in his face. His eyes dulled;

the tautness went from his limbs; the huge body became spongy and slack; and Barbet hated him. A sickness and pressure of anger was in his throat. He heard his own voice, reviling Blachère, emerge from the outcry of voices that drowned Marcotte's whimpering lamentation; then heard it alone, giving orders. The heat went out of his indignation, which became separated from its cause; Marcotte and Marcotte's ship had no longer any place in his mind; his hatred was coldly directed against Blachère personally; his decision was clear and required no effort of him. Three men held Blachère, who made no resistance. He was put in the punishment cell and sat on his plank while it was cleaned. Barbet locked the door and closed the shutter on the grid. Across the courtyard, Marcotte was still on his knees among the fragments of his ship, picking them up, peering at them and tossing them away as a monkey throws away the shells of nuts or allows them to drop from his hand as though he had forgotten them. At sight of Barbet, the old man came to him at a shambling trot in vague expectation of comfort, but Barbet had no heart for him. He sent him and the other prisoners to their cells. The day's work was over and dusk was beginning to fall.

When he returned to the kitchen, the deaf woman, Madame Garbut, was seated at the stove, her hands folded placidly on her apron.

"Is the supper ready?"

She could not hear him, but his manner brought her to her feet. It was her quietest hour, when nothing was required of her except to stir the pot now and then, and she could not understand his shouting or the signs he made. When at last she understood that he was demanding the prisoners' supper, she replied: no, no, how could it be ready? it wouldn't be ready for over an hour; her voice shrilled with resentment of what she felt to be an injustice; she stuttered and turned up her shoulder against him, frightened by the unreason of his having asked for the supper an hour before its time. "And often, when I have it ready, it is you who forget about it; you are out, and everyone has to wait."

He stood at the kitchen-door with his back to her, staring at the tops of the pine-trees that appeared above the break in the ground. His mother came in, but he did not shift, and her little steps brought her to the doorway, where she looked up into his face and suddenly closed her fingers on his forearms.

"What have you done? What have you done, Barbet?" and she looked at his hands.

He shook his head and shook his head but could not answer, and went out, walking at first slowly, without determination, then fast through the pinewoods, down the hill, down the steep path to the low meadows, across the meadows to the river's bank. There was a small beach there, a scoop among the willows, and he dropped on the turf breathless, gathering his knees to his chin, clasping them with taut muscles, his head down, his eyes shut, his whole body stiffened. In a little while, he began to breathe more slowly and his first knowledge of the stillness of that September evening was in the discovery that the noise to which he had been listening inside the crouching blackness of knees and arms had been the noise of his own breath, now quieted. His hands loosened their grip and moved inward along his forearms, recognizing the warmth of his own flesh, until they met over his forehead and came away suddenly from the matted wetness of his hair. Though his mother had looked for blood on him, this wetness was not of blood. He stirred and sighed, like a dog that trembles on the hearth but does not wake, and, shivering still under the seizure of hatred that had been blood's equivalent, turned from the knowledge of it and of himself, and pressed down and down into the forest of his eyes.

But now, instead of the sound of his own breath, the sound of the river was in him, the long swirl of water moving slowly and without intermission, the steady whisper of the central current, the little clap and slip of the shallow beach, and the sound was not of to-day or of any passion, but a timeless sound out of the earth itself, a pulse of his own body proceeding from the earth. He stretched himself out and stared, seeing the earth for the first time as though he were being born.

Great dragonflies were out hunting. A line of gold, fast narrowing in the western sky, shone through their wings as they skimmed the surface and soared abruptly against the poplars' darkness. From the opposite bank, above a reed-bed a-flutter with house-martins, over meadows sloping to the river from high ground beyond Bellis came the barking of a dog—a sound so remote, so small and yet, within its tone, so clear that it enlarged the stillness of evening. When it ceased, the distances of hearing lay open to a wide expectancy; for away a brown owl's hooting wound its long, plaintive rhythm through the dusk, to be challenged near at hand by a sudden trill of wanton splendour flung out by a robin from a neighbouring thicket. Barbet looked up and searched but could not find him. Only the brown owl continued. The poplars deepened their mass as the sky closed in upon them. Separated from the water by a bank of which the form was each instant dissolving, they and the willows appeared for a time to float in the air above the river's gleam; then to settle and stiffen to their watch. A thinning of the clouds let in a milkiness of stars which swam and vanished, and a low sheen, as of glass laid upon darkened silver, appeared on the areas of smooth water between the midstream eddies. Night flowed up and a final calm grew upon the scene.

Barbet remembered his prisoners by way of their supper, for he too was hungry. How long it had been dark he did not know. He stood up and began to walk home with the delight upon him of release from pain and of a mind from which poison had been drawn away. Sometimes, in the morning, when daylight awakened him, he had felt the pulse of happiness before he remembered its particular cause. Now he experienced the lightness of a decision made, without recalling or attempting to recall the process of decision. He saw clearly what he would do and had already done it in his mind when he reached the pinewoods. What lay before him was not in doubt or argument, but presented itself to him as a physical re-enactment of scenes already a part of his experience.

The kitchen door was shut and locked, as he had supposed that it would be, Madame Garbut having tired of waiting and gone home. He let himself in with his own key, and felt his way cautiously to the embrasure in which the lamp would be standing. This he brought out and lighted. On the table, held in place by a spoon, was a sheet of paper on which his mother had written: "Going to bed. All quiet."

The pot, left at the side of the stove, was warm but not sizzling; he shifted it nearer the fire and increased the draught; then laid on the table six bowls and beside them meat, bread, wine and cheese. Lamp in hand, he went to his own workroom and, taking an iron box from the safe, carried it into the kitchen and opened it. After this, he went to a cupboard built into the passage leading to his workroom and brought from it in five bundles the clothes worn by the prisoners when they came to the Maison Hazard. Returning to the kitchen table, he prepared five packets of food and put a packet, with twenty francs taken from the iron box, into a pocket in each bundle of clothing. The box was relocked and put back in the safe. This done, he looked round him at the familiar kitchen to be sure that he had forgotten nothing. It is ready, he said. It was as he had seen it as he walked up from the river.

The time had now come to light the lamp which he was accustomed to take with him when he made his nightly round of the walls. When it was swinging from the leather bracelet by which he fastened it to his wrist so that he might have both hands free to test the bars, he thought: I shall never test the bars again, and remembered, with a smile at the conflict of ideas, how much of the life of birds he had learned while performing this duty. A song—as yet no more than the stirring of a tune—came into his head. Bless my soul, he said, it's weeks since I gave Fontan a new song; this isn't the moment to be tune-making; and, having lowered the wick of the kitchen lamp that it might not smoke in his absence, he took the prison keys from their place inside his shirt and set off down the covered way. At the entrance to the courtyard he saw the pistol in its niche, and because everything, even a pistol, had upon him a power of association or companionship, as though it were alive, he touched the pistol as he might have touched the head of a dog that he was leaving behind.

The prison was quiet, though all the prisoners, except Blachère, were awake. What is it? they said, haven't you brought supper? Marcotte was standing at his door-hole, looking out into the dark, and he said only: "I saw your lamp coming. It was swinging low. I knew you hadn't the tureen."

"Your supper is in the kitchen to-night," he said. "You can go there now."

They did not understand. "What kitchen?"

"My own kitchen. An order has come for your release."

"Release? All of us? Release?"

"What does it mean?"

"It must be an amnesty," said Balze.

Marcotte, with respect for a word he did not understand, asked what an amnesty was.

"It will be a political amnesty," Balze replied with a townsman's assurance. Then an idea struck him. "What has happened? Is there a war? Is there an Emperor in France?"

"No," Barbet said, "there isn't a war or an Emperor."

Blachère's cell was the last to be opened.

"Blachère!"

He rose, blinking at the light. "What is it?"

"You have had no supper."

"Where am I? This isn't my cell?" He stretched out his arms and touched the walls.

Barbet took hold of him and led him out. The other prisoners were visible on the fringe of the lamp's circle. The excitement of their voices was communicated to Blachère who, not yet understanding what was afoot, backed into the doorway of his cell. Seeing before him the small figure with the lamp and how isolated it was and how defenceless, he swung on the balls of his feet and drew back his arms to strike. Barbet raised the lamp to the level of his face and said: "I am unarmed, Blachère, and all the doors are open." As he said this, Blachère ceased to be dangerous; his intentness broke, his impulse swerved as though a cloth had been drawn across his eyes. His great body threw its weight back on his heels; the menace and agility went out of it; the head turned from side to side; the gaze dulled and wandered. The power of evil in him was displaced by a fugitive cunning, and crying: "The doors are open. Now! Now! Go for the doors!" he put his head down and plunged blindly into the darkness.

The others, who had stood hitherto without initiative—for, in the night, they had not seen that the doors to the courtyard were open, awoke now to their opportunity, and, a fear seizing them of some betrayal which might snatch from them the liberty so long desired, they were swept by Blachère's panic and would have gone at his heels; but, as they were in the instant of flight, Barbet said: "You can go now or later, but if you wait for me I will give you food and clothes." He spoke with so steady an assurance that they believed him, and followed him across the courtyard, through the double doorway and into the kitchen. Here impatience again shook them. An open door leading into the night set their minds flaming with the instinct to escape, Marcotte eyeing it continually with covert avarice and edging towards it with his back to the wall. "There's nothing to be gained by running for it," Barbet said, and thrust into Marcotte's hands the bundle of clothes that belonged to him. "There's food and money in the pocket. Lie low for a time. Get clear of the district. There'll be no hue and cry. As long as I can keep the secret, no one shall know you are gone."

A little reassured but still questioning, the four men began to tumble out of one suit of clothes and into another, pausing now and then to sup the broth poured into their bowls and chattering in disconnected phrases, each of himself, his rediscovered possessions, the fit of his old clothes, his darting memories of this shirt, this jacket, chinking his money, tossing from palm to palm his packet of food— as excited as a starling in the reeds.

The stress of delay was more, Barbet knew, than Marcotte could long endure. He was dressed, fumbling with his buckle, edging step by step nearer to the door, and soon would be gone. Barbet went over to him and, though he began to grumble at sight of them, put into his breast pocket the depised spectacles bought in Angoulême, then looked at him for the last time and turned his back. "He's gone!" cried Fontan. When Barbet looked round, Marcotte was no longer in the doorway.

"Are we free to go?" said Balze cautiously, speaking for Heim and himself.

"If you want to," Barbet answered with a light in his eye.

"If we are caught, we shall be punished for prison-breaking,"

Heim began in the voice of a man suspicious of injustice and determined to contend for his rights.

"You are not prison-breaking. No one can punish you for walking through an open door."

"I want a paper—signed," said Balze.

"A release-paper," said Heim. "What I don't understand is why you are doing this. Why are you giving us money?"

"Well," Barbet replied, "you can give it to Fontan if it burns you."

The idea that any man should give money away troubled Heim. He was afraid that he might afterwards be accused of having stolen it.

"A release-paper," he said again, "and write on it—no, write on another piece of paper that you gave us the money."

"Certainly I will," Barbet said, "but it makes no difference, you know," and he went into his workroom for pen and ink. When he returned, Fontan was alone in the room.

"Where are they?"

"Flitted."

"But the papers they wanted?"

Fontan shrugged his shoulders. "They took the food and the money out of Blachère's clothes and then—" He spread out his hands.

"And you?"

"Yes," Fontan answered, "I shall go. I must go."

"You are free to go or stay."

Fontan shook his head. "Where is the spare mandolin? There used to be another. Still at that inn?"

"The Cheval Pie."

"Where the girl came from," said Fontan.

"Why do you ask? Do you want it? You can't carry a mandolin where you are going?"

"No, I don't want it," Fontan replied, his thought so twisting in reluctances and delays and desires that he lost track of it. "I was thinking of Eugénie. I shall look for her. She may be still at Lyons. . . . It will be strange here to-morrow—no one in the cells. Had you thought of that? Who will write down your music for you?"

"I hadn't thought of to-morrow," Barbet said. "If one does, you know, one never gets out of prison."

Fontan stood up and looked at the door and at Barbet, then slowly round the room, wishing to be gone but afraid to go.

"You are lucky," he said, "to have a home like this. . . . And I used to teach music to young ladies. In winter, it was always too hot or too cold. If you shut the window, there was the stove; if you opened it, there was a draught. The door didn't fit. . . . But that is of no interest of you." His face twitched, he held out his hand, and, when Barbet had taken it, overwhelmed by the sentimentality of his violent and timid heart, he stammered: "I hate last times. That's it. Silly, isn't it?" He laughed shrilly and tears came into his eyes. "I don't think it was any good putting me in prison. A man like me. What I did was all over, long before they took me. I suppose the idea is that I might do it again. But that's silly too. A man like me. How could I try to kill anyone again? Not twice. It isn't possible." He was still clinging to Barbet's hand. "You are brave!" he exclaimed, dropping the hand in extreme embarrassment. "To let us go. To open the doors and say—'shoo'! That is seeing everything in one—not in bits and pieces—everything in one. Shoo! It is done! You are yourself again! You are brave. Like a lion."

Barbet reached for his bowl and emptied it. "Look," he said, "I'll see you on your way."

Fontan replied with clinging eagerness. An expression of confidence came into his face, for he would not now have to go through the door alone. They went out together, past the musky scent of the garden, past the barred windows and the edge of the wood, and at every step Fontan's spirits rose. He stretched his arms, he smelt the air; so entranced was he by the sensation of freedom that his fear of its strangeness fell from him. On the road north of the prison, running east and west towards Roussignac and St. Brice, Barbet halted.

"Which way, Fontan?"

"I have a brother at Surgères."

"That is a long way," said Barbet. "Watch the sun in the morning. Keep north-west. Listen—along this road for a kilometre; then

to the right, to the north, away from the river. Nercillac. Follow the
Soloire. Make for St. Jean d'Angély."

"St. Jean d'Angély," Fontan repeated. "I have money. I can
take a train." The idea of finding himself in a train overwhelmed
him and, forgetting Barbet, he began to run as though he could hear
the engine puffing in a station. But he did not run far; his footfall
slackened to a walk and was long to be heard, for the night was still.
A dog barked and was answered by another.

There, said Barbet, turning homeward, it is done. As he crossed
the front of the house, he saw a light in his mother's window.

"Have they all gone, Barbet?"

"Yes, mother."

"I counted only four."

"There was another went first. Blachère went first."

"Ah," she said, "that is as it should be."

He went into the kitchen and she came down to him, her head
so wrapped in a shawl that her face was no larger than a pair of
small apples. Together they made the prison clothes into bundles
and put them away in the cupboard.

"You are not still troubled about anything, Barbet?"

"No, mother."

"Ah," she said, "that, too, is as it should be. Now I will make
some strong coffee and we will drink a glass of cognac. . . . No, no,
Barbet. Don't deny me. I know what is right. After a battle and
before a marriage—always a glass of cognac."

Chapter 3

WHEN HE OPENED HIS EYES NEXT MORNING, Barbet's first thought was that he had not yet decided with Pierre on what day they should begin to pick the grapes and he sat up in his bed with the idea that he would go out at once, as soon as he had drunk his coffee, and look at the vines. Coffee. Last night, late, he and his mother—and suddenly his mind was flooded with the whole knowledge of what he had done. He went to the north window of his bedroom and looked out on the courtyard, remembering how, last night, all the cell doors had stood open.

Downstairs he saw Madame Garbut's back. She was preparing the prisoners' breakfast. Barbet shrugged his shoulders and made for the outer door, at the moment caring only that he should escape before she knew that he was in the room and began to upbraid him for having forgotten supper last night. He gained the open air and would have gone to the vineyards, but on the way saw Quessot and hailed the old man and walked on at his side to the coopers' shed. Their way took them round the angle of the house that they might enter the west courtyard by its own gateway, and Barbet wished the way was longer, so pleasant was it to listen to Quessot's even voice and to walk with his content.

"When I was in Paris last time—or, rather, it was at Vernon—I was talking of you, Quessot."

"Of me? And what were you saying of me?" Quessot asked.

"Only that you were wiser than I am. The oak's more alive to you than it is to me."

"That may be. But then I have only the oak. You have more windows to your house."

They understood each other perfectly. There was no need to say what both knew—that, in speaking of the oak, there was nothing they did not speak of. "You'll soon be having new brandy to put in the casks," said Quessot. "It's an early year. Not many weeks now before you are distilling. That's what I like. If my casks were like great bottles that held the fluid and no more, where should I be and where would my oak be? It might as well be iron or glass. But without my oak to suck, where would the cognac come from? Years my oak works after it's gone from my hand, and years before it comes to me." He jerked a thumb towards the prison. "Are you making coopers of them inside? They'll have to serve a long sentence." Quessot let himself into his shed and prepared his work for the day. "What would you do if you woke up one fine morning and found they were all gone?"

"I should walk out of the house, Quessot, and I should see you on your way to work, and we'd walk round together, I dare say, and you'd get your tools out as usual, and we'd talk a bit and no one would be a penny the worse."

"That's true. The oaks wouldn't stop growing, you may be sure," he continued in muffled tones from inside an old smock he was pulling over his head. "It seems to me prison's like a glass bottle. Cognac doesn't mature in it; nor men. If men have to be shut up, better find some oak to put 'em in." His head now emerged and he poked his chin forward. "Now, what is it?" he said. "You look different to-day"—and he came a step nearer. "I haven't seen you look like this since you were a boy and up to your games."

But Barbet had not dared tell Quessot the truth. Having given the prisoners their freedom, his business was to preserve it by allowing none but his mother to guess that they were free. It was not easy, though his mother aided him and regarded deception as a delightful game. After a few days had passed, she could not resist—and, indeed, did not try to resist the temptation to invite Madame Vincent to supper and to invent for her little anecdotes, which were supposed to have been brought to her by Barbet himself, of what Fontan had said, of what Marcotte had done.

"And Blachère—the one who used to disturb you so by his shouting, dear Emilie—Blachère is a reformed character. He gives Barbet no trouble at all. I feel sure he will give no trouble ever again. You see, I am not always wrong."

"What do you mean—that you are not always wrong?"

"You will remember, dear Emilie, that once Barbet had a little trouble with his prisoners. And Pierre would have used the pistols and you said—"

"You said what I did, Chouquette. There was no difference at the time."

"At the time," Madame Hazard agreed. "But then I learn, Emilie. That is the difference between us. I learn and you don't."

"You mean," said Madame Vincent, "that you are everlastingly changing your mind. That is all it comes to." Madame Hazard opened her mouth to say that she disagreed, but her guest was too quick for her. "Now! Now!" she cried. "It is useless for you to say 'I disagree! I disagree!' You say it like a parrot. The truth is, Chouquette, though you call yourself a Bonapartist, you are a revolutionary at heart."

"Certainly. But are they not the same thing?"

"No," cried Madame Vincent, "they are not, and, if they are, they ought not to be. You think one thing at one moment, another thing the next. I can remember that once you were very proud of your consistency. 'What I have said, I have said!' Even that has gone. You are a thoroughly unstable character—that's the long and short of it." Madame Vincent stiffened herself to deal a final blow. "And so was Bonaparte!"

"In any case," said Madame Hazard, "if we were to stop talking for a moment, you would know by the silence that Blachère is a reformed character."

The two ladies pressed their cards on to the table, cautiously face downwards. Not a sound came from the courtyard.

Nevertheless, deception was not easy. Madame Vincent might be entangled in a rhetoric swifter and more irrelevant than her own, but Madame Garbut was deaf; only action would persuade her; and it fell to Barbet, at the intervals long established by custom, to carry into the courtyard tureens and dishes for prisoners who by now were

far beyond the range of St. Jean d'Angély. At night, when Madame
Garbut had gone, a part of these supplies could be brought back, but
the broth had to be poured away that the tureen might be returned
empty, and cheese, meat and bread would dangerously accumulate.
Hating waste, Barbet nevertheless disposed of them. "There's no
doubt about it," he said to his mother; "if you don't do what the
community expects, you are landed in all kinds of absurdities. Never
should I have believed that one day I should go out secretly from my
own house and bury meat and bread in a pinewood." A smile spread
over his face and his cheeks wrinkled. How Thérèse would laugh! he
thought. There's a song for Thérèse!

He had already begun a letter to Thérèse and from time to time
continued it. Some day he would put it in the post, but not until
the secret was out.

"When I let them go," he wrote, "I did not think of what would
happen afterwards, and I am glad I didn't. Some things have to be
done for their own sakes or not at all. But now you have a song, if
you want one, about Barbet in a pretty mess, and happier in it than
he has ever been in his life. Everybody lives ordinarily in a kind of
balance, held in it by dozens of strings, which are what people expect
of him and what he has come to expect of himself. Cut one of them
and everything goes. A gaoler who doesn't keep his prisoners or a
rich man who gives his money away at once finds that not only is
one string cut but that all the others have shifted and all the rules
which the world made for him have ceased to be relevant. And
they become fantastic too. Every day I carry in food to men who
are not there and, after nightfall, carry it out again and bury it.
Madame Garbut expects this of me. And I have to buy the food
no one needs because the people who sell it expect me to buy certain
quantities regularly. And I have to draw more money than is spent
on food because Anton would become suspicious if he didn't pay
it out on the appointed days. For the moment, I keep the money
apart and shall somehow rid myself of it. But money isn't like meat.
Put it in the pinewood—and there it remains; it becomes a buried
treasure. I suppose I could throw it into the river. Anyhow, Thérèse,
there's the subject of your satirical song on what happens to Barbet—

or to anyone for that matter—if he does the opposite of what people expect of him."

The heats of the year were over, the grapes almost fully ripe, and the country was in its second spring. After resolve and action, Barbet's mind rested, but he knew that more was required of him, his action being not yet complete, and one evening, after a day spent in examining his casks and in the arrangement of labour for the vintage, he asked his mother what she would do when he was gone.

"They will not leave me here, mother."

"No, Barbet. I understand that. I have felt for a long time that we were both going away, you and I."

"You could stay if you wished. Pierre can manage the property well enough."

She shook her head. "No. I'll not be a dead stick on any tree."

Still unsure of her understanding, he told her plainly that, when the truth was known, he would be sent to prison.

"God will not leave you there," she answered—so quiet an answer that, if she had said no more, Barbet would have left it to bear whatever meaning her thought laid upon it; but she added suddenly, in her voice of mischief and delight: "France will not leave you there!"

"I don't understand, mother. If it comes to that, it is France who will put me there."

"Ah," she said, "the law may put you there, the Government may put you there; that is as it should be—an eye for an eye and a tooth for a tooth; but France will not leave you there. You will see!" She laid her arm in his and walked across the garden at his side. "It is one of Emilie's favourite quotations: 'When Paris is angry she marches to the Bastille; when she is tortured, to the Rhine; but when she laughs, to the Élysée.' You will see. France likes men whose ideas are their own and who put them into effect. She knows how to be grave and how to laugh"—Madame Hazard patted his hand with a firm, imperious touch—"and when she laughs the angels are her cavalry."

Barbet turned his head sharply. "Who said that? Is that another of Madame Vincent's quotations?"

"No," said Madame Hazard with composure, "it is not."

As soon as the vintage was in and fermentation had begun, Barbet astonished his brother by asking him to summon a family council.

"What for?" asked Anton. "You have never asked for such a thing before."

"That's because I hate argument," Barbet replied. "This won't be an argument—at least, I think not. It is only something I have to say, and I would rather say it to all of you at once than have to say it a dozen times to each in turn."

On the appointed day, he first visited his lawyer in Angoulême and made provision to supplement his mother's personal income. It was arranged that, on his return to Roussignac, he should be met by Pierre, who would have Madame Hazard beside him in the tilbury. Together they would drive to the house with the gargoyles where the family would be assembled.

In fact, Victor, Bette, Anton and Madame Vincent had come together long before Barbet's train was due. That Barbet should ask for a family council was unprecedented; that Madame Hazard should attend gave it a significance that had set all heads wagging; and in Bette's stateliest room, formal preparations had been made. She herself, in a whaleboned dress of deep maroon which creaked when she moved, was established on a small sofa with her back to a window; her mother was beside her, a few inches advanced towards the sofa's edge, for she felt uncomfortably at a disadvantage when authority was reversed by her being a guest in her daughter's house. The two ladies' heads, one a fringed pile of fair hair, the other high-bonneted, stood up against a triangle of window-light bounded by the looped curtains and the sofa-back, and above them hung a bird-cage, planned in the Gothic style and decorated with alternate ruby and frosted panes. From this ecclesiastical structure death had kindly released the bird.

On Madame Vincent's left hand, at a writing-table drawn out

from its place by the wall, was Victor. He had been taking, or was prepared to take notes, and was trying to pluck from his nib a hair that was the result of his too conscientious use of a flannel pen-wiper. Beside Victor and close to him was a low plush stool which, as the Vincent family clung together, had been reserved for Pierre. A circular piece of satin and rosewood awaited Madame Hazard in mid-floor. Anton himself stood with feet widely planted on a flowery rug at the centre of this half-circle. On his right, separated from the rest, was a sociable with two compartments facing in opposite directions. The windows were shut; the atmosphere was heavy with the smell of washed muslin and of varnish that had softened in the hot weather.

Anton, remembering that Barbet acted with the merchants at Bercy on behalf of several small proprietors who were his friends, had it in his head that his brother was about to demand a partnership in Hazard and Vincent. Madame Vincent suggested as an alternative that he was in debt and had come for a loan.

"If he had run into debt, it could only be in Paris," said Bette, "and, if he had been extravagant there, we should have heard of it."

At this Victor pricked up his ears. "He openly admits having met Thérèse Despreux. I can of course make the necessary inquiries. I heard not long ago that she——"

"Oh, nonsense!" Bette cried in exasperation. "You and your system! I used to be afraid of it! I don't believe in it any more! How long is it since you told me that you could drive Barbet out and that we should have the Maison Hazard? How often did you tell me that Thérèse Despreux would ruin herself? Well, she hasn't. And now you are going to suggest that she and Barbet—nonsense, Victor! You have told me yourself that Monsieur de Courcelet is her man. Do you suppose she'd risk him for Barbet? For such a girl as that, Courcelet's a big fish!" Victor replied, as best he could, that he had not suggested that Thérèse—but Bette talked him down. "Don't speak to me of your precious system! There is Barbet still in posses-sion of the Maison Hazard and all we have is the Cheval Pie. 'They go together!' you said. Well, my poor Victor, they don't come to-gether."

At this point brother and sister fell into an exhausted silence, and Anton returned to his theme of the partnership. His point was that as shippers, to whom supplies of genuine cognac were becoming more and more precious, Hazard and Vincent could not afford to sneeze at the product of a vineyard hitherto exempt from the phylloxera, and if Barbet was going to offer them his reserves as well as his futures, he had something to bargain with that would be hard to resist.

"But a partnership!" Victor protested.

"If he insists! Only if he insists!" Anton replied testily. "The game is in his hands. The value of his reserves has risen. As for the phylloxera, it cuts both ways. There is still a risk that his vineyards may be hit, but they haven't been and, as they stand, they are worth half again what they were. It all fits in," Anton added. "I thought this June, when he came to renew his agreement with me, he would put up the price. But he didn't. There it stands as it has always been since father's time. Victor says it isn't a legally operative agreement anyway, but—"

"Nor is it," said Victor. "Barbet undertakes to sell to no one but you and, if to you, at an agreed price. But it is always open to him to say: 'In fact I won't sell at all except for a higher price, and if you want it—' "

"Ah, you are too clever, Victor," Anton interrupted. "Barbet won't do that. The agreement is convenient between two brothers. It is useful to have a price understood between us. Anyhow, there it is. If at any time in the next twelve months he wishes to sell, he will offer the property to me at a hundred and sixty thousand francs. A hundred and sixty thousand! Bless my soul. That was father's figure. It has always been worth more than that, and now—why, I'd give him two hundred thousand tomorrow! And why do you suppose he didn't put up the price? Because he doesn't care. Because he doesn't mean to sell at all. Because he means to *buy*—and buy a partnership in Hazard and Vincent!"

The argument was interrupted by the arrival of the tilbury. A silence fell. The family eyed one another with the air of people in the waiting-room of a railway station who have long ago tired of one another's company. At the sound of footsteps in the hall, Anton nodded to Bette and went out to receive his mother. Everyone rose as she came in, and sat down again after the necessary greetings.

"We thought you would sit there, Barbet," Bette suggested, pointing to the sociable.

"Thank you," said Barbet, and, perching on the seat farthest from Bette, he looked at her over its back. "You know," he continued, "I am sorry if I have inconvenienced you. It's true I did say that, if everyone were here, it would save explanations later. But I didn't picture it like this."

"Like what?" asked Madame Vincent.

"Well, look at us," Barbet replied. "Who would have thought there were so many? Six—and seven when Pierre has tied up the pony. Even that leaves out Renée." He looked at his brother. "I gather from Pierre you didn't invite her—or rather, that you told him not to bring her."

"That was Victor's idea," Anton replied.

"This is a family council," said Victor. "She is neither Vincent nor Hazard."

"She is my niece," Madame Hazard put in.

Madame Vincent bestirred herself. "That makes no difference, Chouquette. No doubt you have a dozen nieces."

"Pah!" Madame Hazard exclaimed, "do marriages make no difference? Mine does, I assure you. I wasn't born Hazard myself and here am I on the best chair and there is Anton on the rug. Both consequences of my marriage—not to speak of Barbet. And as for you, dear Emilie—my father was a sergeant at Quatre-Bras and yours—"

"Come, come, mother," said Anton, "this is not a time for joking."

"Isn't it? How do you know it isn't? Do you know why we are all here?"

"In fact," Barbet remarked, "I'm sorry Renée isn't here. It concerns her."

Anton, Bette, Victor and Madame Vincent exchanged glances. If Renée was concerned, all their guesses had been wrong. Anton looked at his brother with puzzled eyes, wondering how he had credited him with so good a business head, and Barbet, kneeling on the sociable, turned towards the door, through which at that moment Pierre was entering the room, and said:

"Good, Pierre, I'm glad you are here. I was saying that this concerns Renée as well as you. Now we can begin."

"Where am I to sit?" said Pierre. "Concerns Renée, does it? What has anyone to say against Renée?"

"Sit there!" Bette cried. "On the stool. Sit down and don't talk."

There was a brief silence.

"I shan't keep you long," said Barbet. "As you know, I have just come back from Angoulême. I have made preliminary arrangements there. I am willing to sell, Anton."

"To sell what?" Victor threw in.

"But what else?" said Barbet and returned to his brother. "The Maison Hazard, of course."

Anton was without words.

"At what price?" and "Why?" Bette and Madame Vincent asked together.

Barbet looked at the two ladies and began to smile because the pile of Bette's hair reminded him of Mademoiselle d'Austerlitz. "There's no question of price. Each June Anton and I sign an agreement by which, if I sell at any time in the year following, I give him an option to buy at a hundred and sixty thousand francs and he accepts that as the value of the place. Well, Anton?"

Anton's impulse was to accept at once. Indeed he had opened his mouth to do so when Victor interrupted him.

"One moment! One moment!" he said. "These matters cannot be decided in an instant."

"Why not?" asked Barbet.

"The reserves must be disclosed and valued; this year's vintage must be taken into account; there are many—"

Barbet smiled at him. "Listen, Victor—"

"Yes," said Madame Hazard, "listen, Victor Vincent. If my two sons like to do a piece of business together without a middleman to take a commission—well, you may lose the pickings you have hoped for, but—"

"It isn't a question of that," exclaimed Bette, who cared nothing for Victor's disappointment but was determined to bargain. "The point is, Barbet, that your vines may be touched by the phylloxera. How do we know they are not? Do we take your word for it?"

"Yes," said Barbet, "you do. Do I look like a swindler?"

"And you can take my word for it too!" Pierre put in, too proud of the vines to allow them to be disparaged even by his own family.

This was a blow to the Vincents but they struggled on. A hundred and sixty thousand was, they knew, a low price, but it happened also to be the first price mentioned and it was against every principle of good bargaining to accept it.

"Even if it's true," said Bette, "that the vines are at present untouched, the danger remains. That reduces the price."

"No, it doesn't," said Barbet.

"And why not?"

"Because the price is an arranged price. The danger is certainly not more than it was in June. And there's another reason: the reserves and the scarcity offset the risk; a hundred and sixty thousand is less than the market price. And there's a third reason: I am not here to bargain; I am here to sell."

Anton pushed his thumbs into his waistcoat pockets and braced himself for decision.

"The trouble is, my dear Bette," he said with a smile, "you can bargain with business men, but innocent chaps like Barbet are hard as rocks. Isn't that so, Barbet?"

"Now look," said Barbet, "Victor and Bette have been wanting me to sell for years—and at this price. We all know how this discussion is going to end. Why waste time?"

"There will be formalities to be gone through and details to settle."

"Certainly," said Barbet.

"There's the question of running the place, for instance."

"I assumed that Pierre would manage it for you. That's why I said it concerned Renée."

Anton nodded. "And the prison," he said. "That will have to be considered."

"Perhaps," Barbet answered, "but I don't picture you considering it for long."

Anton took a deep breath. "A hundred and fifty and I'll take the risk." Barbet smiled at him. "A hundred and fifty-five," said Anton. Then he laughed a short, heavy laugh and held out his hand. "All right, a hundred and sixty. I buy. Bette, a glass of wine."

"There is one question I should like to ask," Madame Vincent put in. "If it is not the phylloxera, what has decided Barbet to sell at this time?"

"I am expecting to be called away before long," Barbet answered. "Where I shall have to go I am not sure, but away from here certainly, and that is what matters."

"That," said Bette, "sounds extremely mysterious. Are you going to be married?"

"Oh no. I am going on a voyage."

"And leaving your mother?" said Madame Vincent.

Madame Hazard straightened herself in her chair. "You know, dear Emilie, it isn't surprising. Barbet has always talked of voyages, ever since he was a little boy. I thought it was nonsense then. But now I think differently. I shall go on a voyage myself."

Chapter 4

THOUGH THE FORMALITIES OF SALE AND PUR-
chase were soon completed and the documents were ready for
signature, they were not at once signed, and Anton seemed not to
intend to take possession of his property until he must. What he
cared for was control of the supplies and he was in no haste to make
Pierre manager of the estate. So that Barbet might be tempted to
stay, he was careful not to intrude upon him or his mother. "Bless
you, I know the place," he said when Barbet invited him to inspect
it. "I'm not buying a pig in a poke. You seem to forget that I was
born there. I suppose I must take steps at headquarters to make new
arrangements for the prisoners, but there's time enough for that."
But he took none. As long as the prisoners remained, Barbet must
remain, and to keep Barbet through the months of the distillation
would have suited Anton well. "Meanwhile," he said with a casualness intended to conceal his masterly delays, "I should like to have a
look at the reserves. They are what interests me."

He made a careful list of what he was shown and asked whether
any more cognac was stored in the prison courtyard.

"No," said Barbet, "I thought that might be unwise."

"They sound quiet enough," Anton replied. "I haven't heard a
sound of them since I came here."

"No," said Barbet, "nor have I."

He knew, however, that his time was running out. A visit by the
inspector of prisons, though not as yet probable, might be made at
any time. There had been no news of any of the prisoners; by now
they were as safe as they would ever be, and Barbet cared little how
soon discovery came. Fermentation was over; distillation had begun; October was well advanced and the chatter of the elections

was dying down. Thérèse sent the news of Paris. There had been a riot outside the offices of *Le Gaulois* and Monsieur de Courcelet was of opinion that France, in an attempt to read the Government a lesson, had overstepped herself and returned more royalists than she had intended. Barbet read this without interest; only when she told him of herself did his mind respond; and when he visited the courtyard, on the pretence of taking food to the prisoners, he found, contrary to his expectation, that he missed very little the habit of life that they had represented. It was as if, having made all his arrangements for a journey, he were liberated from the past. For that reason he loved the present more than ever and observed the familiar scene of his countryside after the vintage more than ever closely, not with any sadness of farewell but with joy in the recurrence and endurance of this familiar life, greater than his own and independent of it, which would not miss him, but continue, when he was gone, as though he had not been.

The winter wheat had been sown, the vines were turning yellow, and on his way into Roussignac he would meet on the roads the old two-wheeled waggons in which the small proprietors, who had no distillery of their own, would send casks of their wine to be distilled. When he was between boy and man, he had often driven these waggons himself, pleased to wear the thick tan homespun of a driver's smock, proud of the dark lines of blue or red with which it was decorated, and delighted to find himself on the piece of stretched canvas, the porte-fainéant, that was the driver's seat. They belonged to November rather than to October's later days, but this year everything was early, and one morning, encountering a driver he knew, Barbet drove with him into Roussignac, though he had set out to make the journey on foot.

"So you'll be leaving, I hear?" the driver said. When Barbet had answered yes, he asked no more, but talked of his own realities, the vintage and the phylloxera, until Barbet climbed down from the waggon at the outskirts of Roussignac and set out for the Lion Rouge. He had brought with him the money accumulated on account of the prisoners' upkeep and now went to Anton for more. When this was done, he visited the Protestant church, put a half of what he had into the poor-box, and continued his way to Lancret's church where he left what remained. As he turned to go, he saw Lancret in the doorway. I hope he didn't see me put money in the poor-box, he thought. It was too much; it will make him curious when he takes it out.

If Lancret had seen, he said nothing of the poor-box and, with the habitual reticence of priests, showed no surprise at Barbet's presence in the church. They said a few words, then went into the air and continued their conversation, each feeling that they had more to say than had yet been said and, therefore, reluctant to part.

"Are you busy?" asked Barbet.

"No."

"Then let me come into your house for a little while before I begin to walk home."

They sat in the parlour, under the photographs of the popes.

"As you are going away, this may be the last of many talks we have had together," Lancret began. "I am glad you asked yourself in. I wished to invite you, but should not have done so. Right or wrong? I don't know, but that is how I am made." Having said this, he was for a moment silent, with a silence of resolve, not of hesitation; then said: "Now that you are here, it would be a form of lying not to ask the question my mind is asking—" But at this point he swerved, and Barbet knew that it was Thérèse's name that his lips refused. In a moment, he recovered himself and continued: "In fact, there were two questions, but perhaps one includes the other. Where are you going? They tell me you said—'on a voyage.'"

"I think," Barbet replied, "that I am going to prison."

The priest did not shift his gaze. "Do you wish to tell me what you have done?"

"Yes. I had no intention of telling anyone, but I should like to tell you. I have let my prisoners go."

"Ah, when shall I be able to say that!" Lancret exclaimed, his fingers clasping and unclasping themselves. "How often is any man able to say that!" Then he smiled, a rare, wintry smile that yet had sweetness in it. "And now you will go to prison yourself?"

"It seems probable."

"Even that," the priest said, "is not freedom. It is not freedom in itself. You feel now that all chains have fallen from you. I felt that when I entered the priesthood. To enter it, seemed to me then a form of imprisonment, a voluntary imprisonment comparable with yours and acceptable because it was a way to final liberation. But I have failed, Barbet. I am still in my prison. I free others but I cannot free myself. I knock, but the doors are not opened to me. But the time will come. Jesus is not denied in the weakness of his servants; truth does not wither because my faith is dry; some day—" He broke off suddenly and passed his hands over his face; then looked up and said in a different tone: "Do you know why I am envious of you, Barbet? It is because you do not *know* what you have done. At once, when you tell me the simple fact, I compare and analyse it. Why did you let them go?"

"Because it became necessary," Barbet answered. "Until you asked I had forgotten that evening. I wonder why. I had clean forgotten it. It hasn't come back into my mind until this moment. But I can tell you. Certainly I can tell you. I went down to the river. It was last month, you know—a very still September evening—and, when it became quite dark, sound began to carry further and further as it always does in September—and after a little while—" He stopped abruptly as though memory were failing him. "And after a little while—"

"When you come out of prison," said Lancret, who had learned when to speak and when to listen, "what shall you do?"

"I think I shall be a cooper," Barbet answered.

"In Paris?"

"Where the work takes me."

The priest chose his next words carefully and spoke them with reluctance: "You said to me once that you loved Thérèse."

"It is true," Barbet answered. "It is natural for us to love each other when we are together and when we are apart. But our lives are independent."

"Independent? Can the lives of two people who love be independent of each other? You mean that you and she will work and live independently—yes, that is possible if you both have wisdom

and patience enough. But is she wise and patient?" The priest's
lips smiled in an unsmiling face. "You must not forget her heredity,
Barbet." The making of this little joke, and the effort it had cost,
overcame him. His wide-open eyes filled with tears which overflowed on an unmoving face; then, suddenly, the face was transformed by an uncontrollable seizure of grief and longing and despair. He rose and turned to the wall. "Even now," he cried,
wrenching his body to encounter Barbet again, "even now, how contemptible a man I am! How contemptible and how selfish! If I
heard that she had taken the veil, I should be satisfied—but I should
be satisfied not in gladness for her vocation but because, through her,
I should have absolution from my own sins. While she leads the life
of the flesh, my life in the flesh continues; in her sin, mine is multi-
plied and perpetuated; until she repents, my own spirit is incapable of full repentance." He threw up his head. "And to believe
that, to doubt the independence of my own redemption, is in itself
a sin. Sin upon sin, confusion upon confusion! What shall I do?
. . . Come," he said swiftly. "You must leave me. Until I have
been on my knees, I am not fit to be any man's companion."

They went up the narrow passage together and Lancret stopped
at his front door. He did not hold out his hand or make any attempt
to say good-bye, but stood propped against the door-post.

"When you are ready," Barbet said, "you will know what to do.
. . . That was said to me not long ago."

"By whom?"

"It was said to me twice—by my mother, but first by Thérèse."

"By Thérèse," Lancret repeated. "I can hear her voice saying
it. But she would not have said it to me."

"Perhaps it is through me that she now says it to you," Barbet
answered.

The priest did not at once reply. "No," he said at last, "I will
not deceive myself. No woman would say that except to a man she
loved."

There was a bleakness in this answer from which Barbet turned
away, but he came back and took the priest's hands in his.

"Do not be troubled for me," Lancret said. "It is true—when I am ready, even I shall know what to do. A man in doubt must believe that or perish. And after all, that promise, like every other, is in the gospel itself: 'Knock and it shall be opened unto you.' We invent new phrases and it is well that we should do so, but there is no hope that Jesus has not already given." And he added: "There is no sponge but His to hold to the lips."

Barbet walked home through the woods. He visited the stills and watched the work in progress there; then, in his own room, added a paragraph to his unfinished letter to Thérèse. Other letters, which said nothing of his having released his prisoners, he had sent her meanwhile, but it was to the letter which could not yet be posted that he added an account of his talk with her father. This evening he finished and put it in an envelope, feeling that the time to send it was nearly come.

When this was done, he went into the kitchen and played piquet with his mother at the kitchen table while Madame Garbut prepared supper. A couple of hands had been played when a trap drove up to the door.

"It is Monsieur Anton," said Madame Garbut.

Barbet stirred to go out, but his mother would not be interrupted in the playing of her hand. "Time enough! Time enough!" she said. "If Anton has come to count more hogsheads, he can wait. Let him find his own way in. Come away from the door, Garbut."

Madame Garbut, not hearing, remained at the door. "Monsieur Fricard is with him," she said.

Barbet at once laid down his cards. That Monsieur Fricard, the head of the police in Roussignac, should call at the Maison Hazard was not in itself surprising; that he should arrive in Anton's company could have but one meaning. Fortunately, this did not at once occur to Madame Hazard and she greeted him warmly.

A small man with hollow temples, ruddy cheeks and a thin, neatly pointed moustache, he was an infrequent but welcome visitor, for, though an official himself, he had an ingrained contempt, which Madame Hazard shared, for the whole machinery of government.

Her reasons were political; to her, administration was necessarily incompetent that was not napoleonic; to him it was contemptible because, as he never tired of saying, it was "clumsy." There did not exist in his vocabulary a stronger word of condemnation, for he himself was an orderly man; precision was his god; his collection of postage-stamps, though not of great value, was set out in patterns of flawless symmetry; he darned his own linen because no one else could darn so well; whatever he used—a pen, a collar-stud or an emotion—was at once put back, when he had used it, into the place where it belonged and where he could find it again; and his pleasure was to perform conjuring tricks, not with elaborate apparatus, which he scorned, but by naked sleight of hand. As a young man, he had dreamed of becoming a great detective, but an unappreciative bureaucracy had ruled against him. "These big-wigs in Paris," he would say, "they will never understand the *science* of detection. They think only of achieving a great coup that will startle the newspapers. They expect to catch fish without troubling to mind their nets. Whenever, in my humble way, I have any contact with them, I discover how inaccurate they are. Why, only last month—" And he would produce example after example of their follies. "Clumsy!" he would say. "All thumbs! No nicety in their methods. No science. No system."

This evening, walking in behind Anton from the early twilight, he was evidently in a state of extreme embarrassment, for, though he greeted Madame Hazard, he had none of his little jokes for her, and, while Barbet was persuading the newly-lit lamp to draw, fell back into the shadows. There, at some distance from the table, he found a chair and seated himself upon it with the special, drooping melancholy of a man, naturally cheerful and talkative, who finds himself in circumstances that forbid his talent. Anton, in answer to his mother's question, had begun to say no, he hadn't come to count the reserves; that was done, in any case; he hadn't come about anything connected with his purchase of the Maison Hazard; in that matter, he was perfectly satisfied. His rotund phrases, his jocular avoidances, might have gone on for ever, and Monsieur Fricard began to wriggle in his chair.

"Well, Anton," said Madame Hazard, "come to the point. What is it you want?"

"It is foolish, a little mistake, a matter of no importance at all," Monsieur Fricard said in a voice so shyly apologetic that no attention was paid to his words. Anton continued to explain that sometimes, in life, little confusions arose, little misunderstandings sprang up, which in his opinion it was always best to remove at once—

"But I said that, if only we waited until the morning," Monsieur Fricard put in, "they would have discovered their mistake for themselves and—"

"At once," said Anton firmly.

"Very well," said Monsieur Fricard, "as you please. But I know how inaccurate they can be. If only we could wait until—"

"Now, now, now!" Madame Hazard cried. "One of you trumpets like an elephant, the other squeaks like a mouse, and there's no sense in either. One might suppose that someone had committed a crime."

Was it possible, Barbet wondered, that, even now, she had not guessed why they were come? Was Monsieur Fricard still, to her, the polite little man who chattered pleasantly about the bureaucracy and did conjuring tricks for her entertainment? Did it not enter her mind that he was here now as a policeman? Or did she know this and was she playing an elaborate defence? He watched her face and Anton's, in the ring of lamplight at the table, as though his personal fortunes were not included in the scene, and saw, beyond the ring, the dimmer rectangle of Monsieur Fricard's brow and cheeks; and, as he watched and listened to their voices, not his lips, not his mind only, but the very spirit within him began to smile because their circumstances and his own were incongruous with the peace in his heart.

"But these fellows in Paris," Fricard was saying. "Really, one can't help laughing at them. The mistakes they make! The bungles! They are like some juggler at a fair who lets everything slip through his fingers. And why? Why, I ask you? They have brains, they have resources, sometimes they have even imagination—but they are *inaccurate,* madame, that is the truth. You ask for a document relating to—shall we say?—Jean-Baptiste Dubois dated the 5th of May '81 ; you wait a fortnight, you write again, you find that your request has been mislaid—they can't even keep their correspondence in order. You repeat your request. You wait a month. At last the document comes—and the name on it is Jean-Baptiste Dubois but the date is the 5th of May 1880. A mistake, you will say, of one figure only—but the document is valueless, and now—"

"We are not concerned with Jean-Baptiste Dubois," Anton interrupted. "The point is that a most extraordinary thing has happened in Paris. An escaped prisoner—"

"That," said Monsieur Fricard, "is not strictly accurate. It presupposes something which we have no right to presuppose. All we know is that an old man, who was brought in on suspicion of having attempted to pilfer in a cutler's shop and who refused for a long time to reveal his identity, at last broke down and wept and said that he was tired and that they could do what they liked. In fact, they had no fresh charge to bring against him and would have let him go, but I suppose they were curious, I suppose they pressed him to say who he was and where he came from, and he fell back on the old trick of saying he was someone else. He said his name was Marcotte. He said he was a prisoner here. They don't know whether to believe him or not. You see, it is always the same with them. Marcotte? they say. Roussignac? they say. Off they go to their files—and something is wrong, some paper is missing, there is muddle, inaccuracy, as there always is, and so they say to me : 'Go and see for yourself and report.' "

"Pah! Pah!" Madame Hazard exclaimed. "How can one man be in two places at the same time? Do you see that pot on the fire? There is his supper."

"Evidently," Monsieur Fricard answered.

"Besides, if the man had escaped, would not Barbet have been the first to know it?"

"Besides," Monsieur Fricard rejoined with an affable air of taking Madame Hazard into his confidence, "the exchange of identities is a perfectly familiar criminal trick. At some time, this man, no doubt, was an associate of Marcotte's. He would know some of his characteristics—the spectacles, for example."

"The spectacles?" said Barbet.

"Isn't it true," Anton demanded, "that you once told me you had a pair of spectacles made for him in Angoulême?"

"Certainly I did. But what happened in Paris?"

"Well, as I understand it, this man, as soon as he had claimed to be Marcotte—"

"Of course, as always when anything comes from Paris, we haven't been told the whole story," said Monsieur Fricard, intervening in a tone of authority, "but if one has a little intelligence, one can put two and two together, and what seems to have happened is this: At first, at any rate, they didn't believe him; they knew Marcotte was safe in prison here and, as they had no charge against the old chap, they told him to be off. At that he changed his tune. He wouldn't go. He said he had a *right* to be in prison. He demanded arrest. For what? said they. For being an escaped prisoner, said he. Pooh, said they, be off with you and don't waste our time. And then he complained about his spectacles. How could he earn his living? He couldn't see. His own spectacles, he said, had been broken in the prison; those he had were of no use for fine work and anyhow he had no chisels, no knives, no tools. How could he earn his living? There were still months of his sentence to run. He was entitled to live at the expense of the State. He was entitled to his spectacles. He hadn't escaped from prison; he had been turned out against his will. And so on. And so on. . . . It seems to have impressed them. 'Is he mad or is he Marcotte?' is what they want to know."

"He is Marcotte," said Barbet, and he could have given no answer more certain to convince his brother that Marcotte was safely in his cell. It was Anton who had been suspicious, who had taken alarm, who had insisted to the sceptical Fricard that they should not wait for the morning but go to the Maison Hazard at once. Perhaps Marcotte had escaped and Barbet had been afraid to confess it? Perhaps this was the meaning of Barbet's "voyage" and of his decision to sell the Maison Hazard? And yet Barbet had taken the money for all the prisoners' upkeep and Barbet was not dishonest. Anton had swerved, doubted, suspected, and suddenly, almost in a panic of suspicion, had decided that at all costs he and Fricard must satisfy themselves of the truth. Now, confronted with the truth by Barbet himself, he shied at it violently, fearing that Barbet was leading him on, was laughing at him, and that in a moment Fricard too would be laughing at him as a credulous fool. To prove his worldly wisdom and that he was not being duped, he laughed himself, strode across the room and clapped his brother heartily on the shoulder.

"Good!" he exclaimed. "Very good! So Marcotte is in Paris and his supper is here! You won't catch me as easily as that, Barbet."

Madame Hazard, with swift guile, saw how the wind had changed and set her sails to it.

"Now, Anton, what was it put that idea into your head? If Marcotte had escaped—" She too began to laugh and seized Barbet's hand and patted it. "Come along," she said, "take them their supper, Barbet." Then to Fricard. "Now, my friend, tell me: how many are there who know of this? You and Anton. Any others?"

"None," said Fricard.

"Good, good. Garbut is deaf. Stone deaf. She has heard nothing. We don't want Anton made a laughing-stock. . . . And now, both of you, draw up to the table."

"That is extremely odd," said Barbet. "But the world itself is extremely odd. Don't you believe, Anton, that the man in Paris is Marcotte?"

"No," Anton replied with a grin, "I do not."

"Bless me," said Barbet, "how shall I persuade you? How does one persuade a man to believe the truth?" His mother tried to interrupt him. "No, mother," he said, "have you forgotten? We are going on a voyage, you and I?"

Her composure had left her; the light of fanaticism burned in her eye as it had in the days in which she had believed her son to have the power of miracles. She could think only that he was threatened, that the remote terrors of the law had come into her own home, that he must be protected from them; and she began to patter to and fro with short, quick steps, now clinging to his arm, now pressing her hands together, her lips moving silently in prayer for those fires of heaven which she expected to descend. At sight of her, the bristles of Anton's misgiving rose again.

"Come and see," said Barbet. "You will not find Marcotte in the courtyard. Come and see for yourselves."

The lamp was lighted and slung over Barbet's arm. As Anton and Fricard were about to follow him into the covered way, and Madame Hazard, standing beside the kitchen table, covered her face with her hands, Madame Garbut, unaware of all that had happened, came forward with the pot containing the prisoners' supper. Rather than argue with her, Barbet smiled and took it.

"Allow me," said Fricard; "you will need to have your hands free for the keys."

At the door to the courtyard Anton said, "Do you go in unarmed?" and Barbet, rather than argue with him, replied, "Very well, Anton, you take the pistol."

They went in order: Anton with the pistol, Fricard with the supper, Barbet with the lamp. In the failing light, the courtyard seemed wide and bleak.

"Look," said Anton, "this is beyond a joke. What did you mean when you said that man in Paris was Marcotte?"

Without replying, Barbet went ahead of them until the cells could be seen plainly. Then he stopped.

"You had better satisfy yourselves. All the doors are unlocked."

Anton and Fricard went from cell to cell and returned, but still Anton feared a trick or hoped for it.

"Where have you put them, Barbet? What are you up to?"

"They are all gone," Barbet said.

"All?"

"All."

"My God, do you mean you let them go? Are you mad?"

"Now, now," said Fricard nervously, holding the pot before him, "let me put this down while we discuss the position like reasonable men. There is, of course, a misunderstanding. I think we must put joking aside. I think the time has come at which you should explain to us—"

"My dear Fricard," Barbet answered, "I can do no more than tell you the truth and show you the truth. You must persuade yourself to believe your eyes."

Fricard turned to look again at the open doors.

"But even so," he said, "how did they get farther? That gate is shut; it is built in. Did they scale the walls?"

"No, I let them out through the kitchen—by the way we have come."

"But, then," Anton demanded, "what is Fricard doing here with their supper and why have I a pistol in my hands?"

"You asked for it, Anton."

"And in that case," said Fricard, his voice rising in consternation as the truth was borne in upon him, "I shall have to arrest you."

"Evidently," Barbet answered.

"But not next week, not to-morrow," Fricard protested, looking about him desperately as though he hoped that even now the prisoners might rise from the ground and deliver him from his predicament, "I shall have to arrest you now."

"Evidently," Barbet repeated. "Shall we go?"

"But why did you do it? Why did you do it?" Anton cried. "Didn't you count the consequences? You were bound to be found out."

"I know," Barbet replied. "But it was my way, Anton. In the end, you know, one has to take it."

BOOK FIVE

The Voyage Begins

Heureux qui, comme Ulysse, a fait un beau voyage . . .
JOACHIM DU BELLAY

Chapter 1

THE NEWS OF BARBET'S ARREST WAS BROUGHT TO
Thérèse by Courcelet. Her engagement at the Divertissements
was ended, her return to a glorified Écurie was announced for the
first week of December, and she had spent the afternoon in rehearsing
old and new songs with Templéraud who, having begun to tire of
Annette, was light-heartedly preparing for a new campaign. Thérèse
felt that she was invulnerable; neither Templéraud departing an
hour ago nor Philippe de Courcelet arriving now had power to disturb her. Glad that Etienne was not professionally lost to her and
that her affection for Courcelet had matured, she was comforted, and
a little surprised, by her self-possession.

Courcelet, when she had admitted him, sat down with her in
front of Het Vaderland.

"It is the most comfortable stove in Paris," he said.

This delighted her; she loved to have her possessions praised; but
as it was a form of flattery that he seldom used, it stirred her suspicions and she said: "Of course it is! It is mine. I chose it. . . . But
that is not what you have come to say?"

"No," he admitted, "it isn't. I have bad news, Thérèse."

He was fumbling in his breast pocket for a neatly folded copy of
a newspaper. She held out her hand for it and began to read the
column he had marked.

"How did you come by this? Do you subscribe to the press of
Cognac?"

"Never mind," said he. "It is my business to be informed."

She read in silence.

"They seem to consider it a joke," said Courcelet.

"Ah!" she cried, "so it is! And more than a joke. Don't you see that— Look! look!" She spread the paper on his knees. "A gaoler lets out his prisoners. . . . The mayor carries a pistol, the chief of the local police carries the broth. . . . A prisoner demands to be put in prison again. . . . Look, Philippe, don't you see? Don't you see what has happened? Everything has been turned topsy-turvy—and Cognac and Jarnac and Châteauneuf and Angoulême have begun to laugh." She leaned back and smiled. "Etienne was here this afternoon. He said: 'You know, Thérèse, what we need is a new twist to the Barbet songs.' "

Courcelet stared at her. Not a word of pity for Barbet! Even his arrest was no more than material for her songs! But it was a rule of his detached and tolerant life not to allow opinion to rush to extremes, and he preferred to believe that he had misunderstood her than to condemn her as heartless.

"Your songs," said he, "—yes. But what of Barbet himself?"

"He will be acquitted."

"You think so?"

"Certainly. Don't you?"

"No," said Courcelet. "If you read the whole story, you will see that, altogether apart from his responsibility for his prisoners, money is involved. He has continued to draw what was due to him for their upkeep."

Thérèse gazed at him. "You mean that they will put Barbet in prison?"

"Yes. You had better face it."

"Face it!" She rose and walked across the room. "Very well," she said, wheeling round at the window, "I will face it. Listen. I have many friends—in the Chamber, in the newspapers, everywhere. They are all looking for a stick to beat the Government. This story will spread like a prairie fire. It is a story that makes authority look foolish, and in France—" She broke off and, sitting again at Courcelet's side, checked her excitement and continued in a steady voice. "You are too much committed to authority to help directly," she said. "I don't ask it or expect it. But you can help indirectly by advising me. I have a plan, but it is new, I haven't thought it out, it may be foolish. If you can persuade me that it is foolish and useless, I will give it up. Then, if you like, I will sit about, wringing my hands and pitying Barbet, but not until then."

"I don't picture you wringing your hands, Thérèse; it is not one of your gestures."

"But you thought me heartless? Just now, when I spoke of my songs?"

"Well—"

"Yes," she said, laying her hand on his arm, "you did. People do. I am not heartless. I am active. Why should I sit here for ten minutes, moaning and wailing, and *afterwards* begin to think of what might be done? I miss out a step, that is all. Is that callous? It is the callousness of a general who knows when to counter-attack."

Courcelet, smiling, mocked her with one of her best-loved rhymes:

> " 'Bon, bon,
> Napoléon,
> Va rentrer dans sa maison!' "

"Precisely!" said she. "Now, tell me. Give your mind to this. It will take a long time to put Barbet into prison—first one examination, then another—I know nothing about legal processes except that they last for ever. That is the first point. The second is that at heart the public is always on the side of prisoners who escape, unless they have a particular reason for hating the prisoner, and this man, Marcotte, with his story of his spectacles and his model boat is already half-way to being patted on the back as if he were a schoolboy who had run away from his lessons—and Barbet is the schoolmaster who had the grace to wink. And not only that," she continued, "—and this part ought to interest you, Philippe, as a student of human nature. You may say—and it's true—that we French are a logical, unsentimental people, but isn't it true also that just because, hour by hour and day by day, we are logical and unsentimental, and because, at the same time, we are at root Catholic, and because, still at the same time, we are the children of Voltaire, we love a— well, what shall I call it?—we love and we worship a sudden and complete topsy-turvydom, a—"

"A comic and a holy paradox," said Courcelet.

"Well?" said Thérèse. "If that is true, is my plan unreasonable? In Paris, Barbet is already a name to conjure with. The story will grow. The whole press will take fire." She touched the newspaper. "Look, it has begun. . . . And as the lawyers argue and argue, no one will talk of anything else or laugh at anything else but the absurd solemnity of the people who are trying to put the comic paradox into prison. And I," she added, "shall have a new programme for the Écurie. The whole of France shall sing my songs! Now tell me, tell me honestly, is that fantastic and impossible?"

"It is fantastic," Courcelet answered, "but by no means impossible. Nothing is impossible in France under the presidency of Monsieur Grévy. A few parades, a few music-hall songs, a handsome face, a martial air and—who knows?—any paltry general might execute a coup d'état. No politician with his ear to the ground can rule out the possibility of that. And if the music-halls can overthrow the Republic, I should be a rash man to say that Thérèse Despreux cannot make it appear dangerously ridiculous to put Barbet into prison for having let the others out. Nevertheless," he said, "I think it would be unwise to make the attempt."

"For my own sake?"

"Not only for your own sake, but because, though it is not impossible that you should succeed, it is probable that you will fail. . . . Oh yes, you can make the lawyers and even the Government look foolish—I don't doubt that; but you won't keep Barbet out of prison. You forget one factor—the money." Courcelet spread out his hands. "Probably there's an explanation of that. Still—he continued to draw it. I dare say you can make the authorities wish to let Barbet go. I dare say you can make them wish with all their hearts that he didn't exist. But the more you mock them, the more it will become a matter of prestige, and prestige in governments is like pride in men—it makes them hang themselves in their own rules. You may do the Government harm, which isn't your purpose, but you won't save Barbet from prison, which is. Be a realist, Thérèse."

"How you respect governments!" said she.

"I? Respect the Government? I?"

"Not 'the Government,'" she answered, "but government as such.

Anything, my dear Philippe, to avoid inconvenience—that is your realism. What does it matter, you are thinking, if Barbet goes to prison for a few months?"

"No, Thérèse, I'm sorry for him. I like him. But life isn't a comic paradox. Things must take their course. Anyhow," he added, "what is the good of running your head against a wall? Whether you like it or not, whether the Government likes it or not, however much sympathy may be aroused, things will take their course. He will go to prison. What then? The whole thing will peter out."

For a moment Thérèse hesitated, for she valued Courcelet's judgment.

"I expect you are right in the single fact," she said. "He will go to prison. But what you don't see is that his going to prison is the one thing needed. The thing won't peter out then. I won't let it. It is when the key turns on him that it will really begin. I have a song ready for that."

"A new song? So soon? You are quick, Thérèse," he answered with a sceptical smile.

"No," she said, "an old song. So old that all France knows it already. Change a few words and it becomes a revolutionary song. Have you forgotten Royan? I thought of it there. I have never used it. Thank God, I have never used it! I can now—with Barbet in prison. Listen," she exclaimed, her eyes alight. "This is just a sketch of it, but—listen:

> *"Au clair de la lune*
> *Mon ami Barbet.*
> *Grévy prends ta plume*
> *Pour sa liberté . . .*

Do you see?" she cried. "We can improve on that. But I have the end—

> *"Sa chandelle est morte,*
> *Il n'a plus de feu.*
> *Ouvre-lui sa porte*
> *Pour l'amour de Dieu."*

The old tune touched Courcelet's heart. He had sung it as a child, and as a young man, happily journeying in Haute Vienne; he began to sing it now, joining his voice with hers, and, as he sang, the rebel stirred in him, his imagination stirred.

"O my Thérèse," he cried, taking both her hands, "no doubt I shall be cautious again in a minute, but now—"

"Now? Cautious again already?"

"No. No. A little mad, I think. Heaven help poor Grévy if they sing that under the windows of the Élysée. Let us sing it again, Thérèse."

They sang it together.

"Well," she said, "you *do* persuade me! If I can make a rebel of Monsieur de Courcelet, the world is at my feet."

Barbet's letter to Thérèse, which for so long he had left unposted, reached her that evening and confirmed her resolve. Templéraud threw his heart into collaboration with her, and the programme they had designed for the Nouvelle Écurie was re-shaped. Plence at first hesitated. "The public likes variety," he said; "they shy away from a single emphasis."

"Now," Thérèse answered, "have I ever let you down? It is my career, though it may be your theatre. *I* am the variety; Barbet is the political sensation. What more do you want?"

It was Plence's merit and the root of his success that he did not haggle with his own decisions, once made. Having looked at Thérèse and paused an instant, he said: "Good. I want no more. Have your own way," and she knew that thenceforward he would be with her without hedging, without regrets. He did more than acquiesce; he made Barbet's cause his own and by talk, by advertisement, by visits to his friends, served it with the fanaticism and tenacity of his race. As the days passed, the story of Barbet spread from the provincial to the Parisian press. As the weeks passed and the wheels of the law began to turn, the outcry increased and Thérèse's opening at the Écurie choked the roads to Montmartre with carriages. Those who had known Barbet personally basked in a new fame. A legend sprang up of his appearance at Maubant's, Quérignon's version of the story being transformed into a tale that Barbet had seen Héloïse and Abélard in a vision. Schnetz, being asked whether he also had seen the visionary figures, answered: "No. Why should I? I am not a saint," and his answer went the round of the clubs and became a headline. He worked untiringly and with an optimism more assured than Thérèse's own. "Even the lawyers," said he, "are not mad. They will find a means to acquit him." His overriding confidence persuaded all he knew that, in supporting Barbet, they were backing a winner. Acquittal became for him an article of faith. "Don't talk to me," he said. "I *know*."

After three months of doubt, the day came that proved him wrong. Barbet was sentenced in mid-February. That night, at the Écurie, Thérèse sang none of the new songs introduced since his arrest but reverted to the old ones that he had made for her. At the end, it was the audience that compelled her to "Au clair de la lune," but she would not sing her own words to it. She shook her head and shook her head and, when there was silence, she said:

"Forgive me. The battle is not over. But I dare not sing the new words to-night."

She had meant only that she could not trust herself to sing them, but the audience interpreted her differently; there was a turning of heads, a scrutiny of unfamiliar faces; the room was swept by rumor that Thérèse Despreux had been threatened by the police. At first she knew only that the mood of her audience was changed; she felt their anger while doubtful of its cause; then understood and used it.

"I *dare* not sing the new words to-night. Barbet must be allowed to sleep quietly in his prison and Monsieur Grévy at the Élysée." Then she smiled: "After all, the old words have the same tune."

They obeyed her and sang as if they were singing a conspirators' hymn. Outside the Écurie a crowd gathered round her as she left the building, determined that the police should not touch her, a crowd that increased continually, flowing in from the side streets as she drove to Maubant's under escort. Far down the street she heard them singing:

"Ouvre-lui sa porte
Pour l'amour de Dieu."

On the way home, she called upon Courcelet at the Palais Royal. Never before had she thus disturbed him, but he had been out of Paris in January, she had not seen him since his return and to-night, flushed with the sensation of victory though it was to-day that Barbet had gone to prison, she felt that she must at all costs see Courcelet before she slept. He would tell her whether she was standing on her head or her heels.

He renewed his fire and stood beside it in his dressing-gown while she told him what had passed.

"What will happen, Philippe? That mob was roused. You would have felt it if you had been there. Have I done well? Do you say 'Good, Thérèse'?"

"You have fought magnificently," he answered. "But you have failed."

"Is that failure? To have Paris shouting in the streets?"

"Barbet is in prison."

"Yes, yes, you were right. But I too was right. The story doesn't end here. This is where it begins. What will happen now?"

"Poor Thérèse. It will peter out. I know the mob of Paris. They are like champagne; the fizz goes off. Poor Barbet."

"It may be 'poor Thérèse.' Certainly it isn't 'poor Barbet.' He is worth more than that. Oh dear," she said, "how odd it is! I suppose I am doing all this for myself. He doesn't see himself as a persecuted hero or as a visionary or a worker of miracles. I have had letters from him, you know. There was one written a week ago in which he said—listen; I have it here; I carried it about to show you." She took it out and held it to the lamp. "He says: 'What I am told is happening in Paris surprises me. I am very grateful to you, Thérèse. No one wants to go to prison and in that I am like everyone else. But if I do go to prison, it won't *matter*. Don't imagine what isn't true. My mother, who seemed once to have become free in her mind, has returned to her delusion that to put me into prison is different from putting other men there. She has it in her head that I am entitled to special exemption—a kind of spiritual exemption. I have never claimed and don't feel the least claim to anything of the kind. My story isn't some miraculous legend: the newspapers puff it up into nonsense; I'm not in the least a sublime fool or "The Simpleton of Roussignac." All I am is a good vine-grower and a man who hates to be attached to anything—tied to it, I mean, by ties that he makes for himself. To be tied by force, by other people—to be in prison even, is still to be free. The terrible thing is to let chains grow in one's own mind—not to be able to walk out of a room though all the doors are open. And if there's anything odd about me it is that I don't grow chains for myself and I do walk out if the doors are open. Hatred and fear are chains; I was beginning to hate and fear Blachère; so I let myself out. At the time, I confess, there wasn't much reasoning about it. It seemed to happen—as you said once—like waking in the sun. But I have been made to think about it since then. They ask me so often why I did it, and, when I tell them the truth, they won't believe it. But you will. If they put me in prison, don't be disappointed or troubled. When I put myself in prison, it will be time enough for you to pity me.'"

"Do you understand that?" Courcelet asked when she had finished reading.

"Certainly. Don't you?"

"I understand it, of course, with my mind. But I don't feel it. I don't know what it feels like to be an unattached human being. How, for example, can a man love and yet not be tied to his love by chains of his own making? Or is this the answer—that we are tied only by our appetites, by what we desire to consume and possess? Is that why men who love God say not only that they are unfettered by their love but that their love is itself freedom? It is an interesting speculation and I suppose the reason for my being unable to discover any answer is precisely that it is to me only a speculation. And to you, Thérèse?"

"Go on talking," she said. "It amuses you and it amuses me."

Chapter 2

AS WINTER MOVED INTO SPRING, COURCELET ATtended Thérèse's performance at the Nouvelle Écurie whenever his evening was free. He grumbled a little at having to drive to Montmartre after dinner, but his age had revived in him the romanticism of boyhood and it gave him adventurous pleasure to go to a place of entertainment which, though now fashionable and prosperous, still had an odour of disreputability. He liked to take his friends with him and to apologize in advance for having to desert them when the entertainment was over. "You understand, she often likes nowadays not to sup in company after a performance. We drive quietly home. Very suitable to my advancing years." This was said in such a tone of gaiety and challenge as must persuade all who heard it of his virile youth, and his special delight was to take with him younger men who had formerly been her lovers. To say good night to them, to climb into Thérèse's carriage under their eyes, to believe, though it was long since he had been in effect her lover, that she kept faith with him was compensation for all the disappointments of his life.

Was she faithful to him? He did not seriously doubt it, having applied all his shrewdness to suspicion. By virtue of his connexions with the Ministry of the Interior, he had the best of opportunities to reassure himself, and for three weeks of January, while he was out of Paris, she had been watched. The reports he received were as satisfying as the welcome she had given to his return or as the compliment she had paid him by knocking him up that night of February and being his audience while he philosophized in a dressing-gown. Not that he had doubted that she was genuinely fond of him, for he admired her as she wished to be admired, and treated her with that mixture of sympathy in all her moods, of kindness in all her difficulties and of severity against her transgressions which gave her, at the same time, the sensations of being free and of being ruled. If she was disobedient where he required obedience of her, he imposed penances which she accepted, perhaps for her own sake, perhaps for his. All this he could understand better than most men, for a part of his mind ran with hers, but that she should be so long content with suppers, drives, conversations and chastity puzzled him. They were what he liked, what he needed, what he was capable of, but, aware of their inadequacy to so young a girl, he exercised himself to provide charming compensations. It astonished him that they sufficed. What was she playing for? Marriage? Or were her own passions becoming quieter?

He determined to ask her, not only because he wanted to know but because he had found that such direct challenges were a whet to conversation; and one evening towards the end of May he went to the Écurie and watched her performance with the thought in his mind that, when he and she were alone, he would say: Why aren't you bored with me, Thérèse? Why don't you want younger men? At first she would answer that men of his age pleased her; then that he was a selective connoisseur; then that no one she knew could talk as well as he—all the replies of flattery and convenience; but at last, because she was Thérèse, she would tell the truth.

He went to the Écurie alone. Was it because he was critical in solitude or because he had heard them so often that her Barbet songs seemed to him to have become stale? The audience was rapturous, but this he was inclined to attribute to her prestige. Not to applaud the Despreux was to confess oneself a fool; and certainly he himself applauded—the Petits Chevaux in particular, for in these monologues her voice, her attack, her characterization of the unseen players delighted him; and the old songs—the song of the soldier on the march and the country girl's comment on cities— filled him with warm memories of the early days when she was less famous. But the songs about Barbet—well, satire at the expense of the Government fell flat when the occasion of it was past, and, for him, all the songs about Barbet, and not only those composed after his arrest, were, in effect, satire against the Government. How deep was Thérèse's interest in him? Why, though the songs should have been long ago out of fashion, did she so evidently put her heart into them? Bless my soul, thought Courcelet, when he let out his prisoners and all France was chattering of it, the joke was good, but hasn't he by now been in prison long enough to be forgotten?

On the way home in her carriage he decided that the moment had not come to speak of what was in his mind. She was in no mood to accept criticism. She was proud because the fête in the Tuileries gardens, the torchlight processions, the spahis in their great cloaks, had not affected audiences at the Écurie. "Nor has the war," she said. "By the way, how is the war?"

"What war?"

"Phaleron Bay. The Greeks."

"Oh," said he with a smile, "the Greeks! C'est arrangé là-bas, c'est fini. Why did you take all that so seriously, Thérèse? Tonkin, too. You were always fussing about Tonkin."

"War's a mess," she answered. "Poor devils. When they come back, you give them ribbons. And I stay here singing my pieces."

"Have you renewed your contract with Plence?"

"No."

"I thought that was to be done to-night."

"He brought it again."

"Well?"

"I didn't sign."

"But, my dear Thérèse, surely time is running short. Your present contract has only a few days to run. I can understand your wanting a break, but he must be allowed to know what your intentions are. If you won't sign for the future, he may engage someone else."

"I have told him he can if he likes. I have told him I mean to take a holiday."

"In June? Certainly. But a holiday with a contract at the end of it. You can have what salary you like."

"I have told you and I have told him," she exclaimed, turning in her seat, "that it isn't a question of salary. I am going to take a holiday without a contract at the end of it."

"But why?"

"Let's not talk of it," she answered. "Here's a May evening and an open carriage. Aren't you glad for once that I work in Montmartre and live in the Île St. Louis?"

He was so glad, so proud to be at her side, that he wished to prolong the evening and urged her to sup out with him. She shook her head.

"Are you tired, my darling?"

"Tired? No. You always ask me if I am *tired* when I don't want to do what you suggest. There's supper at home. I want to sup in the window and watch the river."

He acquiesced, and, when they were in her flat, he said: "I have no need to be early to-morrow."

"Which means you will stay? Good. We can talk at leisure— or not talk, as you please. I shall undress before supper. Open a bottle meanwhile."

A door between the two rooms stood open. She walked to and fro while she undressed. When two glasses of Montrachet had been poured out, she paused at the table to drink.

"Listen," he said, "I have something serious to say."

"In these clothes?"

"Why not?"

She made her gesture of obedience. "What I like about you," she said, "is that you have a sense of the incongruous." She carried her glass with her and lay upon the sofa. "Well, what have I done?"

He told her that, in his opinion, the Barbet songs had had their day.

"Did the audience think so?"

"You have great prestige."

"By which you mean that the applause was a compliment to me? That they are tired of the songs? Now, listen. Did they applaud the Barbet songs less than the others or less than the Petits Chevaux? Did they? . . . You see, you are talking nonsense. I will not have you interfering. I will not have you interfering with my work. Anything else—yes. My work—no."

"You have said that before, Thérèse, and have agreed afterwards that my judgment was good."

"Perhaps. But not this time. Naturally you hate the songs. It's your friends in the Ministry who are responsible for his being in prison."

"My dear Thérèse, I have told you a thousand times that he was tried and sentenced in the ordinary way."

"For embezzling the money for the prisoners' upkeep?"

"Precisely."

"And you know he didn't. He gave it to the poor."

"What he did with it isn't the law's concern. He took it. His trial and sentence followed as a matter of course."

"He could have been pardoned."

"But he was guilty."

"He was morally innocent. You knew it. The Government knew it. He fooled the authorities, made you a laughing-stock. That's why you keep an innocent man shut up. The laugh of Paris—of all France—was against you. Those songs nearly brought the Government down. They will yet."

"I admit they were dangerous," said Courcelet, "but they aren't now. That's my point. The thing is stale."

She looked at him. "Is it?"

"Barbet is forgotten. Except à propos of your songs, not a soul speaks of him. Some of the songs stand on their own merit, but some are strictly topical—or were. Are there any other topical songs you have held for so long?"

"But the audience isn't tired of them. They applauded and applauded. You said so yourself."

"You know well enough," he answered, "that you must stop a song *before* the audience know they're tired of it. Anyhow, you have always known it until now. What your personal reasons may be—"

"They don't count."

"What do you mean?"

"Precisely what I say. In the work I do, nothing personal counts. If the songs are stale, they're stale. All right, have it your own way. I will drop them. After this contract ends I will drop them. I don't care whether your ridiculous Government stands or falls. Which are stale?"

How much this swift decision cost her, Courcelet knew, for as she flung her question at him she rose with tears of rebellion in her eyes and thrust past him on her way to the bedroom. To have clung to the songs would have been to obey her sentiment; to reject them was, she now believed, a part of her integrity; and Courcelet was wise enough not to console her. He counted on his fingers the songs that were to be condemned and called their names through the communicating door. She received them in silence.

Out of this silence she asked unexpectedly: "Do you think we outgrow things?"

He tapped out a cigarette just lighted and his expression hardened: "As one grows older—" he began, but before he could continue she was out of the bedroom, her unfastened wrap afloat behind her naked body, and had twined her arms round him.

"I didn't mean that. I didn't mean you. I wasn't talking about that at all. How often am I to tell you that you can do or not do what you please? Come to supper."

"Then what did you mean?" he asked. "Yourself?"

"Myself?" For an instant she was puzzled. "Oh, I haven't outgrown desire, if that's what you're thinking of. I should be a dull mistress if I had. For example, I shouldn't have run in with my dressing-gown flying, should I?"

"Perhaps you hadn't time to fasten it."

"No, my dear, but just time to unfasten it. Was it a good entrance?"

He was enchanted and took her hand. "What is it, then, that you have outgrown?"

"I'm not sure," she replied, beginning to eat her supper. "Not my appetite anyway. . . . But it was interesting, you know. Six months ago I should have been outrageously proud of having had the will to drop those songs. They'd have been a glorious sacrifice to my divine ambition! 'Nothing personal counts. Nothing personal counts' —it has been a watchword for me. And to-night—oh, it's nonsense.

of course; I'm as ambitious as ever or I shouldn't have consented. You have no idea what those songs stood for in my mind. I thought I could rouse Paris with them. I thought I could *make* the Government let him go. But you're right; they are going stale; if I went on with them, they would begin to damage my performance. Very well, I drop them, and Barbet can stay in prison. But in there, while I was reaching for this wrap across the foot of the bed, I was suddenly *not* proud of myself. I used to feel the hell of a great woman when I was ruthlessly ambitious. To-night—"

"To be, in your own line, the greatest performer in Paris—isn't that something?"

"Good God," she replied, "of course it is. For me—"

"Everything?"

She was silent.

"That is what you were going to say?"

She nodded and laid down her knife and fork.

"Then why not say it? Isn't it true?"

"Oh yes, it's true," she answered. "For a moment I wished it wasn't. That's all."

"But Thérèse—"

"'For a moment,' I said! Don't argue. The moment is past."

Chapter 3

HIS SUCCESS IN PERSUADING THÉRÈSE TO DROP
many of the songs that she and Templéraud had devised on the
subject of Barbet had been enough for Courcelet that evening. He
had learned that it was unwise to follow up a victory over Thérèse.
To remind her that she had yielded in anything was to provoke her
to recant. After each shaking, her self-will must be given time to
re-settle.

He had, therefore, surrendered himself to the delights of her
company, but three days later, having taken her to drive with him
in the Bois, where his friends might enviously remark his privilege,
he led the conversation towards the subject of his curiosity; her
failure to renew with Plence the contract that would expire to-
night, her reluctance to sacrifice the Barbet songs, and her surprising
constancy to himself. On the evening of the dressing-gown—it was
by such visual incidents that he labelled his evenings with Thérèse
—he had for a moment cautiously approached the third and the
most important of these problems, but she had instantly produced
cards and threatened him with piquet. She could scarcely suggest
piquet in the Bois and he began again to send out his analytical
scouts.

She would say no more of Plence than that she wished her existing contract to lapse before she signed another. Why? Because she
wanted, for a time at any rate, to be free. "As I walk out of the
Écurie this evening, I want to be able to say to myself: perhaps I
shall never come here again."

"A charming pretence," said Courcelet.

"Pretence?"

"Surely?"

"Don't be so sure!"

He shrugged his shoulders. "You will be telling me next that the Despreux is giving up the stage."

"And if I were to say that?"

The question alarmed him. "I should say you were a fool."

"Why a fool? Is it the best of all lives, do you suppose, to be a singer in café concert?"

"For you, yes. It is the life you have chosen. It is the life to which you have trained yourself. What is more—you can do it better than anyone else. I know, my dear," he added more gently, "that from time to time everyone, whatever his profession, grows tired of it, but—"

"'Tired! Tired!' Every man has a word of his own. Even Barbet had. 'To-morrow!' was his word until I taught him 'to-day.' Your word is 'tired.' I'm not tired. Why can't I be free even for a few weeks? I want to feel that, if I want to, I can go on a voyage. I don't say I'm going to. I want to feel I *can!*"

"Very well," said Courcelet, "as long as you don't. I dare say that sometimes the routine of your life is tedious to you—"

"It's not tedious!" she exclaimed. "Tired! Tedious! What words!"

"I dare say," he persisted with irritated patience, "that sometimes your life is tedious to you. No doubt you have dreams of becoming something altogether different. We all do. I imagine that some day I shall give up politics and write history—history was my passion when I was a young man—but I shan't. Why? Not because the man inside me is changed. Not because I love history less. But just as the way one lives marks the face, so it marks the mind and harnesses the will."

"You mean that no voyages are possible?"

"Voyages?"

To avoid the question, she slipped her hand into his arm.

"I'm sorry," she said. "I snapped at you."

He patted her glove. "There's a penance for that."

"I know."

"But this time," he continued, "the penance isn't what you think."

"What is it, then?"

"To continue our conversation where you broke it off. What did you mean by 'voyages'?"

"I wonder whether I can tell you that," she answered, "—tell it, I mean, in a way you would understand? A 'voyage'—it's not my word, you know, it's Barbet's—a 'voyage' is—"

"Escape?" he prompted.

"No. That's what people always say. Was Columbus 'escaping'?"

"Ah, so you're going to discover a new world?"

"Why not?"

"Because the only voyage to a new world that would suit you, Thérèse, is a tour in New York. You are almost famous enough."

She was stung by the "almost." "I have already been offered that!"

"Have you? Wasn't the salary high enough?"

"Why do you think that's all I care for? Why *should* you think it?"

He shrugged his shoulders. "I'm not accusing you of being mercenary. I say only that you are a professional actress. If you imagine you can be anything else, you are deluding yourself—that's all. Marie Antoinette playing at being a milkmaid. . . ."

"You are wrong," she said. "You think you are right because I play my part so well. I had no heaven-sent vocation for the stage, but I was alive, I had talent, I wasn't going to rot in Roussignac all my life or sell hats in Angoulême. I had to get *out*—and the stage was my way out. First I put up my own stage in the garden of the Cheval Pie; then I climbed on to it; and *after that* I invented the heaven-sent vocation. Do you understand that?"

"But—'voyages'?" said Courcelet. "You're wandering from the point."

"I'm not. I'm coming to it. . . . I hypnotized myself; you have to, if you're going to the top." She turned on him. "That's where you fail, my poor Philippe. You didn't hypnotize yourself; still you are partly a historian, partly a connoisseur, always slightly despising your own job; that's why you are not président du conseil. That's no good to me. Whatever the council is, I'll be president of it. That means self-hypnotism. People of my sort are like a chicken with its nose on a line of chalk; so was Bonaparte, so was Balzac. You look about you and criticize the landscape; you don't get anywhere; we do. We stay on the track and we're happy as long as we keep our noses down; but if we look up——"

"Doesn't the landscape please you?"

"That may be," she answered. "But the spell is broken. The hypnotism doesn't work any more. If we look up, we see the white line as what it is—a track, an obsession. Then one of two things happens. A giant—Balzac—goes on; he substitutes a deliberate, undeluded will for the obsession, and he goes on. That is a great artist. I'm not that. I can go on; probably I shall; and I shan't despise my job—I shan't be *tired* of it, it won't be tedious to me; you can get that out of your head—but I shan't be hypnotized any more; I shall never be able to re-hypnotize myself as Balzac did—as the giants always do when they come up from the chalk line. But there's one other thing I might do. I might break away from the chalk line altogether. That's the meaning of a voyage—not to be earth-bound, not to be stage-bound or money-bound, not to be *bound* to anything."

"My dear, everyone thinks at one time or another that they could buy salvation for the price of a ticket to Tahiti. Unfortunately, when they get there, the same soul comes out of their valise."

"Look," she said, "I want you to understand this. I really want you to understand it. I'm not a vague dreamer. I'm a professional actress. I know that as well as you. But I am by one degree more realistic than you are, and I'm not stage-struck any more. It was a drug; I'm cured of it—*as* a drug; that's all. I can do without it. There have always been other ways in which I might have lived, but I'd forgotten it. Now I know it again. My nose is up from the chalk line. That's what a voyage is. And don't imagine that I am not capable of it."

"Dear Thérèse, you are capable of anything—but not, I think, alone?"

"By which you mean?"

"Only that the companion of your voyage will have the devil of a time when you grow tired of it. Have you thought of that? One ought not to share one's St. Helena."

"Oh," she said with a sigh, "you know how to be cruel, don't you?"

The horses were being rested in the shade. Nothing pleased Courcelet better than to sit with Thérèse in a carriage drawn up by the roadside so that all who passed might see him on his throne. To be still, to be near her, to draw off his gloves, and feel the warmth of the carriage-cushion under his hand, to smell the leather and the horses, to hear wheels bowling past him and see the glitter of their spokes, filled him with a sense of well-being; for he was afraid of death, of its cold exile—as he understood it—from the pleasures of a connoisseur, and often would sit still for a long time, thinking only: I am alive. I am still alive. And Thérèse filled him not only with a sense of life but with a sense of power. A docile woman bored him. A reserved, aristocratic woman appealed, if at all, only to his intellect. Thérèse was wilful, intractable, like a vicious mare, but she played her game by the rules understood between them. In the last resort, he was master. She would die in argument rather than surrender her opinion, but, commanded, she would obey; and now, though she was silent, neglecting his question, he was content to warm himself in the enchanting miracle of her known obedience. If he said: Thérèse, I want to drive home alone, she would make her little gesture of acquiescence—an outward movement of her palm—and leave the carriage.

Instead, he ordered the coachman to drive on and watched the sway of her body at the jerk of the traces. The horses' pace was quickened. Trees and grass and little knots of people flashed past. Thérèse leaned forward, then swung round in her seat, having recognized a friend.

"Stop," she cried, "stop," and raised herself, perilously swaying.

The carriage drew up. "I'll get out. Wait for me here. . . . No, no, I should never catch up. Turn the horses. Drive slowly back."

But all her vigilance could not re-discover the figure she had recognized.

"Very well," she said at last. "It's hopeless. Drive on again."

After a little while she looked at Courcelet. "Don't you want to know who it was I saw?"

"Not if it's another abandoned lover produced from the sleeve of your inexhaustible memory."

"My poor Philippe! The sleeve's empty. I've told you about them all."

"Good."

"This wasn't a lover. It wasn't even a man. It was an old woman. I thought she was Madame Vincent."

"Vincent?"

"I have told you about her. Quotations run in her head. Anyhow, they did, though I'm told she's less sure of them nowadays. You remember? A friend of Madame Hazard."

Courcelet, to whom Victor's name was familiar in his list of agents and who had long known that Madame Hazard had come up from Roussignac, thought swiftly.

"It's not impossible," he admitted. "Madame Hazard is in Paris, of course."

"*She* is in Paris! How do you know?"

"I know everything. . . . I supposed that you did. In fact, she has been bothering everyone who's fool enough to see her. She's mad, I believe—or near enough."

"In what way?"

"A saint has been imprisoned. She is the mother of the saint. . . . But interesting. I saw her myself as a matter of curiosity. She says that the Republic will fall, that the Emperor will return—though whether it's to be the first or only Napoléon le Petit seems not to matter, and whether he is coming back to rescue her son or deliver the vines from the phylloxera she seems not to know. Anyhow she swears that the only way to save the Republic is to let Barbet loose."

"My God," said Thérèse, "I believe that even I have more heart than you. What did you do—laugh at her?"

"I was extremely courteous."

"I have no doubt you were. And where is she now?"

"That I don't know."

"Of course you do—or can find out."

"She came first to the Hôtel Bagnolet, but moved into the suburbs. I will have inquiries made if you wish it."

"Why didn't you tell me of this before?"

"My dear Thérèse, if you will forgive me for saying so, I have heard enough of the precious Barbet without going out of my way to remind you of him. You have dramatized the whole thing. Men have been to prison before."

"That's not the point."

"What is the point, then? You're not in love with him?"

After a momentary hesitation, she replied: "No. I'm not *in love* with anyone. And that, perhaps, is the answer to the question which is always in your mind—that explains the chastity which you find so astonishing. It has always been my habit to be in love with someone and—"

"A cheapening of the great passion, the romantics would say," Courcelet put in.

"I am not speaking of 'the great passion.' I didn't say it was my habit to love someone but to be in love with someone."

"Is there a difference, except of phrase? I thought you were a realist, Thérèse, not a metaphysician. Very well, I accept your distinction for the purposes of argument."

"I am not arguing," she replied. "I am telling you. You asked whether I was in love with Barbet—"

"Very well, I amend my question. Do you love him?"

"That is a question I won't ask myself for your entertainment."

"Then I will ask another question. Are you still my mistress?"

"Have I yet refused you? Until this afternoon you have never bored me. And you are not exacting, my dear Philippe."

"Until this afternoon, you have never insulted me."

"If that is what you think, you can punish me," she said. "That will be a consolation. But perhaps not? I had better ask you a question: am I your mistress still?"

He nodded as he did when a waiter submitted a dish for his approval before serving it.

"Then you will get me Madame Hazard's address?"

"Certainly."

"It is remarkable," she said, "how well we understand each other —you and I. I wonder sometimes whether we shall ever be able to part. Nothing is so important as to be able to quarrel with lucidity."

That evening, her last at the Écurie, she shook her head again at Plence's offer of another contract, and, refusing all escort, looked forward to driving home alone. At the door, as she was about to enter her carriage, she saw, among the crowd on the pavement, Madame Vincent's face. She halted and asked those who were pressing upon her to make way. Madame Vincent was evidently exhausted and her mantle crushed by the pressure of the crowd. Thérèse took her hand.

"I will drive you home. We can talk in the carriage."

The old lady had expected a long country welcome as though they were meeting ouside the Lion Rouge in Roussignac, but she understood what was required of her and at once behaved as if to drive away from the Écurie in the Despreux's carriage were, for her, a habit—certainly a right. She sat erect in her place and composed her long, heavy features in an expression of authority. When the wheels began to turn and the throng on the pavement to wave and shout good night, she shared in Thérèse's acknowledgments, raising her left shoulder, tucking her jaw-bone into it, and tilting her head sideways like a gaunt bird.

"Tell me," said Thérèse, "where is Madame Hazard?"

But Madame Vincent had a story to tell and would tell it in her own way.

"At Vanves," she replied and, before she could be interrupted: "I saw you in the Bois, Thérèse."

"I saw you. At least I thought I did. But when I turned the carriage, there wasn't a sign. Where had you gone?"

Madame Vincent had concealed herself. "I was at the kiosk, but I kept my back turned." She admitted it with rigid solemnity; then paraded her reasons in order. In the first place, Thérèse had not been alone; in the second—and this was sternly said—the old gentleman in the carriage had seemed to be of the type which— "well," said Madame Vincent, "we will pass over that—not a type sympathetic to me, shall we say? And in any case—"

"What?" Thérèse prompted.

"You must understand," Madame Vincent replied, patting Thérèse's hand as though she were speaking to a child whose understanding was in doubt, "that Chouquette and I have been in Paris some time. She has been very strange; it is, she says, her siege; in time, she says, the walls will fall down. What walls I can never be sure— perhaps of Paris, perhaps of Barbet's prison, perhaps of Jericho. She has worn herself out, seeing people, sitting in waiting-rooms, standing on doorsteps. But always she has said: 'Whatever we do, we must not go to Thérèse Despreux. Barbet would be angry. Barbet would not allow us to interfere with her life.' That is why I turned my back this afternoon. But this evening I came."

"I'm glad. You saw the show?"

That this question was as necessary to an actress as the breath she breathed did not appear to Madame Vincent.

"I waited on the pavement," she said.

"But why?"

"The entertainment would not have interested me."

"I'm sorry," said Thérèse, who admired so much plainness. "But you are a woman of the world? You don't disapprove?"

"That," said Madame Vincent, "is not the point. Poor Chouquette—"

"How is Madame Hazard?"

"That," said Madame Vincent, "is the point. She has taken it into her silly head to die. She is, in consequence, dying. All nonsense, of course. She was never a reasonable woman. . . . I am very fond of her, you understand."

Only the profound earnestness, the abrupt emotion, with which these words were spoken prevented Thérèse from laughing at them. Like Courcelet, she had delight in the incongruous and it pleased her to watch a black bonnet shake its ribbons against the street lamps where his silk hat might have been.

"Where are we going?" Madame Vincent demanded, looking about her in sudden alarm.

"The Île St. Louis. I live there."

"But I am staying at Vanves."

"You can't possibly go to Vanves to-night. Do you know what time it is? You must stay with me to-night. We will go to Vanves in the morning."

Thérèse felt her companion stiffen to resistance. "But—" she began.

"You had better allow me to take charge, dear Madame Vincent. I think you have done enough for to-day. There is some supper at home. You can tell me everything then."

For a moment the warrior contemplated battle for her independence; her forearm became rigid; then, feeling Thérèse's fingers interlaced with her own, she tightened her grip as children do when they are on the verge of tears, and said:

"You are kind, Thérèse Despreux. I didn't know you could be so kind. . . . Yes, I have been on my feet all day. Oh dear!"

Her body relaxed. She leaned back against the cushion. A gleam on her cheek told Thérèse that her tears were falling.

"You have a very comfortable carriage," she said. "Is it your own or hired?"

"My own."

They drove on.

"Oh dear," she said, "what will they think—the Verviers—if I don't return to-night?"

Thérèse did not ask who the Verviers might be. She was afraid the old lady might faint and looked into her face anxiously.

"I will explain everything to the Verviers. Don't trouble about anything at all."

"But you have a spare-room?" Madame Vincent demanded.

"No," said Thérèse, "I haven't, but I have a very large bed. It is called Castor and Pollux."

Suddenly Madame Vincent burst out laughing. "I am a large woman," she said and laughed no more.

As the carriage stopped, Thérèse was hoping that Courcelet might use his key that evening and find Madame Vincent on his pillow.

"Red Riding Hood," she said.

"Why Red Riding Hood?" asked Madame Vincent.

"I'm afraid there are several flights of stairs," said Thérèse. "Give me your arm."

At supper, Madame Vincent came to life. She was so interested in the management of Thérèse's small household that, until her curiosity was satisfied, she could not speak consecutively of Roussignac. She wanted to know at what time the maid, who had evidently laid the supper, went away, at what hour of the morning she returned and what wages she demanded. Why was there supper laid for two?

"There's always supper for two," Thérèse answered, "in case I bring someone back. After a performance I'm never sleepy. I like to talk."

"And if you bring no one, supper is wasted?"

There was much else that Madame Vincent wished to know. Why, for example, was the bed called Castor and Pollux? "Because," said Thérèse, "it is shaped like a swan," and Madame Vincent pursed her lips sceptically over the story of Leda and the father of the gods.

"Well," she said, "I shouldn't have thought it practicable."

"You wait until you get into it," Thérèse exclaimed. "It's the most practicable bed in the world, and the wings keep out the draught."

"I didn't mean the bed," said Madame Vincent. "I meant the story."

At last, propped against the quilted satin of the swan's neck, she gave Thérèse her version of Barbet's trial and sentence and of the events that had followed it.

"The world, you see, my dear Thérèse, isn't as simple as men like Barbet suppose."

Again and again they had asked him why he let the prisoners out and he had always given the same reply: that it had seemed wrong for him to keep them shut up. But didn't he know the law? —yes. Didn't he respect the law?—yes. Did he suggest that all prisons should be thrown open and all punishment cease? He had answered that he suggested nothing at all. He wasn't a ruler or a judge. He had no power to open other prisons, but he could open his own, and he did.

Then they had examined him about the money for the prisoners' upkeep. He said it hadn't entered his mind that he would have to continue to draw it. After the prisoners were gone he had seen that, if he ceased to draw the money, inquiries would be made before they had had time to go to ground. They would all have been recaptured. As it was, only one had been. The Court had been puzzled. But hadn't he known that sooner or later the secret must come out?—yes. And he had been prepared to take the consequences?—he hadn't looked ahead to the consequences. But that was absurd. Everyone looked ahead. Everyone ought to look ahead.

At this point in her narrative Madame Vincent drew up her knees under the bedclothes and shook her finger at Thérèse.

"Sometimes," she continued, "Barbet is as foolish as his mother. To answer as he did isn't the way to get on with men of the world. He made them angry. 'I don't agree,' he said. His mother is like that. 'I don't agree,' she says and you can get no more sense out of her. 'What do you mean—you don't agree?' they asked. 'I mean,' said Barbet, 'that for some people—anyhow for me, I can't speak for others—the only way to do a thing is to stop arguing about it. If I hadn't argued and looked ahead, I should have done this long ago. Well, I stopped arguing and did it.' "

"I understand that," said Thérèse. "I ran away from Angoulême."

Madame Vincent shrugged her shoulders. "But you can't run away from facts. He went on drawing the money. It's true he put it in the poor-box, half in the pastor's and half in the curé's, but that didn't help him. 'That's a pretty thing,' they said, 'to be charitable with the State's money. What credit do you take for that?' 'None,' said Barbet. 'Then what have you to say?' 'Nothing,' said Barbet. 'But we understood that you were a saint? We understood that you performed miracles? Probably you wish to reform the world?' 'No,' said Barbet. 'Then you are content with the world?' 'No,' said Barbet. 'Then why do you not wish to reform it?' They were trying," Madame Vincent added, "or at any rate Victor says that they were trying, to prove that Barbet was subversive, that he was revolutionary. The next question they asked him was: did he know that songs were being sung about him in Paris?"

"My songs. What did he say?"

"He said yes."

"No more?"

"They asked whether he had arranged that these songs should be sung, whether he had friends in Paris, why he went to Paris regularly. To sell cognac, he said. . . . Oh, he answered all their questions quite simply. But they weren't clever answers. He seemed not to know they were trying to confuse him."

"If he were burned at the stake," said Thérèse, "it wouldn't occur to him that the executioner wished to burn him. Do you despise him, Madame Vincent?"

"No."

"You did once."

"That is true. I like a man to defend himself."

"And he didn't?"

"No, certainly he didn't. . . . Oh, I don't know what it is. I don't easily change my opinions. But, do you know, at the trial, I kept thinking of what Barbet's mother used to say of him when he was a boy. 'You can't get *at* him,' she used to say. 'He's a good boy and he's not a fool. But he does foolish things,' she said, 'and it's no good arguing, it's no good punishing. He doesn't complain or struggle or defend himself, but you can't reach him, you can't get at him, you—' There," Madame Vincent went on after a pause, "it's very odd, but I didn't even feel sorry for him at the trial. He was perfectly happy. He didn't need defending. When it was over and he was given a chance to make a few arrangements before going to prison, he said to Victor: 'Well, Anton has the property. Everything is settled.' Victor couldn't help asking: 'What shall you do when you come out?' and Barbet laughed and said: 'At the moment, Victor, I haven't an idea. Would Hazard and Vincent give me a job as a cooper if I asked for it?' But Victor says he wasn't really asking a question. He didn't wait for an answer. He sent a message to his mother that she was to live quietly as if he were there. Then he went away. And of course," Madame Vincent added, "she hasn't lived quietly. After a time, she went off to Paris by herself and no one could stop her. In the end I came up—not before it was time. She'd have been in prison herself in another day. She always was a silly woman. I can manage her better than most but even I couldn't stop her going where she meant to go and seeing the people she meant to see. The extraordinary thing is that they let her in. But they did. In the end, she got through any door she chose. 'There,' she said, 'you see, my dear Emilie, I'm not as mad as you think.' I went with her. If I hadn't been there for them to wink at—well, no matter. What I was afraid of was that she might think of the Élysée. And one day she did. 'To-morrow,' she said, 'we go to the Élysée. That will be the end. That will be the end. The President will grant a pardon. You mark my words: that will be the end.' But that night, in the house of those skinflint cousins at Vanves, she began to shiver. Her face was burning and her feet like ice. We put her to bed and kept her there, but all through the fever she was at the Élysée or the Tuileries. She led us a pretty dance through history. Any President would do—Thiers, Grévy, anyone you please; and if it wasn't a President, it was Napoléon III, and if it wasn't Napoléon III it was Napoléon I. I thought she would die but she didn't. And do you know she was disappointed, as though a door had been slammed in her face. She tried to lift her head from the pillow but she could only turn it—first to the left, then to the right—looking at the room. 'Still at the Verviers,' she said, as though she expected to be at the gates of Paradise."

Madame Vincent stared at Thérèse. "Do you understand?" she demanded. "That is why I came to you. Chouquette means to go through that door as she went through the others. It was as if she had taken a ticket to heaven and come back to the place she started from. 'Still at the Verviers,' she said."

"But listen," Thérèse answered, "if you remind her that Barbet is still in prison—"

"No," said Madame Vincent, "I have tried that. I have even said: 'My dear Chouquette, you have not yet been to the Élysée.' 'The Élysée,' she answered. 'It is not necessary. The Emperor has signed the order of release.' And she has made up her mind to die —and die she will." Madame Vincent was examining the embroidery of Thérèse's sheets. "I am," she said, nodding sleepily, "at the end of my resources. But perhaps in the morning we shall know what to do. . . . Tell me again, I have forgotten the story of Leda. A swan, I know—but did you say an eagle?"

"It was Venus who became an eagle," Thérèse explained. "Leda was a woman, dear Madame Vincent."

"Oh, fiddlesticks," replied Madame Vincent, "the whole thing is impracticable. You yourself told me she laid an egg."

Chapter 4

NEXT MORNING, THE LAST SUNDAY OF MAY, Thérèse drove out to Vanves and stayed long with Madame Hazard, less in deliberate kindness than because the old lady, drawing near to death, had acquired so strong a resemblance to her son that Thérèse was fascinated by it. In watching her, she began to understand that Madame Vincent had been wrong in supposing her to be mad and in believing that she was arrogantly or foolishly knocking on the door of death. Sometimes a cloud of delirium passed over Madame Hazard's mind and she spoke of the first Napoleon as if she had been in his presence; but what had appeared to Madame Vincent as madness was only an extreme simplification of life, something child-like in the sense of being faithful and penetrating, a reliance upon nature and upon a goodness inherent in it. Madame Hazard had, indeed, been what Madame Vincent called "a silly woman," fussy, bubbling over, given to agitations, but these were gone from her now, the dross was gone; she neither clung to life nor clamoured for death, their continuity having appeared to her. The "silly woman," even the vain and pretty girl she had been once, could still speak with her lips, but there was within her a tranquil because an accepting spirit.

She could no longer be surprised and did not ask how it had come about that Thérèse Despreux was at her bedside. "Barbet," she said, "will be glad to find you when he comes." Later she said: "I remember. I thought you had a wicked face. But he was right. I see now." And in the late afternoon, when fine rain had begun to drop from the rail of her little balcony, and the white of her hair and of her pillow to shine in the premature dusk, she said: "After all, there is nothing to be afraid of."

"You mean—in death?"

"I mean: in life. He thinks the door is shut, but it is open."

"Who thinks the door is shut?"

"Barbet," said Madame Hazard. "It is raining outside. I can see it sliding on the leaves. I think I could sleep now for a little while."

During the days that followed, of which she spent a great part at Vanves, Thérèse was at first glad that her contract with Plence had not been renewed. Since she had become celebrated, intervals between her engagements had been few and short, and on each occasion to be in Paris and not to work had been for her a kind of desolation; as the time approached at which she would have gone on to the stage, she had begun to ache and be frightened, and no book, no company, no diversion had appeased in her the hunger for an audience; but now she did not feel this hunger, the planes of her reality shifted, she no longer thought of the Écurie as her real life and was able even to forget that she was an actress.

On Tuesday evening, about seven o'clock, she left Madame Hazard's room and came into the little garden or courtyard that lay in front of the Verviers' house. It was a square patch of gravel and evergreens, divided by a palisade of ornamental sheet-iron and a gate from the footpath up which she must walk to her carriage. Monsieur Verviers had returned from his desk at the Crédit Lyonnais; he had hung his bowler hat and his jacket on a branch and was smoothing the gravel with a wooden rake. His wife, a close-eyed, aquiline woman with a bodice that held her arms always a few inches from her sides and gave her the appearance of having been stuffed, was watching him in silence. They had at first been suspicious of Thérèse but were no longer. She had pleased Monsieur Verviers by asking him questions about finance, which made him feel that he was more than a bank clerk; she had discovered that Madame Verviers, in her youth, had, like herself, worked at a milliner's and their discussions had been ardently professional; and she had made them laugh. For years they had found nothing in particular to say to each other, and to laugh together was a relief in

their long matrimonial silence. When Thérèse came from the house,
they were, with reserve, glad to see her.

"And how is the patient?"

"No worse."

"So the doctor said this morning."

"But I wanted to ask you, monsieur. You are her cousin and—"

"Her second cousin."

"You are her second cousin and I of course am not related.
Nor is Madame Vincent if it comes to that. Neither of us has any
authority. It is for you to decide, but we thought that the people
at Roussignac—"

"By all means. By all means send for them," said Monsieur
Verviers. "A wise precaution, I'm sure. How many will there be?"

"Anton certainly and Bette, I suppose. She would never miss a
funeral. And Victor—Madame Vincent's son—he won't let Anton
out of his sight for long. Perhaps Renée, if Pierre lets her come.
Pierre will have to stay to look after the Maison Hazard."

"A married couple, then," said Madame Verviers, reckoning on
her fingers. "They could have the back room on the same terms.
The others we could lodge with the neighbours."

"If I sent a telegram as I go—"

"As urgent as that?" Monsieur Verviers interrupted. "Is it
necessary to waste a telegram?"

"At my own expense."

"Ah, I see. . . . Well, living as we do, I suppose we don't understand the ways of the stage." Monsieur Verviers set to work
again with this rake. "A telegram—yes. A different life. A different
life altogether."

Thérèse smiled, but suddenly the planes of her reality shifted
again. I suppose the truth is, she thought, that I am capable of
playing any part—even the part of a woman who has ceased to be
an actress. Sitting in Madame Hazard's room, I play the part appropriate to that room and that company, and thinking of her and
Barbet and the life at Roussignac I hoodwink myself into believing
that the Écurie isn't my real life after all—just because for a couple
of days I haven't hankered after it. It's a kind of romantic vanity,

I suppose. Philippe was probably right: "Just as the way one lives marks the face, so it marks the mind and harnesses the will."

Although Parliament was sitting, Courcclet had arranged to go out of Paris for a wedding in the neighbourhood of Tours. On Wednesday Thérèse had luncheon with him before he took his afternoon train. He would be away, he said, three or four days, and she was careful not to ask him to be more precise. It was his habit to give no account of his movements. He had her kcys, he liked to use them unexpectedly, and she was content that he should enjoy his privilege—the more content because she had no impulse to deceive him. At luncheon she enjoyed his company as she always did, for he could listen as well as he could talk, and there was nothing she could tell of the Verviers that did not interest him. He appeared to regard them as sociological specimens. He wanted to know what they said of politics, what clothes they wore, what newspapers they read, and she phrased her account to entertain him. From the subject of Madame Hazard he slid away, for to die was to him a solecism that it was embarrassing to discuss. He played with the bread beside his plate, he tapped his glass with his fingernail and Thérèse said to herself: Now what is it that he has on his mind? what plot is he hatching? He said "yes . . . yes" distractedly, turning his head away from the new earnestness in Thérèse —always turning away until she repeated Madame Hazard's words: "He thinks the door is shut, but it is open." Then he swung round. His eyes lighted with curiosity, as though the words had some special significance for him.

"Say that again."

Thérèse said it again.

"Did you ask what she meant?"

"I asked: who?"

"Well? What did she answer?"

"Her mind was wandering."

"What did she answer?"

"Something about Barbet and the trees."

"Do you remember her words?"

Thérèse laughed. "Why should I?"

"You have a memory. What did she say? What, precisely, did she say?"

"I said: 'Who thinks the door is shut?' She said: 'Barbet'—but I doubt whether she was answering me. She was just thinking about him. Then she said: 'It's raining outside. I can see it sliding off the leaves.'"

"Could *you* see it?"

"What?"

"The rain. You said it was becoming dusk. She's an old woman. Is her eyesight as good as that?"

"I don't know. I suppose so. . . . Are you mad, Philippe? What on earth has all this to do with you?"

"Did you see the leaves yourself?" he persisted.

"I didn't look."

"Try to remember, Thérèse. Was there in fact any tree within sight of her pillow?"

"Possibly not. There are trees in the Verviers' garden but— what are you getting at? Have you turned into a policeman?"

"Tell me," he said, "one thing more. What time was this?"

"About six."

"After or before?"

"After six. . . . And now," she said, "will you tell me what all this is about?"

He would not. Though she went to the station with him, he did not return to the subject.

On Thursday, Thérèse found Anton, Bette and Victor in possession at Vanves. She was allowed to visit Madame Hazard but not to stay in her room. Bette considered her coming impudent and her presence a contamination. When Madame Vincent said that Thérèse had been kind and that Madame Hazard liked to have her in the room, a battle of words began between the two women, and Madame Vincent, a sturdy fighter not given to surrender, quailed and yielded. She became inwardly ashamed of having brought into the house an actress whom Bette still thought of as the tart from Angoulême, and Thérèse, when she understood this, lost courage. She went into the patch of garden in front of the house and stood there on the gravel, wondering what would become of her when the years of her celebrity were done. Except among people of the theatre, she was an alien; all others, whether like Bette they were censorious or like Courcelet of a freer class and temper, considered her to be different in kind from themselves, to be scorned, played with, tolerated, desired, even worshipped, but always with the reserve that she was alien among them. They would not trust her beyond the entertainment she gave. She tried to believe that this was because she was an actress or because she had had lovers; but the world had accepted actresses and wantons as it would never accept her; and she remembered that Courcelet had said: "You ruin yourself by talk. It's not even that you have been wanton, my dear Thérèse; a woman can grow out of that; but you have used your wantonness as an advertisement. It is a placard that wrinkles on the wall."

She drove away from Vanves in a rage of melancholy. Perhaps that's true only of Paris, she thought. If I gave up the stage and went away, I'm still young enough to—but she saw her life of the theatre as a prison to which she had become accustomed. "He thinks the door is shut, but it is open." And if I went out, what then? Do I want the life of the Verviers? Now, when I get home, what then? I wish to God I had renewed Plence's contract. I wish I had a theatre to go to. I could sing to-night. I could cut them to pieces and send them out gaping and squalling. She had made no engagement for that evening and leaned forward with the intention of telling the coachman to drive—but she could think of no one whom she wished to see and fell back again in her seat. At her flat was a note from Templéraud asking her to go with him on Saturday to the Battle of Flowers in the Tuileries, and suggesting that afterwards they should dine together. With a wry smile, she returned it to its envelope. Since she and he had ceased to be lovers, she had learned to look back upon her suffering at that time with an iron indifference as though it were the suffering of another woman with whom her intimacy had been lost. Templéraud and she had met seldom except to work, and always under the constraint of a friendship deliberately preserved. And now what does he want? she thought. To be seen about with me—or more? She shrugged her shoulders. She had no longer any desire for Templéraud, but—it would do Courcelet good, if he returned, to learn that the placard wasn't yet wrinkled on the wall.

This mood of reckless defiance, which in the past had served as her answer to all the rebuffs of the world, could not be preserved. She struggled to preserve it; it had been an escape from thought, a form of intoxication; but now, in spite of herself, she no longer wished to "go out and get drunk" and the notion of reverting to an old lover bored her. A new one, then? But what new lover would sit up in bed next morning and, while drinking his coffee, watch the sparrows pecking at the window-boxes, and make her laugh with stories of Roussignac, and suddenly take her breath away by saying: "Do you know, Thérèse, I suppose we are as unsuitable a pair as ever woke on the same pillow, and yet whenever we are together it seems to me always the most natural thing in the world." She had laughed then and slid her hand under his and shaken her head at the impossible, but nothing ever said to her, no praise, no swearing of love, had so warmed her heart or given her such enduring happiness. It was an inward happiness which, without reversing the theory of her life, had changed its practice. Not her morals but her tastes were altered. What's the matter with me, she said to herself, is that I'm not a tramp any more.

Because she had promised, she went with Templéraud to the Battle of Flowers. The wheels of her carriage and her sunshade were garlanded, and from a great basket at their feet she and Templéraud replied with handfuls of flowers to bombardments by friends and strangers; but rain spoiled the festival, the military bands were driven into a marquee, men in silk hats turned up their trousers above their ankles, splashed through the puddles and threw wet flowers from inverted umbrellas used as baskets. Small boys did a new trade in picking flowers out of the mud, holding them under jets of water and selling them again. She found that even the bitterness she had once felt and controlled in Templéraud's company was gone, and could remember without a pang—as an actress may remember the genuine emotion of last season's play—that she had once discussed with the young man at her side the romantic pleasures of their taking a house together. Thinking of Barbet and of his continuity in her life, she said amiably to Templéraud: "I wonder who is living in the house we might have taken in Burgundy?" To be able to say this gave her the satisfaction there is in writing an epitaph.

After less than an hour, she ordered her carriage to drive home, shook off her companion, changed and sat down to neglected letters. Even Madame Vincent's news that Madame Hazard was sinking failed to stir her. "I think she cannot live more than three or four days," Madame Vincent wrote. "Come if you can on Monday afternoon or evening. If she is no worse, Anton and Bette will be away then, perhaps Victor, too. It seems that the vines at the Maison Hazard have been attacked by the phylloxera. They are to have a meeting with a lawyer (they have had two already) to discover, I think, whether there isn't some way out of Anton's purchase of the property from Barbet. They want to suggest that he knew before he went to prison; they say *he* told them the vines were free of disease—in other words that he cheated them. Not that they say much to me. Bette tells me nothing; Victor little. He says that they haven't a legal leg to stand on; he wants them to keep away from lawyers and take their chance that Barbet himself may think it unfair to hold them to their bargain. Oh dear! Oh dear! what bitterness! I believe it wasn't so much poor Chouquette as this phylloxera that brought them to Paris. I said as much to Bette. She has become a hard woman. 'Two birds with one stone,' was all she said. When I think of her as a little girl—I used to be angry with her then for being so soft! People change in that way, women more than men. What she says they want is permission to visit Barbet. The man who can give permission, or obtain it, is Monsieur de Courcelet. Victor knows him or says he does; but at the Ministry of the Interior they say that Courcelet is out of Paris—back on Saturday night, perhaps Monday. You, dear Thérèse, will know the truth of that?

I didn't mention our meeting in the Bois, though Victor, of course, knows already that you have influence in that quarter. But you needn't worry. Victor would come to you but Bette won't allow it. I said that I thought your advice might be useful. But I'm getting old. Bette and Victor are no longer my children. They don't listen to me any more. Come on Monday. Chouquette spoke of you on Thursday and I shall be glad to see you. Do you know that Chouquette said to me only an hour ago that she would like a game of piquet? I had even to get out the cards, but when they were there she didn't notice them. She had forgotten. That's how it is. Come on Monday, if you can."

Thérèse looked at her calendar. Monday, then—the day after to-morrow—and she wrote: "Vanves." Her clock said that before long Templéraud would return to take her out to dinner. If he wished to be her lover or supposed that she wished it, their evening would be spoiled. But after all, she thought, as she began to dress, there's always a good chance that he feels as I do.

When he came, she said: "Tell me, do you feel as I do?"

"About what, Thérèse?"

"Us."

He hesitated, smiling. "I expect you have fallen in love," he said. "Annette and I are together again."

"That's all right," she said; "now we can dine comfortably. Whether for peace of mind or for the pleasures of anticipation, it's always best to know at the beginning of an evening where one will drink one's last cognac."

"You are an astonishing person, Thérèse. What were you afraid of?"

"Only," she said, "that we might go to bed together out of politeness. I did that once. So did he."

"And wasn't it a success?"

"In fact," she said, "it was."

"Why, then," he asked, "what happened?" and he put her cloak over her shoulders.

"The sparrows," she answered, "would eat the flowers in my window-boxes."

"Good," said Templéraud; "couldn't we make a song of that?"
"No, we couldn't," said Thérèse. "Is it still raining?"

Late that night, she was reading in her window-seat. Templéraud, who had been a good companion at dinner, had come in for a last cigarette with her and had been gone more than an hour. Supper for two was on the table, but the silver covers had not been moved from the dishes and the cork was undrawn.

She laid down her book and said to herself: I suppose I have gone mad, but it is true I love Barbet. Since that night—no, long before that—since the day I went to sleep in the sunshine at St. Cloud; before that—since the evening when I saved his life, the evening of my albatross. And I'd rather be at Vernon with him to-morrow than in any other place with any other human being on earth.

The river was gleaming under her. She leaned from her window and stroked the damp stone of the sill. The idea entered her mind that Barbet was in the room behind her. For that reason, she dared not turn, but continued to watch the Seine, and the figures of two men approaching each other on the bridge. When they had passed and were out of sight, she withdrew from the window. The clock on the mantelpiece began to chime.

There was a knock at the outer door. Courcelet had forgotten his key. For a long time, she had been silent, and now did not move. Unless he had searched for her light as he left his cab, he could have no certainty that she was in. But he might look up at the window of the sitting-room as he went away. She blew out the candles and stood in darkness.

He knocked again and, because she was resolved not to admit him, she stayed in mid-floor, trying to smile at the trick she was playing him, but her mouth remained shut, her arms were stiff at her sides and the muscles of her flanks were so tautened that her legs began to tremble. A third knocking was followed by a shuffle of footsteps in withdrawal, and they were not Courcelet's footsteps. She wished in an agony to move and could not; then, with a little cry of intaken breath, moved to call back, before he was gone, this departing visitor. There was darkness in the passage of the flat and on the landing also. From the well of the staircase, only silence came up, no footfall descending. Near to her was that inaudible stirring which informs the senses that darkness is occupied. He was not gone. She drove her wrist against the brooch she wore and heard her own deep sigh. He was waiting, perhaps within reach of her hand, but, when she stretched it out, she encountered nothing. She felt her way along the wall, pressed against it as though she were on a narrow ridge overhanging a precipice. What her fingers touched at last was an oilskin coat, then by clumsy chance the stubble of his chin, and she said: "Barbet. . . . It's Thérèse."

"Yes."

"Wait until I bring a candle."

"No, Thérèse." With his shoulders he thrust himself away from the wall. "I'm all right. I can follow you."

"Give me your hand then."

When he was in a chair and two candles were lighted, she opened the wine.

"You always have a corkscrew, Thérèse."

He tried to laugh but the sound ended abruptly in his throat.

"Oh, Barbet!" Giving him the wine, she put her face against his, and said: "Your hair's dripping. Your feet are soaked. I'll light the fire. Wasn't I clever to have this kind of stove?"

As soon as the fire was lit and a kettle put on to boil, she undid the swollen laces of his boots. "Gently," he said, "they won't come off easily. Let me do it." He leaned forward with hand stretched out; then fell back. "Sorry. I leave them to you." And when at last the boots and the oilskin were off, she brought a towel and dried his head. The hair stood up, the socks began to steam. She took off his socks, dried his feet and gave him Courcelet's wool-lined slippers. Until coffee was made, she spoke only of little things, content not to be answered. Asked whether he was hungry: "I was," he replied, "but I've gone past it for a bit. Don't worry, Thérèse. There's nothing I want. I'm happy to be here." She brought a dish from the supper-table. "Presently," he said. Meanwhile he held a bunch of grapes in the palm of his hand and ate from it.

At last she said: "Have they released you, Barbet?"

"No, I walked out."

"Then you may be recaptured? You may be taken back?"

"I suppose so. But I don't think that will happen." He put down the grapes and held out his coffee-cup to be refilled. "You see, it all came about in this way. The warder comes round the cells at regular times. That evening—"

"Was it on Tuesday?"

He counted with the fingers of one hand on his knee. "One night in the open, then the barn, then a railway truck—yes, the next was last night—four. I suppose it was Tuesday. It seems a long time ago."

"Was it at six o'clock? Soon after six?"

He nodded without surprise. "Afterwards, in the square, the clock said a quarter to seven. I was on my way then."

Before continuing his story, he put out his hand and touched her shoulder, as though the contact were necessary to establish in his mind a distinction between actual and remembered experience. "The warder went out and shut the door," he said. "Between then and lights-out isn't an easy time. It's the longest part of the day. As I walked round the cell I was thinking that just through the wall, there'd be grass growing up against the stone; if I could put my hand through, I should touch the grass and, if I *was* touching the grass, I should be free. It doesn't do, in prison, to think in that way. You may get it into your head that, if you walked straight on, you'd go through the stone; that's how men go mad and dash themselves against walls. I always turned away from thoughts of that kind; they boil and curdle in the mind; there's no outlet. So I stopped walking and knelt where I was and set myself to remember that my being shut up didn't change things at Roussignac. Everything there was going on just the same. It was still the mois de Marie—"

"It wasn't," said Thérèse. "It was the 1st of June."

"Perhaps it was," Barbet answered. "I thought it was May. I saw the boys and the young girls and women going to church in the evening and I remembered that when I was a boy it was always in

May that I wished I wasn't a Protestant. You know, even Victor was happy in May. It's what I remember about him. The Vincents put up a shrine in their house: the Virgin in white with a blue sash—"

"I remember it!" Thérèse exclaimed. "I went there with mother. A tiny figure on a star-spangled globe."

"You know," he continued, looking past her, "the silence in a prison is an extraordinary silence. Sometimes there are sounds—boots in the passage or a man howling—but they only increase the silence. You have to fill it. So, as I stood there, off I went through the Long Wood. You remember the two spurges—the leafy-branched spurge and the wood spurge—the two differing greens, like two sisters? Often I heard, near me, very near me, inside my cell, the flute of the golden oriole. I looked for him but he wasn't there. When I came out of the wood and had walked into the town, I found my own squirrel and the yellow wallflower that grows wild on the church and in your father's garden his big yellow roses drooping as if they were as heavy as wax. And, Thérèse, listen, I went on to the Cheval Pie, expecting to find you there, but suddenly I remembered that you were in Paris and everything shifted. I was in prison. You were in Paris. Outside the wall there was grass and I had to twist away from the grass and walk and walk in the cell before I could be still again. By that time it was the binetu I heard. I was in the vines and my mother was with me. She would always have it that she was the first to hear the binetu, so I pretended not to hear it. For some reason she began to whisper. I couldn't hear. I stooped down to hear what she said. 'The door's open,' she was saying. 'The door is open.' As I stooped, my shoulder touched the door of my cell. It rattled and came away from the frame two inches. So I opened it and walked out."

"Listen, Barbet," Thérèse said, "you say that as if it were the most natural thing in the world. The warder must have locked your door."

"I thought so, of course. I thought it was shut, but it was open. That's all I know."

"Go on," she said. "Isn't there a gate to the prison? When you came out of the cell, you weren't in the open?"

"I was in the big courtyard. All the cells opened on a covered way that ran round the courtyard. As I came out, there was a little knot of workmen, six masons with their tools, walking ahead of me down the covered way. I walked behind them. I made the seventh. Against the wall were some barrels of cement and on the barrels they had left their oilskins and oilskin hats. When they had taken their oilskins, two were left. I put on one and walked through the gate with them."

"Didn't they count? Didn't they notice they were seven, not six?"

"But why should they, Thérèse? Why do you make everything so complicated? If you were a mason at the end of your day's work, would you stop in the rain and say: 'One, two, three, four, five, six?' Would you?"

"No. But the oilskins, the two extra oilskins."

"I suppose two men were working late."

"Doesn't it occur to you that all this happened because—oh, I don't know," she said. "It all seems simple to you. And you walked to Paris. There must have been a hue and cry, there must have been descriptions out. How did you hide yourself?"

"I didn't," Barbet answered. "I asked for what I needed and people gave it to me. I don't think there is a hue and cry. I saw two newspapers. There wasn't a word. Surely there would have been? When I let my own prisoners out, the newspapers became excited about it as if it were extraordinary, as if I had done something against the Government. If they knew I had escaped—"

"*If* they knew!" Thérèse cried. "Now I understand. The newspapers haven't been told. That's what Philippe was getting at! He must have known on Wednesday that you were out but he wouldn't tell anyone—not even me. Oh, Barbet, if only I were singing at the Écurie! I could make France laugh! I could have all Paris in the streets by to-morrow night! That's what Philippe was afraid of."

"But, Thérèse, who wants to have all Paris in the streets? I don't want to give trouble to poor Monsieur de Courcelet and his friends. Someone, after all, must govern France."

"What do you want, Barbet?"

His body slackened and he looked at her with dazed eyes. "Sleep, I think."

"And to-morrow?"

"Oh," he said, "to-morrow . . ."

He had fallen asleep suddenly with the plunge of exhaustion that is a drowning. When she brought him to his feet and helped him to undress, he swayed like a toy soldier on a lead rocker, returning to the upright with a jerk that opened his eyes. His lids at once began to droop again. When he spoke, his words were so deeply muffled that she did not know whether he was awake or asleep. She put him to bed in a silk nightshirt of Courcelet's and stood beside him while he curled himself into a ball.

In the sitting-room, beside the chair he had used, were his clothes, his boots, the glass and the cup from which he had drunk. She gathered his clothes, put them into the bedroom and closed the communicating door. So he's in there, she thought. It's very odd. I suppose what happens next is that I undress and climb into the same bed. There's nowhere else to sleep. I shall be the first to wake; he won't find me there. He'll imagine that he's still in prison or in a barn or a railway truck, and he'll wake up and find my swan—

A key was moving in the lock of the outer door. A flood of laughter and delight warmed her body and she greeted Courcelet with an enthusiasm that overwhelmed him.

"Well," she said, "what did you come for if you're not pleased to see me?"

"Of course I'm pleased. . . . You have a fire?"

"Isn't it cold enough?"

"Whose cup is this?"

"I made some coffee."

He walked across to the table and examined it.

"I've had a guest," said Thérèse.

"So I see. He appears to have eaten my supper."

"Very little of it."

"Very little of it!" he repeated. "You haven't eaten any at all."

"I wasn't hungry. I'm not now. You can have mine."

"Thank you. . . ." He sat on the edge of a chair, clasping and unclasping his hands. "Thérèse," he said, "something has happened. There's a chance you may be able to help. Why in heaven's name are you laughing?"

"I wasn't," she replied, holding her face between her hands. "Anyhow, not at you."

"I adore you," he said, "but you are an infuriating girl. Whatever you were laughing at is irrelevant. This—"

"Oh no, it's not," she cried. "It's so relevant, I shall die if I'm not allowed to laugh. My cheeks are aching. Oh! . . . All right, I'll be good and listen. What has happened? Another note to Greece?"

He hesitated. "Is it of any use to tell you? You wouldn't help if you could. And yet you'll have to know with the rest of France. What has happened is that Barbet Hazard has escaped."

"You might have told me that on Wednesday afternoon before you went to Tours."

"You knew? How could you?"

"I didn't."

"You mean, you guessed?"

"My poor Philippe, you were very conspiratorial."

He spread out his hands, baffled. "Anyhow," he said, "the point is that we managed to keep it quiet. He had no money and as far as was known not even a change of clothes. We thought the police were bound to have him within twenty-four hours. Then back he would have gone and nothing need have been said. As it is—"

"But, Philippe," Thérèse asked, "if you wanted to catch him, surely the first thing to do was to publish descriptions in newspapers."

"Thank you. Not of Barbet Hazard."

"But why?"

"Because he's dangerous. And you know it, Thérèse. It's partly your songs that have made him dangerous. For good or evil, the surest way to get rid of a government in France is to laugh at it."

"France is a great country," she replied with a smile. Then with the utmost gravity, the corners of her mouth twitching, she went on: "But, Philippe, a harmless little vine-grower—what can he do to you?"

"To-morrow a great deal. The news is out to-night. Some workman in the prison lost a suit of oilskins. The oilskins were seen next morning in fine weather coming out of a barn ten miles away. Two and two were put together. A journalist got on the scent and the warders have chattered. Anyhow, the newspapers have it. To-morrow all Paris will be roaring it. 'Barbet releases himself.' 'Where is Barbet?' 'Barbet defeats the Government.' You can imagine it. There can be no end to it. If we don't catch him, we shall look fools. If we do catch him—"

"You can't send him to prison again," said Thérèse.

"We must."

"No, Philippe. If you don't catch him, people will laugh—that's true, and you'll have to bear it. But if you do catch him—listen, there are things that no government can do twice. If you put him in prison again, France will stop laughing."

Courcelet poured himself out a glass of wine.

"You are becoming a politician, Thérèse. I assure you, we have no malice against the man. All we want is to hear the last of him."

"That's easy."

"Is it indeed?"

"Whoever wants to be the most popular minister in France must first catch your bird, then let him go."

Courcelet smiled. "We haven't caught him yet." He yawned and stretched himself. "Well, let us wait until to-morrow. It's useless to try to conceal his escape any longer. His description is being officially published."

"That also," said Thérèse, "is a placard that wrinkles on the wall. You'll find it so."

He missed the allusion. "I'm tired. And sleepy. You don't mind if I stay to-night?"

While his question was being asked, he had taken off his tie.

"In fact . . . the truth is . . ." Thérèse began, putting out her hand to prevent him from unfastening his collar.

All his experience had not taught him that, if she had wished to be rid of him, she would have lied with accomplished smoothness. Her hesitation, her faltering embarrassment, now awoke in him the suspicions she had designed. He stood up, tie in hand, bristling.

"What do you mean? What are you trying to say?"

"Only that I'm tired, too."

"I shan't disturb you."

"But—"

"So you weren't expecting me? Is that it? Who was your guest at supper? Or are you expecting someone now? He's late, my Thérèse?"

"I'm not expecting anyone. And he's not late."

"That's a lie."

"It is precisely true."

"Well, then—" he said, not knowing whether to believe her, searching her eyes, guessing for her mood.

She smiled and shook her head. "Still you can't stay, my poor Philippe."

"Why?"

"There isn't room. He's here already. He's asleep."

A lilt in her tone, a light in her eyes, informed Courcelet that his anger was misplaced; she was playing a prank on him; no one was there; he was being laughed at and could save face only by laughing at himself. In any case, jealousy, anger, all high emotion was out of the part that he had chosen in life. His scenes were the comedy of a discreet and smiling indifference.

"Now," he said, putting his arm round her shoulder. "Tell me the joke."

"I'll show it to you. Come and see."

They went into the bedroom together. Barbet's head was so deep in the pillow that he seemed to have burrowed his way into sleep. The lace flounce had curled over him and wisps of his hair stuck through it.

Courcelet, applying his rule against the obvious, forbade himself any exclamation of surprise.

"Well," he said calmly, "it's a big bed and a small man, but there's not room for three of us however sleepy we are. . . . Good night, Thérèse. I have not been here, you understand." He was about to go, when the vitality, the latent energy of that sleeping figure claimed him. He took an observant pace backward and cocked his head as if he were appraising a statue. "My God, the little chap's alive! I wonder what he's dreaming about?"

"He's not dreaming," said Thérèse. "When he's awake, he *is* awake, but when he sleeps, he sleeps."

Chapter 5

BARBET SLEPT SO WELL THAT HE DID NOT STIR
that night when she lay down beside him or next morning when
she awoke. She made plans while she dressed. There was no cause
for immediate alarm. When her contract at the Écurie ended, she
had given a holiday to her maid, who was still with her family at
Sens; and, because it was Sunday, the woman who came in to clean
the flat would not appear until the afternoon. Thérèse's temptation
was to find a reason to be rid of this woman and to keep Barbet at the
Quai d'Orléans, but, though she trusted Courcelet, she decided that
this was impossible. She was too closely associated with Barbet in the
public mind. If there was a hue and cry and his name was again to
be on the lips of Paris, her flat would probably be watched and
certainly besieged by callers. He must be moved elsewhere, and
quickly.

She decided to go to Cugnot for help. He had the kind of recklessness that was unaware of personal risk, and would give Barbet
shelter for the plain reason—the only good reason—that shelter is
always to be given to a friend who asks for it, whether or not the
police happen to have set a price on his head. At her walnut desk
she scribbled a message for Barbet, telling him where to find materials with which to make coffee and commanding him at all costs
to open the door to no one—"not even to me," she wrote. "I have
my key and will let myself in when I return." This note she put upon
a chair at his bedside, and was about to turn away when there came
to her a recollection which, though its form was indistinct, yet
halted her. It presented itself as a belief that she had lived through
this scene before, and her mind, groping for precise correspondence
between the present and the past, swayed between delight and fear,

doubtful of the truth that would be revealed when the mists fell away. Gazing at Barbet while he slept, she felt that knowledge was approaching her which, if she could but grasp it, would change her understanding of her life.

When knowledge came, it disappointed her at first; it seemed trivial and no match for her boundless expectancy; and she said to herself: It was only Frédéric talking nonsense! as though the truth were necessarily mean and of no account because it had been spoken by Frédéric. On the day on which she had given a performance in the prison, he had said that she would never be at peace until someone who was in trouble came to her, tired and dull, useless to her, and she gave him safety and put him into her own bed and let him sleep. This had been the recollection she sought, this saying—so unlike anything that Frédéric had said before or since—was the evocative scent towards which her memory had struggled. She shook herself and blamed herself for a fool and set out for Cugnot's studio.

There she told Cugnot and Madeleine of all that had happened. Madeleine had been out and had seen a poster in which Barbet was described, but the news that he was in Paris and in Thérèse's flat set them laughing by its unexpectedness. "The police give no date of his escape. I had thought of him far away, hiding in barns," Cugnot said, "and here he is, brought on a magic carpet, asleep at the Quai d'Orléans. By to-night, certainly by to-morrow, Paris will be talking of nothing but Barbet. You had better bring him here at once and not come near the place again yourself. You will be followed—if you haven't been already."

"But will he consent?" said Madeleine.

"To come to you? Why not? He loves you and Cugnot."

"But will he consent to go into hiding at all?"

"Why not?" said Cugnot. "He's not a fool. Do you mean—because his mother is ill? Thérèse need not tell him that."

"I shall," Thérèse answered. "One doesn't lie to him. He runs his own life better than any nursemaid can run it for him. He knows what to do."

Madeleine put in: "That, in a way, is what I meant. I wasn't thinking of his mother's illness. I meant what I said : will he consent to go into hiding at all?"

"In any case, he isn't likely to force an issue," Thérèse answered. "He won't go out and give himself up. Whatever happens, he will allow to happen naturally. I am beginning to understand Barbet. He is never bound by any particular circumstance. The fact that he is a fugitive is an accident; it isn't important to him; and he will behave as if he were not one."

It was agreed that she should go at once to the Quai d'Orléans and bring him back with her. She found him dressed and unaware of the strangeness of his appearance in the clothes he had worn on his journey. He had made coffee.

"Nothing seemed to have been used," he said. "Did you forget to make coffee for yourself?"

She had forgotten, but was now hungry and, taking the cup he offered her, sat down beside him. He held his own between his hands and, as he tilted it to drink, looked at her over its rim.

"Vernon," she said.

"Why?"

"Do you always hold your coffee-cup as if it were a bowl without a handle?"

"I expect so. I like the heat under my fingers."

He was completely tranquil as though to be an escaped prisoner were a situation that touched him neither with a sense of danger nor even with curiosity.

"I have been to Cugnot's," Thérèse said, steeling herself. "I want you to stay with him, at any rate to-night."

His face fell. "Must I go from here? I imagined myself coming to you, Thérèse."

His disappointment so rewarded her and touched her heart that she took his hand before she replied : "And if I hadn't been in?"

"I should have waited."

"But I might have gone into the country!" she protested. "I have finished my job at the Écurie. I might easily not have been in Paris."

"But you were," Barbet said, unperturbed. "Since I have been shut up, all my happiest, all my surest thoughts have been of you, Thérèse. We haven't gone away from each other?"

"No," she answered, "and this morning, when you were still asleep, I felt that we were nearer than we had ever been—much nearer," she added, "than we were at Vernon. But that was my fault. It's a fatal habit of mine to invent phrases and then stick to them—like a journalist whose article goes wrong because he has a bad first line. I said that we went to bed together out of politeness. Why did I say that? In some way, at the time, it was necessary to me to say it—playing light comedy, I suppose. There's a kind of pride or stubbornness in me that won't let me take a revolution at a gulp. It was my way of saying that I became your mistress for neither of the reasons that have always been my only reasons— neither because I chiefly and intolerably desired you nor because you chiefly and intolerably desired me—not because to lie with you was a need as important as hunger—but because we loved each other. I wouldn't admit out loud that anything in love was more important, more *real,* than that hunger." She checked herself and sighed. "I am going back on all my old creed," she said. "It was much easier, you know, to be a plain, hungry animal than to love a man as I love you. And anyhow, Barbet, at Vernon, you didn't contradict me."

"No," he agreed, "I didn't contradict you. It is dangerous for lovers to argue about love. No one has ever been persuaded to love, or to love in a particular way and not in another. It is a revolution that is made alone. It was true of your prison as it was of mine: when you were ready, you would know what to think. That was why I didn't argue—and because I didn't want to." He leaned towards her, drawing her arm across his body, and kissed her. "But our experience at Vernon wasn't false, Thérèse. Why are people so intolerant of the moods of love? One is sentimental, they say; another is theatrical, another romantic, another animal, another spiritual or real or true: and they condemn one or other of these moods as fiercely as sectarians condemn their rivals' way of worshipping God. But true love is all of these, and what we thought and felt on the balcony at Vernon is no less a part of love than what we are thinking and feeling now. Perhaps the balcony at Vernon was theatrical and perhaps a part of our conversation over coffee next morning was absurd; but only proud and pitiless minds put love on its dignity or mock the foolishness of lovers. Do you suppose that Héloïse and Abélard were never foolish or animal in their love?"

She was filled by an impulse to tell him what Frédéric had said and how, this morning, she had remembered it, but it would be hard to put into words the significance she attached to the saying. It was a long story, and Barbet did not know the beginning of it. Instead she asked:

"What has happened to us, Barbet? It is true that we are nearer to each other than we have ever been. It is I who have changed, not you. Until now, I have always loved because I was hungry. I have always said that love must have something to feed on. But our love has had little to feed on—for months, nothing—and yet it has grown and deepened."

Even now, she thought, I must separate myself from him; though we love each other, it is not safe that we should be together; and she cried out silently within herself: Shall we never be together, he and I? and she wondered whether their parting would drag at his heart as it dragged at hers.

"I must take you to Cugnot's," she said. "We must not stay here."

He reached for her and held her, all his long absence poured into the present touch.

"Let us stay a little while," he said.

That he should long for her and beseech her was too sweet for her resolve.

"Let us stay, then. . . . Barbet," she added, "remember sometimes that I have not the consolations of philosophy. The reach of your hand is that to me—even if you are too far away to touch me. When I believe you love me, I am proof against all fear, temptation and loneliness. Only give me evidence sometimes that I am in your heart. Oh, you are lucky to be the magnet! I know what it is to be that too—but it doesn't ache as the steel aches."

Chapter 6

RINGING AND KNOCKING AT THE DOOR WERE left unanswered; it might reasonably be assumed that Mademoiselle Despreux was out of Paris on a Sunday in June; and it was not until the late afternoon, when the charwoman's coming threatened them, that Barbet and Thérèse left the flat, remaining separate on the stairs and in the hall, and not rejoining each other until Thérèse was already in the cab she had summoned and Barbet climbed in beside her.

The first thing he asked of Cugnot was a razor, but it was refused. "No," said Cugnot, "you will need a change of clothes and none of my own will fit you; I am twice as long as you; but once there was a merchant skipper in a picture of mine. Here is his kit—jacket, trousers, cap, everything—but you must provide the beard." Barbet put on the clothes and wound a scarf round his neck. "And the advantage is," Cugnot said, "that, whoever comes, you needn't hide unless it is someone—Schnetz, Quérignon—someone who is bound to know you. I will begin a portrait of you now and Madeleine a pencil drawing. If a visitor comes by daylight, I am painting you— and you are the model; if by night, Madeleine is continuing her drawing—still you are the model."

"Good," said Barbet. "Thank you. Can I smoke a pipe? But, you know," he added, "I shan't be a guest very long. Soon I must go out and find a cooper's job and take my chance. Besides, Thérèse has told me that my mother is ill. How ill, Thérèse? Have you told me the truth? Is she dying?"

"I shall be able to tell you to-morrow," Thérèse answered. "I have promised to visit her. You stay here. I will bring you news."

474

"I am sorry, Thérèse. I shall come with you or, if you think that is unwise, I shall go alone. You can drive. I can go by train from the Gare Montparnasse."

Cugnot protested. "But it is madness. Your relations are there, Thérèse says. Your brother and—"

"Victor, Bette, Madame Vincent, the Verviers themselves," Thérèse recited with an emphasis, at once amused and despairing, on each name. "Well? What do you suppose will happen? Do you suppose that they won't recognize the bearded merchant seaman?"

"I'm sorry," Barbet repeated. "I can't look ahead to that. If my mother is ill, I must go. I will go independently from Montparnasse."

Cugnot would have intervened again, but Thérèse waved him aside.

"No," she said to Barbet, "we will drive there together."

It was against reason that he should appear at Vanves. If the balance of argument had been only of filial duty against danger of recapture, or if another man had been concerned, she would have resisted fiercely; but she had learned how to enter into the acceptances of Barbet's mind; because she loved him, she did not mistake his detachment for rashness or fatalism; and, when Cugnot would have spoken, she laid her hand on his arm to silence him.

"Now," she said, "don't argue, dear Cugnot. A man who walks out of prison and arrives at *my* flat on a magic carpet is entitled to drive to Vanves if he's mad enough to want to. Besides, we don't want to argue. We are very happy this evening. While you begin your portrait, may we have a drink? I think the merchant seaman loves me. And that, if it is true, entitles me to two drinks."

"And to a feast," Madeleine said. "First there will be a pâté, then a coq au chambertin, then cheese for the intelligent or, for those who share Cugnot's tastes, there are mille-feuilles with a Greek jam of rose-petals. Now I shall leave you and attend the coq."

Cugnot set out his palette and began to paint. "But what will happen," he exclaimed presently, "if someone calls after the light has gone and Madeleine hasn't begun her drawing?"

Madeleine was sent for, Thérèse took her place in the kitchen, and, when the drawing and the coq were far enough advanced, the sitting was abandoned. They sat down to the pâté and to Clos de Grenouille that Courcelet had bought in Chablis and given to Cugnot. At first, while the others talked and Barbet was full of gaiety, Thérèse was silent, unable to enjoy the evening because it must end and she return to her empty flat on the Quai d'Orléans; but when Barbet, without pause in his imaginary autobiography of the merchant seaman whom he had named Paul Dermoz, reached across the table and put his hand over hers, she was suddenly happy again.

"The magnet to the steel," he said.

" 'Paul Dermoz'?" said she. "Why did you choose that name?"

" 'Paul Dermoz' was a barge."

"Near Tripleval? You saw it?"

"Or Port Villez."

"What are you two talking about?" Cugnot cried. "Magnet? Steel? Tripleval? Port Villez? Are you talking in code? Go on with your story."

"Yes," said Barbet, "I'm sorry. We were talking in code," and he continued the fantastic adventures of Paul Dermoz.

Then it is true that he loves me, Thérèse thought; and she dreaded no longer her return to her empty flat on the Quai d'Orléans. The old despairing and bitter mood might return; but this evening was happy, this evening was in brackets, and she began with delight to dispute with Barbet the authentic history of Paul Dermoz.

"I ought to know," he said, "I am Paul Dermoz. These are his clothes. This is his beard."

"If it comes to that," said Thérèse, "I ought to know. I loved him. I have had trouble with his beard."

"Did you go on voyages together?" Cugnot inquired.

The question, asked innocently as part of the game they were playing, struck at Thérèse, but she did not drop the gaiety of her tone. "Together? But yes, there were voyages in bateaux-mouches; there were voyages on the Seine."

"And on the high seas?"

"As for them," said Thérèse, "you will find their history inscribed on my monument in Père-Lachaise."

She could not resist a temptation to call at the Palais Royal on her way home. To her delight she found Schnetz with Philippe de Courcelet. He was on the edge of a chair, wagging his finger and evidently boiling over with excitement and projects, while Courcelet, leaning far back and with his eyes fixed on the ceiling, was as certainly fighting a battle of defensive indifference. They rose as Thérèse was announced, Courcelet with eyes alight and eyebrows raised in warning, Schnetz eager to give her his news. Had she heard that Barbet was free? She admitted that she had been told that posters were out.

"Posters?" Schnetz exclaimed. "They were out this morning. I can tell you, I have been about a bit to-day. I have heard what people are saying. Yes, yes, I admit that last time I was wrong. I said that they wouldn't put him into prison—and into prison he went. But this time I shall not be wrong. If they catch the little chap, they'll never dare to put him back again. Already the people are singing in the streets. Not much as yet. Groups here and there. Your song, Thérèse:

"*Ouvre*-lui *sa porte*
Pour l'amour de Dieu!

Bless my soul, you must have heard them yourself. It's not so long ago. Which way did you come? The Rue de Rivoli?"

Thérèse dared not admit that she had come from Montmartre, and not from her own home. She thought quickly before replying:

"I came by the Quais. I didn't turn up until the Oratoire."

"Ah," said Schnetz, "that explains it. But you wait for to-morrow! Wait for the morning papers. I have told Courcelet. He ought to warn the Government. If Grévy doesn't give that man a pardon, he'll be laughed out of the Élysée. More than that—he'll be howled out."

"Certainly," said Courcelet with a deliberately incredulous smile, "if, as you seem to expect, my dear Schnetz, the barricades are up in the morning, I will convey your warning in the appropriate quarters."

"You see!" Schnetz exclaimed, pointing at his urbane host, "he doesn't believe me! What do you say, Thérèse?" Before she could answer, he continued to Courcelet: "I tell you it is true. You may think it absurd. This isn't a political issue and you imagine that nothing except a political issue will ever move Paris. But this has appealed to their sense of justice. They see Barbet as an innocent man who is being needlessly persecuted. And Grévy isn't liked, the Government isn't liked; they are weak and pompous—like soft balloons. This thing will prick them. I repeat: I have been about Paris to-day. I have made plans. I will tell you what I have done. First I called on—"

"You had better not say what you have done," Thérèse put in.

"Why not?"

She indicated Courcelet, who said: "I confess that if I were planning a revolution, I should observe a certain discretion, my friend. I am called The Barometer. Your experience must tell you that I am not a very trustworthy person."

"Not on this?" cried Schnetz.

"By no means."

"But you are Barbet's friends. You are Thérèse's friend."

"Still," said Courcelet, "it is for me to record every change of temperature and pressure. Besides, to be frank, I think you are talking nonsense."

Schnetz rose. He was deeply and bitterly indignant. "Then I have no more to say. May I drive you home, Thérèse?"

"Thank you. I shall stay a little while."

"Good God! Have you gone over to the enemy?"

"By no means," she said. "I have come to tame him."

When Schnetz was gone, silence followed.

"Well?" said Thérèse.

"You might suppose," Courcelet replied, "that an old man as fat and fiery as that was completely harmless. But it is not so. The harmless men are those with balanced, critical minds to whom life is a comedy that they will not allow to swerve into tragedy or farce. Have you ever noticed how many revolutions have been made by men who might have been clowns? Schnetz, ridiculously enough, is dangerous. He pulls a thousand strings and has, in fact, been pulling them. But he is dangerous chiefly because he happens to be right. I still hold the view that no injustice has been done; but that is an academic view; in fact—and only facts matter—Paris has begun to take the bit between its teeth. Before you came, Schnetz was prating about revolution like a student; he wagged his finger at me and flourished 'Forty-Eight under my nose. That did not alarm me. Whatever Schnetz may do or think, your beloved Barbet won't overthrow the Republic. If there is a row, we can crush it in a day. But I look at it from the opposite point of view. Here is a chance of positive gain, very cheap at the price. Give him a pardon, set him free, flourish the trumpets of liberty a little, point out—what is true—that the Prussians would have put him in prison again, and all the women in France, including you, my dear Thérèse, will give the Government a pat on the back. And, heaven knows, the Government needs a pat on the back."

"Then I have persuaded you?" said Thérèse. "Or was it Barbet himself who persuaded you?"

"No, I cannot admit that," Courcelet answered, stretching out his hand for her glass. "No injustice has been done, but I see where advantage lies. A wise Government stands firm against stones when there is no alternative to stones, but when, at no cost but a stroke of the pen, stones can be converted into bouquets— In fact," he continued, watching Thérèse's face, "Schnetz isn't the only man who has been busy to-day. I too have paid my calls. I began naturally at the Ministry of the Interior."

"And then?"

"The Ministry of Justice."

"With what result?"

"At present none; but Government departments are like actresses —their appetite for bouquets increases."

"To-morrow, then?"

"Ah, Thérèse, I am not a magician, but to-morrow at eleven I am to call at the Élysée to discuss—well, no matter what it is that I am to discuss."

"Not Barbet?"

"In fact, the Bourse."

Thérèse smiled. "You are stubborn, Philippe. I wish you would admit that you are persuaded and that it is Barbet himself who has persuaded you."

"Well," said Courcelet, "you know me. You must judge for yourself. Is there any other man who, if I found him in your bed on Saturday night, would send me off to the Élysée at eleven o'clock on Monday morning? Your vine-grower has never worked a more improbable miracle. The odd thing is that he should have worked it in his sleep."

Thérèse called early at Cugnot's studio and drove out to Vanves with Barbet at her side. If she had delayed until the afternoon, as she had intended, she might have found none but Madame Vincent and Madame Verviers in the house; arriving in the morning, she must, she knew, face Anton, Victor and Bette, and she tried to warn Barbet that she would be unwelcome.

"I shall not be allowed to see your mother."

"Certainly you shall see her," Barbet answered. "We will go to her together."

"But Anton and Bette—oh, Barbet, they will argue and argue. Not only about me. At sight of you, they will hold up their hands and cluck. How did you escape? Where have you been? How does it happen that you and I are arriving together? And there's the phylloxera. I didn't tell you of that. The phylloxera has struck your vines. Anton and Victor want to go back on their bargain. They want their money back."

"Nonsense," Barbet answered with a firmness that surprised her, "the place is sold. What is done is done. As for their questions— leave them to me, Thérèse."

She was so well accustomed to fighting her own battles that to find all initiative taken from her by him was a cause of happiness and peace in her. He had a single purpose—to be with his mother—and, though his manner was as gentle as ever, throughout that day he allowed nothing to stand in the way of it and would look forward to nothing beyond it. Finding the gate and the front door open, he walked in unannounced. In the Verviers' little parlour the whole family was assembled, except Madame Vincent and Monsieur Verviers, who was presumably at his bank. As Barbet was about to enter, he took Thérèse's hand for an instant, then released it. In the room, he greeted them all generally, and before they could question him, said :

"I have come to see mother. So has Thérèse. Will you take us to her?"

"Thérèse—" Bette began.

"Thérèse is with me."

The questions began to flow.

"Yes," Barbet said, "it is true. I have escaped from prison. As you see, I am in Paris. As you know, there is a price on my head. I have a beard because I have grown it. I am wearing these clothes because they have been given me to wear. That covers the whole ground. You can tell the police I am here or not tell them. It makes no difference. All that will come afterwards. Meanwhile, which is mother's room?"

They told him—up the stairs, the second door on the right.

"Is no one with her?"

"Madame Vincent," Anton replied. "The doctor has been. He has just gone. He was talking to us in this room. That is why we are here."

"How is she?"

"Sinking."

"Dying?"

"For the most part unconscious."

"I will go up."

Thérèse followed him. Why did one always smile at the strength of his will? If some loud-voiced man, called ruthless, had shouted the company down, had rejected all questioning and stridently insisted upon having his own way, she would not have smiled. The effect had been the same. All the difficulties and discussions and delays that she had foreseen as they entered the house had been cut through. Not three minutes had passed; they were on their way upstairs together.

In his mother's bedroom, Barbet's method was as calmly determined.

"Thérèse and I will sit with her," he said to Madame Vincent. "Are there any instructions?"

"None. There is no more we can do. Even when she is conscious, she recognizes no one."

"Perhaps you would like to rest," Barbet said. "But you love her. Perhaps you would rather stay?"

"I will stay. And if she comes round, I am to call Bette," Madame Vincent said. "She will call the others. . . . Quite useless, I am sure. She doesn't know who they are."

"Never mind," Barbet answered. "Now let us sit down quietly."

Madame Hazard was lying on her back, her head turned to the right so that she faced the window. Only the movement of an edge of linen at her throat indicated that she was breathing; her eyes were open, but she seemed to be asleep. Thérèse and Barbet drew up chairs at the side of the bed nearer to the window. Madame Vincent sat behind them, against the wall, in the shadow of the curtain.

On a bracket behind Thérèse was a clock which, she had noticed while Barbet and Madame Vincent were speaking together, was of wood, in the form of a Swiss châlet. At first, while she watched Madame Hazard, she heard its ticking, but afterwards became unaware of it, the sound being absorbed in the quiet of her mind. As though a frame had grown up about the area of her vision, the scene before her eyes became intensified. In watching the head on the pillow, and in her consciousness that Barbet was watching it also, she seemed to be looking into a mirror that held within it reflections of infinite depth, which, as she strove to penetrate them, receded, drawing her on and on, until she herself was within the mirror and a part of the scene she observed. The head on the pillow was Madame Hazard's. She did not lose grip on this knowledge or recognition of the features; neither her seeing nor the normal distinctions of her mind were blurred; but she felt at the same time, and with a sense of fulfilment rather than of contradiction, that it was Barbet who was lying there. The walls dividing the individualities of mother and son were dissolved for her also and she knew that for an instant she was a sharer in Barbet's own perception. The instant passed. She saw Barbet sitting beside her, his legs crossed, his hands clasped about his knee, and she heard the clock again.

This vigil continued many hours. Others came and went, and Barbet was not disturbed by them. Twice he rose and touched his mother's face, then returned to his chair. In the late afternoon, her eyelids closed and she said:

"The door was open, Barbet."

"Yes, mother."

"It was foolish of us not to know it until then."

For an hour, she did not speak; then she began:

"I supposed once that you would raise me from the dead. It is not necessary." After a little while she added: "When you grow old, Thérèse, do not say good-bye to the nightingale. It is not necessary." She sighed deeply. "Nothing vanishes." Then, in a stronger voice, her normal voice: "Barbet, please take my face between your hands." When he had done so and kissed her, she opened her eyes, and continued to live until the evening, saying no more and, it might have been supposed, sightless. But Barbet did not take his eyes from hers until she died. Then he stood up. There were by this time others assembled at the foot of the bed, even Monsieur Verviers, returned from his bank. Barbet looked at them, then again at his mother. He took her hand and held it between his own that once more, while it was warm, he might feel the smallness of it. He patted it, as he had often in the past, and, laying it down, bent over to whisper in her ear. Then he straightened himself slowly and went out, signing that Thérèse should follow him.

At the head of the stairs, where the bracket-lamp had not been lighted, he compelled himself to say: "I will take you to your carriage." On the last words, his voice shook; as he went forward, he misjudged the step, stumbled, and recovered himself with a hand thrust against the wall. Thérèse put her arm under his, half afraid that he might not accept her help, but he did not withdraw. Trying to speak and failing, he yielded a part of his weight to her.

Outside, darkness was falling. After hesitation at the door and an uncertain turning of his head to right and left, he allowed her to take him across the gravel drive towards the gate. This momentary dependence upon her so moved her to grief and happiness that she felt the scalding of tears behind her eyes, and, because the muscles of her own face were tautened, she touched his that she could not clearly see. He was crying, but soundlessly, without agony, in the release of one who at last permits himself to sleep when he has long been tired. As he moved the garden gate, its bell jangled. Telling her to stay, he went up the road to the stables in which her carriage had been lodged and, after a time, returned in it.

"I shall see you to-morrow," he said. "I shall stay here to-night. I wish to settle with my family."

She accepted this and drove back to Paris. Barbet remained in the house of the Verviers. He had intended to answer whatever questions they wished to ask, to be final, to free himself, but at their melancholy supper they were too decorously mournful to speak of anything but the dead and of the arrangements that must be made for transporting her body to Roussignac and for the printing and distribution of funeral cards. After supper, Anton, evidently spurred to it by Victor, drew Barbet aside and broached the subject of the phylloxera. He suggested that there was at least a moral obligation on Barbet to resume the estate and return the purchase money; Victor was for the most part silent, knowing perhaps that any argument of his would work against his case; but Bette, mistaking Barbet's stillness for docility, ventured to assume his consent, implying that a man so unworldly as he would not, for the sake of profit, insist on the letter of the law. Barbet waited until they were done; then replied that his life in the Maison Hazard was over, that he would not return to it, and that he intended now to lead a new life.

"I told you long ago," he said, "that I was going on a voyage. That is what I meant."

At this, Victor raised his voice.

"I have no more to say," Barbet interrupted.

Anton was alive to the inflexible in his brother's mood. He had, moreover, enough good-humour to make him a diplomatist such as no Vincent could be. He resolved to play for time.

"Look here, Barbet," he said. "You are tired to-night. Leave it over until the morning. Leave it over until we are in Roussignac."

"How can he come to Roussignac?" Victor put in. "He is a fugitive. How can he show his face anywhere? If it comes to that, how can he touch his money unless we act as intermediaries? He daren't show his nose in a bank." Then he turned to Barbet. "How do you propose to live this new life of yours?"

"As a cooper—openly, without concealment."

"You will be recognized."

"Perhaps."

"And what do you suppose will happen then?"

"I don't ask." For the first time there was a note of anger in his voice. "Will you never understand? It is simple. I do not ask. Should I have come here if I had first asked whether you would betray me?"

Victor's lips tightened and his face darkened; his mind was quick with arguments by which he would persuade Anton that they must inform the police if they were not to be Barbet's accomplices.

"I am tired," Barbet said. "I am going to my room."

Anton rose with him. He was overawed by the fact of death and ashamed of having discussed business to-night; he would have preferred to postpone such an argument until his mother was in the ground. To make amends, he said:

"You will be visiting her on the way. We will go together, Barbet."

Barbet answered: "No, Anton, her body is dead."

"I sat there all the time with you," said Madame Vincent who had been silent throughout the evening. "I wish she had spoken a word to me. She cannot have known I was there. I should like to go to her now, but I cannot go alone."

"I will go with you," Barbet said and took the old lady's hand.

He and Anton and Madame Vincent went upstairs together. He left them in his mother's room and went to his own and slept.

Chapter 7

IN THE MORNING, HE FOUND THAT THE DOOR OF his bedroom was locked. Victor's intention was clear. How very odd, Barbet thought. People have a passion for locking doors uselessly. Why should Victor suppose that I wish to escape, or in any case, that I should escape in that way? He washed in water from his jug, dressed in his seaman's clothes and looked out of his window. Well, bless my soul, it's too easy; and he let himself down by the water-pipe.

As he turned the corner of the house on his way to the front door he met his brother walking in the garden, restlessly and alone.

"Good morning, Anton," he said. "On patrol?"

"No. Just strolling," said Anton in a jerkily casual tone, as though he had been caught stealing apples. "You came down the drain-pipe of course. I told him you would."

"Then why did you lock the door?"

"I didn't."

"Why did he?"

Anton shrugged his shoulders. "Why do wasps sting? . . . And partly, I suppose, because there have been men about the place. The doctors. Undertakers. Don't want them to see you."

"But why, if you are going to give me up?"

Anton scraped the gravel with his boot. "Awkward; awkward in many ways." He looked round in embarrassment, wishing to heaven he could think of something to say, and, his eye falling on the blinded windows of the villa, he jerked his thumb at them. "Looks wrong in the sun. Like that old doll's house of Bette's with the windows painted black." Then he gripped Barbet's arm, as he had when they were boys adventuring together, and, with a swift move-

486

ment to a pocket, thrust a bundle of notes into his hand. "Look," he said. "You make off. Take your chance. You make off now. That way. Through the chicken-run. There's a gate there. Make for the woods and out the other side. I haven't seen you."

"Thank you," Barbet said. "I'll keep the money for a bit if I may. I shall probably need it. And I don't want to be a nuisance to you, Anton, but if once I start running away I shall never stop. What will happen I don't know or how it will all work out, but I intend to lead my own life in my own way."

"And if a house caught fire, wouldn't you walk out of it?" Anton asked.

"Yes," Barbet answered. "And if France were invaded again, I should fight. And if a boy threw a stone at a window beside which I was sitting and the glass flew, my eyes would shut to protect themselves from splinters. There are things that a man resists naturally —different things in different men; and if he says 'No; I have a rule; I won't resist them, I'll let the splinters fly,' then *not* to resist becomes an obsession and his nature breaks up; he isn't a whole man any more. But to be put in prison again is not, for me, an evil of the kind that I resist naturally. It would be much worse to spend my life thinking how I might avoid being caught. I want to keep my mind clear, that's all, Anton. To do that, I must live patiently as regards others, and accept what they do. It is a kind of private civilization after all," he added with a smile. "I don't try to reform the world."

"Do you mean," said Anton, fastening on the point that was of concern to him and speaking with hopeful astonishment, "do you mean that you don't mind going to prison again?"

"I would rather be a cooper. Why? Are you going to put me there? Poor Anton, don't worry about it. They'll let me out in the end, or perhaps they will leave the door open again. Listen!"

There were footsteps on the gravel. Victor came running from the front of the house. At sight of the two brothers quietly talking together, he halted, aware of something incongruous in his panic.

"I went to his room," he exclaimed. "I unlocked the door. He was gone."

"Evidently," said Barbet. "I wish you wouldn't talk about me, Victor, as if I weren't here. I am here. I am not trying to escape. But I am hungry and should like some coffee. Why haven't you already sent for the police?"

Victor's plan had been carefully and rapidly matured. Anton had objected that, if Barbet's own family were to hand him over to the police, they would be brought into contempt. "Very well," Victor had replied, "officially neither of us will appear in it. We will take Barbet to Monsieur de Courcelet and wash our hands of him. Courcelet will do the rest. He is discreet. He will keep our names out of it. You can rely on him. As you know, I have acted for him on more occasions than one."

Anton had unwillingly agreed. As mayor of Roussignac, he could not face the charge of having shielded his brother. Victor and Bette had the capacity of making whatever they proposed seem unavoidable; he knew they were wrong but could think of no answer to them, and his vanity, his fear of their livelier wit, hemmed him in. In any case, if he did not act with Victor, Victor would act alone. He was in a trap and could see no way out of it, now that Barbet had refused to take his chance; but the gloom of the Verviers, the darkened room, the hushed voices, the tiptoeing in homage to the dead, Bette's silent glee and Victor's fiddling with the detail of his triumph—his orders for a hired carriage, his finger-licking over the pages of a railway time-table—irked him as they stood round the parlour table, drinking their coffee.

These damned Vincents! he thought. These damned Vincents! and he had the rebellious impulse of a bull on a chain. He imagined himself saying to Barbet: Look, come and join the firm. Join the firm and run the Maison Hazard with me and somehow we'll get all the Vincents out! But Bette was a Vincent. He looked at the formidable pile of her hair, the rolls and curls that seemed to have been baked and glazed. He remembered the steady grinding of her voice when she was determined, and his heart failed him. Postponing the distress of his mind, he said aloud: "Anyhow the coffee is hot. What good coffee it is!"

"Thank you," said Madame Verviers. "I am glad it pleases you."

Anton gathered his strength together and, unable to say: No, I won't go at all, substituted for it a lesser rebellion—a salve to his conscience or his pride.

"Anyhow, I won't go in your train," he declared, raising his voice with the bluster of a defeated boy. "We will drive all the way. You can put that time-table in the drawer."

Victor would have resisted, but Bette was wiser.

"Sh—sh!" she said in a whisper, pointing at the parlour ceiling. "Not so loud, Anton. Remember poor mother. Of course you are quite right. You shall drive all the way. Victor, you will need a pair of horses."

"Nonsense!" cried Madame Vincent at the top of her voice, beating her spoon against her saucer. " 'Poor mother' indeed! Who is your mother? I am."

"Hush, mother, hush! You forget yourself."

"Yes," said Madame Vincent, crestfallen again. "Poor Chouquette. We had a game unfinished, Barbet. There's the score on the shelf. She was winning, too." Madame Vincent's face was suddenly contorted by grief. She wheeled round heavily, as though she had been struck; but the blind was down, she could not look out of the window, and she turned back, her long face awry, and shook as she stood, like a great crow that has battered itself against glass.

To be again in the light and the open air was so great a relief to Anton that, as the hired carriage drove away, he threw up his head and grinned, for all the world as if he were driving out for a day's holiday. Having done so, he was ashamed of himself. Was not his mother dead? Was he not taking his brother to prison? He adjusted his features to the gravity befitting the mayor of Roussignac in such circumstances and slid a glance at the captive seated between Victor and himself.

"I'm glad I am not going home," Barbet said. "I should miss the sound of her, Anton. She pattered, she took such tiny steps. Odd things one remembers. Physical things."

"Yes," said Anton with a rhetorical sigh, "poor mother!"

"Oh no," said Barbet. "But, in this sunshine, she would have laughed and clapped her hands. That is gone."

He had placed his seaman's cap on his knees, which were pressed together because Victor, unable to believe that no escape was contemplated, had insisted that all three should squeeze into the back seat. Fortunately the carriage was open, the sun was warm and the birds were singing. Odd to take a chap to prison on such a morning, Anton thought, and he nudged Barbet with his elbow to express this feeling as well as he could.

Barbet appeared to understand him perfectly.

"Of course," he said, "if one is going to escape from prison, one ought always to do it in the early summer. I escaped on June the 1st." A recollection striking him, he slapped his knee so violently that the seaman's cap rolled to his feet and Victor seized his arm. "June the 1st!" he repeated, disregarding Victor. "I had clean forgotten it and so, I think, had she; but it was on the 1st of June that Victor Hugo was buried."

"She?" said Anton.

"Thérèse." Barbet's eyes sparkled. "I remember her saying that no one ought to be buried on the 1st of June. . . . Or put in prison, Victor."

Victor frowned but made no answer. As the journey proceeded through the Porte Brancion, clinging to the railway as far as the Place du Maine, he found that he was inexplicably in the company of two men who were enjoying themselves. He unbuttoned and rebuttoned his jacket and straightened his tie. Barbet began to talk to his brother about the Maison Hazard as if there had been no dispute on the subject the night before.

"Don't worry about it, Anton. Leave it to Pierre to dig up and burn. The thing won't spread. In any case, the place is worth more than the money if you hold on. All the vineyards will be replanted some day. You mark my words—they'll find an American root that will flourish even on chalk. If you want to gamble, buy vineyards in the Grande Champagne. I said so once to Pierre, but Pierre hasn't the cash—unless Victor lends it to him."

Perhaps Victor did not hear. He was leaning forward and tapping the driver's back with the knob of his walking-stick, for the carriage had unexpectedly turned into the Rue de Vaugirard.

"Hé! Hé! Straight on. Don't you know your way? We aren't going to the Luxembourg."

"The road's up," said the driver, "at the crossing of the Boulevard d'Enfer," and he drove on steadily, turning into the Rue Cassette. Here, on the left, above a high wall, a little church was striking the hour on a cracked bell, and Barbet was sorry to leave it behind and find himself again in the Rue de Rennes.

A minute later, at sight of St. Germain des Prés, he cried out: "Stop. There's my café. If I am going to the scaffold, let us at least give the horses a rest."

Even Victor could not refuse to sit at a table in the sunshine, though he looked continually at his watch and emptied his glass while Barbet and Anton were sipping theirs.

"If we don't go on," he said, "Courcelet may have left his rooms and gone to the Ministry of the Interior. He looks in there, I believe, most mornings."

So it was. They were turned away from the door in the Rue Montpensier.

"Why do you want to take me to Monsieur du Courcelet?" said Barbet. "Why not to the police? I have asked you that before and you didn't answer."

"I act for him," Victor answered.

"Do you, indeed? In what way?"

"I act for him," Victor repeated impressively. "He would expect me to report to him personally a matter of this kind."

"But—"

"That is enough," said Victor.

"Oh, leave him alone," said Anton. "It does no good, Barbet. It does no good. Better Courcelet than the police."

Outside the Élysée a crowd was assembled, a good-tempered crowd, laughing and singing and cheering.

"I didn't know the President was so popular," said Barbet. "And what an odd song for a crowd to sing under the windows of the Élysée."

"What was it?"

"Well, I thought it was 'Au Clair de la Lune,' but it can't have been."

At the Ministry of the Interior, Victor asked for Monsieur de Courcelet and filled in a form on buff paper. As he handed it in he said to Anton: "I have written a special word on it. We shall be seen at once."

"Did you put my name?"

"No. I thought it better not. I thought that, in any case, you would prefer not."

"Oh," said Anton, "that's as may be. But I should have thought that, if you had written 'Mayor of Roussignac,' we might have made quicker progress."

"You will see," Victor replied. "When we are shown in, you shall speak first."

After half an hour a porter came into the waiting-room. Its dozen occupants stirred, hoping to be summoned. He held Victor's buff form in his hand and called the name: "Vincent." Victor stepped forward.

"You are to write here particulars of your business."

"Now, my man," said Victor, "I have waited half an hour and that is more than enough. You take that to Monsieur de Courcelet and draw attention to my name. Besides, I have written a word that he will understand."

"You are to write here particulars of your business," the messenger repeated.

"Give it to me," said Anton, shouldering his way forward. "I'm tired of your 'special words,' Victor. Why don't you write sense? Ten to one he has forgotten who you are—if he ever remembered. Give me the pen."

"Your name won't help," Victor protested.

"It won't be my name!" and Anton scrawled on the paper "HAZARD, Théophile" and, with a final, exasperated flourish, added "Barbet," placing it between brackets and underlining it twice.

In less than three minutes, the messenger had returned. Like a prisoner between two gaolers, Barbet was led upstairs and ushered into a great room with gilded doors and a ceiling dimly flushed with cracked cherubs. The light of the most distant windows drew a luminous rim about Courcelet's head and touched his ears with pink. As they made their way across an archipelago of carpets, he gave no sign of recognition.

"Well, gentlemen, what can I do for you?"

At the sound of this remote voice, Anton halted, shuffled and advanced. It was Victor who had courage to speak.

"My name," he began, "is Victor Vincent. No doubt, sir, you remember me."

"Ah yes. Roussignac, is it not?" Courcelet held out his hand to be shaken. "Well?"

"This is Monsieur Anton Hazard. . . . And this—"

Anton rumbled into eloquence. He liked his commission ill enough, but if a speech was to be made he would make it.

"Monsieur," he began, "you will not fail to appreciate the closeness of family ties or how brother is bound to brother. For this reason, I come here reluctantly—with how much reluctance I find it hard to express. My brother and I have lost our mother this morning—or rather last night—we have—"

" 'Lost'?" said Courcelet. "In what sense 'lost'? Are you reporting a disappearance or a murder?"

Anton gathered control. "By death. By natural death, monsieur."

"I offer you my sympathy. But what has her death to do with me?"

"Nothing, Excellency. Nothing, I admit. I spoke of it only to show how reluctant I was to—that is to say, I come here compelled by a sense of duty to lay before you or, rather, to ask your collaboration in what cannot but be an extremely painful and delicate matter when considered from the point of view of—"

As Anton had lost his way, Barbet said: "Wouldn't it be simpler, Anton, just to say I am here?"

"As mayor of Roussignac and as the prisoner's brother, it was right that Monsieur Anton Hazard should speak first," said Victor, smoothly intervening. "But we will not waste your time, monsieur. I myself will say briefly—"

"Prisoner?" said Courcelet. "What prisoner?"

"This," said Victor, "is Théophile or Barbet Hazard. A reward is offered for his apprehension. We have brought him with us. We brought him to you, monsieur, rather than to the police, in the hope that you would allow me to use my influence with you to obtain some mitigation of—"

"What influence?"

"Whatever small influence my services—"

"Very well, Vincent. Let us say you have done your duty. I bid you good morning." He turned to Anton. "I hope things go well in Roussignac, Monsieur Hazard. From all I hear, though these are dark days in the vineyards, there is great hope—I have real hope—that the men of science will overcome the phylloxera. I rely upon you to use all your influence to persuade the more timid to replant."

"Thank you, sir," said Anton, put at ease by this sudden kindliness of tone. "I'm glad to hear you speak as you do. I'll do my best."

"As for the prisoner," said Courcelet, his eyes moving to Victor, "there is none. A petition was lodged with the Commission des Grâces on Sunday. The Commission reported yesterday. The pardon was granted this morning."

"On what grounds," said Victor, "if it is permitted to ask?"

"That is an extremely intelligent question," Courcelet replied. "If it were possible to see the Élysée from these windows, I would show you the answer to it. As it is, you must choose. The grounds of pardon are prescribed: justice, humanity or public order. As you pass into the Faubourg St. Honoré, your eyes and ears will assist your choice. . . . But I should like a word with Monsieur Théophile if he would be good enough to remain."

"And now, my friend," said Courcelet, when he and Barbet were alone, "you have not spoken since you came in. Perhaps you find the room too large?"

"The vine-leaves are wrong," said Barbet. "Whoever painted the ceiling couldn't paint vine-leaves. . . . I hope it is not, so to speak, your personal ceiling, monsieur?"

"By no means. Strictly I don't even belong to the Ministry. They lend me the room, you may say. I have often observed that the men who paint goddesses and their offspring are extremely ignorant of vine-leaves. One would have expected familiarity with one to have implied knowledge of the other."

"Yes," said Barbet. "I am sure you are right, monsieur." Then he added: "I should value your advice, if I might have it?"

"It is at your disposal."

"Whom should I thank? I am sure there is someone whom I should thank. Not the President, of course. The Commission des Grâces, perhaps?"

"No," said Courcelet, "they are high officials of the Ministry of Justice. They are too impartial to receive gratitude. You might, of course, thank Mademoiselle Despreux. She has never been impartial on any subject, though her liking for you and for me argues a certain breadth of mind. I suppose I take an inhumanly detached view of the whole proceedings. That is my little affectation; and I confess that nothing in them seems to me more remarkable than her choice of a song. After all, she knows her Paris and there's not a living soul who wouldn't have said to her: 'Paris is bitter. Paris is hard. There has never been a time when satirical songs burned with a more cruel acid. If you want your song to bite, the sharper the acid the better.' And yet she, to force the hand of the Government, has the crowd singing 'Au Clair de la Lune'!"

"Yes," said Barbet, "I heard them. I suppose it worked just for that reason."

"For what reason?"

"That it was impossible. . . . But I am taking up your time, monsieur."

"No. . . . Well, yes. . . . Will you dine with me to-night?"

"That is kind of you. I had thought, perhaps, that Thérèse and I—"

"That shall be arranged. Eight. My rooms in the Palais Royal."

Courcelet walked with him towards the door. "What are your plans? You understand, of course, that all France is looking for you and that the first journalist who runs you to earth will make a fortune."

"He won't look for me in a cooper's shed," Barbet answered. "I shan't be in Paris and I shan't be at Roussignac. That's where he will look."

"Still a fugitive?"

"Oh no; if he finds me, it won't spoil a barrel."

"And to-night? Presumably not Castor and Pollux? The reporters will be lying in wait on the Quai d'Orléans. Would you like a bed with me?"

"Thank you," said Barbet. "You are very kind, but there is a little hotel to which I always go. No one will look for me there."

After his dinner-party that evening, when Barbet and Thérèse had left him, Courcelet sat down to write:

"If there is an inward monitor, whose approval alone is of value and who alone may be permitted by a free man to impose order upon his freedom—in brief, if I am not utterly deceiving myself—I am happy to-night, for my monitor tells me I am entitled to be happy. I, who am lazy, or affect laziness, have never acted with more energy than during the past two days, paying calls and asking favours with a spirit that seems scarcely to have been my own. Barbet is free; Thérèse is unquestioningly happy; and nothing is more remarkable than the combination of two assurances in me: first, that I did right to secure his liberty; second, that no damage would have come to him if I had failed. He is an invulnerable man because—"

Courcelet laid down his pen and moved from writing-table to armchair. There, on the sofa, Thérèse and Barbet had been sitting half an hour ago, and, remembering their happiness and his own joy in it, he turned away from that didactic "because" and said: deliver us from the temptation to lay down rules. It was the essence of Barbet's nature that he lived by no rules and yet had order within him, the order not of submission to laws or of conformity to the ideas of others but of his own sense of natural values. And yet, Courcelet said to himself, of what use is it to say that? A rebel, a man of anarchical mind, any vague and paltry upstart who wished to be conspicuous in his defiances, might claim to have "his own sense of natural values." The phrase is just a phrase—with truth in it if you know the man, but, if not, meaningless.

He went to his table again and, crossing out his uncompleted sentence, wrote in its place:

"It has been a good evening, memorable to me because there have always been two opposed forces in my life whose opposition has troubled me: this evening my sense of that opposition vanished. I mean an opposition of ideas on the subject of pleasure. I have brought with me from childhood an association of pleasure with guilt; in my maturity I have repudiated that association and my reason has said with Montaigne that pleasure is among life's principal gains. But have I ever, until to-night, fully believed Montaigne in Montaigne's own sense—that is to say, neither with an aloof, intellectual repudiation of the idea of sin nor with a self-justifying greed for pleasure, but with an acceptance of it as necessarily good in itself because it is a means of communication and to communicate is to live? This, perhaps, has always been Thérèse's belief or, rather, her intuition; it gives a special strength to her vitality which has made her dear to me beyond the desire, or the vanity, that first drew me to her; but I understand this retrospectively, having seen her with him; she was too reckless or I too suspicious for it to have been possible for me to learn it from her alone. But Barbet, so different from her in all else that the idea of love between them is conventionally incredible, has a vitality that is recognizably the same in kind with hers. He accepts pleasure as he accepts suffering; he is not damaged by them because they do not come to him from outside life but are parts of it; he is not thrown out of his course by 'strokes of fortune' because they are not external strokes. And her sense that her life includes these things and is the more alive because of them gives Thérèse what hitherto I have called her recklessness in pleasure and her courage in disaster. That is why they love each other—not that they live, or are ever likely to live, the same lives, but that they are alive in the same way."

Courcelet read the sheets lying before him.

"How wise I am!" he said aloud. "Too wise," and, unable to escape from a view of himself playing his little scene, he wrote: "Perhaps. Perhaps. Perhaps," and dropped his pages in the waste-paper basket. How depressing it was to know that, in the morning, he would take them out again!

Chapter 8

WHILE THEY WERE IN COURCELET'S ROOMS AND the moment of parting was still separated from them by hours of good company, it had seemed easy to Thérèse that Barbet should go into the country next morning and she stay in Paris. Soon they would meet again.

But after they had left the Palais Royal and were driving across the river to the Hôtel Bagnolet, Barbet asked her why she was troubled. The question, piercing her guard, showed to her that she was guarded.

"I'm not, Barbet. It is best that you should be out of Paris for a time if you are to be left in peace. Later I can come to you or you to me. We are together; we are each other's; that makes it easier to part for a little while, not harder."

She had been able to say this because, while she spoke, he had still been near her, and even when she had left him on the pavement at the entrance to the Impasse Marcel she held firm in this new assurance of her mind. But though it was a genuine and happy assurance, it was still unaccustomed, and, in the entrance to her flat, she was struck by a gust of her former loneliness and wished that a letter from him were awaiting her. That is foolish, she thought. I am not alone. As long as he is alive, I shall never be alone again.

Nevertheless, before sleeping, she said to herself: We are right. We *are* right. But why should he go to-morrow? Next week would do or the week after; and, in the morning, she awoke uncalled and with the fear in her mind that Barbet's train was steaming out of the station. She looked at the time; it was early—so early that if she made haste she might see him again; Mademoiselle d'Austerlitz would give her coffee; Barbet would come downstairs astonished to find her waiting for him.

She dressed and went out. There was no cab in sight and she decided to walk across the bridge towards Notre-Dame. Her attention was caught by a woman's boot floating in the water. What interested her in it was that it had been an elegant boot, not a tramp's. Who had thrown it away? Sometimes, she thought with a smile, tramps wear elegant boots with uppers of violet silk and tuck them in under their skirts on the way to Mantes. A cab was now appearing on the bridge but the sight of a hat told her that it was occupied. Her attention returned to her own feet, then to the swirling boot. Behind her the jingle of the cab ceased. She had no wish to be recognized and kept her back turned. A hand was laid on her arm.

"Barbet! Why are you here?"

"I came for you. Yesterday, you know, I bought some clothes and a bag to put them in. When I woke this morning, there was the bag—packed."

She smiled at him, understanding too well the melancholy of luggage to miss the train of his thought.

"I was on my way to you," she answered. "It isn't that I had changed my mind. I was coming to see you off. At least I think I was."

"I might have been in prison to-day," Barbet replied. "If I had been, I should have thought: 'If only I could have to-day on the river with Thérèse!' What is to-day?"

"Wednesday."

"I mean the date."

"The 9th of June."

"We will have it on the river, Thérèse. Monsieur de Courcelet's journalists won't look for us in the Gabrielle d'Estrées. I will go to-morrow instead of to-day."

"To-day!" she answered. "Forget to-morrow. What shall we do until ten thirty-one?"

They paid the cabman and seated themselves at a café at the farther end of the Pont St. Louis where it joined the Quai aux Fleurs.

"The President may have reprieved you yesterday but we have

reprieved ourselves to-day," Thérèse said as she drank her coffee. She was filled with the magical joy of contrast, comparing the delight of what was with the emptiness of what might have been, and though Barbet took his pleasure more steadily she knew that he too was thinking: All day! All day! Some instants are so precious in themselves that they cannot be used; the art of life is to waste them; and she prayed that Barbet would not move or suggest that they should go.

Stay at table till I've *finished.*
Stay in bed till I'm *awake!*

So well was her prayer answered that, in the end, it was she who paid the bill without his noticing that she paid it, and said: "Come and walk in my back garden. It is mine because I see it from my window," and they went towards the river across the space in which the archbishop's palace had formerly stood, she, in her imagination, watching them from her window as they walked. A shudder of sadness passed through her—that tick of a clock in an empty room which lovers hear when they are happy and together.

"Suppose," she said, "we were to stop here by that fountain. After all, there are dragons and angels. Suppose we were to stop here and not move."

"I know," he answered. "I feel that. Thérèse—in spite of the dragons and angels—I want to kiss you here."

"Kiss me," she said, and afterwards: "Why?"

"Because, for a moment, it does stop the clock. . . . Now, Thérèse, we walk round the cathedral. In front of it we find a cab. The cab takes us to the Gare St. Lazare."

For another moment she hesitated: "Good-bye, dragons and angels."

"Never say good-bye to the nightingale, Thérèse. It is not necessary."

"I wonder."

"In any case," said Barbet, "it's a June morning and no war."

The train left so punctually at ten thirty-one that clocks seemed to be on their side, not against them, and at Mantes the stress of happiness gave place to its ease, its urgency to an infinite leisure. Each forbore to ask the other where they were going—to Vernon? to La Roche? Distance as well as time should be unquestioned; in any case there was, as they knew by experience, time to spare before the Gabrielle d'Estrées began her voyage. This evening, Thérèse thought, we shall dine together in Paris, and for a moment was glad; then drove the thought away. She would not think of this evening, nor to-day would she count the hours.

When, as they came downhill towards the river, the bridge lay before them, they were still so early that they turned back and to the right, passing through a narrow street into the wide sloping square from the crest of which the church looked down, its two towers reaching up into an enchantment of sunlight and windy clouds, its loveliness fortified by its high solitude. No one was in the square but an aproned child with a great roll of bread under her arm, and no one was on the steps of the church. Barbet and Thérèse looked in through the open doors at five distant windows throwing down their blue.

"There is a bird in the nave," said Barbet. "I wonder how long he has been here. Look, he is tired and resting."

"He will never get out," Thérèse answered. "He will fly and fly and hurt himself and never get out."

Barbet took her arm and withdrew her into the shadow. "He will have seen us move. We may have shown him the door."

They waited silently. The bird flew past them through the door as if he had always known his way.

Thérèse's hand tightened on Barbet's arm; her fingers moved on his wrist. "I should feel as if I had found the last line of a sonnet," she said.

"Why?" Barbet asked. He walked with her across the face of the church, forgetting to seek an answer to his question because above one of the doors was a carving that interested and puzzled him—a battered carving of an angel, perhaps the angel of the resurrection, at an open tomb. From the tomb were protruding cerements that had been cast off, and beside it a knight in armour lay upon the

ground. Above him another armoured knight appeared to be floating in the air. What this carving had lost in the years and what it
represented they were uncertain, but it carried their minds and their
talk away to another day long ago as full as this of breeze and sunlight, with the same tension of the body, the same taste of life upon
the lips, and they thought of the unknown sculptor working on the
stone and afterwards standing where they stood to look at it and
walking home to his dinner. To their left, there was an archway from
which a flight of steps ran down to narrow streets. "This is his short
cut home," Thérèse said. Barbet followed her. Together they leaned
on the parapet at the head of the steps, looking at the pair of mean
alleys, the Rue du Fort and the Rue Monteclair, which, twenty feet
below them, clipped the houses in a thin V. In them Thérèse saw
the life of the old town and imagined her sculptor disappearing
down the Rue du Fort.

"I agree with Philip Augustus," she said. "We will go into the
church and visit him. Do you think they would bury me here if I
asked them?"

"I thought you had chosen Père-Lachaise—next to Rachel."

"Well," she answered with the delight she had always in Barbet's
playing her game with her, "it's hard to choose. Rachel is near to
Héloïse. But might not my heart, like Philip Augustus's, still be
buried in Mantes?"

It did not trouble their minds that time was passing. They went
into the church together and walked through it slowly, glad of its
coolness. When they came out, they had but to return to the bridge
and follow the plane-trees sloping down to the Quai de la Tour; at
the end of the slope they would find the café at which they had
waited a year ago, and at the landing-stage the Gabrielle d'Estrées
would be lying. When they found that the Gabrielle d'Estrées was
gone, they felt no shock of surprise. It was as if they had known she
would be gone.

"That," said Thérèse, "is the second time we have missed the
Gabrielle d'Estrées."

They went on the landing-stage together and looked across the river at the poplars and willows of the Île des Dames, and at a small boat approaching them under sail, leaning on her bow-wave, the wind abeam.

"You would think," said Barbet, "that to miss the only boat of the day—it's very odd; I don't feel in the least as I should if I had missed a train."

The sailing-boat put her helm down and came up sharply alongside. Her occupant, a man of not more than middle-age but with wrinkles so few and deep that they appeared to have been sliced in his face with a knife, handed her along the landing-stage towards a ring to which he made fast. He then disembarked, acknowledged Thérèse's and Barbet's existence with a nod and a good morning, and began a lively conversation with a youth who had run out of the café to meet him and whose employer he seemed to be. Thérèse looked over her shoulder at the café and read on its board the name of its proprietor. What had served for Monsieur Jugiaud at Vernon would serve again here and she said to the stranger:

"Monsieur Guélin?" He bowed and declared himself at her service. "We were admiring," she said, "the way you came alongside. Until the last moment, it looked as if you were going to run us down."

"Never," he said with a wink, "not if you know your boat. I've known this one too long."

"Too long?"

"Oh, she's a good boat. But she's old. I have a new one on order. Should have had her by now. This one," he continued, giving her gunwale an affectionate jolt with his foot, "she's good enough when she's running but you can't keep her close to the wind."

"I suppose you wouldn't let her to us for the day?"

Monsieur Guélin looked from her to Barbet, estimating his seamanship. "Where do you want to go to?"

"Down-river," Thérèse replied at hazard. "La Roche perhaps."

"La Roche! Well, you might get there with the wind and the stream, but you'll never come back, mademoiselle. Never in the world."

The subject appeared to be dismissed. He turned to the youth from the café: "Where's that board?"

A board mounted on a pole was lying face downwards on the landing-stage. It was given to him and he began to set it up in the stern sheets. On it was painted: Boat for Sale.

"How much?"

The wrinkles deepened and the intervening table-lands of brown and glossy flesh came up about the eyes. "Three hundred francs."

She took the money from her purse and held it out.

"Thérèse," said Barbet, "she's not worth half of that."

She continued to hold it out. Monsieur Guélin took it with becoming shame.

"She's yours," said he.

"She is," said Thérèse, "if you include provisions in the price."

"Why, yes," Monsieur Guélin replied. "You are welcome to what we have. Would you come in and choose?"

Barbet, at the prospect of seamanship, had dropped on his knees to examine the tackle.

"What on earth do you carry so much money for?" he asked over his shoulder.

"To buy ships," said Thérèse.

It was true that the wind's direction was that **in** which they wished to go but the river moved in wide curves and Barbet had need of his seamanship. After a little while, he found their boat easy to manage, lazy but good-tempered and without vice. While he sailed, he had leisure to watch Thérèse against a background of trees and water that changed continually and to talk to her of little things belonging, minute by minute, to their present experience together. The handling of rope and sail was as pleasing to him as the use of a cooper's tools, and the steady flow of the water, the pull, the slackening and the refilling of the sail gave to the morning and the early afternoon a timeless continuity that rested all questioning.

In the full bend of Rolleboise, where the river, turning under the cliff, embraced, in its right bank, a great curving stretch of cultivation and wood, he let down his sail and allowed the boat to drift.

"Your tiller," he said. "Keep her in mid-stream if you can while I unpack the food and drink."

He became aware then that she had not his tranquillity.

"What is it, Thérèse?"

"Everything with us," she said, "happens half by chance and half by intent—just as everything with you seems to happen half by reason and half by miracle. You laugh away the miracles. I wonder why. You say they happen 'naturally,' but that is only a word."

He gave no answer, knowing that she was making an approach to what was in her heart to say, and soon she continued: "When I bought this boat—that was half by intent. Only half. I hadn't changed my mind. But when we came down to the landing-stage, wasn't the river empty? I looked. I know it was. And yet when we knew we had missed the Gabrielle d'Estrées and were on the landing-stage, there was this boat coming straight towards me. In a moment, she was at my feet."

"Monsieur Guélin was flesh and blood all right," said Barbet with a smile. "What theory are you spinning?"

She hesitated and looked at him with entreaty. "I can't say it. . . . Yes I can. I can say anything. I think there's a fate in this, Barbet."

He came up from the bottom of the boat and sat beside her. "Say what you have to say, Thérèse."

"You can't live with me. I mean, you can't make your life with me in Paris," she said, hardening her tone in obedience to the will in her to speak reasonably and without extravagance. "It would be a vile life for you—a cage. You must go on your own voyage, Barbet; I know that. But I can come with you. I can make your life my life. If you want to be a cooper in one place, I will live with you and cook for you—I am a good cook. If you need to wander, I will wander too. I won't be Thérèse Despreux any more. I'll pretend that—" She broke off, hearing her own words. "No: I will become—" She could say no more. Her hand that was not on the tiller moved up to hide the tears she felt gathering in her eyes, but neither in life nor—she remembered suddenly—on the stage can a face be hidden easily by one hand, and, in despair, she let it fall again into her lap.

"It's no good," she said. "I *am* Thérèse Despreux. I say I can, I think I can, but in fact I don't let my prisoner go."

They were drifting in to the bank. He moved to hoist the sail and the boat drew forward again. Thérèse yielded the tiller to him and allowed her fingers to drag through the water. Though she had spoken harshly of herself, she was not unhappy or without expectation. And what am I expecting? she thought. To be with him always? To cook and mend for him? Nonsense. I am I and he is he, and life doesn't work out that way. Some day, I suppose, people will learn that, though domestic happiness is the right end to some love-stories, it isn't the right end to all of them because it isn't their true end. He and I could force it, but it would be like growing an apple on a pear-tree; there are different kinds of love and different fruits belong to them.

This was a hard creed for a woman who, in her heart and against all reason, wished that a romantically domestic scene might be given her to play in her own life, but she would not hoodwink herself; she clung to her own truth, and permitted to romanticism only the indulgence of hearing her voice say:

"Why, if we love each other, can't we be together? I know it is impossible. . . . Why is it impossible? . . . All right," she cried. "I know the answer. Because we are on separate voyages. And because we aren't liars. . . . And yet," she continued, smiling and puckering her forehead, "I am happy and so are you, Barbet. Is that only because now, for a few days and nights, we shall be together?"

"No," he answered. "That isn't the reason."

.She put her hand over his on the tiller. "You overestimate me," she said. "But it's true—I haven't gone far, but I have begun, perhaps."

It was possible that they would sleep that night at La Roche Guyon or perhaps at another place, now unknown to them, which would become as precious in memory. To-morrow they would set out on the river again towards Vernon, and on the following day—

The days would come to an end, but she did not fear it. Even partings she could endure in the knowledge that they would not be endless, for she felt no longer that she was in a cage, whether of time or of her own individuality. What lay before her she knew no more than she knew what stretch of country would be opened out by each bend of the river, but she looked forward, with confident expectation, not, as in the past, to a particular attainment, a special triumph of her own to which life should be compelled to contribute what she demanded of it, but to a less exacting, an enfranchised happiness. Certainly, as yet, her life and Barbet's would not be lived together; perhaps they would never be. This she was able to accept as a true condition of their relationship and a part of its nature. She loved him the more, counting her own future the less, and, because she was aware of her own increase, which discounted all the chances of possession and loss, was hungry for nothing and despaired of nothing.

"Well," she said, "here is our life beginning; together or apart— *our* life. What shall we do with it? Shall we make a plan?"

"Not now," Barbet answered. "When we are ready, we shall know what to do."

LONDON—JARNAC—PARIS—LONDON
Summer 1936 to June 1st, 1940